P9-DNZ-848

The
MIDNIGHT BAND
of MERCY

Also by the author

The Desperate Season

The MIDNIGHT BAND of MERCY

MICHAEL BLAINE

SOHO

Published by
Soho Press, Inc.
853 Broadway
New York, NY 10003

Library of Congress Cataloging-in-Publication Data

Blaine, Michael.
The midnight band of mercy: a novel/Michael Blaine.
p. cm.
ISBN 1-56947-371-4 (alk. paper)
1. Minorities—Crimes against—Fiction. 2. Poor—Crimes against—Fiction. 3. Landlord and tenant—Fiction. 4. New York (N.Y.)—Fiction. 5. Murder for hire—Fiction. 6. Conspiracies—Fiction. 7. Journalists—Fiction. I. Title.
PS3552.L3454M53 2004
813'.54—dc22 2004005793

Book interior designed by Kathleen Lake, Neuwirth and Associates

10 9 8 7 6 5 4 3 2 1

for anna tasha and rose

this city of words

author's note

The events depicted here are based on a true story. The Midnight Band of Mercy operated in New York City during the early 1890s. Their highly contradictory statements to the *New York Herald* have never been reconciled, but the Midnight Band did have a tangential relationship to the period's wider reform movement, and its leader did go on trial in an extensively reported case. Some of the figures drawn here were admired for their good works, others for their low crimes. The rest are my inventions, brought to life to explain the mystery behind the Midnight Band, as well as to live and breathe on their own.

Within a narrow range, the dates of certain events have been reshuffled for dramatic purposes. Otherwise, I have tried to create an accurate historical picture of New York City during the Panic of 1893.

—Michael Blaine

The ambiguity is the element in which the whole thing swims . . . so nocturnal, so bacchanal, so hugely hatted and feathered, yet apparently so innocent.

—Henry James

Says Dinny "Here's my only chance
To gain myself a name
I'll clean up the Hudson Dusters
And reach the Hall of Fame"
He lost his stick and cannon
And his shield they took away
It was then that he remembered
Every dog has got his day

—Hudson Duster Gang victory song

chapter one

APRIL 11, 1893. 5:25 A.M.

Max Greengrass pushed himself away from the faro table. All night the layout, thirteen spades glued onto an enameled tablecloth, had mesmerized him, but now it was time to cash in. For once he was ahead, four dollars and thirty-seven cents to be precise. His lungs felt sticky with cigar smoke. He had to stretch his legs.

Out on Perry Street he could breathe again. He loved the last moments before the sun came up, the streetlamps going pale, the cool air blowing off the river, the solitude. Searching for one last fare, a fly cab prowled Bleecker Street. The hollow sound of hooves on paving stone echoed in the stillness. As he walked, the luminous gray light intensified, wrapping him in its subtle glow. He jingled the coins in his pocket. Life wasn't half bad.

He'd slip a buck to his mother—his father had a religious allergy to work—and another to his sister Faye. He wished she would stay away from the Mrs. Winslow's Soothing Syrup, but she claimed various mysterious pains, especially after doing three shows a day, and he hated to go hard on her.

Barely watching where he was going, he had to skip sideways to avoid stepping on them. Four dead cats laid out in a perfect row in front of a dusty Waverly Place building. The unnatural order of the display teased his imagination. When Max picked up one of the creatures, its head rolled loose on its neck. With the tips of his fingers, he grasped the cat's delicate skull. Manipulating it was easy, too easy.

He recoiled, his throat closing in disgust. Repelled, but fascinated, he placed the tabby back in the same position on the sidewalk. Then he stepped back and wondered. Why had the creatures been so carefully arranged? The cats' tails had been configured just so, each lined up parallel to the next. Did they represent some dark hieroglyphic? Was he looking at a pattern, or the shape of his own hunger?

A space-rater at the *New York Herald*—he was paid by the column-inch—Max couldn't afford to pass up any story, even the least likely. He had already scrambled for pennies at the *Brooklyn Eagle*, the *Tribune*, and the *World*, but the best stories, and a full-time position, had somehow eluded him. He couldn't figure it out. It wasn't any one thing. At the *Trib* he'd gotten into it with an editor named Burgundy-Jones, a high-hat bastard if there ever was one. At the *World* he'd missed a few days on a bender. At the *Eagle* some toff from Columbia showed up out of the blue, and before Max knew it he was being eased out.

Max wasn't reflective, but once in a while a terrible thought would creep into his mind: he was getting older. In February he'd turned twenty-five. What would he do if he never found a secure spot in the newspaper business? This fear would flash white across his mind, paralyzing him for a second, but then he would find fresh material, he would lose himself, and forget his terror completely.

The feline corpses at his feet intrigued him. Sitting on a nearby stoop, he gazed at the dead animals, trying to decide if he could squeeze two hundred words out of their demise.

A man with ginger-colored muttonchops emerged from the parlor house next door. At the top step, the sack-suited businessman straightened his tie and plunged onto the sidewalk, stepping blindly onto one of the furry victims. Staggering, he cursed under his breath and hopped to safety. His mouth pursed in disgust, he glanced down and muttered one more imprecation before marching off toward Sixth Avenue.

Max wondered if he should chase the sportsman. To flesh out an article, he would need quotes. He'd quit the faro bank with money in his pocket, he'd avoided the bow-bow wine—a raw brandy the management offered gratis—and now he had the price of something better at Fitzgerald and Ives around the corner. But he moved up the steps into the deeper shadows instead, watching and wondering.

A few minutes later, Mrs. Jabonne, in a brilliant black-and-red kimono, threw open her door and looked up and down the street. Shrugging, she set a dish of milk on the top step. Then she caught sight of the crime scene.

Barefoot, she rushed outside, lifted a beribboned white cat into her arms, and let out a wail.

Max knew her. He had visited her establishment several times, but had left with mixed feelings. She ran a nice house with clean girls, but some of them were thirteen, fourteen at the most. She claimed they hadn't had a dose yet. Such small bones, such pure, unblemished skin. Now he hesitated. Pressing himself into the shadows, he watched her hug the soft animal to her breast and take a few steps back. Then she thought better of it. Looking both ways down Waverly Place, she dropped her former pet back onto the sidewalk before anyone could catch her.

Max pushed off.

Inside Fitzgerald and Ives he bought the last round.

"You're a white Jew, Maxie," Officer Lynch said, lifting his stein. Unbuttoned at the throat, his voluminous blue coat featured a row of brass buttons.

Far from taking offense, Max appreciated his acquaintance's backhanded compliment. Yanking up his shirt cuff, he displayed his white-skinned forearm. That got a laugh.

Max's father could never have comprehended his love for a fresh beer in a decent saloon, or how easily he got along with the street cleaners, touts, shoulder hitters, hod carriers, ward heelers, and cops who graced a polished brass rail. Then again, who cared? Hadn't the old man already chanted the prayer for the dead over him? Let him shuffle around the house all day in his felt slippers with his prayer shawl over his head, praying after the sun came up, praying after washing his hands, praying after every damned thing including lightning and thunder, and meanwhile forgetting to work for a dozen years.

What a bunch of mumbo-jumbo. The old man had a saying: What you want to do that for? What you want to go to a show, go to a dance, go to a lecture or a dime museum? His father was opposed to pleasure on principle. What was wrong with Fitzgerald and Ives, a run-of-the-mill joint with sawdust-covered floors and the usual chromos? Around noon, two nickel beers would buy a free lunch of cold cuts, salted cod and pickled fish of uncertain origins.

"You got something today?" Officer Schreiber asked, pointing at the pile of newspapers at the end of the bar.

Schreiber's daughter Margaret played the violin. His son Carl had died of diphtheria. Max made it a point to remember these things. Without cops, where would he get half his stories? Schreiber's tall helmet added to his considerable height. Max felt dwarfed next to the towering policeman.

Without realizing it, Max arched his back and rose up onto his toes. Then he slid a folded copy of The *Herald* down the burnished wood surface, in answer to Schreiber's question.

"Lower left," he directed. Stretching, he sipped his beer, then pushed his hat back on his head.

MEASURES FOR MATES

Prof. Johnson Broward of Harvard has measured thousands of heads and has come to the conclusion that seventeen cubic inches separates the Anglo-Saxon cranium from its less developed peers. His scientific investigation led him to measure the skulls of Northern and Southern Europeans, as well as Poles, Russians, Slavs, and Negroes.

To ascertain cranial capacity, Prof. Broward filled his skulls with measures of white pepper seeds.

"The Slav's forehead is low and sloping," Mr. Broward told a Cooper Union audience last night, "and the back of the Southern Italian's head is often sheared off, severely limiting cranial capacity,"

Mr. Broward admitted that professors tended to have high foreheads and ample domes. While not in the market for a wife at the moment, Prof. Broward said, "Heiresses, who after all are carrying the blood of superior stock, might do best if they got out their tape measures before mating."

"Lookit Lynch, he's got a head like a horse," Schreiber responded. "Nice one, Max. Beats the shit out of smackin' yeggs for a living."

The metro editor, Stan Parnell, had cut the article from the bottom up, leaving only the first three grafs. At $7.50 for a full column, his squib had been worth exactly two dollars and seventy-nine cents. Still, the *Herald* was better than the *World*. You could starve waiting for Pulitzer to cough up your carfare.

A sharp rap on the door caught their attention. Peering through the plate glass, the bartender recognized Mrs. Jabonne. "Hey, Schreiber, your little twist is lookin' for you."

"Which one?" Schreiber cracked.

Mrs. Jabonne marched in, wearing a black skirt, an immaculate blouse with flashing pearl buttons, and a cape of deep purple.

"Hey, Minnie," Schreiber said, barely looking up from his beer.

Taking a wide stance in the middle of the floor, Mrs. Jabonne replied: "They're killing cats now. Up and down. They murdered my Sally. While you're drinking yourselves blind, some crank's getting his satisfaction."

"Wadda we look like, the goddamned ASPCA?" Schreiber snapped.

Mrs. Jabonne didn't back down. "I got four dead cats in front of my house. Ain't there a law?"

"I'd say lay off the hop," Schreiber answered, winking at his companions.

Max wondered. He might be able to make something out of it after all. So far, his longest *Herald* article involved a riot at a St. Marks Place wedding—the bride's side had tried to charge the groom's relations for drinks.

"I'll take a look, and if I need you boys to keep the peace, I'll call you," Max offered.

"Who put you on the force?" Schreiber demanded.

Soon Max and Officer Schreiber were trooping after Mrs. Jabonne to view the great cat massacre. Out of the corner of his mouth, Schreiber half-whispered, "She's loaded. They say she's got property all over Brooklyn Heights."

When they reached Mrs. Jabonne's, a guttersnipe in overalls and a rag of a shirt was balancing himself on the iron fence. Max noticed the way the boy's bare toes gripped the black rail like a monkey's. How could they run around like that, even when it got ice-cold?

When he spied Officer Schreiber, the kid leaped off the fence and took several steps back, his eyes darting toward the closest alley. Maybe he was the one who had killed the creatures littering the sidewalk, or maybe he was looking for a handout to finger some other guttersnipe. The one thing Max liked, the thing he thought might sell the article to Parnell, was the way the four cats had been lined up, their evenly spaced tails telling some obscure story.

Before the boy could get a word out, Schreiber flew at the scrawny kid, flailing with his nightstick. "You murdering little bastard," he swore, aiming a full swing at the guttersnipe's head. "I'll fan ya'!"

"You idiot!" Mrs. Jabonne spit, grabbing at the towering cop.

In a flash the boy took off across the street, hopped a plank wall, and pressed himself into a black sliver of darkness between two buildings. The snaky little bastards could get in anywhere. Cellars. Warehouses. Litters of them slept under wagons parked along the North River piers. And there were as many of them as there were cats, screeching insults, grabbing from carts left and right, setting bonfires, sleeping in old sewer pipes, in nests on the hay barges.

On Printing House Square they curled up on sidewalk grates to catch the steam from the booming presses below. All winter he'd seen them in stairwells, passed out in mewling piles, bottles of blue ruin scattered round them.

Ruefully, Max watched his story disappear. Then he wondered if the little rat might pop up around the corner. Without another word he started running too, slipping in the ankle-deep horse muck along the curb, flailing, barely keeping his balance on the slick Belgian paving stones.

chapter two

Max scanned Greenwich Avenue, but the street was almost empty. A woman on the third floor of a rust-colored building rested her elbows on a pillow as she gazed out the window. In some invisible courtyard, a busker was singing a ballad. Max wished he were there, watching the girls dance in pairs under the waving wash. Wasn't it too early for singing beggars, though? The whole city sang to him, even in his sleep.

The kid had vanished. Maybe it was just as well. A few dead cats. It wasn't much of a story.

Then out of nowhere the boy materialized. He was sauntering down Greenwich Avenue, confident he'd outrun any danger. With a darting hand he picked off a baked potato, so swiftly the vendor, who had looked away for a split second, remained supremely unaware. Max didn't want to startle the guttersnipe again. Instead, he cut across the street at a sharp angle and followed the barefoot child as he wandered east, then south through the waking streets.

Near the corner of Sheridan Square, a stringy-haired woman staggered out of a dive called Langdon's, a tin growler full of beer gripped tightly in her hand. Dragging a yellow car, a pair of tram horses, their wrapped fetlocks stained with blood, strained past him.

Skulking along the edge of Washington Square Park, and then down Sullivan Street, the boy entered the Italian section. Max kept pace a quarter of a block behind. A few Negroes, the remnants of the Little Africa neighborhood, were still hanging on, but now the men with the slouch hats and stogies and the dolorosas with the black shawls dominated the sidewalks. Fresh-cut macaroni hung from tenement windows, drying in the breeze.

Apparently feeling safe, the kid sat down on a basement step to wolf down his last bit of potato skin.

Max waited one more moment, watching the scrawny boy eat. He chewed furtively, but with a desperate urgency. Max could buy the guttersnipe a meal, but what good would it do? These kids were like wild dogs: if you petted them, they were liable to bite your hand off.

"I got a penny for you," he offered, standing a few feet away.

"For what?" the boy asked warily, sensing a trick. Max could be one of those settlement-house workers, or from the church, or one of those hoisters who promised you a warm bed and then sent you out west to work on a farm like a slave. He'd heard it all from his older brother Jimmy. He didn't go near nobody 'til he was sure of him.

"Back there, you saw the cats." Max opened his hand and displayed the coin.

"Give it here," the guttersnipe replied, now up and circling Max. He had sky-blue eyes and a scattering of freckles high on his exposed cheekbones. Still, he looked like a tiny, shifty man. "C'mon, give it here."

"First tell me what you know."

"I don't know nothin'. Give it here." Lithe and quick, he danced out of reach.

"Nothing doing. Did you see who killed those cats? Who lined them up like that?"

"I seen it. Gimme two."

Max dug in his pocket and pulled out another penny. "Okay, here." He flipped one coin to the boy, who backhanded it with sudden grace. "And one more when you tell me what you saw."

Now the kid broke out in a smile so childlike and innocent-looking that Max was reminded that he was talking to an eight- or nine-year-old. "I seen a man with a great big sack." Miming, the kid stretched his arms out to describe the bag. "And he was breakin' their necks, and he looked like a ghost, and he was tall, real tall."

Up close, Max could see how narrow, how pigeon-boned the guttersnipe really was. A handful of craters, the remains of some old pox, marked his right cheek.

"How tall?"

"I dunno. When I seen him, he looked like a ghost."

"As big as me?"

"Yeah. Bigger. He was a giant, but you could see right t'rew him, too." The little bugger was having fun with him now. "Can I have the other one? I'm hungry, mister."

"What's your name?"

"They call me Famous."

"Seamus?"

"Nah, 'Famous.' Famous O'Leary."

"Ah. Did you ever see this man before?"

"Oh, yeah. He lives near the park. He's got a million crappy cats in his house. I dunno. He could find nice ones."

"Which house is that?"

"In the middle somewheres," Famous replied.

Max assumed Famous O'Leary was making it all up as fast as he could. Why was he wasting his time on this street rat? "And how old are you?"

The kid shrugged. "Eleven or twelve."

Max knew it was hopeless. A twelve-year-old who looked eight, a full-grown street arab who didn't know his own age. If he offered Famous O'Leary as his major source for the cat story, Stan Parnell would run him out of the newsroom. He could see the metro editor gazing down at him from his platform in complete disgust.

Licked, he tossed the kid the second penny and turned his back. He'd have to go back and interview Mrs. Jabonne after all. She'd probably recognize him as a former customer. If she did, she'd have the upper hand, though he couldn't quite explain why. And then what? He might end up with a few column-inches, or else nothing at all.

Dragging himself back to Waverly Place, he knocked on the imposing woman's door. It opened a crack, but he could barely make out the figure inside. "The lady ain't here."

"Are you sure? I only need her for a minute. It's business," he added ambiguously.

He cooled his heels on the top of the stoop for five more minutes, but to no avail. "She says to tell you she's asleep," the same languid voice informed him.

A penetrating hunger seized him. If, instead of chasing after meaningless squibs, he lit out for West 16th Street, he could get back to his boarding house in time for breakfast. His current landlady, Mrs. DeVogt, was no Mrs. Cohen, who had the nerve to serve week-old tongue and beef like leather. Mrs. DeVogt laid it on like nobody's business. Fresh butter and eggs and thick slices of ham. His sister's boyfriend, Danny Swarms, whose room was down the hall from Max's, had talked him into spending the extra dollar a week, and it was worth it.

He slipped into his room, washed his face in the porcelain basin, changed into his second shirt, rinsed his mouth, and tended to his facial hair. With a straight razor and a sure hand, he rapidly scraped away at his cheeks, his squared-off chin, and his pale throat. Then he took out a small scissors and carefully clipped any errant hairs that might disturb the shape of his luxuriant black mustache. There were men his age who still hadn't established one nearly as thick or graceful. Max liked to snip and shape, letting the hair curl just beneath the corners of his mouth until the whiskers fell in a rakish droop.

He had a high, well-formed forehead, hazel eyes, a slightly beaked, slightly crooked nose twice broken in bare-knuckle exhibitions, and a thin but expressive mouth. Growing up, he had used his fast hands to good effect, but his formal pugilistic career consisted of only three fights, the last at Harry Hill's where Vinnie Avenoso, a hungry Carmine Street lightweight, carved him up good and proper. Although he preferred wrapping his fist around a pencil now, he still followed the manly arts in the *Police Gazette,* whose pink pages chronicled the fortunes of The Nonpareil, the Boston Strong Boy, The Corkscrew Kid, and Little Chocolate in between classifieds for rubber goods and pinholed cards.

He ran the edge of his thumb over his humped nose. Still, he wasn't half-bad looking, he thought. He never lacked for female company, but he wasn't ready to settle down. When he found the scratch to afford a decent flat, when he earned a steady paycheck, when his father started pressing clothes again, when Faye got on her feet, when he paid off his small gambling debts, then he could get serious with a woman. He dreamed of the shining moment when he would resolve every one of these nagging problems, a moment of brilliant stillness. Meanwhile, he didn't have to answer to anybody.

He wondered what the other boarders would think of his little cat tale. At the right moment, he'd drop the story into the conversation to see how they'd react.

The breakfast room, a nook whose papered walls were crowded with small silhouettes in hand-tooled frames, could barely accommodate all the lodgers. The sideboard displayed blue and white crockery decorated with colonial themes, a slightly bedraggled Japanese parasol hung in a corner, and the drapes featured a Turkish motif.

At the head of the table, Mrs. DeVogt was lecturing her young charges, who were too conventional for her taste. She had lived through far more idealistic times, she loved to point out, during which Mrs. Woodhull had published her radical views on marriage—she didn't approve of it—and Henry George had thundered against the vipers who oppressed the poor.

She had participated in the Natural Dress movement, and she never tired of reminding her female boarders of the dangers of tight-laced corsets. As she spoke, she kept glancing at the young women, Gretta Sealy and Belle Rose, each of whom managed to maintain a respectful expression.

"I know you girls don't take me seriously, but believe me, I've seen some terrible cases. First of all, the birth canal narrows in reaction to the pressure of a tight lacing." She paused for effect after pronouncing these risqué words in mixed company, her black eyes mischievously scanning her charges.

Danny Swarms fingered his puffball of red hair and winked at Max, who did his best to hold back a laugh. Max wanted to steer the old lady away from her favorite subject, but it was definitely the wrong moment to bring up the catricides.

Gretta maintained a smooth mask during this familiar lecture. Her brushed-back chestnut hair showed her high forehead to good advantage. She had a broad face, but her wide-set eyes, her straight English nose and full mouth were finely proportioned, giving the illusion of thinner, more fashionable features. When she fixed Max in her clinical blue-eyed gaze, she shook him to the root.

She pushed back one gigot sleeve and leaned over her plate, the play of muscles in her forearm perfectly visible. Through the corner of his eye, he caught the swell of her chemise-cloaked breasts. The organdy's silver underthreading imparted an elusive sheen that suited her. Smooth as her skin, he thought.

Facing her across the table, he stretched his leg out, hoping to brush the tip of his shoe, however accidentally, across her ankle. He shifted to the edge of his chair, extended his leg further, imagining Gretta pressing back, staring straight through him. Finally, the tension became unbearable, and he straightened up.

Then he caught Danny running his eyes up and down Gretta's lush figure. Since Swarms was squiring his sister Faye around, Max felt justified in delivering a sharp kick to his friend's ankle. Danny just smiled and shrugged.

Gretta was barely aware of the two men. Instead, she was wondering how to light Mrs. Seymour Bethesda-Clarke. The woman's face was asymmetrical, and it was hard to decide which was her better side. And when she didn't get her sleep, Mrs. Bethesda-Clarke developed dark, baggy pouches under her eyes that were almost impossible to touch up. Mrs. Bertha Van Eggles, who ran the studio, depended on Gretta to make unpleasant blemishes disappear under her quick brush, but she thought the owner's demands were becoming more and more unreasonable.

Belle shot Max a furtive glance. Did she mean to encourage him? She had thick black hair fixed in a bun, warm brown eyes, a delicate nose, and a bud of a mouth. There was a trace of the steppe to her looks, the way her eyes narrowed to slits when she laughed. Barely over five feet tall, with a thin, graceful figure, she hardly looked like a visiting nurse, but she had lived and worked at the Rivington Street College Settlement House for a year. Now, roaming the tenements, she treated everything from nits to scarlet fever every day.

Her room was just down the hall. It could all happen spontaneously, Max daydreamed. In the middle of the night they could bump into each other in the dark hall. He could feel how easy it would be to sweep her off the floor; he could feel the shock of her lips, her smooth face, her breasts, her thighs, encased in silky material, pressing against his legs. He smelled her perfume—or was it Gretta's? Suddenly the breakfast table was saturated with the smell of roses.

Mrs. DeVogt went on, her soft, round face glowing. "So when it's time to have a child, if you've been tight-lacing you'll go through the worst ag-o-ny imaginable."

"Mrs. DeVogt!" Belle admonished her. The old bohemian would say anything to shock them. She admired her landlady, but sometimes she went too far.

Max tried to forget Belle's body. Otherwise he wouldn't be able to stand up when breakfast ended. Under the table he rearranged himself, praying his pulsing hard-on would fade away. When could he mention the cat corpses arranged so neatly on the sidewalk? He waited for an opening.

"Don't laugh. I knew a woman who tight-laced herself to a nineteen-inch waist. She died a week later, and do you know what the doctor said?"

Getting into the spirit, Danny asked, "What did he say, Mrs. DeVogt?"

"He said she'd cut her own liver in half!"

Max attacked his fatty steak, which he was having trouble keeping on the plate. Swallowing hard, he managed to offer a question. "With all due respect, Mrs. DeVogt, but is that possible?"

A titter ran through the boarders. For all her radical ideas, Mrs. DeVogt sounded as ridiculous as the rest of the older generation.

"Certainly! There was an autopsy. Not to speak of all the idiots these women bring into the world. The babies' heads get squeezed like melons!"

Gretta, who had been trying hard to keep a straight face, burst out laughing. "Mrs. DeVogt, now you're exaggerating!"

The landlady had little sense of humor on the tight-lacing controversy, however. Instead of responding, she hit the bell next to her and Eileen, the serving girl, took the dishes away.

"And what did you type today, Mr. Greengrass?" she asked, turning to Max.

Max hesitated. If he revealed the triviality of the story he was working on, he risked looking like a lightweight. On the other hand, if he got a strong reaction from the table, he might find out if he was on to something. "A story about cat murders, Mrs. DeVogt. Four cats, to be exact."

Gretta leaned towards him. "How awful!"

"Some crank?" Danny asked, his interest piqued. "The public, they lap that up."

Belle's eyes widened. "Why would anyone do such a disgusting thing?"

"What do you know about it?" Mrs. DeVogt asked Max, apparently hooked as well.

"You'll have to look for it in the *Herald*," Max said, digging himself deeper into a hole.

chapter three

Danny rapped his walking stick on the steps. "Downtown?"

"Sixth Precinct house."

"Ahh, too bad." In his boater and tight blue suit, Swarms looked ready to step on stage.

"I've got to keep on the case," Max explained.

Danny tapped his cane to some inner beat, a faraway look in his transparent blue eyes. "There's a singing waiter I gotta look up anyway. Izzy Ballin. He's been beating down my door with some new song. I'd like to publish it. Nice hook it's got. 'Ida, Ida . . . dadumdeedumdadadumdeedum. . . .' You know how many copies of 'After the Ball' Ditson's in Boston ordered? Seventy-five thousand. One lousy hit, you're made for life."

"You see Faye lately?" These days Danny knew more about his sister's peregrinations than he did. Max held his breath in trepidation.

"Oh, Jesus. I forgot to tell you! She got a new part."

Relief rippled through him. Faye was always telling him to stop expecting the worst. "What is it?"

Danny stroked his weak chin. Talking out of the side of his mouth, the actor imparted a deep secret. "She's playing a grasshopper."

"A what?"

Danny flashed his sunny smile. "She's makin' good chink. What else you need to know?"

"Is she—?" Max tilted his head back and sipped from an invisible bottle of Mrs. Winslow's Soothing Syrup. In the past, he had known just how to deal with Faye's boyfriends. He didn't trust a single one. Now that Danny was dating Faye, though, hope, that subversive emotion, was undermining his natural suspicion.

"C'mon. Faye's a good kid. This job'll set her right up."
"Right up where?"
"Gotta hustle, kiddo."

At the Sixth Precinct house a woman, wild-haired and wobbly, was waving a heavy chair leg and shouting at Officer Schreiber. "He's got the nerve," she bellowed, gesturing toward a bald man with a gash high on his cheek. "He even brings her into the building to do his business with her."

"Lay off the hard stuff, why don't you?" the man snarled.

"Shut up, the both of yez, or I'll cram this down your throats." Schreiber showed them his meaty fist. The man fell to muttering under his breath, but the woman remained unrepentant.

"He's a yellow dog. That's why he runs to her with his tail between his legs." Unsatisfied with this jibe, she spit at the bald man for emphasis.

Casually, Schreiber smacked the woman flush in the mouth with the back of his hand. She flew straight back, slamming into a wooden bench and falling into stunned silence. The bald man bowed his head, waiting for a blow that didn't come. Schreiber just pointed to the other end of the bench with his nightstick, and the misguided husband scurried to follow the policeman's suggestion.

Schreiber turned to Max, a smile breaking out over his generous features. Max stole a peek at the woman, who was cupping the blood pouring from the corner of her mouth. She might have been holding her front teeth, for all he knew. Schreiber had really hauled off on her. But what could he say?

When he started out at the *Brooklyn Eagle*, he might have questioned Schreiber's tactics, but now he knew better. Anyway, he wasn't some mincing good-government fanatic—some goo-goo—like the Reverend Parkhurst. Precinct houses were flophouse and jailhouse rolled into one. Who wouldn't get fed up?

"I thought you were knocking off," Max said to the policeman.

"Yeah. Listen, Maxie, I got something for you. Let's get out of this shithole for a minute."

Once they hit the sidewalk, Max contributed his last decent cigar, Lillian Russell gracing the paper band. Schreiber slipped it into his pocket.

"So I went back to Fitzgerald's after I seen you, and guess who shows up? Morris from the 19th. You know him, don't you?"

"*Sergeant* Morris, right?"

"That's the one. Anyways, Morris says he ain't seen nothing like it. A half dozen of 'em was laid out two doors down from the station house on West 30th. Maybe it's an epidemic. They got the cholera in Jersey City again," he added. Max couldn't follow this line of reasoning, but Schreiber went on serenely. "Morris says the 19th is crawling with strays. Maybe that has something to with it."

"You mean they may have a disease?"

"Sure. Maybe they're comin' off the ships with some new kinda cat typhoid. The goo-goos will make hay with that one." Schreiber let go a brown ball of phlegm. "A man gets the shits, they blame Tammany. If the sun forgot to go down, they'd blame Boss Croker."

In fact, Schreiber's remarks were politically astute. The reformers had attacked Tammany ceaselessly over its slipshod sanitation efforts, which amounted to giving out contracts to Tammany cronies. Who knew? Politics was crazy. An epidemic among cats might affect the next election.

On his walk uptown, Max couldn't help noticing every cat he passed. They lounged on stoops, slipped in between ashcans and under delivery wagons, they sunned themselves next to pushcarts and raced in between the children who flooded the sidewalks. A healthy striped tabby nosed at a horse, bloated and dead at the curb. Nearby, two barefoot girls rolled a hoop back and forth. But the cats he observed showed no signs of wasting away. On the contrary, they looked healthier than some of the hollow-eyed men who stood in clusters in front of lodging houses, in doorways and on the steps of open cellars, men who occasionally sidled up to Max and whispered, "Got some coin?"

Were there more of these panhandlers now than last year? It seemed that way, but they were so quiet and furtive that it was hard to tell. And when you were hustling until your tongue fell out, like Max, the tramps became a damned nuisance.

Sergeant Morris, it turned out, was more than happy to relate his tale. Max's racing pencil could barely keep up with the policeman.

A middle-aged man who had risen to his position after a long career, Morris had a mottled complexion and a spider's web of exploded veins in his fleshy nose. "Right down the block, on the steps. Sammy, the doorman, this mornin' on his way in to work, he found 'em. Then there was the fairy from Proctor's, he paints those drapes, the whatayoucallems. . . ."

"Scenery?"

"Yeah, the sign painter. He found a bunch in front of his place on West 25th." He looked down at his ledger. "In front of Fifty-One West Twenty-Fifth. Eight, he says. Then the janitor from next door walks in and says they're stinkin' up the street. Well, I says, what do I look like, the bleedin' Health Department? If we catch the lunatic's pullin' this shit, he'll get what's comin' to him. What'd a cat ever do to nobody?"

"Did they look sick?"

"How the hell do I know? Why don't you get your damn newspaper to make a stink, 'cause makin' a stink's the only thing's gonna stop the crank pullin' this shit."

"Somebody's on a rampage, huh?"

"We never had this many before. It's a record for the precinct."

"You mean this isn't the first time?"

"Well, last June there was some, but we figured people was goin' away for the summer, they was getting' rid of their pets. Or maybe some of Schwab's boys were having a picnic. But this is out of hand. The people are gettin' nervous."

"What would Schwab have to do with it?" Was Morris talking about Schwab's saloon on East First where those blowhard anarchists wasted their time? East First was nowhere near the 19th, and cops usually confined their thinking to the boundaries of their fiefdoms.

Max, who had been surprised by Morris's fury, watched as a sleek and well-fed black cat rubbed up against the sergeant's leg. Leaning down, the cop gently stroked the animal's head and was rewarded with a satisfied purr. "This one's called Nig. He been with us since before I got to the 19th."

"Schwab the Red?" Max asked.

A woman in a shapeless housedress interrupted them. Bits of straw stuck out of her lank hair. A swarm of bleary children clung to her hem and ran squealing around her. "C'n we stay the night again, Sergeant?"

"Get here early, mind you," Morris replied, patting a small boy absently on the head. "Ahh, where'd they go if it weren't for the station house? Anyway, this is how I figure it. The Reds don't necessarily have to do the big job to nobody. What they want is to get everybody nervous all the time.

They do all kinds of little things, maybe murdering a few cats, they get everybody lookin' sideways. Then later, when they're stronger, they start throwing the bombs. Like that crank they arrested who was threatening Mayor Gilroy."

Morris's theory sounded about as far-fetched as Famous O'Leary's tall, ghostly catnapper.

"What was the address of that scenery painter?"

"He calls himself Cristofaro. John Cristofaro. They're bringing guineas over to paint our pictures now."

The artist, who was under pressure to finish a turreted castle for the Offenbach opera at Proctor's, said, "Can we talk and walk? I'm so far behind with the new flats, they might as well shoot me now."

A light drizzle began to fall.

Cristofaro went on. "You'd think the city would show some consideration. We're trying to live in this . . ." stalking along the sidewalk, he groped for a word. "Oh, I don't know what to call it! You don't find eight animals in a row like that unless somebody's using poison."

"Lined up in a row?"

"Yeah. Heads this way, tails that way."

"Did they look sick or healthy?"

Cristofaro gave Max the fish-eye. "I didn't have my stethoscope on me. This is the third time, too!"

"The third time?"

Falling harder, the rain splashed over the Proctor Theatre's low tile roof. Before Max could pursue the cat matter further, Cristofaro hurried past the box office and disappeared into a side entrance. At least the artist had corroborated Morris's report.

Now he'd have to canvass Waverly Place.

Starting from the middle of the block, he began working his way east, knocking on one door after another. At the third house, he found a distraught Mrs. Winston McCall, a woman whose treasured Angora had turned up in a mound of dead cats in Grove Street Park. He kept his excitement to himself, but clearly the phenomenon was spreading.

"You wouldn't understand," said the widow, who, though restrained, was clearly in deep distress. "When a pet dies, one goes into mourning just as if a close relative had passed on."

"I do understand," Max assured her. In fact, he couldn't fathom how a person could mourn an animal. Maybe Mrs. McCall was a little touched. Still, he was moved by the quaver in her voice.

"They ought to arrest the monster who is doing this!" she added with sudden ferocity. "They should hang him from a tree!" With that, Mrs. McCall slammed the door in Max's face.

Back at the office, he began fooling with leads.

"Death is stalking the cats of the Tenderloin," he wrote, and then he quoted Sergeant Morris and Cristofaro, the scene painter. He took this tack because Stan Parnell was partial to headlines involving the Tenderloin. If the metro editor thought the murders might have a salacious angle, all the better. Then he worked his way back to the massacres at Waverly Place and Grove Street Park, the latter confirmed by the local precinct, and closed with Mrs. McCall's cry for vengeance. Best of all, he kept it to six grafs. No point in overreaching.

He waited for the right moment to approach Parnell, who reigned from his platform—the "throne," the reporters called it. Blocking Max's way, William Walter Scott, the portly theatre critic, was monopolizing the city editor just because he was eminent enough to do so.

Another stringer, Billy Webster, stood right behind Max, fingering his own story. "Look at Scottie up there. He's licking the cream off his lips. He's just like Croker. Every day he's working for his pocket," Billy added in a low whisper. "The producers, the press agents, they're crawling all over him. You think he lives on what Bennett doles out?"

Billy knew the score. Did Lily Langtry's press agent want to see her name in the paper more often? Did Tony Pastor need a plug for his latest attraction, the English ventriloquist with the Cockney automaton? Who could help them more than William Walter Scott?

With a little luck, a reporter could find himself perfectly situated.

Finally, Scott hauled himself down from the throne and brushed by Max without a word. Max leaped onto the platform before anyone else could cut in and thrust his copy into Parnell's hands.

Parnell started scanning the copy. A rail-thin man of indeterminate age, he read without moving a muscle—until he found something he didn't like. Then he jabbed his sharpened pencil straight into the page. Max felt every stab.

Raising his colorless gaze, Parnell spoke. "Don't ever mention an epidemic unless the Health Department says so."

"It was the cop who said—"

Parnell cut him off. "Where'd he study medicine? The Health Department. Period." Flinching, Max waited to be dismissed, his copy tossed into Parnell's wastebasket. Instead, the editor offered him a lipless smile. "The whole city's on hairsprings. They think there's an anarchist under every mattress. The *Herald* ought to catch this crank in the act. Now, that would give circulation a shot in the arm."

Max plunged in. "I could stake out the locations."

Parnell didn't say yes, but he didn't say no. He simply raised his eyebrows. "Copy boy!" he shouted and Max, seeing his article sanctioned and sent off to the printers, experienced that ancient thrill. His words would see the light.

chapter four

At six the next morning, Max sat in City Hall Park reading and rereading his story. Bench-sitters were rubbing their eyes after a restless night on the boards. A man nearby was setting up shop for the day. His sign read "I CAN EAT ONE HUNDRED EGGS IN ONE HUNDRED MINUTES!" Ten-year-old girls, the hot corn vendors, were taking their stations. A sidewalk salesman was offering the latest craze, rubber masks fashioned to look like cartoonish New Yorkers—Bowery b'hoys, muttonchopped businessmen, dark-haired dagos, a mab with a red gob of a mouth. Newsboys filtered through the park, hawking the day's papers freshly printed directly across the way on Newspaper Row. Above, the first light of day reflected off the *World*'s gilded dome.

Max's article had made page six, sandwiched in between accounts of an assault at the Hotel Viano and the Right Reverend Bishop Potter's shocking stipulation that he be buried in a wicker coffin.

DEATH STALKS MANHATTAN'S CATS

Carnage in the Tenderloin
Residents of Waverly Place Weary of
Dodging the Silent Slain at Their Doors

Piles of dead cats are turning up with remarkable regularity in widely separated sites around town. Sgt. Morris of the Tenderloin has been flooded with complaints of catricide in the 19th precinct. John Cristofaro, a Proctor's scene painter who resides at Fifty-One West Twenty-Fifth Street,

> observed eight of the slain felines lined up in a row in front of his house.
>
> In the Sixth Precinct, Officer Schreiber reports that ten dead cats, at least two owned by Waverly Place residents, appeared on the sidewalk yesterday morning. Grove Street Park has also been the location of a great cat massacre.
>
> Yesterday morning, dead cats lay deep on the sidewalk before 176 Waverly Place, and when Mrs. Jabonne, who lives over that way, discovered the slaughter, she found her own beloved pet among the victims. A Waverly Place widow, Mrs. McCall, who also lost her feline friend, said, "They ought to arrest the monster who is doing this! They should hang him from a tree!"
>
> While it may be well that the halt, the lame, and the blind in the cat kingdom should be put out of their misery, some of the victims appeared to be in fine health. At any rate, citizens who live in the vicinity of these assassinations have deeply rooted objections to picking their way through the slain which lie stark and still before their doors at dawn.

Satisfied, he marched west to the Rector Street stop on the El. It was only six-twenty. He had plenty of time to get back to Mrs. DeVogt's and lay down his article as casually as possible on the breakfast table. He knew he had serious competition for Gretta's attentions—she had been dating a swell named Martin Mourtone—but at the moment his confidence was surging.

Max had first met Martin Mourtone when the toff picked Gretta up in his glassed landau. The chattering dandy had tried to convince him that he knew every blind pig and opium den in town.

"Slummer-dummer," Danny observed when the couple had departed.

"Knows all about the tongs in Chinatown, no less," Max had laughed. Police Superintendent Byrnes himself couldn't decipher the latest tong warfare.

Mourtone also turned up at the Hoffman House bar where Max delivered his weekly loan payment to Sim Addem. The Italian Renaissance

Hoffman House, on Broadway between 24th and 25th Streets, acted as the inner sanctum, the unofficial Democratic Party headquarters, as well as the watering hole of well-off sportsmen, businessmen, and the theatre crowd. When he had an extra dollar or two, Max would meet Danny there to watch the dignitaries on display.

Uninvited, Mourtone slid over and took a sip of his brandy while Max settled with Sim, who was building his pile to finance a run for alderman. After Max paid him, he allowed the young reporter to buy him a drink. Then he turned around and fit the small of his back into the bar. Max followed suit, and a moment later Mourtone did as well.

"That's what I call a painting," the horse-headed Sim intoned, pointing to the Hoffman House's prize possession, Bouguereau's *Nymphs and Satyr*. Displayed below a red velvet canopy, the painting's vast, waxy surface featured a goat-faced satyr being pulled mischievously into the water by four nymphs. "Lookit the way he lit up her rear end," Sim added with pride.

"Very accomplished," Mourtone put in, but Sim ignored him.

Max felt giddy in the crush of well-heeled men in black silk and beaver toppers, his ears picking up scraps of conversation about Mayor Gilroy and Tammany's tight-lipped Boss Croker, real estate, watered stock, and Lower East Side bomb throwers. Though he felt like an imposter now, he dreamed that one day he would be able to wander as a matter of course into the Hoffman House. The men pressed against the brass rail would be pleasantly surprised to see him, and the bartender would produce his favorite cocktail. So he didn't mind running into Martin Mourtone. He imagined that Mourtone might mention to Gretta that he had seen Max there, and she would surmise, however erroneously, that he belonged in that charmed circle.

Martin bought the next round, teasing a grunt of recognition out of Addem.

"I was down at Suicide Hall the other night," Mourtone confided.

"McGurk's?" Sim asked, incredulous. Of course Addem knew McGurk and how he squeezed a nice dollar out of barrel fever. "You touched?"

"He likes the atmosphere," Max explained maliciously.

Addem snorted and knocked back another drink, not even bothering to cover up his contempt. After Sim drained a whiskey and half a beer chaser, he began expounding on the goo-goos' latest legislation. "So they order from on high, from their friggin' thrones, that the age of consent is . . . Presto! Sixteen. Maybe ten was too young," he added, referring to the previous law, "but wadda you goin' to do about human nature? And do they think for one second about takin' the bread out of the lady's mouth?"

"Reverend Weems gave that sermon last week." Max noted.

"Don't worry, he gets his end wet." Sim's long jaw split in a grin.

Mrs. Jabonne's thirteen- and fourteen-year-old charges with their unmarked skin and air of innocence flashed through Max's mind. The subject made him faintly uncomfortable.

"I got other business, fellas," Sim said, pushing himself away from the bar.

"Another for my friend here," Martin called out before Max could shove off too. "So what do you think of *The Century*?"

"What?" Max was determined to down his fresh pilsner and make his getaway.

"You know. Gilder's magazine."

"Oh, that one. I can take it or leave it." In fact, he rarely looked into *The Century*'s genteel pages. Its long sentences on cultural topics put him to sleep, and he didn't see why they had to throw around French words when plain English would do, but he also worried that he was missing something. Martin was educated and probably worshipped the damn thing.

To Max's shock, Mourtone launched into a tirade. "Dead in the water, if you ask me. What city is Gilder living in? I've been thinking of starting a magazine that would put in everything Gilder leaves out. Plenty of photographs. Have you seen Gretta's pictures?"

"Her portraits?"

"No, no. Her photos of the streets. Fantastic. The most objective eye you've ever seen. She's not like Riis and the rest of them. She's something new."

"Really?" He felt envious, regretting that he hadn't understood Gretta's work better. Evidently her still features and smooth manners hid accomplishments he hadn't fathomed.

Max waited for the usual smutty innuendo, but Mourtone veered off in another direction. "Speed is what I'm looking for. You go out into that street and what do you see? Streetcars, cabs, wagons, elevated trains. Preachers. Cutthroats. Bond salesmen. Pushcarts with last week's chickens. Chaos. Meanwhile, *The Century*'s blathering about Carthage."

Max couldn't resist. "You could call it *This Instant!*"

"That's good, that's good. You see, I need reporters like you."

"Your father's in what?"

"Insurance. Raising money won't be a problem," he added bluntly, before launching into another exposition. Max listened in wonder. How could he have been so wrong about the man? He had ideas, energy. He wasn't some City College brain blowing smoke in Sachs's Café. Why wouldn't Gretta care for him?

Still, Max's natural skepticism asserted itself. "I'll take half what they give Harding Davis."

"That shallow quiff? You're worth twice as much!"

"I always thought so."

"By the way, I saw your sister the other night."

Immediately, his stomach tightened. Where? What had she been up to this time? "Faye? How'd you meet her?"

"I ran into Danny Swarms right here, and he dragged me over to Cremone Gardens. No offense, but I couldn't take my eyes off her. What a voice!"

Christ. Faye in her mask of powder, stomping and bellowing away in front of a two-piece band. Munchie on violin and Crow on viola. They sawed fast and sometimes in tune.

"She's got a foghorn all right." From the first time she stood up on the kitchen table, pressing her fat knees together, she had the voice. As her older brother, he'd wanted to knock her down as fast as possible, but the sound coming out of her, solid, ringing, stunned him like a blow between the eyes.

His mother was clapping, and Faye was dancing closer and closer to the edge of the table, and he didn't know whether to push her off or catch her before she fell.

When Max woke up the next day with a paralyzing body hangover, he wondered what part of his newfound admiration for Mourtone had been composed of whiskey and what part hot air. Nothing compared to the intimacy that developed between two men on a drinking spree, and nothing felt worse than the headache the morning after. This one was like needles behind his eye.

At breakfast, he took several slices of ham and some extra gravy for his potatoes. He also left some space on his plate for Mrs. DeVogt's delicious scrambled eggs, which she flavored with onions and peppers.

The landlady, with a worried expression on her face, asked, "What do you think of that bank in Omaha, Mr. Greengrass?"

Max had no idea what she was talking about, but he took a flyer. "Another run?"

"Yes. What do the people on the paper say?"

"Just another farmer's bank, Mrs. DeVogt. Once the silver mania dies down, everything will be back to normal." Seeing an opening, he made his announcement. "I did get my little cat story into the paper today."

Perhaps the other boarders were distracted by their own affairs, but no one leaped to see Max's work, which he had folded and placed next to his plate.

"May I?" Belle asked finally, reaching for the *Herald*. In a glance, she took in the article. "Ach, terrible!" she said. "I wouldn't be surprised if the owners of these cats were responsible. And why not? Maybe they can't feed them, with all the jobs drying up."

"Uh-oh," Danny said, winking. "Blood-sucking businessmen, is it?"

"You should listen to Belle," Mrs. DeVogt chimed in. "Henry George is turning over in his grave."

Self-consciously, Belle fingered the fleshy beauty mark high on her cheek. Shifting her gaze, she caught Max staring at her. Her brown eyes held his gaze for a moment, brown eyes flecked with gold, and he could feel a swelling in his chest. He never thought her type would be interested in him. Belle believed in fighting scarlet fever and rapacious landlords, she believed in pure milk and clean sheets and socialism.

Max didn't believe in anything and was proud of it. Ideas blinded you. At the same time, he envied people who had names for themselves: Anarchists. Methodists. Zionists. Free-silver fanatics. Gold bugs. They could share delusions and church suppers. There was no name for what he was.

The conversation wasn't going in the direction Max had hoped. Belle was paying attention, but Gretta hadn't evinced the slightest bit of interest. Instead, encased in a dreamy silence, she kept cutting her meat into bite-sized portions. He especially liked her broad, full mouth. Yet most of all, she gave off a sort of indefinable glow. Perhaps it was simply animal health, but Max thought it was something deeper. What had Mourtone been babbling about? Her "objective" pictures? What did that mean?

Unable to contain himself, he asked her directly. "And what does Miss Sealy think?"

She looked at Max blandly. "I think you ought to write about some less disagreeable subject."

Danny let go a barking laugh.

"Sometimes the city can be very disagreeable," he replied stiffly.

"But you don't have to rub our noses in it, do you?"

"Well. . . ." Max coughed to cover his humiliation.

"Come on, he doesn't have a choice," Mrs. DeVogt said, rescuing him. "That's his job. Will you be away long, Gretta?"

"Just a few days. I haven't seen my family in Staten Island for three weeks."

"I was on my way down to the ferry myself," Danny said.

"Oh, that's all right, my friend Martin's taking me."

A few minutes later the elegant Mourtone did arrive, his landau drawn by a pair of chestnuts with fashionably clipped manes. They shook their heads in the spirited way of fine horses. Ray Allen over at the *Brooklyn Eagle* had told Max the secret of this picturesque equine mannerism. Barbed bits.

While Gretta prepared to leave, Max crawled up to his room, fell onto his bed, and stared at the ceiling. Why had he imagined that his small success, if it could be called that, would impress Gretta Sealy? She had mentioned tennis at her country club, and bicycling with friends around the countryside. She spent her days arranging backdrops and elegant bric-a-brac, chatting with society matrons about coming-out parties and charity balls.

He didn't have time to feel wounded, though. He would put it out of his mind. Hadn't Stan Parnell given him an opening? Shouldn't he be out there hustling? Yet a deep lassitude gripped him, pressing him into the mattress. His arms and legs felt weighted down as if they were underwater. Finally, he fell into a profound, paralyzed sleep. He was drowning, yet he couldn't get his limbs to fight the weight of the water. Then he began to see, despite the darkness, sinking, flailing animals, cats drowning along with him. They drifted right past his face, their eyes wide with fright, their claws extended, their tails snaking back and forth. Then he became a clawing cat, writhing helplessly, unable to fight to the bright surface.

When he finally woke up, his jaw aching, he found himself entangled in moist sheets.

chapter five

"Fayefaye."

Max's sister sat up in bed. She was still lounging in her silk robe, red Chinese dragons warring on a field of blue. Smudged and faded, her penciled eyebrows looked as tired as her eyes. Rearranging her pillows, she patted the bed for him to sit down. "Cig?"

Her flatmates, the dancers Judy and Joanne Connolly, were rattling pans on the coal stove. He looked out the window. Down below, behind a hash house, the cook was sitting on a stone step, a lapful of potatoes in his apron.

"Just a used cigar."

"Ugh. Look over in the ashtray there. There's a broken one I left." Faye was dark, like their dumpling of a mother. Black-eyed and curly-haired and pretty enough, he supposed, but he didn't think about that. She was his sister.

He lit the butt for her. "So what's with the grasshopper? It's a part? Danny says you're making out good."

"If Gordon meets the payroll, I'll be the Queen of Sheba." She picked tobacco from between her teeth and looked at him cross-eyed. "You busted too?"

He pulled two bills from his purse but held them between his fingers, high over her head.

Bouncing on the bed, she snatched the money from his hand and kissed him on the cheek. The sudden movement woke her baby, Leon, who sniffled, yawned, and started crying. "I'm a scene-stealer. You'll see. Why don't you come with Danny tomorrow night?"

He had dropped by to give her the money, but to talk to her, too, about the cats and Gretta and the damned space-raters' bench and a dozen other things, but the smell of her milk, and his nephew's filmy stare, spooked him. "Who's watching Leon now?"

"Oh, I have a new woman. Mrs. Darling, she's called. She's a real professional. When I get home from work, he's dead to the world."

"She's probably sticking that Soothing Syrup in the bottle."

"Don't start up, worrywart."

"I wasn't saying a thing."

"You're always saying something, even when you keep your trap shut. I can hear you thinking." She planted a small fist on his back and laughed. "Daddy didn't know that about you. He always thought you were a gangster."

"Ahh, what could he understand?"

"Ach, you're just like him. Watching me all the time."

"What're you talking about? I'm dead to him, remember?"

"I gave him better reasons."

"The time he went at you with his shoe? I had to pull him off you. Then right away he throws a tallis over his head and starts davening. You know what? That man's afraid of his own shadow. I used to watch how he crept around, and I said to myself he's more dead than alive. He never leaves the block. He has the same friends he had when he got off the boat. I said to myself, do the opposite in everything, and you'll be fine."

"You're the opposite, all right. A little the same, though."

"So, you staying away from the stuff?"

"You see! The next time Danny has to scrape you off the sidewalk, I'll tell him to leave you there." She stuck her tongue out. Nothing bothered Faye. No matter how shaky things got, she had a wisecrack.

"You're still carping about that? I was a kid. It was five years ago."

"That's not what I hear." She pecked him on the cheek. "Now go away so I can feed Hungry Man here."

"Let me see him first. Leon, say hi. Say hi, Leon." The sallow-cheeked boy gave him a glassy stare. A pint-sized human being with a world of clouds in his head and Fayefaye for his mother. Jesus.

Faye should have weaned the kid half a year ago, in his opinion. The boy was almost two. "Say hello, Leon."

Coming to his senses, Leon brightened. "Unca Max."

"Lookit that. He's a genius."

Leon laughed and showed Max his gums. The kid had a purple,

star-shaped birthmark near his hairline. He'd have to comb his hair over it. Love, fear, and melancholy pierced Max in a single bolt of emotion.

Faye retrieved the child, tossed him over her shoulder, and started burping him. For the moment, he quieted down. "Go, go. Thanks for the loan. I'll pay you double."

"So what's the news with you and Danny?" All he knew was that Swarms, whom Faye had met backstage at the Coronet half a year ago, wasn't Leon's father and that sometimes, when he took Faye to their favorite lobster palace, he didn't return to Mrs. DeVogt's until the next morning. What they did together, Max purposely blurred in his mind's eye. His sister and his best pal, it was too damned complicated.

She twirled her curly black hair and made her Fritzie Labonza face, the one she had invented when she was ten. Sucked-in cheeks, tongue out, eyeballs almost disappeared under her lids. She could make him fall down laughing with that expression. "Don't lie and say he doesn't tell you everything. The two of you."

"On the subject of you, he's a closed-mouthed S.O.B. What're you, blackmailing him?"

"The baby needs breakfast, do you mind? Kiss?" Drawing Leon to her, she threatened to expose a swollen breast.

"Okay, I gotta go to work anyway. 'Bye, little guy." Danny might be in the picture for a while, but who was the kid's uncle forever? What a mess. Still, the little guy was his flesh and blood. What could you do?

Gazing intently at Max, Leon said, "Ba."

"Ba to you, bub."

She was strange, his sister. She refused to see how appalling her situation was. No, that wasn't it: she didn't notice there was a problem at all. What really maddened him was how cheerful she was. He'd come over determined to have a serious talk with her, but before long she'd tell him a blue joke she heard at Nigger Mike's or sing a few lines from a new show, and soon raising a kid on the fly in a tenement flat with a pair of chorines who couldn't come up with their share of the rent half the time seemed liked a good plan.

On the other hand, she was still keeping Leon's existence secret from the rest of the family, so she wasn't all that free and easy. Lurking below the surface was the uncomfortable question: What was *he* going to do about it? Was he ready to cough up for the kid every week? Was he willing to give up faro banks and eye-openers at Fitzgerald and Ives? Not on your life. He'd never confused himself with the Reverend Dr. Parkhurst.

He tapped down the stairs on his toes.

Every door was open to catch some air from the stairwell. On the landing below he saw into an apartment identical to Faye's, three rooms counting the kitchen. Several Italian women were jabbering away as they picked at a huge mound of walnuts, plucking the meat, separating the shells, pouring the cleaned nuts into jars. The youngest one, a daring girl of about twelve with a purple scarf tied over her head, waved to him. He touched two fingers to his forehead.

Out on Sullivan Street, a vegetable wagon rolled to a stop. With a look of disdain, a wizened dolorosa poked an eggplant. A peddler with a cigar box tied around his neck was hawking pipe cleaners and broken candy. The sun poured down, washing the rust-red buildings. A senseless elation took hold of him. Another cracked day, another chance.

He wasn't about to give up on Mrs. Jabonne. She'd lost her pet, and eventually she'd want to talk. Once again he pounded on her door, and this time the mistress of the house opened up herself.

"You?"

Max quickly slipped his left foot over the doorstep. "All I need is one minute of your time, Mrs. Jabonne."

"One minute, tops. You've been around here, ain't you?"

"Maybe. Do you have any idea who's doing the cats?"

With a slicing motion of her hand, she cut him off. "Who else? They're out all night, smoking, stealing who knows what, forcing little girls." Her disgusted expression made the moral high ground where she dwelt quite clear. "Where's their mother and father?" she demanded.

Max wasn't interested in Mrs. Jabonne's reform tendencies. "Where can I find them?"

"Who?"

"The kids, the ones you think—"

"They're up all night makin' a racket on Hudson Street. They're always sneaking into The White Stag and getting pie-eyed and makin' their messes in the street. I know it's them because I've seen 'em. For fun they'll swing a cat around by its tail and laugh their brains out."

"Did you see them kill yours, though?"

"No," she said reluctantly. "But they've got queer minds from living like they do. It's just like 'em to think it's funny."

"Where can I find the ones you're talking about?"

"Go to The Stag around ten or eleven. You'll catch 'em, I'll bet. Then you can wring their skinny necks 'til they choke."

"You're very kind. Thanks for the tip."

"You can't go to the store without they're putting their paws in your pocket."

He didn't have to wait for nightfall. A band of local street arabs was lounging in Grove Street Park, and among them Max recognized Famous O'Leary. He didn't share Mrs. Jabonne's venomous attitude toward the boys, and Famous, with his birdcage of a chest and rounded shoulders, seemed more sinned against than sinner. Still, these guttersnipes, some of whom were aspiring to join the Hudson Dusters when they grew their first chin hairs, would mob a man with a dozen picking hands. They had their share of razors and knuckle-dusters, too.

Before Max even reached the mob of small fry, Famous rushed him. "Got another penny? Got a nickel? C'mon, mister, you got loadsa coin, you know ya' do. Help a little kid out, I got nowheres to sleep tonight."

In the middle distance, a boy with a broken-brimmed derby set rakishly on his head stared at Max without blinking. Unlike Famous, his face was flat, expressionless, all trace of the child worn away. A ruddy-faced companion was playing with a longshoreman's hook, burying it over and over into the slats of a bench.

"Who's that?" Max asked, pointing to the flat-faced kid.

"That's the Cham-peen. C'mon, mister, what's a penny to you? Don't be a cheapskate."

"I got two cents for you if you can get the Cham-peen to talk to me."

Famous sauntered over to open negotiations. The first offer came back at a full nickel, but Max finally bought a consultation for three cents. There were six boys, including The Great Napoleon, a tubercular thin waif with rabbit's teeth, and The Basher, master of the docker's hook, but Cham-peen stood out. Aside from his rakish hat, he was wearing a pair of cut-down gabardine pants held up with a rope and an enormous suit coat that fell to his knees.

"There's a guinea works in a stable," Cham-peen confided, poker-faced. Max looked over Cham-peen's shoulder, noting that the other street arabs could barely contain their laughter. "Over on Hudson. He's the one. He smokes guinea stinkers."

"He's got a pile of horsecrap this high!" Famous put in.

"What does he do with the cats?" Max asked skeptically.

"He puts 'em . . . in a big pot," the sober leader replied. Max was impressed by the boy's self-control, if not his powers of imagination.

"So why are so many cats still on the street?"

"They's the leftovers."

Famous O'Leary hooted. The Great Napoleon threw himself on the sidewalk and flung his arms out. Two others followed in excited imitation. Famous took the opportunity to step on The Basher's stomach, but the victim twisted O'Leary's ankle and flung him down too.

"You boys go uptown at all?"

"Fourteen Street?"

"Further."

"Nah, Fourteen's the dead line. Enemy territory."

"Yeah, we t'row rocks at their heads," Famous explained, brushing himself off and grinning.

"The stable guy . . . he does this business every night?"

"Nah, only when there's a full moon," Cham-peen theorized. Pressing themselves around their leader, the boys barked and howled.

"All right, all right. I'm busting my sides. Does he go into The Stag?"

"Yeah, he sucks it up 'til he bust. Alla time."

"So, where's he going to do the job next time?"

"Where there's cats, stupid," Famous shouted. The Basher pounded Famous's shoulder.

"Watch your mouth, mister!" Max balled his fists in imitation of John L. The boys fell to shadow-boxing. Max slapped The Basher lightly in the stomach and gave The Great Napoleon a tap. They may have been mocking him, but maybe some day one of them might tell him the truth.

In fact, he was starting to suspect them as much as Mrs. Jabonne did, but these street arabs didn't venture out of their territory, and with good reason. Max couldn't prove it, but he guessed that they did some work for the Hudson Dusters, possibly for the delivery wagon thief, Ding-Dong. Max had seen another Duster luminary, Rubber Shaw, being arraigned at police court on an assault charge. Jackie O'Neill from the *World* pointed out the way Shaw's nose was running and confided that almost all the Dusters had a problem with the white powder.

The Fashion Plates were always crossing the Broadway border to the east, and the Marginals and the Pearl Buttons were forever sticking their noses into dock business. These professionals were perfectly capable of batting the brains out of a transgressing street arab and tossing him into the river. So even if Cham-peen and his acolytes were causing the mayhem on Waverly Place and in Grove Street Park, why were there so many catricides in the 19th Precinct where yet another gang, the all-powerful Gophers, held sway?

He could stake out a location where cats were really swarming, but which one? He couldn't walk down a single street any more without noticing the calicos, the midnight blacks, the yellow and brown toms, the occasional escaped Persian or Siamese licking themselves, eating hard-won scraps, stretching languidly in the sun, hissing on stoops, curling into the shadows. They congregated behind restaurants, around ashcans, under pushcarts, in alleys, at construction sites where there was always a fresh supply of rodents. When they yowled at night in their peculiarly painful congress, who could go back to sleep?

"How do I know you guys aren't choking the kitties for fun?"

A dark look passed over Cham-peen's flat mug. "Wha'd we get for that, mister? Waste our time? Them things'll scratch you blind."

Max saw the kid's point. It wasn't that Cham-peen was above doing away with a few animals, but what was in it for him, for the gang? They had serious business to attend to every day: where to steal a scrap of food, what to crawl under if it started raining. Killing a cat wasn't worth one red cent. It was a luxury.

By eight, The White Stag was roaring. Standing outside, Max heard a piano and violin grope through a ballad, a few voices joining in the verse:

Sweetheart, I have grown so lonely
Living thus away from you.

He wouldn't have minded wetting his whistle and singing along, but instead he circled the few blocks surrounding Grove Street Park. Arc lights blazed on the Ladies' Mile, but not on these back streets. For a while he sat on a bench, just outside a pool of gaslight. The neighborhood was alive in the night, mothers calling their children, babies wailing, doors slamming, carriage wheels rattling, the crisp sounds of hooves on cobblestones. The air was redolent of boiled cabbage, burning garlic, frying fish, and fatty chops.

The swarms of children struck Max. The youngest were practically naked, and, as far as he could tell, no one was watching them. One small boy in nothing but a nightshirt urinated happily at the curb. A tiny girl chewed a corncob at the mouth of a tenement. On the spiderweb of fire escapes, kids raced up and down like circus performers, fearless, sinuous as monkeys. All around him they squealed, hopped over sidewalk cracks and, whooping, raced in and out of a dark stable.

"Stay away from Blackie, he kick your guts out," the stablehand, who was finishing a skinny cigar, warned them.

Max waited a few minutes and then sidled up to the man, who was trying to revive his black stogie. Max offered him a fresh match. "I'm doing a story for the *Herald*," he explained. "What's your name?"

"Buri. John Buri. They got a dead pig. Nobody take it away," the Italian said right off. "They make chickens back there, too. Nobody come."

"That's City Hall for you."

"They say to me take away, but why? I am horse man, not pig."

"You ever have trouble with the kids around here?"

"Kids? I call them rat pest. They hide in here, in the hay, then I chase, and they set fire. They think maybe they make a big joke. Me, the horse, we could get kill."

Evidently, by pointing the finger at John Buri, Cham-peen had been pursuing a personal vendetta. The sly little bastard.

"You ever see them killing cats?"

"No cat. Rat, yes. They play a game."

Max didn't want to know the rules.

For two days he patrolled the area, staying out later and later, getting more and more exhausted. He developed a route that looped from Waverly Place to Grove Street Park and then around to The White Stag.

He chatted every night with John Buri, hoping the man might have seen something while lounging outside his stable doors. But it was no use.

Finally, on Friday night he decided to change course, heading up Broadway toward the 19th precinct, past the extravagantly illuminated theatres, the glittering hotel restaurants, the cafés and concert saloons, merging himself into the current of businessmen, gawking tourists, peddlers, sidewalk knife sharpeners, organ grinders, and tight-waisted, befeathered women who flew across the sidewalks like silk birds. The omnibuses and carriages clattered over cobblestones, red-faced hacks shouted comments about certain blind drivers, barefoot flower girls cried out, the music from small orchestras poured out of the better cafés. Wheels scraping, barrels banging on carts, and every five minutes a Sixth Avenue Forney steam engine roaring a mere two stories above—the din was impossible. He loved it all, loved it helplessly.

He rode the rapids of human beings without thinking, just to feel alive.

Before the window of the Gilsey House restaurant he stopped to admire a lyre of beef tongues framed by sugar cupids, covered with white sauce and decorated with truffles. *Foie gras* molded into apples and tinted with what appeared to be bits of spinach completed the display. He thought of grabbing a quick drink at the stately Gilsey House bar—Danny and his actor friends frequented the establishment—but then changed his mind.

Now he was ready to take on the Tenderloin's side streets. He headed west and then edged a few blocks uptown. On West 28th a pair of brightly rouged professionals sauntered toward him, but he gave them a wide berth.

"Want somethin' sweet, honey?" one of them called out.

On the second floor of one house, a window flew open and a pudgy woman leaned out, exposing her breasts and hooting. Lines of jostling, flush-faced men blocked the sidewalk in front of several buildings. Out-of-tune pianos jangled against one another. Finally, Max took to the center of the street to escape. A couple of blocks north, things quieted down a bit.

Then he saw the hat, a wide flat-brimmed hat with a veil that seemed to float in the soft gaslight.

Dressed in a black silk dress with fashionable leg-o'-mutton sleeves, the woman under the hat possessed an aristocratic bearing. On her arm she carried a large basket. Max sensed something about her. She looked so out of place navigating the brothel traffic, she kept pausing and gazing around—was it furtively?—so he followed her at a discreet distance. At the corner of West 30th Street, she paused, grasped an iron railing, and then half-disappeared down some basement steps. Holding his breath, he picked up his pace, darting across the still street, approaching within a few feet. Only half the woman's body was visible now, but Max saw her flat-brimmed hat tilt down as a large white handkerchief flashed and disappeared.

Now he stepped close enough to watch her work. Several scrawny alley cats rubbed up against her ankles as she scattered bits of fish around her. The three overflowing ashcans on the basement landing had already attracted some of them. With a swift gesture, she snapped open the lid of her long basket and extracted the handkerchief, after which she bent down and quickly covered a striped victim's face. In her grasp the animal fought desperately, clawing, writhing, its muffled cries muted by the cloth pressed down over its mouth. Her jaw set, the woman held the struggling animal fast.

Slowly, the cat's efforts to cling to life faded. Every twist and turn of its body looked like the ghost of the last. Its claws waved weakly. Its tail drooped, just a bit of loose rope now. Suddenly, she snapped the cat's head back and cracked its spine. Lips pursed, she held the tom up for a moment as a few weak spasms rolled through its body. A beatific expression passed over her face as the animal went limp in her grasp.

In a matter of seconds she deposited the tom in her hamper. All around her, the other animals ate in deep concentration, devouring the fish she kept raining down on them. Then she snatched a second victim, engulfing its head in her ample handkerchief and holding it away from her bodice. A black sable, the animal looked as plush as could be.

This one fought back harder than the last, somehow tearing the handkerchief off its small face, flailing and howling for its life. The woman's mouth turned grim as she repeated her routine. Seizing the animal by the scruff of its neck, she held its head fast a second time and covered it with her smothering cloth. Almost in the same motion she cracked the cat's neck with an audible popping sound. Max was close enough to smell a powerful chemical gust.

Standing on the sidewalk above her, Max's mind raced. Should he try to stop her? In truth, he didn't know what to do. He didn't quite believe what he was seeing.

In a swift movement, the dark-clad matron tossed the second dead cat into her long, padded basket. Apparently satisfied, she climbed back to the sidewalk.

Before she could see him, Max hid in the adjacent basement stairwell. It was almost impossible to hold himself back now; he wanted to leap out and confront her, but he controlled himself as she arranged the limp cats on the sidewalk.

Emerging from a nearby brownstone, a clean-shaven sportsman in evening dress gave the woman a quick look, then turned on his heel.

Max approached her. "Excuse me," he said softly, eyeing her empty basket.

She turned toward him, an imperious expression on her face. A light web of wrinkles marked her sharp features. "Can't you tell I'm working?"

Now Max saw a badge affixed to her breast, but he couldn't read the legend stamped on it. "Sorry. What does your badge say?"

"I am Mrs. Warner, and we are the Midnight Band of Mercy. There are a number of us ladies out doing these acts of kindness." Her diction, her bearing, her tone all suggested the high-minded reformer.

Max could make no sense of her answer, but he knew he might never catch one of these angels in the act again. "Ah. So you're a philanthropic organization?"

"Exactly. We are directed to this work by our president, Mrs. Edwards. Our mailing address is at 1397 Broadway if you wish to contribute."

Eyeing Mrs. Warner to see if she objected, he quickly jotted down the address. She seemed not to notice or care, so he kept his pad in full view. "Why might you be working in this district?"

"Just look around you. This area is full of unwanted cats, sick cats, and it is our mission to protect them. I've been up and down this area, from Fourteenth Street to Thirty-Fourth, already once this night, and I'm not in the least tired," she offered proudly.

Mrs. Warner's remarks belied reality. He sensed in the woman a profound strangeness, an alien quality he couldn't define. The thought that she had comrades in arms, if it were true, was even more disturbing.

"Do you get a salary?"

"Oh, no. We receive no pay. We do our work for pure love. How do we keep our work going? Oh, our expenses are light."

In the police courts, Max had seen more than one babbling vagrant sent off to Bellevue, so he searched this woman's face, her gestures, her clothes for signs of mental disturbance. Unfortunately, her appearance and demeanor argued for sanity.

Just to keep her talking, he asked, "Don't you think you might spend your time better by visiting the poor and the sick?"

"No, I don't. There are other persons to look after the sick and starving people, but no one else to help the poor cats."

Evidently, she saw no contradiction between ministering to one's charges and murdering them. "Do you kill every cat you find?"

"As many as possible. What business is it of yours? Are they your cats? If so, why don't you keep them in your house? They have no business being out on the street after eight at night."

"Aren't you killing some people's pets? Some that are well-fed?"

She became indignant. "Then why are they running wild at all hours? And as for your starving families, there are other societies for them. Join one. We minister to the cats."

"We weren't talking about other people, we were talking about what *you're* doing."

"It's nature's way. Since the monkey climbed down from the trees."

"I don't understand."

"Modern philosophy? Progressive thinking? You've heard of them?"

Now he was truly lost. He couldn't make any sense out of her argument. Before he could interrogate her further, the woman whirled and stalked away.

He pursued her down the sidewalk. When he caught up to her, he touched her elbow. "One more question?"

She shook him off, her basket striking Max's side with surprising force.

"Where do you meet? And when?"

"Do I snoop into your private business?" She glared at him the way, he imagined, she stared down one of her servants. "Shoo, fly!"

Watching her disappear, he couldn't shake his revulsion, or his fascination. What sort of human being was this Mrs. Warner? She killed with efficiency, with casual aplomb and yet reasoned with fury. Her strange way of thinking disturbed him as much as her actions.

He hoped that 1397 Broadway didn't exist and that the Midnight Band was Mrs. Warner's own fevered invention. Imagine dozens of Mrs. Warners, all suffering from the same delusion. On the other hand, if the Midnight Band had an address, a charter and officers, his story would carry much more weight than yet another account of a solitary crank on the loose.

The Broadway address turned out to be a bookshop. Mr. Wiggins, the manager, a man with limp hair and a complexion that had never seen the sun, seemed irritated to see a customer so early. Before Max could get a word in edgewise, he said, "If you're looking for a copy of *Trilby*, go someplace else. We've got a standing order for thirty of the damn things, but we can't seem to get our hands on a single one. It's easier to find a Trilby contest than the book. What do you think of that?"

Max knew about *Trilby*, of course, though he'd never read that popular tale of Oriental intrigue. He preferred newspapers and hadn't read a book since he left the City College in his first semester. To his taste, a good newspaper was more alive and believable than any tripe by that bore Howells.

He'd seen Trilby hats popping up everywhere, though. "Contests?"

"Trilby contests. Know what's the latest? Who has the perfect Trilby feet. The girls stand behind curtains and take off their shoes."

"That's fresh. Listen, there's a group, it's called the Midnight Band of Mercy—"

"You're not after the book?"

"No, the Midnight Band—"

"Oh, certainly. They keep a mailbox here. They're some kind of charitable organization, they told me. Their members selected the cat business."

"How long have they had this box?"

"Oh, at least a year."

So it was true. The Midnight Band wasn't a figment of Mrs. Warner's imagination. He was both grateful for the story and sickened to find out that other Mrs. Warners were roaming the streets. Sickened, but also in a state of wonder. What would drive someone like Mrs. Warner to go out on the hunt at night without regard for her own safety? Who had taught her to smother cats, then snap their necks with such efficiency? What lay behind her impulse? A perverse pleasure? An obscure hatred?

"Do they get much mail?"

"Oh, now and then. A few envelopes."

"And they post letters back?"

"What're you, a cop or something?"

"Sorry. Max Greengrass. *New York Herald*." He showed his card.

"Okay. Yeah. They've got quite a correspondence going."

"And how many ladies do you think are in the organization?"

"Well, I've seen a few. And they *are* ladies. They can recite the Bible, chapter and verse. They're not like these *Trilby* fanatics."

"Would you have names and addresses?"

"I'm not an informer, Mr. Greengrass. I sell books."

"Well, who picks up the mail? What's her name?"

The bookseller gave him a stony look.

At least he had enough material to prove the Midnight Band was a real organization, but Max wasn't sure he could communicate how Mrs. Warner's rampage had affected him. The Midnight Band's followers needed drive, nerve, and even a perverse courage to carry out their mission. Not only that; Mrs. Warner seemed to be proud of her vocation, and to enjoy it as well.

He felt giddy. Parnell would have to give him ten, maybe a dozen column-inches.

chapter six

In the end, he managed to work all the key facts into his article, but he worried that he hadn't adequately captured the sensation of discovering Mrs. Warner in the act. How to communicate her mixture of cool efficiency and otherworldly fervor? Finally, he decided that describing the moment's utter strangeness was outside the scope of his article. How could he explain what he didn't understand? Mrs. Warner apparently believed in her credo—killing defenseless animals to save them—but he couldn't grasp her reasoning or her passion.

The subhead told a compelling tale to The *Herald*'s faithful. Better still, Parnell had allowed Max's indignation full play up top.

EPIDEMIC OF CAT KILLINGS

**Women of the Midnight Band
Permit No Cessation of the
Feline Carnage**

An organization calling itself The Midnight Band of Mercy has taken responsibility for the slaughter of cats on Waverly Place and in the 19th Precinct. A *Herald* reporter has personally witnessed one of the group's assassins committing indiscriminate acts of murder on cats of all types and classes. It was a most extraordinary and disturbing sight. Worse still, the Midnight Band's crusaders vow to con-

> tinue their terrible campaign, which they consider their moral duty.

It went on, a full eleven inches, listing every fact and key quote. How could they keep him off the staff now? Parnell was definitely warming toward him. Hadn't he ordered Carlson to clear Max a desk and give him a decent typewriter?

More significantly, he kept Max on the story. "Find the chief cook and bottle washer and interview her. If you run her down, and she'll stand for it, we'll order up an illo." Parnell would never break down and say something as simple as "nice work," but the promise of an illustration was worth far more.

Max raced back to the bookstore and left a message for the Midnight Band's leader, the so-called Mrs. Edwards. That evening he cruised the 19th. The swollen cat population looked as healthy as ever. A three-foot-high garbage mound on 24th Street had attracted several warring tomcats. At the bottom of a stairwell, a gray with a white chest was nursing her mewling brood. A black cat darted under a wagon. An old warlord with a tattered ear sauntered right across the sidewalk. Max couldn't stop seeing cats, but their enemies were nowhere in sight.

Sergeant Morris hadn't heard of any slayings that evening either. Schreiber said the Midnight Band was making itself scarce for a reason.

"John Law's after their skinny necks. They're scared outta their wool drawers now," the patrolman speculated. Max wondered if he'd squeezed the story dry.

At the dinner table, Danny was the first to point out Max's article. "A good piece of work, but don't tell me you didn't gild the lily." In a complicated dance, the corner of Swarms's mouth rose, as did the lines in his forehead, indicating he wasn't in the least bit serious.

"I was this close to the woman." Max touched index finger to thumb.

"Why didn't you stop her?" Belle asked. She hated to admit her fascination. Wasn't Max's tale exactly the kind of cheap sensationalism her boyfriend Jake always railed against?

Irritated, Max shot back, "Oh, I did, after I got over the shock of it." A white lie, but what was he supposed to say?

"I picked up a turn at Tony Pastor's," Danny announced, raising his fluffy eyebrows. "Just a fill-in."

"Oh, that's marvelous," Gretta said. "What will you do?"

Max was impressed. In Pastor's high-class acts, the women covered up and the comics toned down their blue material. It was a big step up for Danny, who usually scrambled in the concert saloons and begged singing waiters to try out his songs.

"The usual, but fresh."

"Hey, we'll all catch you. We'll drag Faye along too," Max said. Was Danny on a joyride with Faye, or was it more serious? Then he thought of his sister's smeared eyebrows, her puffy face, the milk stains on her Chinese robe. Maybe he shouldn't ask any questions.

"Why not? Make a party. We can go to Pete's over on Irving Place later."

"Your sister? The one you two are always talking about?" Belle asked.

"Fabulous Faye," Danny replied. "Another night, we can go see her show."

A spirit of affection suffused the atmosphere. They all knew that Danny had knocked on a thousand doors and that a turn at Pastor's was a great break. Swarms had so many strikes against him—his premature baldness, his putty-like face, his slight frame, his poverty—yet his talent made a man forget these deficiencies. As Danny basked in glory, Max flushed, as if the date at Tony Pastor's were his too. If he felt a twinge of jealousy, and he did, he was only human.

Faye would be a fool to drive Swarms away, especially now. She had already run through an aspiring clog dancer, a dog trainer, and a mind-reader from Flushing who was willing to put her into his act. Every time she jettisoned one of these Lotharios, Max was secretly thrilled, though he made sure to act irritated. Danny Swarms was so perfect for her, though, and for him too. A brother-in-law and a drinking buddy all rolled into one.

His little sister Faye ran like a groove through the center of his brain. She had had scarlet fever when she was five, and he still remembered the heat of her forehead under his palm. Certain she was going to die, he locked himself in a closet and cried with his fist in his mouth. Naphtha fumes had burned his eyes.

An older Faye threw her report card into a storm drain, and he'd had to organize three friends and a crowbar to retrieve it. She liked to pinch and scratch, she came to school with wax teeth in her mouth, and she learned piano at her friend Marsha's flat. *Once Faye's straightened out. . . .* The phrase had a practical sound to it. He just hadn't found the right formula.

A flood of angry letters poured into the *Herald* offices, though not all of them were critical of the Midnight Band. Happy to keep the controversy boiling, The *Herald* printed these missives and their calls to arms several days running.

Speculation ran high that the cat killers were in it for the money. One letter writer argued that "a catgut, divided into sixty-one threads by the professional violin string maker, furnishes four E strings at 30 cents each, 15 D strings at 40 cents and seven A strings at 25 cents each, for a total of $8.95. These women are making a very nice dollar."

A little girl wrote to say that unless the Midnight Band was put out of business, she and her pussy would move to the country. A Waverly Place resident demanded that the miscreants be brought to justice. Still, Mrs. Warner stirred up more support than Max had expected.

An insomniac wrote, "All honor and glory to Mrs. Warner, the cat killer. Send her down to Clinton Place and receive the blessings of one who cannot sleep at night by reason of the midnight racket made by cats."

Though he still wasn't getting a salary, Max claimed his far-corner desk every morning, ostentatiously typing useless notes when he had no serious business to transact. Copy boys raced up and down the narrow aisles, reporters banged away on their upright typewriters, clusters of men waited their turn at Parnell's throne. Cigar smoke rose, bells rang, voices bellowed. Nowhere else did he feel more at home.

Meanwhile, Mrs. Edwards and Mrs. Warner eluded him. No one seemed to know where they lived. Max inquired at Superintendent Byrnes's office on Mulberry Street, but the police department's upper echelons showed little interest in the case. Finally, after camping out at the police chief's door, Max was rewarded with word from an assistant. "We're looking into it, but we got our hands full with the two-legged beasts."

He spent the weekend roaming the Waverly Place area and the 19th, but there were no fresh Midnight Band outbreaks. Parnell wasn't giving him any new assignments either, and the story was dying.

His mood grew darker. Of all things to pin his hopes on! A few madwomen and piles of dead cats. He'd always been prone to sudden shifts in his spirits. Most of the time, he pushed his terrors into a corner of his mind and pretended they didn't exist. He'd stay on an even keel for weeks at a time, but when the horrors started leaking out, he'd plunge right down a black shaft. Only Faye knew about these panics, and only Faye could talk him out of them. She understood how to take him seriously and make fun of him at the same time, and soon his heebie-jeebies would fade. Only his fear's ghost would remain, all the more frightening because it lived on, disconnected but eternal.

He treated the cat saga lightly at the boardinghouse table, but interest there had grown intense. Even Mrs. DeVogt had become less dismissive. At least she had stopped referring to him as a typist. Only Gretta failed to show any regard for his tale. In his black humor, he didn't wonder why. She was a tennis-playing Staten Island beauty. Why should she be interested in him?

By an act of will, he managed to stop gazing at her across the table, engaging anyone else in dinner conversation before addressing her. Following her into the hall, he watched her smooth, graceful walk, the way her dress flared out, her square shoulders. If he looped his arms around that waist and pressed her to him, he would feel the full shape of her breasts, her hips, her thighs. All of his proud resistance melted away.

When she actually touched his wrist, a shock ran right up his arm. She smiled at him with a sympathy she had never shown before. At first he didn't notice the envelope in her hand. "Martin sent you this note. He's been reading your stories, and he thinks he can help you."

"What gave him that idea?"

Laughing, she replied, "I haven't the slightest idea, but he seems to think you're quite the character, Mr. Greengrass." Her tone was mildly skeptical. "I had to remind him that I dine with you regularly."

He stood there dumbly, looking down at the expensive stationery. Why couldn't he think of something to say? He was never at a loss for words. "You look beautiful tonight," he blurted. Too blunt! His cheeks burned.

She seemed to take his remark in stride, though. "Thank you, but I'm really all dragged out from work."

Why was she working so hard? It dawned on him that her circumstances might not be as comfortable as he had assumed. "Why don't you take a few days off?"

"Well, there's too much business at the moment. I can't exactly walk away from my job." She must have sensed his surprise, because she went on quietly. "My father passed away a few years ago, so I contribute. To my mother. And my uncle does too. He's a sea captain. Now, he's quite a character!"

In one exchange she shattered all of Max's preconceptions. Why hadn't he asked her these questions before?

They had to stand close to one another in the narrow, awkward space, but Gretta didn't draw back. Perhaps she didn't mind.

"Sorry about your father."

"Oh, don't be. It was hard, but time. . . . He's the one who taught me to take pictures in the first place. He was a chemist. . . ."

"Ahh. And Martin, what does he do exactly?" On their pub crawl, Mourtone had dodged every question on the subject.

"Oh, he's in his father's insurance office. They have him going around collecting weekly premiums to learn the ropes, but he despises it."

"He has a territory?"

"Yes, from Thompson Street west. Part of it is called Little Africa, I think."

"A small part, now," Max said absently.

Max knew the area well. It had the highest tuberculosis rate in the city. In rear tenements where blacks and Italians were living ten to a windowless room, the white lung ran wild. These same people were the most likely to eat tuberculosis tainted meat and drink cholera-infected milk.

"He can't possibly be selling insurance policies on Thompson Street, can he?" Max asked.

"Maybe not there. But the policies only cost a few cents a week. Some of the people who are a little better off take them, I think. I know he loathes his work."

He couldn't summon up much pity for Martin Mourtone, but he said, "It must be very unpleasant for him."

"Yes, it is. Well, I hope you'll confide in me if Martin's information is worthwhile. I couldn't pry a word out of him."

"Of course, but we get dozens of leads. . . ."

After she left, he lingered in the hall, breathing her perfume. He liked to think he was no novice when it came to women, but Gretta's beauty made him go weak in strange places. The backs of his knees, deep in his chest. Now that he knew she needed every dime, she seemed less ethereal, and that excited him even more.

Idly, he ripped open Martin's envelope. The note said, "It's a vicious joke, but it might explain things. I can meet you tomorrow at Stephenson's on Bleecker at about 2. Nobody we know goes there." No salutation, no signature, just Mourtone's barely legible scrawl.

Martin was right about Stephenson's. The dive was a notorious black-and-tan, infamous for fostering relations between white women and any variety of the colored, from American Indians to Mexicans to local Negroes. For a slummer like Mourtone, the forbidden couplings no doubt added to Stephenson's allure.

Max would have preferred an expensive drink at the new Metropole on Forty-Second. Through its tall windows, you could see every hot bird in town strut past.

You had to be careful about what you drank in a stale-beer dive like Stephenson's. The management was renowned for its skill with knockout drops. Who cared about the black-and-tan's clientele? They were perfect marks. Many were seamen off foreign vessels, the rest bootblacks, barbers, coal shovelers, rag men, and members of the lost sisterhood. Naturally, the police levied a small tithe on the establishment. That Stephenson's had been open twenty-four hours a day for over a dozen years demonstrated its high standing in the community.

Early the next morning, Parnell sent Max out to Williamsburg to cover a story: two hundred steers had dodged the Johnson Avenue slaughterhouse and were stampeding up and down Bedford Avenue. At noon he interviewed Dr. Alphonse M. Wallace, whose arm had swollen to twice its normal size after a Bellevue patient bit him to protest a diagnosis. By the time he knocked out these stories, he was running twenty minutes behind schedule.

It took Max's eyes a moment to adjust to Stephenson's shrouded interior. The joint was eerily quiet. He searched the gloomy interior for some sign of Mourtone. The deeper he penetrated, the stronger grew the smell of musty beer and piss. A bartender in a stained apron stood stock-still, a rag in his hand, and the single patron, a black man in work clothes, stared at Max wide-eyed, in apparent shock.

A fluttering gas light revealed a bar framed by a pair of husky, tooled pillars. Behind the bartender, a ragged collection of liquor bottles reflected the faint illumination. Max heard the shuffle of his own feet in the sawdust and the sound of his own shallow breathing. In a chair whose back tilted against the scarred wall, Martin perched, his head flung back. Too far.

Max could only see the lower part of his face, his exposed nostrils, his down-curved mouth, his pointy chin, his young, sharp Adam's apple. A painting of a schooner hung off-kilter behind Martin's head. There was something about the way he was balanced back on the chair, and the way the picture tilted in the opposite direction, that gave Max vertigo. Fighting the urge to toss his dinner, he edged closer. The scratched wall looked moist. Max didn't want to look too closely, but the back part of Mourtone's head seemed to be missing. Yet the mask of his face was still intact. His lips were half-parted in an ambiguous expression. In death he stared, his eyes without light, at a vague middle distance.

A dented, liver-colored hat had skidded to the far end of the table. An ash-tipped cigar lay dead beside Mourtone's curled fingers.

"Did you see what happened?" Max's voice sounded thin, not his own.

"What right's he got comin' in here?" the bartender replied. He had a flat plate of a face, small black eyes, and a voluminous mustache spilling down toward a prognathous jaw. Pink at the nostrils, his nose lay flat in the heart of his face.

Clearly terrified, the African remained frozen at the bar. A spattering of white marks on his cheek looked like burns from hot fat.

"You saw what happened?" Max asked again. How could he go home and tell Gretta? He didn't want to see her face crumple, he didn't want to know how much she might have loved this lifeless body.

The bartender deflected his question. "He a pal of yours?"

"Acquaintance." Of course, the police would inform Mourtone's parents. It wasn't his responsibility. But Gretta knew he was going to meet Martin. How could he dodge her questions? He would have to find some conventional words and manage to behave in a conventional way. And never reveal that some small part of him was elated that his rival had suddenly ceased to exist.

Then he thought of that night at the Hoffman House, Martin's glee as he tore apart the stuffy *Century*, his half-baked plans, his praise for Gretta's pictures. And now he was nothing but a husk. Acid scalded the back of Max's throat.

"I got Sodder's warehouse knockin' off work in a few minutes, you think those boys'll wanna have some laughs with that thing around?"

"What about you?" Max addressed the husky, yellow-eyed black man. His overalls, missing the hook on the left strap, were nothing but patches.

"He's a deaf and dummy, he don't know shit," the bartender cut in.

Still as a statue, the Negro didn't react. Maybe the rag was telling the truth. Max figured the odds at one in ten.

"Did you see who shot him?" Slowly, Max swam through the stifling atmosphere toward the bar. Stunned, he was still operating like a newsman. He felt like a ghoul, but he could turn Mourtone's murder into a major item. Martin's ambiguous note. Its connection to the cat killings. The dead man's social standing. The father's flourishing business. As a lurid setting, Stephenson's would play perfectly. Parnell would love it.

Despite the realization of his good fortune, Max had to fight waves of nausea, swallowing to keep down the bile that threatened to pulse straight up his throat. He hadn't seen a corpse in a while, and he had asked all the wrong questions about that one.

Stephenson's bartender swiped his flattened nose with the back of his forearm. "Look, I got no Western Union here, I can't leave the joint. Why don't you be a good feller, run over to the station house and bring the au-thor-o-ties."

Max put both hands on the bar and straightened his shoulders. "Listen, I'm from the *Herald*. What did you see?"

"Ain't you my favorite turd? Every minute he's layin' there, I lose business. I don't talk to no newspapers. Get me Johnny Law."

When the rag ducked down, Max knew what was coming. By the time he heard the slung shot slap against the bartender's palm, Max was already backing away. "All right, don't get so hot. I'm on my way."

A drizzle muted the afternoon light. A few sticks of wood and canvas protected Stephenson's doorway. Max caught his breath, making a point of not running. He wouldn't give the sonofabitch the satisfaction. Instead, he squared his shoulders and fixed his hat. Police headquarters was located on Mulberry, blocks south of Houston, but Max didn't trust any of the local buttons. He was better off going straight to the top.

A detective would understand that Mourtone came from a well-connected family and that the department had to jump to. Then Max could follow the police back to Stephenson's to get a look at the bartender's face when he was forced to talk. Even if the cops barred him from the interrogation, he could quote the investigator and insert his own observations as well. He could play up Martin's note in the lead, tying the insurance agent's homicide to the wave of cat killings.

Stephenson's door smacked open. Shoulders hunched in the rain, the rag bellied up to Max. "What're you loiterin' for, Jocko? Ain't you diggin' up some help?"

At first Max didn't notice the bulldog-mugged boy nearby. The hulking barkeep pressed closer and showed his underbite.

"I know my business," Max retorted, balling his fists.

Turning to the aproned boy, the bartender jabbed a thumb at a mucky mound of curbside refuse. "What'd I tell ya'? I'll tan your hide before you can say Jack Robinson."

Why was the man's nose so raw, so shapeless?

A glancing weight struck Max's shoulder, and he almost lost his balance. Racing through the puddles, the black man, his head bare, pounded past him down the sidewalk, then veered onto Thompson Street. The thought was only half-formed before Max started racing after him. The Negro might have seen the whole thing. A deaf and dummy could shake his head yes and no, he could tell the story with his hands. In the middle of the block, the fading figure in the tattered overalls darted into an alleyway.

His heart scuttling up his throat, Max rushed after him. As he groped down the dark walkway, the soft rain grew heavier, turning to a sudden downpour.

Emerging, he found himself in a rear courtyard just in time to spy his witness plunge into another alley. Soaking wash hung unattended on a line. He heard shouts, singing, coughing, babies crying. Inside a tunnel-like passageway he felt the sewage slop up to his ankles. The rain tasted of coal dust. Inadvertently, he tripped over a soft, indescribable mound. He didn't look down. Behind a fence, geese yawped.

Then he came to a T in the alleys. He ran left for fifty yards, then turned and ran in the opposite direction. Hemmed in by sheer tenement walls, he had no idea which way to turn.

The African had disappeared. Max shrugged and picked his way toward Houston Street. Runny mud seeped up his suit pants, spattering his calves. He trudged on, praying for a lucky turn into civilization, but the lane ended at a brick wall. Now he had to retrace his steps, unsure but stubborn. Finally, he broke out onto West Third Street.

Drenched and shivering, he plodded south, crossed Houston, and headed downtown on Mercer Street. A shift of chattering garment workers, Eastern European Jews and Italians, poured from a loft building. With their shawls over their heads, in twos and threes, they moved in shapeless black clots towards the Grand Street train station.

He'd caught a chill. Waves of heat and cold swept through him. Hunching forward, he drove himself through the downpour. Small figures hung back but kept pace with him.

Stephenson's boy had shed his apron, but not his pushed-in features. In a smashed plug hat, he was pedaling a bicycle with a deformed front wheel. Wobbling, the boy rose into the air and then fell at irregular intervals. Max squinted but couldn't place the other little bastards. He searched for Famous, Cham-peen, even The Basher, but he couldn't identify these street arabs. They occupied different turf, sidewalks patrolled by the full-grown Fashion Plates.

Were they stalking him on their own inspiration, or were they doing the rag's bidding? It hardly mattered. One way or another, charity was not their stock in trade.

The bike rider's confederates ducked into basements, hid behind piles of garbage, skittered under parked wagons. But they followed every twist and turn Max made, even when he whirled around and started to retrace his steps. The gang did look familiar, though. Yes, he'd seen the same stunted figures staggering pie-eyed around a Lafayette Street ashcan fire.

Had the barkeep dispatched his minions to stop Max from reaching police headquarters? But why? He hadn't seen who had killed Mourtone. Still, he had stumbled on the aftermath. Cooing to each other, the arabs drew their noose tighter. A pale devil tossed a pebble that glanced off Max's forehead. In the backs of their throats, the boys made a cawing sound. Then they let go a shower of stones. Max threw his arm up in front of his face. Setting his feet wide, he steeled himself for the onslaught.

Then he heard voices; he was reprieved. The Saint Bernard Hotel, an infamous roaring house, loomed in the mist. Nearby, a sign featuring large gilt teeth flapped in the wind. Dr. Minsky's Painless Dentistry. A liquor shop legend announced "Sherry with a Big Egg in it, 5 cents." Inside the doorway of a cast-iron building, a peddler, a stack of derbies on his head, stood still as a photograph. Max heard the racket of wagon wheels on cobblestones and the rhythmic clatter of hooves on paving. He took a breath, relaxing now. Then he heard the explosion.

Schwab's boys? They were always babbling about a well-placed bomb, but so far New York had been spared the terrors of Barcelona, or even Chicago. Still, with Johann Most and Emma Goldman on the rampage, and all those tramps in the streets, his mind jumped to the obvious conclusion.

Running loose, a horse raced past in terror, its harness trailing. Max watched its slick haunches disappear around a corner. Capes of rain enveloped him. He moved toward the cursing voices. Teamsters? Some kind of ordinary fracas. If he could blend into the crowd, he'd be safe.

A tangle of vans, carts, broughams, and coaches choked the street. A deliveryman in a white smock stood on the roof of his vehicle trying to make out the cause of the impeding carnage.

Max saw the trouble. One delivery wagon was overturned, completely upset, its chestnut horse on its side, whinnying pathetically, trying to rise, slipping, falling again in a snarl of ruptured traces. Nearby, an empty carriage's side was smashed in, exposing its elegant padded interior to the rain.

Two drivers went at each other's throats. One of them, in boots and loud checked pants, was small and nimble. Ducking and dodging, he kept slipping his opponent's bear hugs, raining blows down on the stolid man's hairless skull. With a terrible scraping sound, the mad chestnut rose, snorting, dragging the cart on its side across the paving stones before falling again, spewing manure, pissing in terror. Racing toward the downed, gasping animal, the driver flailed with his whip, searing long fresh wounds into the helpless beast's flesh. Then he paused to kick the animal in the side.

The wagon driver seemed to think that by kicking the horse and slashing it over and over with his hissing whip he could force it to its feet, but instead the chestnut's eyes glazed over, poached eggs in its long face, and the life leaked out of him.

The racket of bumping, packed vehicles, the drivers' screeching curses, the dull thwack of boot on horseflesh ached inside Max's brain. These men couldn't help him. He was alone.

In full sight of the accident the street arabs showed themselves. There were half a dozen, maybe more. With that off-kilter bump and bump, the bicyclist bored straight at Max with teeth bared in his bulldog mug. He barely made a sound when Max landed a punch high on his forehead. Invisible hands pulled at the newsman's coat, worked inside his vest, tore at his pockets, hands like clicking crabs, unattached to the street arabs whose pocked faces blurred before his eyes. His body rigid, he fell backwards, his head cracking on stone. They fell on him in a pack. He fought hard, he used his fists, his knees, his elbows, but their pointy blows came from everywhere.

chapter seven

He woke up with bare, wet feet. His boots, even his socks were missing. Inside his cheek his tongue traced raw flesh. Though he felt an overwhelming urge to drift back to sleep, his freezing toes kept him from falling back into the alluring darkness. Instead, he found himself stretched out stiff in a doorway, bootless, sockless and, he realized suddenly, his coat had disappeared as well. In a panic, he groped to see if he was wearing pants. When he was satisfied that he wasn't lying stark naked in the drizzle, a much deeper terror seized him. His own name kept eluding him. He dozed, faded in and out.

Then a man wearing a tall stack of derbies squatted next to him. "They cracked you good and hard, mister, something terrible. You still got a few teeth?"

Had this hat man saved him? Irregular waves of nausea swept through him. He could go to sleep again for a century, but the man wouldn't leave him alone. "Open up. You shouldn't swallow your tongue. I had a friend who ate his and choked."

The idea of a man eating his own tongue struck him as funny, but he repressed his laughter because the derby man seemed so earnest. He tried to recall where he lived and discovered that he couldn't. If he could only concentrate hard enough he knew he'd get it, but the lure of sinking was too sweet, sinking and fading away. He swam in a dream for a while. Only the pain brought him back to the surface, a shooting pain that darted up his jaw into the heart of his right ear. Parts of him felt broken. Like an old mechanical contraption.

Gaslight hissed in a dusty storeroom. A piece of time was missing, but his feet were dry. He looked down and was happy to see feet inside black woolen socks. He was the happiest man in the world. Warm feet: that was all it took. But who was he? Shelves of hats, stacks of hats, signs for hats, handwritten signs for hat sizes appeared, paled, then reappeared sharper still. He was lost in a universe of hats.

The derby man was feeding him.

Even a little thin soup was comforting if you didn't know who you were. He forgot his fears as the warm liquid went down. Bits of gristle got stuck between his teeth.

"A little stove I got."

He was picking at one recalcitrant shred of meat when it came to him. Max Greengrass. But there was something so comical about the sound of it, Greengrass, that he hesitated to commit himself. Maybe he had read about someone with this ridiculous name, and it had stuck in his mind. He didn't want to make a mistake and claim to be the wrong person. But wasn't that who he was? The wrong person? Sensing that this had always been true, he almost laughed out loud.

And what if he showed up at the wrong address? Well, it wouldn't be his family, it would be someone else's family. Now he lost confidence in the name Max Greengrass entirely. The nausea returned with newfound force. He looked at his fresh woolen socks and tried to hold back, but then an uncontrollable spasm seized him and undigested soup showered down on his feet.

"West 16th Street." He was sure he would recognize the house, and the people inside would remind him of his name. He wouldn't ask directly, he'd just wait for them to address him. Broken bits clattered inside his mind. Then he broke out laughing. He was the wrong man because he was dead. His own father had told him so. Read him right out of the tribe. But at West 16th Street they'd recognize the animated corpse. Him.

"Ten cents a pair," his peculiar savior grumbled. "And now you ruin."

"I'll buy a dozen. Just take me to West 16th." His mother worked a mop in a hallway. Where was it? In some unnamed tenement stinking of ammonia. The mop had strings like an old woman's hair.

"A pair of felt slippers. You'll walk on air."

Groping, he discovered one trouser pocket slashed apart, but the other was intact, a few coins buried deep in the lining. "No purse," he explained, offering the man a few coins. "No watch either. Time?"

"Three-thirty. Maybe four," the hat man said, pocketing the change.

Max wondered whether he had paid far too much for the socks and the slippers but didn't have the will to protest.

Greengrass was a made-up name, a prevarication that never fooled anyone. He was an invented man. His father was a lie, his birth an immaculate deception. There was a true story behind it, he could taste it, but it drifted away.

The hat man flagged a fly cab and pushed Max, felt slippers and all, into the coach. "West 16th, he'll show you," he shouted to the cabby, and the rickety horse-drawn vehicle clattered into the traffic, every uncushioned jolt ringing inside the bone bell of Max's head. He started to remember.

Remembering came in fragments. The clawing fingers inside his pockets. Martin tilted as if he were going to fall. The black man's shoulder spinning him around. Wet black alley walls. The choking atmosphere inside Stephenson's. The slap of slung shot against the bartender's palm. The rag's pink, leaking nose.

"Wait, forget 16th Street! Take me to police headquarters! Mulberry Street!" he shouted up at the slouch-hatted driver. Madly, he groped around for Martin's note, but it had disappeared along with his other possessions. His heart sank.

An intense headache still pulsed in his temples, but at least he knew who he was again. At Mulberry Street, he strode right up to the desk sergeant. "There's been a murder over at Stephenson's."

"You sure you ain't the guy on the other end?" the muttonchopped officer replied. A pair of lounging street cops hooted from a comfortable bench.

"Over at Stephenson's."

"That chapel?"

"Listen, I'm from the *Herald*—"

"And I'm the friggin' Queen of England. You take a look at yourself?"

Aware that hatless and in spattered felt slippers he didn't cut a compelling figure, he kept his temper. "Yeah, I know, I got rolled. You can call my editor, Stan Parnell. I'm Max Greengrass."

A bow-legged barrel of a cop pushed through the door. Max recognized him instantly. Jack Sloan. Last September at Fitzgerald and Ives, Max had lost two bits to him on a bet involving the Orioles. "Jack."

"Maxie, what gives? You get roughed up?"

"You know this clown?" the sergeant asked, his skepticism wavering.

"That's Maxie Greengrass. He works for the *World*, don't ya, Max?"

"The *Herald* now. Vouch for me, huh?"

"Sure, Maxie, he's a white man. Who's the gyp did this to ya?"

"Says he seen some hackum over at Stephenson's," the sergeant replied, mollified now. "We got an extra few coats back there, mister. I don't know about no shoes. Who's the stiff?"

"A friend . . . an acquaintance of mine. As far as I know, he's still sitting there with a hole in his head."

Sloan slid over and passed Max a flask. The raw whiskey singed his throat, but he took a good pull. One of the bench-sitters produced a topcoat. "I got some boots back there, lemme look at your feet."

After making a sober assessment, he returned with a cracked pair of boots that actually fit. "They batted me around pretty good," Max said, touching the moist, matted hair on the back of his head. "You got a detective on duty?"

"Stout, over here!"

In the police carriage the veteran, Detective Stout, a sunken-cheeked man with a hedgerow of dark eyebrows, kept up a steady patter. "Yeah, talk about your rat pit. Stephenson's? Any way they can manufacture a shekel, huh? White girls ballin' off niggers. Does than make sense? I mean from a business point of view. Your average nigger don't have a pot to piss in, how much can he dig up to go around the world? This friend of yours, he ain't . . . ?"

"No, I told you. His father's in insurance." This information settled the race question. At least Max hoped so. He sensed a mean streak in Stout, and had no doubt that the detective would soon be referring to him as *that sheeny* Greengrass.

"So you been at the *Herald* how long?" Stout probed him.

"A few months. I was at the *World* before that." The cop didn't have to know he'd been a space-rater at Pulitzer's pressure cooker too.

"You can wipe your ass with either one, right? So you walk in, your pal's got his brains removed, and the bartender is *non compos mentis*."

"That sums it up."

"And we got a deaf-and-dumb nigger in overalls. Christ."

"We don't know that for certain. Consider the source."

"Yeah, right. Can you imagine raising a kid in this cesspool? I moved my wife out to the suburbs, Kings Highway in Brooklyn. So where'd the nigger hotfoot it to? Minetta Lane?"

"No, he ran up Thompson and into the alleys. That's where I lost him."

"You can bet he took his razor with him to Minetta. So how long you been friends with Marty? You cruise these joints with him?"

Max stiffened. "He was just an acquaintance who read one of my stories. I had a drink with him once over at the Hoffman House."

"Kinda an uptown–downtown game?"

"No game. Just what I said."

A colored man in an oily striped suit stood under Stephenson's shredded awning. Max steeled himself for the dreadful sight of Mourtone one more time. He told himself that Martin Mourtone didn't exist any more. The thing flung back in the chair was just that, a fleshy thing without sight, without thought, without sensation. A skinned sack of meat and bone you tossed into a simple hole in the ground. Unfortunately, this line of thinking only made him queasier.

"While you're at it, ask Stephenson's rag why he sicced his boys on me."

"Yeah? How you figure that?"

"The arab that jumped me, he was working for the bartender."

"You seen it?"

"Yeah. He was cleaning up some mess."

The dive was filling up with warehousemen, local carters, janitors, and bootblacks with their kits. Max recognized a policy promoter from Frenchtown, near New York University. The whores over there did a pretty business with the students and the professorship. Not a single woman graced the crude bar. Following in Stout's wake, Max could barely see the barkeep at first, so he made an end run around the detective to get a better look. Behind the bar a bent, hawk-nosed character hiked up his apron.

Where Martin's body had tilted against the wall, an empty chair stood. Missing from the table were Mourtone's hat and his dead cigar. Even the moist spots on the tin wainscoting had been wiped and dried.

Stout sidled back over to Max. "He went to see his mother. In Baltimore."

"What?"

"This joy boy says he didn't see nothin' when he got on his shift. So it must've been your rag that took off to see moms in Maryland. Nice timing."

"That's where Martin was sitting." Max motioned toward the corner.

"I guess they shipped him over by Bellevue. C'mon. You're his last friend in the world."

"Let me ask the barkeep something."

"C'mon, don't waste my time."

But before Stout could restrain him, Max picked his way through the tables and pressed up to the bar. "Listen, you know the other bartender's name? Where he lives?"

The new barkeep shrugged. "MacNamara. I'm fillin' in."

"What about his first name?"

"Joe. Joseph MacNamara. I come in, he's gone. I ain't seen zip. He goes on boats, they says. The whatchacallit . . ."

"Merchant marine?"

The scrawny man leaned down to tap a keg. "Yeah. They say he's seen 'em all. Dotheads. Hottentots. Maybe he shipped out to Japland."

"Or the South Pole?"

"Sure. Maybe."

The morgue squatted on grounds adjacent to the great municipal hospital. A caretaker in a brown denim suit led them to a ledger in which the deceased's height, weight, hair and eye colors, type of clothes, and valuables were recorded. For some reason, few of the departed shuffled off to the netherworld with anything of value.

Three bodies had been delivered in the last two hours. One of the recent arrival's descriptions matched Mourtone's to some extent, so the attendant led them to the chest-high shelf drawers that ran along two facing walls.

"Damn rollers need grease," the attendant complained, struggling and cursing over the heavy sliding compartment.

The chicken-necked man who slid out in the drawer bore no resemblance to Martin Mourtone whatsoever. Max caught a quick glance at a shattered eye socket and turned away. "Nah."

"You sure?" Stout pressed him. " 'Cause if you're sure, you've got one witness who I can tell you right now is nowhere near the fucking city of Baltimore, and you got another one who's dancin' in Little Africa as we speak."

"I'll bet my life he's not cake-walking, wherever he is."

A leaky smile spread out on Stout's face. "And as I'm sure you know, it's against the law to perpetrate a hoax, especially if you're planning to put it into your so-called newspaper." The detective's face tightened. "I remember you from the *World*. The Brian Gallagher case."

Max's stomach sank. In an unsigned article, he had raised questions as to why police Lieutenant Gallagher, after slitting the throat of a barber on Worth Street, had never been charged. He had suggested this with great care, indirectly, by posing certain questions to the deceased's family, but he hadn't fooled a soul, particularly the higher-up buttons.

He didn't have a byline, so he thought he'd be safe, but some sonofabitch had ratted him out to the bigwigs in management, and a month later his space work mysteriously dried up.

"Yeah, so what?"

"You know so what. If some bleeding-heart judge listened to you, Gallagher would be wasting his life in the Tombs."

"Whoever it was, it wasn't me." His ritual denial. Who could really nail the author of an unsigned piece? "Why would I want to kill all my sources? Ask Morris over at the 19th about me."

"You make up shit, there's laws against it."

"Don't go down that road. Bennett's lawyers will be crawling all over you." He had no idea if his publisher, who spent most of his time in Paris, would take the slightest interest in this dispute, but threats were all he had.

Suddenly, Stout smiled and punched him in the shoulder. "Hey, don't get so itchy. It's just a little joke."

Max didn't think it was a joke, but maybe he'd been too quick to lose his temper. "What do you expect? Look at this lousy coat you boys gave me."

"You mean that job ain't yours?"

Suddenly, an immense weariness spread through him. His limbs felt heavy, swollen. "You mean Sloan didn't tell you. . . ."

He was going to explain how he'd been rolled, how he'd been left facedown on the sidewalk, how he'd been rescued by a man wearing a tower of hats, but it all seemed too difficult. "How about a ride home, Stout?"

Without witnesses, without a corpse, he had no story. There was no point in going back to the office.

As they rocked along in silence, he wondered whether to tell Gretta about Martin. Should he sit through dinner masticating stringy beef, making excruciating small talk, and then take her into the parlor? Should he knock on her door directly? Was there a decent way to announce such terrible news? Did words exist that would soften the blow? Or should he hide it from her for a few days and wait for Martin's body to turn up? Wouldn't she hold that against him? The more he planned, the more muddled his thoughts became.

He tossed the ragged topcoat into an ash can, but now he was down to his shirtsleeves. Climbing the simple stone steps to Mrs. DeVogt's house, he hoped more than anything to slip into his room and wash up. He could envision his second clean shirt and his second suit hanging, newly pressed, in his closet. He yearned for fresh linen against his skin, the smell of laundry soap, he craved obliterating sleep. In his hand, the brass doorknob felt like soft skin. He turned it.

chapter eight

He had barely slipped through the foyer when Mrs. DeVogt accosted him. "Mr. Greengrass, what happened to you?"

"Sorry. I had an accident." He began to edge past her, but she pursued him.

"But your face. Look at you!" She waved a finger in disapproval.

Max gazed into the gilded convex mirror at the foot of the staircase. High on his forehead, an abrasion was forming a crusty scab. His left eye looked swollen and purple. A wet skullcap, his hair stuck to his scalp. In the distorted glass, his bruised face seemed to be streaming away from him.

Ignoring Mrs. DeVogt's prying, he said, "Yes. Will Gretta be with us for dinner tonight?"

"Dr. Condon's office is just around the corner."

"Will Gretta—"

"Why are you talking about Gretta in your condition? No, she's with her mother. She's caught the catarrh again."

"Will she be back tomorrow?"

"She said she has to take Miss Goelet's picture."

"I'll just go and patch myself up, then."

He managed to pour some water from the jug and splash his face before toppling onto the bed. Then he plunged into a paralyzing sleep. In the distance, he heard Mrs. DeVogt tapping at his door, and he tried to swim back to consciousness, but he hadn't the strength. When he woke a dozen hours later, he found himself curled in a fetal position on the bed, wearing his borrowed boots.

Clean clothes improved his appearance considerably, but he still looked as if he'd been in a barroom brawl. His entire left side felt stiff and bruised.

His mind was racing. Should he tell Parnell about the murder? Where was Gretta? How might he break the terrible news to her, yet still probe for information?

He wondered how deeply she had cared for Mourtone. The more intimate they had been, the more likely she was to know why Martin wanted to meet him at Stephenson's. Yet, the more distant their relationship had been, the happier Max would be. He prayed she knew everything, and he prayed she knew nothing at all.

At the breakfast table, where he consumed three eggs, ham, several hot rolls, and two cups of coffee, he fended off the other boarders' questions.

"What wall'd you walk into?" Danny teased.

He forced a laugh. "Hazards of the trade."

"You may want to try another profession, Mr. Greengrass," Mrs. DeVogt said.

"Who else will have me?"

"See a doctor or we'll punish you," Belle said. Despite her light tone, her eyes shone with real concern.

Outside, Swarms looked him over too. "Now you've got Belle mooning all over you. She's a nice little package. I ought to get rolled too."

"Nothing like that, Danny. A bunch of street arabs."

Swarms looked skeptical. "I'd get those scrapes cleaned out chop-chop. You don't want to croak and leave me alone with all that gash."

Max couldn't help feeling testy when Danny talked like that. Gash. Birds. Hot numbers. Now that the actor was squiring his sister around, Max felt damned uncomfortable about Danny's wisecracks. At the same time, he was pissed at Faye. He couldn't have an ordinary conversation with his closest pal any more. Somehow his sister had shimmied in between them. Who could he let his hair down with now? "What about the love of your life? Don't I know her?"

Danny grabbed his chest in a heart-rending gesture. "Hey, just kidding. When I'm at the table, I've got blinders on. I couldn't tell you how either of them's built."

Max's irritation dissolved. "My ass. You may be human . . . I suppose."

An evil grin crept onto Danny's thin lips. "Faye's got a little surprise cookin'."

"Crap." He looked heavenward. " Just strike me dead now. One big bolt."

Max knew that Gretta's studio occupied a street-level storefront at the corner of West 25th Street opposite Madison Square Park. The great stores were opening by the time he began the brief hike uptown. In the window of B. Altman's on Sixth Avenue and West 19th, a mechanical butterfly dipped and soared around a draped, headless dummy. Revolving electric stars cast their rays on a mauve silk gown, the material glittering with pinpoints of light.

Along the Ladies' Mile, shopgirls in their French heels and tin collars ogled the latest in silver and jewelry. Knots of well-dressed men seemed to have no other occupation than gazing at young women whose felt hats were adorned with ostrich plumes and snowy egret feathers. Women in alpaca capes fluttered across the sidewalk. A flash of plum-colored silk always drew hoots and applause from sports draped over the windowsills of their exclusive clubs.

As he walked north, then east, his intoxication with the city was more than a distraction; its rhythms matched his own internal, jittery beat. The women, the goods, the noise of the delivery wagons, the cursing, shouting drivers, the sumptuous architecture brought on a nervous excitement he loved for itself alone. Faceless in the infernal uproar, he felt some unnameable thrill, a release into nothingness.

The thought of his mission, so close now, suddenly filled him with dread. His message was truly terrible, he felt its weight more completely now, and yet he had to deliver it. At first he hung back in Madison Square Park, letting his eye run over the stores across the broad confluence of Broadway and Fifth Avenue. Auction rooms, china houses, millinery and dry-goods establishments filled the block. In the center a canvas awning displayed the legend ST. REGIS PORTRAIT STUDIO.

A soft bell tinkled when he pushed open the door. The interior was draped in rich damask. On the walls, three Japanese woodblock prints hung in a cluster. A fringed divan upholstered in an Ottoman pattern gave the waiting room a harem-like air. Behind a low desk, a woman with kohl-smeared eyelids presided.

"I'm looking for Gretta," he said softly. The décor seemed to demand whispering.

"You must be Martin," the woman replied, smirking.

"No, no. I'm Max Greengrass, another friend."

"Ah." She looked at his battered face more carefully, considering whether to announce him.

"We're both at Mrs. DeVogt's."

"I see . . . I'll get her."

Bickering voices drifted out. Finally, Gretta appeared, an annoyed expression on her face. When she noticed his scrapes and bruises, her features softened.

"Mr. Greengrass. Your head. Your eye. Did you bump into something?"

"This? No. Something bumped into me. Is there somewhere more private?"

"What is it? Can't it wait 'til dinner? We have a client waiting."

Her brusque tone snapped him out of his reverie. "Sorry. This can't wait."

"Oh. Violet, would you excuse us, please?" She rolled her eyes in the receptionist's direction.

Finally, he was able to speak directly. Yet he couldn't quite pull it off. "There's been a very bad accident. I need to reach . . . Martin's parents."

Her color drained away, and she grasped his hand. Her scent, her hair, the proximity of her luxuriant body made his heart race at exactly the wrong time. "How bad is he?"

Stepping away, yet still caught in her tense grip, he said, "It's very bad. I'm sorry, I didn't intend to say. . . ."

"He's dead, isn't he? Was he run over? Oh, God, I have to set the lights for Gertrude. Mrs. Swanson will be here in ten minutes."

He had assumed she would introduce him to the Mourtones and help him get an interview with the father. At the very least, the family would confirm that Martin was missing. "Can't you leave for the day?"

"Oh, my God. Is he actually dead? You have to tell me." She dug her fingernails into his skin.

"Please, come with me. It's too complicated to talk about here."

"I can't, I can't! I'll lose my job if I walk out now! I have to go back in a minute." Her desperation confirmed his suspicions: she couldn't live without her weekly wage. What about the genteel Staten Island country club, the tennis and bicycle expeditions? He sensed her panic, her fear of losing a single dollar, and his heart sank. What could he do about it?

"You're not giving me a choice."

"No, I'm certainly not! Just tell me." She pushed him away and smoothed her skirt.

"I went to meet him at a bar called Stephenson's. About the note you gave me? When I got there he'd been shot." He withheld the phrase "in the head" just before it passed his lips.

"Uhh," she gasped, hunching over as if she'd been struck in the stomach. "Oh my God, it's not . . . it can't be . . . uhh . . . he's definitely. . . . There's no question?"

"No, no question as to that. I'm sorry to be the one . . . telling, saying this . . . unspeakable thing."

"M'mm." She nodded slowly. Her long fingers stroked her shirtwaist buttons. "Well, we have a client coming. . . ." Instead of leaving, she sank onto the ottoman. "I have to prepare the plates. May I have some water?"

He found the receptionist, who directed him to a sink in the back. She drank thirstily. "Thanks. So nice of you." Her smile, a polite tic, lit her face, her beauty disembodied, dreadful. To his amazement, she gathered herself and stood.

"You ought to come with me, Gretta."

"Where? What difference does it make now?" Her eyes vacant, she twined her hair around her finger.

As she turned away and headed back to the studio, her movements took on a mechanical quality. Max went to her, certain she was in shock. He touched her elbow and she turned around, staring at him as if were a stranger. "Will you be all right?"

She offered a weak smile. "It's impossible."

"You should go home. I'll take you."

Still she shook her head, apparently intent on returning to the studio. Now, the practical side of his nature got the upper hand. "Would you write the Mourtones' address down, please?"

Like an automaton, she drifted over to the desk and scratched out the numbers. She handed the note to him and offered a peculiar smile.

"I'll see you later?"

She nodded, but gestured for him to leave. For a moment longer he waited, hoping she would change her mind, but she turned and went back to the darkroom, her straight back disappearing behind the curtains.

He had no choice but to plunge back into the streets. He took a horsecar up Fifth Avenue to 42nd Street, then got out and walked along the reservoir's massive walls, gathering his thoughts. Spattered blood on a wall. Mourtone flung back at that vertiginous angle. His rubber mask of a face. The cawing, chattering street arabs. Were they still creeping up behind him? Were they crouching behind that shiny Victoria? In that sliver of an alleyway? Ridiculous. He shook his head, as if he could drive the wraiths from his mind.

One step followed another. How much to tell Martin's parents? Should he even present himself as a reporter? No, let them talk first, and then find the right moment? Was that possible?

Horsecars and carriages thundered over the paving stones, but once he took a few steps off the main thoroughfare a voluptuous quiet took hold. Block after block of fine brownstones stretched out before him, and hardly a soul on the street. The glass roof of a conservatory peeked out from behind a fence. An immaculate brougham stood waiting beneath a *porte-cochère*. Ornamental ironwork, freshly painted and jet-black, ran up stone stairs to doors with highly polished brass fittings. The sumptuous peace was what he relished most of all.

Finally, he came to the Mourtones' address, its entrance a street-level Ionic colonnade. The brownstone building, actually three older structures joined into one, possessed an intimate quality despite its grandeur. A dense growth of ivy curled a story above the front door's awning. In between the second and third floors an iron balcony supported a row of potted trees. Even though he knew they were well-off, he hadn't imagined the Mourtones living on such a scale. Their standing intimidated him, he hated to admit it, but he focused his mind on his terrible task.

After he explained his mission, a manservant led him past a grand marble staircase, through a drawing room decorated with Watteau-style paintings set into wooden panels, and finally to the library, its carefully arranged bookcases filled to the brim with fine bindings. A painted frieze, garlands of roses, ran under the cornice. The richly colored rugs, the brocade curtains, the Second Empire furniture, the electric lighting all conspired to create a mood of splendor and contemplation. He couldn't help resenting Martin for having been born into such a velvet cocoon.

In a few moments Martin's father, a thin man with a drooping white moustache, closed the door quietly behind him. He looked far more the aesthete than the insurance baron.

"You say you know where Martin is?" Sagging blue pouches swelled beneath his eyes.

"I'm sorry, Mr. Mourtone. I did see your son last night. . . ."

"Where is he? His mother is frantic. We contacted the police when he didn't come home, but they're in a fog as usual."

"I was supposed to . . . I did meet him at a bar on Bleecker Street."

"Bleecker Street?" The man was clearly dazed, and exhausted as well.

Max could barely get the words out. He was afraid the senior Mourtone might crumble before his eyes. "Last night. Before I got there, someone shot him. He was dead by the time I showed up."

Mourtone flinched, his head jerking as if he'd been slapped. "How do you know? Maybe he was just hurt? Did you get a good look at him?"

Max spoke slowly, enunciating each word. "I'm very sorry. Yes. I did. He'd been shot, and there was no doubt. He's definitely gone."

Dazed, Mourtone sat down on the edge of a sofa. "You have to be certain. What am I supposed to tell his mother?"

"I can't imagine . . . It's a terrible tragedy. Here is my card. If there is anything I can do to help you. . . ."

For a moment Mourtone stared dumbly at Max's identification. In a bitter tone, he said, "You're a reporter? Don't think you're putting this in your scurvy paper. This is hard enough."

Then he let go a feral noise, a grunt, a growl, a moan combined, an animal expression of grief. How strange coming from such a neat, elegant man.

"I appreciate your distress, but it's my job." Max had never made this statement with a greater sense of shame. For an instant he saw himself, a permanent harbinger of horror sailing into the future.

Recovering a bit, Mourtone whispered, "Do me one simple kindness then. Where is the body?"

"That's the other part. I don't really know. He's . . . the body is lost." The empty chair, perfectly lined up under the empty table. The missing liver-colored hat. The ashtray a clean cup of air. The shape of absence. Dread crept bone by bone up Max's spine.

"What? Lost? What do you mean? A second ago you said he was dead. Now you don't know where he is?" Mourtone's voice shook with rage. "Are you some kind of extortionist?"

"It's a complicated story." In short strokes, he explained that he had returned to Stephenson's with Detective Stout, and that Martin's corpse had vanished.

Mourtone set himself at the edge of an upholstered chair. "I told him to stay out of those blind pigs."

"Well, Stephenson's isn't actually. . . ."

Mourtone rocked slowly, chewing on his lips, talking to himself. "He's dead, he's actually dead? You wouldn't make this up, no . . . it's inconceivable. No, it's not. He wanted to do this to us, he always wanted to. . . ." His eyes glazed, he stared at Max. "What do you want from me? Why did you come here?"

"Well, I was the only one who saw—"

"Your newspaper, that's why, isn't it?"

"I thought I might quote you," Max admitted. "All in good taste."

"Ah, good taste. My son is murdered in a black-and-tan, you'll smear it all over your greasy rag, but you'll exercise good taste?"

"I liked Martin," he mumbled, groping for sympathetic ground. "I thought it would be better than the police—"

"But the police don't know anything about it, do they? All they have is your cock-and-bull story."

"I'm sorry, but it's true. I understand your distress."

"Don't suppose anything, whoever you are." Straightening up, Mourtone eyed Max contemptuously. His lips unpeeled in a sardonic smile. "So it's your word against mine, isn't it?"

"What are you talking about?"

"You can't prove he's dead, can you? Why should I accept your account?" Ashen, clearly exhausted, Mourtone was rallying.

"He's missing, isn't he?" Max reasoned.

"Possibly. Maybe not."

Now Max saw a glimpse of the insurance magnate beneath the aesthete's milk-white skin. Mourtone's voice no longer wavered. "We won't see a word of this in your precious paper, of course. In fact, we won't *allow it*. You say you saw Martin, shot, in this Stephenson dive? I will insist I saw him afterwards. Your paper could get sued for libel, couldn't it? Dragging a decent family's name through that rag of yours. Not to speak of the damage to a grieving mother, assuming you have any human feelings. I think your recklessness, once it was exposed in court, would result in a nice stiff fine and drive you out of your so-called profession for good."

Mourtone had made his priorities crystal-clear. Dying was in poor enough taste. Expiring in Stephenson's was worse than death itself. The threat of legal action, given the insurance executive's resources, sounded all too convincing. Max kept his mouth shut and let him go on.

"On the other hand, we could cooperate."

"How?"

Mourtone kept Max waiting while he poured whiskey from a cut-glass decanter. When he passed the reporter his drink, his hand shook. Liquor splashed on the carpet, but Mourtone either didn't notice or didn't care.

"Sit down. Let's work this out to our mutual advantage."

Max sensed that Mourtone had used that phrase a thousand times while trimming his clients, but the scotch went down warm and smooth. "With all due respect," Max reminded him, "you've already reported Martin as missing to the police. It's a matter of public record now."

Actually, Max had no interest in placing a squib about a missing society swell. The real story involved Martin's murder and what he had known about the Midnight Band's activities. And that information had probably died with him . . . unless Gretta knew more than she had admitted.

"Yes, but it won't be public knowledge unless you print it. You can help our family instead of causing us pain. Don't report the incident now. I can advance you some expenses. Meanwhile, you can keep looking. . . ." His voice shaking, he faltered. "Looking for him, in my employ. You saw him last. You're a reporter. Find the boy."

Rapidly, Max sorted out this arrangement's merits and dangers. If the offer was high enough, he could use the money to wipe out his debt to Sim Addem. He'd have breathing room for once in his life. What had Billy Webster said? Look at Scott, the theatre critic, licking the cream off his lips. Just a little on the side . . . how could anybody survive on Bennett's crumbs?

With MacNamara the bartender wandering in deepest, darkest Baltimore and the black man disappeared down a Thompson Street alley, Max had no story. So taking money *not* to write an article he couldn't publish anyway made perfect sense. He didn't see much of an ethical issue. Well, there might be one, but it was convoluted enough to ignore. And how would Stan Parnell ever find out? Still, he felt nervous. He had never before taken money on the side. But wasn't it the way of the world? He couldn't decide, so he stalled.

"What do I do if I find him?" Carefully, he avoided the words "body" or "corpse."

"That's precisely what I'll be paying you for. Have some decency, for Godsakes. I have a heartbroken woman upstairs. Do you want to kill her? How much? Two, three hundred?"

Stunned by the offer—he could live for months on that kind of mazuma—he still hesitated. What if it cost him his job, was it worth it? But who would ever find out?

Mourtone wanted nothing more than to bury his son and the sorry circumstances of his demise. Two or three hundred? He went cold. The butterflies in his stomach fluttered and died. With that kind of dough he could not only pay Addem, he could live like a king for a while. Get the whole bill of fare at the Waldorf, lamb in mint sauce, canvasback duck, Lobster Victoria.

When he looked up at the Venetian painted ceiling, certainly plundered in Europe by Mourtone's architect, he wondered if he could do better. "Five. And if there are expenses later on, you'll advance me?"

"Would you like cash now?"

Suddenly, a febrile excitement gripped him. He allowed himself a single word. "Naturally."

"We'll want to work with Police Superintendent Byrnes. He's a solid man, completely discreet."

Superintendent Byrnes was renowned for finding and returning the possessions of the better classes. It was almost magical how he could put his finger on a pearl pendant or a gold ring the day after it was stolen. Of course, all the reporters knew how he did it, by making deals with every dip in the city, parceling out zones in which he would tolerate pickpockets, the badger game, faro, stuss, and every twist on banco known to man. In return, the underworld granted him a *cordon sanitaire*, the Dead Line starting just above Wall Street. The financial district, with its immense store of stocks, bonds and bullion, and its well-heeled brokers, traders and practitioners of the darker financial arts, had become the safest place in the city.

Max didn't even blink when Mourtone handed him Howe and Hummel's business card. "First, go to these lawyers, and they'll make other contacts. Do you know this firm?"

He had to suppress a laugh. In the previous year's most celebrated trial, Howe and Hummel had defended Hattie Adams against the Reverend Dr.

Charles Parkhurst's charges that she was running a police-protected bordello. In order to gather evidence, the minister had entered Adams's establishment incognito, observed a can-can demonstration, and engaged in a game of naked leapfrog. On the stand, Charles Gardner, the private detective who had accompanied the Reverend Dr. Parkhurst, admitted playing the frog.

"Who doesn't?"

"You know where they're located?"

"Down opposite the Tombs." In a sense, wasn't he being paid to find Martin, rather than to keep anything out of the paper? He wasn't taking a bribe at all. Why not take a job on the side, when half the time he raced around town for Parnell and had his copy tossed back in his face? Wouldn't it be sweet to commandeer a Hoffman House table? He could set off a wine spree, stand the house at the mahogany-paneled bar, and take drinks in return, his right leg secured on a brass-plated foot rest. Or he could take Gretta to Delmonico's or Sherry's. Imagine having the simoleons to do that! He felt giddy.

A pleading note crept into Mourtone's voice. "Maybe you saw someone else . . . it was dark in there, wasn't it? I can't tell his mother, you understand, until it's certain. She had rheumatic fever when she was young."

"It's a terrible thing. I'm sorry." What barren words, inadequate noises.

Mourtone closed the tall doors behind himself.

The insurance magnate didn't return to the library. Instead, his manservant handed Max an envelope and then led him to the door. Proud and ashamed all at once, he slipped the money into his inside jacket pocket. His fingers kept migrating to the thick packet of bills. There they were, real to the touch. In the muffled quiet of the East Side streets, it was all he could do to keep from whooping out loud. He'd never had more than twenty dollars in his pocket in his life. Five hundred dollars, and he'd negotiated the price up from three hundred! Yes, he felt a twinge of guilt, but a flood of newly found self-respect washed it away. Why not lick some cream himself once in a while?

On his way downtown he deposited $400 in his account at the Madison Square Bank. The rest he kept in small bills. No one had to know why he occasionally dipped his hand into his inside pocket or why he was gliding across the sidewalk, lighter than air.

chapter nine

Across the three-story red brick building at 89 Centre Street, Howe and Hummel's sign ran forty feet long and four feet high. In thick block lettering, stenciled on two windows, and on a pair of flanking columns as well, the partners' names were repeated to numbing effect.

Above the Tombs, wispy clouds blew across a brilliant sky. For an April day, the wind was pouring in, sharp and cold off the harbor.

Max entered the stark waiting room, a pair of raw wooden benches pressed against unadorned walls. In the center of the room, a battered stove leaked a bit of smoke. Nearby stood an enormous safe. Cheek to jowl, the waiting clients had drifted in from different universes. A straight-spined man in a high beaver hat and frock coat sat next to a henna-haired woman whose generous powder, rouge, and lipstick were more mask than makeup. A man with a sun-glazed face and wild stalks of hair looked like a fishmonger. Next to him, but sitting at the farthest edge of the bench, a veiled woman in widow's weeds held herself stock-still.

One client stood out, though, a fierce-looking young woman whose false fingernails appeared to be made of sharpened metal.

Suddenly, a tiny, warty-faced man raced into the room and began twirling the safe's combination wheel. Fascinated, Max watched as the clerk swung the massive door wide, revealing nothing within but an old scuttle. Dashing into a storeroom, the little man, who sported a pair of shiny, pointed shoes, retrieved a shovelful of coal, dumped it in the pot-bellied stove, then locked the implement up again for safekeeping. Max managed to catch the man's flying sleeve before he disappeared again. The Mourtone name produced a magical effect. Immediately, the clerk led Max to an inner cubicle furnished with three plain chairs and told him to wait.

Max had been reading about Howe and Hummel for years, though he had never laid eyes on them. It was common knowledge that the Five Points gang the Whyos and the monosyllabic Tammany leader Richard Croker kept Howe and Hummel on retainer. Howe had represented General Abe Greenthal's Sheeny Mob, a pickpocket juggernaut, and Chester McLaughlin's Valentine Gang, expert forgers. Hummel protected luminaries of the theatre as well. Max had heard that P. T. Barnum used the firm, as did Edwin Booth, Tony Pastor, John Barrymore, and, in order to guard her artistic freedom, Little Egypt.

Abe Hummel was also fond of sending subpoenas to men of substance, invoking their imaginary promises of marriage to certain carefully trained chorines and actresses. These breach-of-promise suits amounted to a genteel form of blackmail that New York's sporting men considered a hazard of their exploits.

Yet Howe and Hummel were so well situated that The *Herald* once ran a laudatory article about a dinner they threw for Police Superintendent Byrnes at Delmonico's. In that anonymously penned piece, the author referred to Howe as "the Nestor of the criminal bar." Max was certain that he had come across other stories about the lawyers in the *World*'s Sunday supplements as well.

Howe's chief fame, however, sprang from his storied performances in hundreds of murder trials. Max knew he had represented Dr. Jakob Rosenzweig, who had earned the name the Hackensack Mad Monster for express-mailing parts of Alice Augusta Bowlsby south of the Mason–Dixon Line. Other bloody-minded clients included Annie Walden, the Man-Killing Racetrack Girl; Handsome Harry Carlton; and Michael McGloin, Whyo captain.

So Max knew quite a bit about William H. Howe and Abe Hummel. Even so, he wasn't prepared for Howe in the flesh. Busy with papers, the mountainous man behind the desk barely looked up, giving the young reporter a moment to absorb the spectacle. A skinny messenger stood patiently at the lawyer's shoulder.

Howe, in a doeskin waistcoat, a green patterned shirt, and a royal-purple suit, offered up a paean to clashing colors. Instead of a tie, a dewdrop diamond, held in place by a cloverleaf of white, pink, and black pearls, glistened at this throat. Hanging from a gold chain, stretched to breaking across his great abdomen, a diamond fob sparkled. A yachting cap with a blue brim was tipped back on his enormous head. Max tried to gauge the man's age, perhaps sixty or so. There was something antique about his garishness, suggesting the days when lawyers attracted their clients less by their skill in the courtroom than with their flashing stones.

Finishing his subpoena with a flourish, the attorney issued orders to his messenger. "Say you're from Western Union, you've got news of an inheritance. That's a good one." Here he turned for the first time, his blue eyes disappearing in pockets of flesh, and melted Max with a smile worthy of a Bowery comedian. There was something both captivating and grotesque about Howe's looks. A strong nose, a high forehead, a generous mouth, but more of each than was necessary.

He continued to instruct his process server, while with a broad wink he drew Max into his conspiracy. "Say you're the milkman, the gas man, the iceman, the butter-and-egg man. Put on a dress. But serve, man, serve!"

After his minion had darted out the door, the lawyer rose, placed his hands on his hips, arched his back and groaned. Without the slightest bit of embarrassment, he squatted slightly and produced a musical fart.

With a darting finger, he directed Max's eye to a series of framed sepia photographs that ran along the wall above a bookcase stuffed haphazardly with leather-bound volumes. "The pantheon, Mr. Greengrass, our pantheon. Have you ever seen the like? And whom do we have here? Queen Victoria. Lillian Russell. Mr. Sullivan, of course. Jake Kilrain, a tough customer but a man of unstained character. And Miss Langtry. A Hall of Fame without them would be a sham. And whom do we have here? A little man with a great spirit and a great brain. Our Mr. Hummel."

To Max's shock, next to the dignitaries and celebrities hung a photograph—from the same series—of the miniature man who had retrieved the coal scuttle. Less surprising was the next portrait in the collection, William H. Howe's. The lawyer's somber gaze under the print's brown finish spoke of philosophical depths, a melancholy, tragic view of life strangely at odds with the man before him.

Returning to his padded seat, Howe went on. "These pictures, you may have guessed, come from the *Police Gazette* Hall of Fame. To members of elevated social circles they may not seem like much, but do you know how many people read the *Gazette* every week? They buy these pictures, sir, for a nominal fee, to dress up their living rooms and foy-ays."

Max noted in Howe's uncertain h's a trace of Cockney. His tone recalled the carnival barker.

"It gives me confidence to know that when I stand before a jury, that one or two of its members has hanging in his dwelling, pictures of little Abie and me over the mantel. He knows our exploits, he knows our good deeds. Now what about this friend of yours, young Mourtone? Nasty business."

Howe's mercurial shift in tone jolted the reporter. "You already know?"

The lawyer nodded his leonine head.

"Apparently, he's been murdered." Max's own words sounded tinny.

"You've been through a terrible experience, I understand. When I was only twelve, I saw a man strangled to death. A harmless man who wouldn't hurt a fly. Oh, I had hair-raising dreams for years. I understand your agitation."

Max had the eerie feeling that Howe really did know about his own cat-clawing nightmares. It was hard to resist the man's honeyed sympathy. He did feel agitated, and he hadn't confided in anyone.

"But what makes you think he was murdered?" Howe pressed him.

"Well, I saw him. He'd been shot in the head."

"You saw it happen?"

"No, I got there afterwards."

"So you're not a witness to the crime?"

"He'd been shot in the head. The back . . . a piece of his head was missing."

Suddenly, Howe leaned forward and bore down on him. "But how close did you get to the body? How dark was it in that dive? Do you have a medical background? Did you perform an examination? Did you find a bullet? The murder weapon?"

"Well, no. . . ."

Howe rocked back and offered an avuncular smile. "Don't worry. I've defended hundreds of witnesses."

What did that mean? Was the lawyer threatening him in some obscure way? "I didn't. . . ."

"Ahh, you're not a witness? Then considering the ambiguous circumstances you've described, your friend could have passed on because of the bleeding white lung, pleurisy, brain fever, any number of foul diseases."

This leap in illogic had a dizzying quality, the more so since Howe spoke with so much authority. At one moment the lawyer's tone was warm, in the next accusatory. Or, paradoxically, by some theatrical trick, he struck both notes at the same time.

"I saw Martin recently, he didn't complain. . . ." Wary, Max withdrew into his own skin. However charming, William H. Howe was not his friend.

"He could have been found anywhere. In a lending library. Under a pleasant tree. In his own bed. I've done a study of this. The number of men who claim to have died in their own beds is suspect. On the other hand, spiritually speaking, we ought to have the right to die anywhere, don't you think? Our dead friends need our protection, otherwise who will take up their cause?"

Now Max's suspicions became fully aroused. The payment to him was a sham. The insurance tycoon must have instructed Howe to keep Max out of any real investigation. "How, exactly, do you mean that?"

"Mr. Mourtone's been a client of mine for many years. Don't worry. No harm will come to you."

"Why should it?" he shot back. Reflexively, he balled his fists.

"Oh, don't take it the wrong way. We're working together on this."

Before Max could sort out Howe's equivocal hints and veiled threats any further, the great man seized a scrap of paper from the chaos on his desk, scrawled on it, folded it up, and handed it to him.

"Call this number tomorrow. We'll see if we can find your poor friend."

Perhaps he had jumped to conclusions. Mourtone must want to find his son's remains, if only to resolve the tragedy in a decorous way. Why not use the last man to see Martin alive? A payoff in return for discretion might be exactly what it seemed.

Max waved the scrap of paper. "Whose number is it?"

A golden smile blossomed on the lawyer's face. "Every day they change them. Who can keep track?"

chapter ten

The wind kicked up, the dust from dry horse apples swirling down the funnel of Centre Street. Then he heard the ancient cry. "Rrrraggggs! Bo-ones! Rrrrags! Bo-ones!" Drawn by a hollow-ribbed nag, the wagon rolled toward him, its swollen cargo threatening to spill out onto the street. "Rrrrags! Bo-ones! Rrrrags! Bo-ones!" The timeless entreaty gave him gooseflesh. Used winding sheets and foul blankets. Soup bones and pigs' knuckles. The hair, the piss, the shit, the phlegm, the blood of the dead stuck to faded scraps of muslin. What were these vehicles but ferries to the netherworld? His throat tightened. Then the driver's stovepipe hat came into view.

There was something wrong with it, the tilt, the height, the proportions, its dull surface. It was a rubber hat, attached to a rubber mug. The face of J. P. Morgan himself. The great financier, with his Dutch burgher eyes and his magnificent, carbuncled nose, peered back at him. A Wall Street baron plying a junk wagon. The driver's rubber mask seemed to grin as it drifted by. "Rrrrags! Bo-ones! Rrrrags! Bo-ones!" Issuing from Morgan's lips, the primitive call sounded so incongruous that Max almost fell over laughing! New York. Everybody had to be a wise guy.

For a moment he lingered in Howe and Hummel's doorway.

What had happened back there? The attorney had told him, in no uncertain terms, that wherever Martin's corpse turned up, Stephenson's would never be mentioned again. And that being a witness was a dangerous occupation. Not only that, Howe had managed to deliver the message in such a light and circuitous way that he could never have been accused of delivering it at all. Max had to be hardheaded. He'd taken the money, and now he had to forget seeing Martin at the Bleecker Street black-and-tan unless the police drew him into an investigation. Somehow, he doubted there would be an inquiry of any sort.

This time he wouldn't ask the wrong people the wrong questions. He'd lay forty bucks on Faye out of the blue. What "surprise" was *she* about to spring? Danny had made a joke of it, but his sister surprised him all too often. In the back of his mind he was always on edge, waiting for the next wicked twist in the melodrama featuring Fabulous Faye and Her Latest Fling.

He'd slip his mother some cash too, but he didn't worry about her that much. She always had a new scheme. Planting vegetables in a neighbor's yard. Giving English classes to greenhorns, despite the fact that she'd never gone beyond third grade in Austria. She took fearful immigrants to doctors for a few cents, and when she returned home she acted out their symptoms. Faye had gotten her inspiration from dramas starring typhus and pneumonia.

What did bother him was the way his mother worked. At the crack of dawn, she was swabbing the halls of the four-family house, dragging refuse to the curb, sweeping the sidewalk, turning down the gas fixtures, and polishing the front door's brass doorknob. From the more recent Polish and Russian immigrants, she'd caught the property mania. Once the old man picked up some work, she claimed, she would put a few dollars away and buy a building herself. His father had said she was dreaming, and, for once, Max concurred. Still, he admired the tiny ball of energy, too. While the old man was wandering around the flat, bound in leather phylacteries and muttering the ancient mumbo-jumbo, she was out in the real world, scratching for a living.

Cockroach landlords, they called them. Immigrants willing to live in their own windowless cellars just to collect one extra rent. He wished she'd come down with a different obsession, but he didn't mind nurturing his own illusions. One day, when he was pulling down Harding Davis–type dough, he'd slap a down payment on her kitchen table. Just to see the expression on her face.

But he had more pressing problems.

What could he say to Gretta now? In the morning he had been dedicated to unraveling Martin's disappearance. Now he had to fend off her questions and do his best to drop the subject entirely. That might look strange to her, though. He'd have to make a *pretense* of investigating. Yet he couldn't help wondering what Martin had intended to reveal about the cat killings. What was the "vicious joke" he had been burning to impart?

To quiet his feverish self-examination, Max stroked the soothing packet of bills in his pocket again.

He had to make an appearance at the office. Perhaps Parnell had something new on the Midnight Band, or a fresh assignment for him as a reward for his good work. He also wondered who had written The *Herald*'s encomiums to Howe, and whether, without revealing his own brush with the law firm, he might get some deeper insight into its workings.

From the throne, Parnell beckoned.

The sphinx-like editor seemed a shade friendlier. Or was it Max's imagination? How could anyone tell? Shifts in Parnell's moods were barely perceptible. Max climbed onto the platform and approached his boss's rolltop desk. Paint flakes drifted down from the ceiling. Fresh cobwebs hung around the glowing light bowls. The uptown *Herald* building was nearing completion; here, dust balls incubated in the old office's nooks and crannies, tobacco juice wreathed battered spittoons, three-legged chairs multiplied, and stuck drawers stayed that way.

Parnell didn't even bother to say hello. "Anything new with the cat business?"

"I've got some interviews, but—"

"We're still getting mail on your last one. You stirred them up with that malarkey. Half of our readers want to hang your little biddies, and half of them want to join the party. Stay on it."

"Great." While he still had a chance, Max thought he'd take a flyer on William H. Howe. "Mr. Parnell, can I ask you a question?"

Parnell just stared at him.

"Who wrote those articles about those lawyers, Howe and Hummel? Is the man still working here?"

"Right over there. Biddle covers them most of the time."

Max gazed across the room at Nicholas Biddle, an aging dandy who always carried a gold-tipped cane, even to the most grisly assignments. Whether he was a Biddle of the Philadelphia Biddles, or an interloper, he had never made clear. It was enough, his elegant manners implied, to act like a Biddle. His limp gray hair, which fell to his shoulders, and his long yellow teeth implied a careless aristocratic pedigree.

Not certain what he was after, Max approached him. Biddle was more than happy to suspend his labors and discuss his fabled subject.

"No, I can't say that I keep the old articles. So you met Willy the Weeper, eh? I saw him once—it's hard to believe when you consider the size of the man—but I once watched him deliver an entire closing statement on his knees. It lasted," Biddle paused for effect, "two and a half hours. The last half hour he used up three handkerchiefs."

"I don't doubt it. I suppose I could look up your pieces if you remember the dates. . . ."

"Ahhh, the morgue's a wreck. Don't bother with them. Here's what you need." Biddle rummaged through a series of pigeonholes, finally extracting a dog-eared pamphlet. "I think they came out with this in '88. It will tell you everything you need to know."

Gretta wouldn't get back to Mrs. DeVogt's for a couple of hours, so Max repaired to Logan's on Chambers Street, where the free lunch stretched out into the late afternoon. He chose from a smattering of sardellen, a pair of summer sausages, spring onions, dried herring, crackers, dill pickles, and pretzels, then settled down with his plate at the bar and began reading Biddle's pamphlet.

Howe and Hummel's opus was entitled *In Danger, or Life in New York. A True History of a Great City's Wiles and Temptations.*

After he drained his first schooner of beer, his tense muscles loosened. Halfway through his second, he had a metaphysical insight. Logan's shining mahogany bar was Mecca, and he was a Mohammedan, down on his knees in supplication.

Howe and Hummel's pamphlet declared, in full-throated piety, "It had been well for many an honest lad and unsuspecting country girl that they had never turned their steps cityward nor turned from the simplicity of their country home toward the snares and pitfalls of crime and vice that await the unwary in New York."

The lawyers sounded like Comstock's Society for the Prevention of Vice itself. Reverend Weems, Holy Trinity Church's minister, would have been comfortable with *In Danger*'s tone. Puzzled, Max gulped down more beer to kill the salty sardellen. Those last few sausages tasted a shade mealy. He read on.

In Danger shifted to a different note quickly, as it described the city's "elegant storehouses, crowded with the choicest and most costly goods, great banks whose vaults and safes contain more bullion than can be transported by the largest ships, colossal establishments teeming with diamonds, jewelry and precious stones gathered from all the known and uncivilized portions of the globe, all this countless wealth, in some cases *so insecurely guarded.*"

Evidently, according to the authors, New York's criminals were employing the most scientific methods to separate these indescribable riches from their owners. A detailed passage explained how to construct a shoplifter's muff. By tearing out the handwarmer's lining and inserting a wire frame, "shoplifting is so easy as to be successfully practiced by novices." Out of charity, the authors offered the mathematical formulas needed to beat the ponies and a way to make an invisible pinhole in a faro deck that would guarantee the last winning hand.

Soon Max began to understand the true purpose of the handbook, especially when *In Danger* dwelt on the mixed motivations of the New York police: "Instead of surrounding thieves with a network to convict them, the New York headquarters detectives furnish them with all the facilities for escape known to modern criminal practice."

The technical and helpful descriptions of "the traveling bag with false, quick opening sides" and "lady thieves' corsets" only served to cement his conviction: *In Danger* was a criminal's handbook. When Howe and Hummel expressed their moral outrage at the practices of nightlife establishments such as Harry Hill's Dance House, Billy McGlory's and the French Madame's on Thirty-Fourth Street, where "the performance is of such a nature as to horrify any but the most blasé roue," they didn't neglect to include addresses.

The treatise concluded with a warning that those who drifted to the wrong side of the law would be foolhardy to hire anyone but the distinguished and compassionate Howe and Hummel. One client for whom they had won a hung jury later retained other counsel and was quickly hung himself. When a Miss Blanchette was wronged by a cad named Theodore, she hired Howe and Hummel and "proceedings were taken which brought the contumacious Theodore to a very satisfactory arrangement as far as Miss Blanchette was concerned." As for their client Mrs. Hazzard, her "lawyers carried all before them like the flood."

Max didn't even realize how loud he was laughing until a barfly asked, "What're you readin', bub? A joke book?"

"You could call it that," he replied. In fact, *In Danger* was the most hilarious piece of self-promotion he'd ever seen. It also made him more wary of William H. Howe than ever.

Max saw Gretta scanning the street in front of Mrs. DeVogt's. He rushed up to her, hoping the cloves he'd chewed had killed the booze on his breath. In a rose-and-yellow-striped overskirt and a hat trimmed with artificial lilacs, she looked anything but the grieving lover. Her somber expression suggested otherwise though.

"Good. I was hoping to catch you here. Would you come to Staten Island with me? Mother's still ill. We can talk on the ferry." Her voice had a strangled quality, but she spoke to him directly, holding his gaze.

He couldn't help admiring her control. "We'd better hurry. South Ferry will be a madhouse around now."

"You'll get to see the cottage."

Unfortunately, rush hour was at its height, so he and Gretta had to press hard into the tightly packed mass of riders just to get onto the train. Max felt painfully embarrassed for Gretta, whose body had to bear the intimate weight of a snickering young man in a straw boater and a bloated character with an irritated wen on the tip of his nose. He also wished fervently that he were the one crushed against her, helplessly and without blame.

The train squealed and rocked on to Fourteenth, then Ninth, and Houston. At Franklin Square, the conductor could barely get the doors closed again.

"Sardines are better off," he said over the straw boater to Gretta.

Out on the river, a Long Island ferry blew its steam whistle.

Her expression remained frozen until they left the train. The ferry terminal smelled of ammonia and saltpeter. A merciless wave of humanity drove them down its length. At the slip, the flat-bottomed boat was already taking on passengers. In a moment they found themselves packed onto an outdoor bench.

Quietly, Max said, "I'm so sorry about Martin."

She replied with a stiff nod. Out in the harbor, a wooden, double-ended side-wheeler paddled toward Ellis Island. Beyond, a four-masted schooner drifted toward the Narrows. She took his hand. "Let's go over to the side."

They stood together silently as the ferry made its clumsy way into the harbor. A sharp wind rose, and they were enveloped in salty spray. Max shivered, but Gretta seemed oblivious, so he hung on to the wide, polished rail. Gulls sailed gracefully alongside the boat, then, screeching wildly, skimmed the water. A tug dragged a low-slung coal barge past. Further out, near the mouth of the harbor, the gray shape of a brig materialized.

Cutting through the choppy bay, a steam yacht sailed by. The wind, the salty air, the spray, the sight of ships suspended on the horizon, the soft rocking of the boat were soothing, hypnotic.

Gazing out at the bay, Gretta spoke in a halting, disconnected way.

"I know you probably thought he was a dilettante . . . he *was,* I suppose, but he was a very dear person. Sometimes he seemed light, I know . . . this may be meaningless to you, but Martin had a very sympathetic soul. He could have sat back and wasted his money, but that's not what he did. He was quite generous. He had a charitable side. He could also be completely ridiculous, silly. . . ."

She had a searing headache. Her eyes were dry as sand. It was so hard to make the words say what she felt. She wished she could come out with passionate speeches like Belle Rose, but how could she explain her emotions when she felt so foreign to herself? Grief didn't feel like grief at all. It was more of a distant ache, a dreamy disbelief. Then there was the money. She had never been sure how she felt about Martin, but she knew how she felt about his fortune. She'd never lied to herself about that. Was she supposed to live in a rooming house the rest of her days? What was she mourning? Martin, yes. She had sincerely cared for him. But she also mourned that lovely studio he was going to build for her, and the lot on East Seventy-First Street where McKim and Meade were supposedly going to build them a modest chateau.

"I understand," Max said, though in fact he heard her damning the dead man with faint praise.

She quickly disabused him of this notion. "I took quite a few pictures out-of-doors on the street with him. I couldn't have done them without him. He knew his way around all these queer places. Rutgers Street. Little alleys off Allen Street. How could a woman go down there and make plates by herself?"

Now she heard herself building Martin up for no reason at all. Or was she making herself look more sympathetic by praising him? What was she saying? She'd hauled her equipment down to the Lower East Side several times without him. Words, slippery words, betrayed her all the time. She had such complicated things to say, yet she sounded so thick, she could tear her own tongue out.

She started biting her cuticles, but she caught herself before she turned them into a bloody mess.

Of course Martin hadn't mentioned their marriage plans to his parents yet. Of course they wouldn't have thought she was suitable, and they would have blocked Martin's scheme anyway. Wasn't that the truth? A middle-class girl who worked for a living? And from Staten Island? Martin never would have stood up to his mother. It had all been a dream. Or had it? Her thoughts were all bits and pieces.

"No, of course not." Now Max's speculations veered in the opposite opinion. She had certainly been in love with Mourtone. If he were ever to gain her affection, he would have to appease this ghost. Yet how could he pursue Mourtone's murderer after taking his father's money to keep out of the affair? But hadn't he taken money just to suppress mention of Stephenson's? No one, neither Martin's father nor William H. Howe, had tried to discourage him from finding out *why* the young man had been shot. Or was he telling himself fairy tales?

He wondered who would answer the telephone at the number Howe had given him. He wondered if there would be anyone at all.

Groping, he tried to keep the conversation going. "I wouldn't have taken you for one of those Kodak girls."

Kodak had been placing ads in newspapers, magazines, and billboards for the past two years, promoting its new light, easy-to-use equipment. These advertisements featured dazzling girls in shirtwaists riding bicycles and taking pictures with abandon.

For some reason, this innocuous comment was exactly the wrong thing to say.

In a sarcastic voice he'd never heard before, Gretta recited her version of the ad copy. "'It matters little whether the subject be religious or romantic or the spot sacred or very ordinary, the Kodak girl will be found around, snap, snap, snapping away.' I'd like to strangle them." She struggled to restrain her fury. She could put out the eyes of every insipid Kodak girl in creation. Did any of them give the world one hard look?

But why was she going on like this? How could Max understand what she was talking about? Why had she invited him to accompany her home? She must have been mad. Not that she didn't like him well enough, compared to the rest of them. Belle with her self-righteous philosophy. That oily Danny Swarms. Even dotty Mrs. DeVogt got on her nerves.

Max was startled by her outburst, but he supposed she was so upset about Mourtone that she didn't know what she was saying. "Sorry. I didn't mean...I know you love your profession."

"Oh, I apologize. You didn't deserve. . . ." Then she turned away and began to cry. After a moment, he put his hand on her shoulder, and she reached back and held it. Max was vulgar, she thought, but he had a kind streak, and she was so glad not to be alone. "I was running around all day like a madwoman. One minute Gertrude locked me in the darkroom, the next minute she needed me to light the better side of Miss Goelet. Miss Goelet doesn't have a better side," she added, laughing through her tears. "I forgot to eat, making deliveries. I couldn't think. My mind felt like an iron ball. Thank you for coming."

She felt her weight fall back against his chest.

He smelled her hair. "Please. Don't thank me."

She took his handkerchief and blew her nose. "Martin was a completely harmless man." What a terrible thing to say. Now she missed him. She missed the way the tip of his tongue probed the tip of his mustache. She missed his musical laugh. The feel of his unruly hair in her fingers. The way his body trembled when they kissed. How could he be erased like that, as if he had never existed? Grief came in waves. She missed him bitterly.

"Somebody thought he wasn't so harmless."

"Do you think it was a simple robbery?"

"Not really." He almost said, Why would they go through so much trouble to make the body disappear? But he caught himself. Gretta didn't know yet, and he wasn't sure she ever needed to know. "But it's possible."

"Are the police looking into it?"

"They've got their best man on it."

She looked at his masculine face, a face with darting green-and-gold eyes, a crooked nose, and a clean, square chin, and she didn't believe him.

chapter eleven

Gretta's house turned out to be a charming, low-slung building. At regular intervals dormers lent variety to the roofline. Her family had moved in just before the outbreak of the Civil War. A five-sided conservatory had been added at a later date. Dense wisteria clung to the batten-board sides. Better yet, the garden sloped down to the water a mere fifty yards away. Still gathering herself before she had to face her mother, Gretta led him through carefully tended flowerbeds and down the lawn, which was punctuated by tall Japanese vases and heavy urns. Standing at the low seawall, Max could see the Narrows with crystal clarity.

All he could hear was lapping water, the wind in the trees. No other buildings were visible. Gretta's house might have been the only building on the entire island.

Out in the middle of the harbor, a black-stacked steamer labored toward the North River docks. Gretta picked out a Norfolk schooner and a full-rigged Calcutta. "My uncle taught me. He used to hold me up and let me look through his telescope."

"What's that heavy old boat?"

"A whaler. Back from the Arctic."

A pair of Indian clubs lay on the embankment. Casually, she picked them up and started tossing them and snatching them out of the air with efficient grace. What a relief to let her body take over. Yet her senses felt strangely muted. A veil hung over the water.

"You're athletic, aren't you?"

"No, I'm an athlete," she replied. A body without a mind, picking Indian clubs from the air.

Her mouth set, her eyes focused in deep concentration, she flung the clubs higher and higher until she winced every time she caught one of the tumbling wooden pins. Far from showing off, she was alone, inflicting pain on herself just to see if she could feel it.

"Incredible."

"Should I join the circus?" A body without a mind was disconnected from pain. She wished she could dive into the bay and swim like a seal, the water streaming off her back. Abruptly, she tossed the clubs up onto the lawn and turned back to him. "So what can *you* do, Max?"

Without warning he flipped onto his hands and palm-walked all around her. A gale of laughter seized her, but she covered her mouth.

Flushed, back on his feet, he said, "Used to do that for pennies when I was a kid." He brushed himself off, caught her eye, then looked away. Had he done the wrong thing? Standing on his hands was easier than finding the proper words for sadness.

Together, they laughed nervously, united in their discomfort.

An excursion steamer, flags waving, chugged into view.

Catching his breath, he said, "It's beautiful here. Why would you ever leave?"

"There isn't much carriage trade here. Gertrude isn't about to move her shop."

"You worked all day?"

"I left after lunch and lay down in my room. I'd already taken off so many days. Mother has caught one sickness after another." A note of irritation crept into her voice. "And my aunt is away with Uncle Lars. He's a sea captain, and he takes her along."

"Isn't that unusual?"

"Well, they're very unusual actually. They met when my Uncle Stanley died on Lars's ship."

"Her first husband?"

She laughed softly. "Exactly. They were somewhere near Sumatra, evidently, and it took two months to get home. Uncle Stanley was stuck in his coffin all that time, but when Tillie got home, she was married again!"

"Isn't this a dark family secret?"

"Oh, no. She brags about it. She always tells me she improved her quarters without paying an extra dime. They bring the most phenomenal things home. . . . Well, you'll see. I hope you don't think I'm awful, talking this way."

"Far from it."

"It's just that if I keep thinking about Martin . . . I feel as if I'm going to fly apart." That was another exaggeration. In her new, muffled world she was starving for breath.

"Isn't there anybody who might know something, a friend, somebody he worked with?"

"Not really. He was always out on his own. He hated his job so much, I kept telling him to quit, but then his father would have been so disappointed."

"Was anybody in the company giving him a hard time?"

"Oh, not that. It was just the nature of the work. He always said the company was the house and the policyholders were the marks. But he exaggerated, I suppose. I'm sure it wasn't that dire."

"Did anybody ever threaten him?"

"Why would they? The worst thing is . . . It seems . . . It's so dreadful. . . . It feels as if someone killed him on a whim, for no reason at all." She sighed. "We'd better go in. I have to make supper." Halfway up the lawn, she paused. "Considering Martin's family, their position, the police will be responsive, won't they?"

"That's quite possible."

She gave him a hard look. "You know about the way these things work, you'll hear about what happens behind the scenes, won't you?"

Instantly, he became wary. She expected far too much of him. "Not if they want to keep me in the dark."

"But you'll pursue this for your newspaper, won't you?"

He squirmed. Why not confide in her . . . part way? How else could he become intimate with her quickly? Yet he had to delay, dispense half-truths.

"I need another source, another witness before they'll print anything." Of course he couldn't mention that Martin's father would deny his son had ever set foot in Stephenson's.

"What about the police? Isn't there a report?"

"I didn't want to go into this right away . . . I'm sorry."

"Please, Mr. Greengrass. Not knowing . . . nothing could be worse."

He gave her a hard look, but she didn't flinch. "You'll find this very frustrating, but everybody's disappeared, the witnesses, the bartender, the Negro who was there. I couldn't tell you everything this morning."

"Oh." She could barely get the puff of air out.

He explained as much as he dared, including the street arabs' assault, but she still struggled to grasp what he was saying. There was no body? No witnesses? No story? She sensed he was still protecting her emotions by holding back certain details. How could she explain that her feelings were all tangled, and that she preferred bald facts?

"What do you mean they've disappeared? Won't the police find them?"

He shrugged and looked away.

A darker look of recognition passed over her face. "Are you saying the police might not investigate at all?"

"No, no . . . it's just that they're in a bad spot without a . . . pardon me . . . without a corpse."

"Wouldn't it be awful if nobody did anything? That seems . . . as bad as the murder." If she never set foot in Manhattan again, would it disappear like a mirage? She would take pictures and ride her bike and smack tennis balls in her lovely Staten Island cocoon forever. To get away from Gertrude, Mrs. DeVogt, Danny Swarms, and that smug Belle Rose, who took too much delight in mentioning those Russian writers with impossible names. She despised these overeducated immigrants who seemed to sniff out her ignorance so easily, but she despised even more her own lazy indifference to learning.

"I didn't say that. It's just going to be difficult." Again he cursed himself for being compromised. His limp response to the murder was gaining him little credit in her eyes. "Don't worry, though. I'll light a fire under Superintendant Byrnes."

Suddenly, she looked immensely tired and sad. "I can't . . . it's inconceivable that he's dead. Vanished. Except from our minds. What a queer way to exist."

"I wish I could say something. . . ."

She shuddered visibly, and he expected her to weep again. Instead, she sighed. "Time for me to get out the pots. Mother's boiled dinner calls."

Lars and Tillie's treasures crowded the modest sitting room's walls. Japanese fans, Indonesian masks, a pair of tusks, and pictures of Tillie and Lars at sea. Bits of coral, sea sponges, and exotic shells were displayed on a long glass table. Gretta led him to the foot of the stairs and pointed at the huge bell hanging from a beam.

"RING THE BELL, AND RING LIKE HELL!" read the legend painted across it.

"The dinner bell?"

"I don't know where they got that," Gretta said, with a muffled laugh. "My mother doesn't approve."

Her dried-up mother didn't seem to approve of much. Thin and sour-faced, she barely uttered a word. Although Gretta made small talk to cover the deafening silence, every clink of silverware against china made Max more and more uncomfortable. As soon as it was polite, he thanked Gretta and rose to leave.

"Would you like a drink before you go? I want to show you something."

She led him into a glassed-in porch and poured some amaretto. "I'm sorry about mother. It isn't you. She's just alone so much, she's getting impossible. Tillie's the only one who can handle her."

Sinking down onto the horsehair sofa, he took a sip of the cloying drink. "Don't worry. My father's about as sociable as a mailbox," he confided in turn.

For once he had said the right thing to her. Her lovely, generous smile made him catch his breath. It would be so natural to reach up and draw her down onto his lap, to kiss her throat, her hair, feel the full shape of her body against his chest. His craving for her gave him the shakes.

"We ought to introduce them. They could sit in a room and say nothing to each other. Would you wait here?"

In a moment she returned with a large wooden box. An ornate script marked its lid: Grierson and Jones, Apothecaries. 11 Chestnut Street, Philadelphia, Pennsylvania. "Mother's medicine chest."

"Mrs. DeVogt has her own supplies, too, doesn't she?"

"Yes, that's what gave me the idea. You said in your articles that the ladies were smothering cats, and that there was some sort of chemical involved?"

She *had* been paying attention to his Midnight Band saga. "I thought you weren't very interested in my cat ladies."

"I hate them, I wish they'd go away, but I couldn't help thinking . . . and Martin was so interested in it." She picked her way through slender bottles of eucalyptus, cocaine, and samplers of Lydia Pinkham's tonic. "Here. This one is very strong."

She spilled a bit on her handkerchief and passed it to him. Immediately, the familiar, powerful odor wafted out. He barely had to sniff the cloth. "What is it?"

"Chloroform. Just a little makes you dizzy. What do you think?"

"I think you have a talent for investigations."

"Really?" For a moment her muted expression fell away, and she smiled. Reaching out, she touched his humped nose. "You broke it?"

"This? Yeah. A little boxing when I was a kid. I was good at taking punishment."

She held him at arm's length, not sure what to make of him. On an impulse, she kissed his cheek. "I couldn't bear to have this awful thing happen . . . and then nothing. As if it hadn't happened at all. You'll keep looking into it?"

Standing so close to her, her kiss still alive on his skin, he couldn't find the right half-truth. "Why wouldn't I?"

chapter twelve

On the ferry ride back to the city, he covered the tent in his trousers with a handy copy of the *World*. Visions of Gretta tormented him: she turned her back and let him unlace her corset eyelet by eyelet, until her freed breasts fell into his palms; an American odalisque, she reclined naked on a velvet divan; he went to her, shedding his clothes in a frenzy: hat, coat, vest, and socks. Wide-eyed and dreaming, he felt the shock of her kiss. He feared his erection would last all the way to the Battery.

He tried to distract himself by turning the *World*'s blanket-sized pages, but nothing in the newspaper Pulitzer called his "great unfinished novel" could keep him from sinking back into Gretta's arms. He could feel her rippling against him. So lush, so warm. He couldn't stand it, but he couldn't stop.

When a bedraggled organ grinder and two children with violins approached him, he tossed them a few coins. Stretching on the hard bench, he took in the tinkly music, the swaying lanterns on the dark vessels nearby, the spangle of yellow lights downtown.

Strangely enough, the organ grinder was cranking out the same tune Max had been hearing all over the city. Dum dada, dum dada, dum daddadum. . . . It was a catchy melody, but he wondered why the Italians had all taken it up at the same time. He'd have to ask Swarms.

Max didn't believe in romantic love. He had spent so many years arguing Faye out of her latest infatuation that he had honed his philosophy to a razor's edge. Love was an illusion driven by lust, at least in the case of men. (He cringed at the thought that Faye might be swept up in the same tides of passion that drove him to Mrs. Jabonne's creamy white girls.) Love was a convenient self-deception, a fig leaf that covered the drive for money, display, position. Love was nothing but self-regard. In fact, treacly writers who couldn't ſathom the freedom of isolation had given the solitary life a bad name. Love was a conspiracy of the weak against the strong, a boudoir Christianity, a haven for the effeminate, a silken prison.

So what should he call his fascination with Gretta? Obsessive desire? Passion of a new order, physical hunger so intense it masqueraded as emotion? Was her character as mesmerizing as her beauty? She was an odd duck in a way, mourning one moment, tossing Indian clubs the next. She could be so direct, her soul seemed to be on the surface of her skin. Then she could be maddeningly obscure, her feelings veiled behind elaborate manners. Despite her prune-faced mother, she had been so gracious that he had almost relaxed at her Staten Island manse. Almost. How could he ever fit in at that house under a strict Protestant regime? He was sure he'd used the wrong fork twice. Yet he was even less at home in the Jewish ghetto, that hive of medieval chants and black gabardine suits.

He acted one way at Fitzgerald and Ives, and another way at Mrs. DeVogt's table. When he was taking a speed walk with Danny, racing from Fourteenth Street down to the harbor, their conversation reeling from women to those vampires called theater managers, to Cap Anson's batting average, legs and words in furious motion, he became himself, but what exactly was that? They rarely talked about anything serious; and now that Danny was seeing Faye, a whole layer of his friend's life had become off-limits.

On their excursions, they increased the pace block by block until they were almost running through the human carnival and he forgot who he was. Then they would find themselves down at the Washington Market or the Battery, eating clams with squeezed lemon, watching paddle-wheeled towboats on the way to Sandy Hook, and chattering away about nothing at all. He wondered if he was himself only when, in sheer motion, he shed the husk of Max Greengrass and became velocity itself.

At times, he felt less like a man than a shifting series of negotiations.

Faye said all he cared about was chasing stories, and in a way she was right. In the hunt, he wasn't Max Greengrass, that pigeonholed creature, he was a flow of words rushing into new, unpredictable channels.

That night he could barely sleep, but when he finally slid under the skin of consciousness he dreamed that Mourtone Senior was slipping into the room and stealing back his thick pack of bills. Max cursed himself for not putting the money in the bank, then he concentrated hard and realized that he had, and that he was dreaming. Soon he fell deeper into the internal darkness, to that place where every nighttime phantom paralyzed him. A peevish Gretta drifted into view, tossing chamber pots at his head, accusing him of some ambiguous indiscretion. As the pots bounced off his skull, he kept apologizing for his nameless crime.

From the *Herald*'s office, he called the number William H. Howe had given him. Just as he'd suspected, no one answered, even after a dozen rings. From his battered desk he took surreptitious glances at Parnell, high up on his throne. Was the editor wondering why he hadn't turned in any new copy? What was he supposed to do? The cat ladies hadn't committed any fresh acts of mercy; none of the precincts had reported any recent carnage.

Of course Parnell could give him a new assignment. Then the expressionless, blade-faced editor looked directly at him—and straight through him—without flicking an eyebrow. Max's stomach clenched, but he ignored the raw taste of panic burning in his throat. Instead, he kept calling Howe's contact every fifteen minutes, letting the phone ring twenty, then thirty times. Obviously no one was there. No one would ever be there. Mourtone had bounced him over to Howe who had bounced him into a void.

Frustrated, he took a quick run over to Logan's, where he downed three hard-boiled eggs with horseradish along with a couple of lagers. Rolling back to the office, he felt positively belligerent. He was prepared to keep calling the damned number all day. On the second ring, a laconic voice answered, "Yeah?"

Howe hadn't told him what to say. Fumbling, he muttered, "Ah . . . Mr. Howe said—"

The flat voice cut him off. "Go down the oyster market on Tenth. The loading dock straight across. Brewery."

The line went dead. What would he do if he found Martin now? He'd convinced himself that Howe and Mourtone had been manipulating him, and that the phone number was simply part of a runaround. Now, if he found Martin's corpse and he called the cops, he'd have what he'd needed all along, a body and a corroborating source. Why not give the cash back and write the story? Wasn't the lion's share of Mourtone's money safely tucked away at the Madison Square Bank, and the rest in his billfold, less a few dollars?

He could report the murder and its connection to the catricides, and in one fell swoop the Midnight Band would be transformed from a grotesque joke into something far more menacing. He steeled himself for the sight of Martin's shorn-away skull, the exposed gray matter in its shell.

To hell with Mourtone and his lawyers. He'd write what he saw, and the consequences be damned.

Yet somehow, he didn't think Mourtone and William H. Howe would allow him to go ahead with this plan, though he couldn't see how they could stop him either. By the time they found out, his article would be hitting the streets. The mere thought of returning the bribe—he had to face it, a bribe is what it was—gave him mental breathing room. Thinking about renunciation didn't amount to practicing it, but imagining a way out calmed him down. He was no prude, but taking money under the table wasn't his style.

Choked with wagons, painted drays, horsecars, and omnibuses, drivers on their feet shouting curses at each other, wheels clattering over uneven stones, West Street was Bedlam itself. Beer skids, barrels, and huge piles of shucked oysters littered the way. Near the shore of the Hudson, a steam tug chugged along. Several docked barks, their rigging dense webs against the sky, projected their bowsprits over the dock. Above him a pair of sailors reefed jib sails. On deck a sun-browned man sat cross-legged, sewing linen. A Royal Baking Powder wagon wobbled by. A sign on the side of a brick warehouse declared CHILDREN CRY FOR FLETCHER'S CASTORIA. A merchant in a plaid vest berated some longshoremen who were struggling to move a mountain of bales. They clawed at it with their grappling hooks.

He took his time picking through the horses and carts. Stopping to get his thoughts together, he stood staring at the floating oyster market. Saltwater wells built into the barge's holds kept the shellfish fresh. On deck, men wrestled with a cargo from Princess Bay, Staten Island.

If he discovered the body, he'd have to send somebody to the precinct house. He wasn't going to abandon Martin a second time. There were always boys around, of course, all too many. He could hire one as a messenger. Perhaps he should find a kid and send him to Mulberry Street right now. He could get a high-ranking detective on the case immediately.

He was thinking so feverishly that he reached Tom's Brewing Co., Malts and Ales, before he knew it. From a short distance he viewed the loading dock. A few barrels stood on its iron lip. In the building's shadow, a drunk lay with his head twisted against a rough plank, his derby tipped off his head. Nobody else was around.

A sick, fluttering sensation seized Max's stomach. In the chilly air, sweat broke out on the back of his neck; but he bit his lower lip, hauled himself up onto the dock, and began walking slowly, inspecting each barrel's contents. The first two were filled with yellow chaff, but the third, surprisingly, was stuffed to the brim with clamshells.

Max looked around. While chaos reigned on the street, the brewery was quiet, its rear door chained shut. Maybe it was out of business. Tentatively, he scraped a few shells off the top layer. His pulse raced, and he realized he was grinding his teeth so hard his jaw ached. Stepping back, he took a deep breath. How to do it? He didn't want to touch anything "too particular," but he had to dig down deeper, just in case. Lightheaded, blood beating in his temples, he plunged ahead as fast as he could, rolling up his sleeve, dipping his hand in and cupping several handfuls of cold clams out of the barrel. Grease clung to his fingers and forearm, congealing into a second skin. Then he hit a layer of chipped ice.

Now he rolled up his other sleeve and began to dig with both hands. Clawing down even farther, he touched the thing before he saw it.

At first he thought Martin had been frozen blue, but that didn't seem possible. The face gaping up at him, its mouth pried wide by a single shell, wasn't blue at all. It was dark brown. Its hair was kinky, its nose broad. Encrusted with blood, its eye sockets gaped ragged and black. In a spasm, he pulled his hands out of the barrel and staggered back.

To keep from getting sick, he took enormous draughts of salty, oily air. Then he braced himself against the wall of the brewery. Waves of nausea swept through him, but he kept breathing and breathing. For a minute or an hour, half-formed ideas swirled around in his mind, but he forced himself to think things through. There was no way of knowing, at least so far, whether the head in the barrel had once been the Negro from Stephenson's.

If the rest of the man was stuffed in the barrel, though, the parts might be clothed in some particularly ragged overalls. He might have those wormy white scars on his cheek.

In his bones, Max knew that was who it was. Why would Howe's contact send him here otherwise? Just to view some random slaughter? That didn't seem likely. With the bartender tucked away in Baltimore, or in another barrel for all he knew, the witnesses to Martin's murder had been neatly eliminated. Had Howe engineered this fresh killing? Was he threatening Max himself?

The plaid-vested merchant seemed to be staring at him. Bobbing over their oyster well, a pair of shuckers gazed at him with keen interest. A fishmonger smeared his hands on his bloody apron and looked in Max's direction. Was the sailor squatting and braiding a rope really Howe's man? Were the longshoremen hauling a crate of bananas simply longshoremen? His heart tried to scuttle up his throat. He knew one thing: he didn't want to end up in pieces too.

He scanned West Street, searching for a likely messenger. The oystermongers couldn't leave their stalls and barges. The drivers couldn't abandon their carts and wagons. Several unsteady men were passing a bottle up and back nearby, but, strangely enough, there wasn't a street arab or guttersnipe in sight. Usually, as he knew only too well, there were swarms of them. Stymied, he stood frozen, unable to examine the barrel again, unable to work out his next step.

He would never abandon this body, no matter how long he had to watch over it. While a Negro in parts wouldn't merit many column-inches, Parnell would like this one. A severed head always made good copy. When an assassin had blown himself to bits trying to slaughter Russell Sage in 1891, Police Superintendent Byrnes had collected the man's head from the ruins and put it on display in a jar. Hundreds of people lined up to view the bomber's twisted features.

Max had to think in terms of word counts and column-inches, but he felt rotten about the deaf-and-dumb Negro too. This one had wanted to live in the worst way, he thought, recalling the way the black man had torn out of Stephenson's and disappeared into Little Africa's alleyways. As if he were running for his life.

Regaining his senses, Max looked around West Street, searching for a single guttersnipe to do his bidding. Then he saw a button rambling half a block away. Without hesitation, he leaped off the dock and went after the cop.

"We could dump the pieces out," the young policeman suggested.

"Let's get him to the morgue. Let the professionals take care of it, all right?" Max argued. Extracting his flask, he offered the button a snort. The cop knocked back a capful of the raw stuff. "Clears out the sinuses."

"You sure you don't wanna see the rest first?" the patrolman persisted.

"Nah. Why make a mess?" His throat was on fire from the rotgut. Across the way, the floating oyster market rose on a sickening swell. He had to turn away.

"Suit yourself. I'll go send for the dead wagon."

It took almost an hour for the varnished police vehicle, drawn by a hollow-ribbed gelding, to get to the brewery's loading dock. Two men, whose job was to scrape corpses off the sidewalk, casually rolled the barrel inside the closed wagon. At a crawl behind the Fourteenth Street horsecar, they passed R. H. Macy's, W. Jennings Demarest, and the old Union Square Theatre. Finally, they reached Bellevue's gates. Caretakers in wrinkled brown cotton suits wandered in and out of the vast complex. From the dead wagon, Max could see a bald woman in gray gingham waving from a madhouse window.

A cloud of chemical stench wafted from the examining room. Max held his breath as the attendant, a hefty man in a butcher's apron, lifted the eyeless black man's head and placed it at the end of the table. Water sloshed around inside the barrel. The ice had melted. Max forced himself to watch without flinching. Inside his coat pocket, his hand groped for a half-smoked cigar. He found the stub, stuck it in his mouth, and chewed, tasting the sour tobacco.

Expressionless, the morgue attendant raised a severed arm. He held it aloft, water streaming off splayed dead fingers. Clams clattered to the stone floor. "Hand me the mop, would ya?" the bull-necked attendant asked, laying the severed limb out on his slab, whistling tunelessly through his teeth.

Max complied. He heard the slap of the soaking swab. He lit his dead cigar. "What's your name?"

"Who cares?" His eyes were hidden in pouches of fat.

"So I got something to call you."

"Grackle."

"You have a first name?"

Fishing out another arm, Grackle shrugged. The mop. A leg. The mop. Finally, the full torso, ribs exposed under mottled skin, a hairless chest. A corona of puncture wounds wreathed the corpse's feminine nipples. Methodically, Grackle placed each body part in its proper place, reassembling the poor man in rough order. In patches, remnants of overalls clung to the Negro's flesh. The head, gap-toothed, smiled shyly on the slab. A chicken's-foot of white scars marked its left cheek.

"When do you think they did the job on him?" Max kept his eyes averted from the African's face, its disconcerting, faintly amused expression. He would have preferred a rictus and bulging eyes.

The attendant poked the corpse's soft belly. "Hard to tell. They kept him fresh this way."

It was all too easy to picture his own blood-drained head on the table. A big piece of wax fruit. Time would dine on him soon enough, but he wasn't ready for William H. Howe to make a meal of him.

"Stabbed him to death?" he asked, pointing to the pattern of wounds around the corpse's drooping nipples.

"Maybe his pal done it after. Who knows? Sometimes they like to bite."

"So what came first, you think? The cuts here," he persisted, pointing to the circle of puncture wounds, "or the rest?"

"You mean was he axed up before or after?" Grackle patted his leather-aproned stomach and gave Max a fishy look. "After. It's always after."

"Yeah, sure." Max shrugged, doing his best to cover his gaffe.

"It only makes sense." Grackle spread his arms and glanced around the room, taking in his slab, his mop and pail, his chest of drawers, his entire empire. One body rolled in after another. The tide came in, the tide went out. You went through the pockets, you found six cents and an ivory comb with broken teeth, a few keys to nowhere, you looked for the usual perforations and holes, and then you filled out the form. What could be more natural?

chapter thirteen

Stan Parnell went for it. "It's the barrel. If he was just another coon sliced up in Minetta Alley, I'd give it an inch, tops."

Padded out with non-committal remarks from Mulberry Street headquarters, Max's treatment ran five full grafs. He'd done his best to make the victim a living, breathing person, but what did he have to work with? The body's connection to Martin Mourtone, the remarkably prescient William H. Howe, the anonymous voice on the telephone line—in short, every compelling detail—had to be kept quiet.

The corpse was both love note and threat. A professional had dispatched the Negro. Why not Max himself? Someone still cared for him, but the African's body was a warning that the affection might last only so long. A spasm of fear ran through him, but he told himself that terror was a good thing. It led to sensible behavior. Yet despite the fact that he had seen danger on a slab, he didn't quite believe it. These things happened to other men, men who weren't careful, men who didn't know the ropes, men tainted by lousy luck.

He was also aware that disbelief was his greatest enemy.

Parnell raised his rheumy eyes from Max's copy. "Nice work, kiddo."

"Thanks."

He wasn't imagining it. The sphinx, the man without emotions, was actually taking an interest in him. "Did Biddle set you straight on Howe?"

"Howe and Hummel? I can't tell whether they're defending criminals or defending their employees."

Parnell made a thwarted sound that died in his throat. Parnellian laughter. "You're making progress! Copy!" he shouted, and a boy came racing over. "Check around, see if any blackies have been reported missing," he told Max. "Come back in a couple of hours. I'll have something for you."

Not wasting any time, Max made the rounds along Thompson, Sullivan, and West Third before hitting Mulberry Street headquarters again, but he came up empty. No detective had been assigned yet, and none would be, he suspected. What was he supposed to do? Wander around the remnants of Little Africa with a lantern?

Back at the office, Max looked around for Nicholas Biddle, who was alternately scratching some words on a pad and staring out the window. With his legs outstretched and his lanky body slid halfway down in his padded chair, Biddle appeared far too relaxed for a man at work. In between bursts of writing, he absently tapped his gold-tipped cane on the plank floor.

Max approached the old reporter. In his hand, he held out Howe and Hummel's opus, *In Danger*.

"Thought I'd return this, Mr. Biddle."

Biddle's gray-blue eyes regarded him with amusement. "Nick, call me Nick. So how did Weeping Willy go down with you?"

"It leaves you wondering. Listen, do you have time for a spot at Logan's? My treat."

"Well, if you're treating, let's go to Pontin's," Biddle replied, thereby upping the ante four-fold. "On Franklin. You know the place?"

"Sure." Max gulped. A few trips to Pontin's, and he'd be making withdrawals from the Madison Square Bank.

Interrogating Biddle wouldn't be cheap, and it wouldn't be easy either. The man was close, perhaps all too close to William H. Howe, but he might give up a detail or two. Did the lawyer have a blood lust for young reporters, for instance? Or did Max's attachment to the *Herald* protect him in some obscure way? Did Howe and Hummel represent Stephenson's? Max recalled that they had defended Morris Tekulsky, president of the Liquor Dealers Association, and by extension the saloon interests.

He'd have to gain Biddle's confidence while keeping his intentions veiled. It was always possible that the old reporter made extra greenbacks by whispering in Howe's ear.

Biddle ordered the Sole Margeury and, without glancing at the list, his favorite wine. "They have a wonderful cellar here, very strong on the French. Now, what do you know about Pontin's?"

"Mostly mouthpieces here, right?"

"Ahh, yes and no. If you look around, you will see the flower of the legal profession. That's Judge Dos Passos over there, a great intellect. And Judge Mallory, a dim bulb by comparison. But the secret of this place is that for the truly elect, there is a separate dining room in the back."

"Judge Dos Passos isn't of the elect?"

"I'm disappointed, Max. Quick, quick," he snapped his fingers.

"Howe and Hummel?"

"Practically their clubhouse. I've seen them do business on a tablecloth."

"So you know them pretty well?" Max probed, taking a sip of the Bordeaux.

"Anyone who claims to know Willy's depths is in my estimation a bleeding idiot." Biddle lit into his filet with gusto. Pausing, he regarded a chunk of fish on his fork. "Fresh, flaky. No one does it like Pontin's."

"Well, after reading their pamphlet, I was wondering. . . ."

"Yes?" Biddle's eyebrows bobbed up and down. On his aristocratic face, the effect was disconcerting.

Max's speculations had gotten a laugh out of Stan Parnell, so he plunged ahead. "It's really a treatise on how to *commit* crimes, isn't it? Do they plan the robberies and then defend the ones who get caught?"

"Oh, *that* old canard. Tell me you weren't laughing while you read it."

"I was, I was."

"Good. Otherwise I would have to revise my opinion of you. That whole thing was a lark, and a nice piece of advertising too. Why would they want to get *their* hands dirty when they're making a fortune on the proper side of the law? Don't get me wrong. It's not that Willy and Abie aren't a little bent. They're not above playing the badger game, in a gentlemanly sort of way. On the other hand, to whom can a chorus girl turn when she's down on her luck?"

"You mean their breach-of-promise racket?"

"Hmmm . . . Stan said you were a quick fox. I'm not too fond of the practice myself, but when Abe Hummel burns papers, they never come back. And the same girl will never bother you again. In a way, he's doing you a service."

A rueful smile crossed Biddle's thin lips, and Max guessed that the old reporter had been caught in Hummel's net too.

Biddle as much as admitted it. "The next thing you know, Abie is buying you first-night tickets or giving you a tip on Saratoga. He writes that racing column, but you know that. You have to admire a little man like that, he's practically a hunchback for Godsakes, and yet he wrings more out of life than anyone." Now Biddle veered back to the original subject. "Let me ask you. Why do you think their own pamphlet makes them out to be felons?"

"Advertising, as you pointed out."

"Yes, true. But think about it. They have a reputation to uphold. They're not selling their services to Mr. Parkhurst or Mr. Comstock, are they? Willy has a genius for making his clientele comfortable. They know he's not judging them."

Max's skepticism must have been written across his face.

"So you don't believe me, my young cynic? Would you like proof?"

"Proof is always attractive."

"For instance, they're quiet as church mice about it, but they do more *pro bono* work than any outfit in town. What's more, if Willy loses a murder case, he can't let it go. It plagues him. Tell me any other lawyer who visits his convicted client, convicted of a capital offense, the client most lawyers want to forget as fast as possible, and tell me the lawyer who stays with the wretch even on the day of his hanging. Would you like examples?"

"Sure."

"You know there is a mania for facts nowadays; it's almost offensive. All right. Carlyle Harris, the wife-poisoner? Willy took his case on appeal, but the first lawyer botched it so badly, there wasn't much he could do. Do you know what he told me after the hanging? When he hears a friend's neck snapping, that hideous sound makes him more determined than ever to keep his clients off the gallows."

Max kept a straight face. Biddle seemed to be forgetting he was talking to another reporter. "You're making a good case yourself, Nick, but isn't this just more self-promotion?"

"Cynical, Greengrass. Cynical. How about this? Do you know who defended Victoria Woodhull when that cretin Comstock brought her up on obscenity charges?"

At the mention of Mrs. Woodhull, Max practically choked on his chop. Why would Howe get mixed up with a radical feminist? Wouldn't that sully his reputation? "*The* Victoria Woodhull?"

"The same one who published the little tale about the Reverend Beecher and Mrs. Tilton. The same one who was dragged before the bar for printing the word 'virginity' in her magazine. You should have seen Willy's cross-examination of Comstock, that mincing prude! Willy quoted Deuteronomy, Shakespeare, and Byron, to see if Comstock would keep them out of the mails, too. Postal Inspector! It's amazing the pantywaist sonofabitch is still in power. Back then, in '73, I thought those Puritans were relics. Now we've got the Reverend Parkhurst biting our ankles. And this Weems fanatic, too. Sometimes I think history is running backwards."

Biddle was beginning to sound just like Mrs. DeVogt. Of course, he came from the same generation, with the same irritating tendency to speak from on high. Still, Howe as defender of free speech and tormentor of the mail censor Anthony Comstock cut an admirable, if incongruous, figure.

"I'm beginning to understand."

"Not to speak of that woman . . . my memory is failing me . . . the one who swore the Republican Party was running a conspiracy to drive her crazy. Willy defended her gratis too."

"No."

Leaning over the table, his striking blue-gray eyes shining, Biddle made one more point. "Do you know how much Western George paid Willy after the Manhattan Savings job? Ninety thousand. It's still the biggest fee in history."

Sipping the last drop of his white wine, Nicholas Biddle rested his case.

"What about the press, Nick? Would Willy defend us?" He thought the question was vague enough.

"Didn't you hear what I just said about Victoria Woodhull? Free speech is Willy's creed."

"He wouldn't use any strongarm tactics against a reporter? You know, if you got on the wrong side of him?"

"You have a sardonic look; did anybody ever tell you that, Greengrass?"

"Yeah, as a matter of fact."

Their eyes locked, but then Biddle broke into mordant laughter. It was impossible to resist Nick's charm, but that didn't make Max any less wary. Suddenly Biddle's features shifted, another face emerging, a face stripped of practiced irony. He leaned over the table, his voice low and serious. "I wouldn't cast Bill in a bad light."

"Who would? He's my hero, fighting those temperance hags."

"Our knight in shining armor," Biddle agreed. "Violence isn't in Bill's nature. He can crush a man like a bug and never leave a mark on him."

Somehow this assertion rang true. Why should Howe soil his hands with insignificant reporters?

"Tekulsky uses him, right?" If the saloon owners' organization employed Howe, there was a good chance the attorney represented Stephenson's too.

"What's your point?" Biddle said sharply.

The reporter's reaction all but confirmed Max's suspicions. The black-and-tan operators were probably Howe and Hummel clients too, along with Mourtone Senior. Who knew if the lawyers mightn't have uttered the abracadabra that made Martin vanish? Now he was jangled all over again. Howe had to know about the brewery's barrel. Why wouldn't he keep a longshoreman or a merchant marine on the pad to keep an eye on dock business?

"Just idle curiosity."

"Ha! You and Torquemada. I'm on deadline. This inquisition is over."

He had two choices. Crouch in terror, his insides churning every time a stranger look at him crooked, or march straight into the lion's mouth. Living in darkness and perpetual anxiety was clearly the greater of the two evils. He would assure Howe that he posed no danger to Mourtone or the rest of his clients. If he could ask the lawyer a few of the questions Nick Biddle had turned aside, all the better. Straight, direct, above-board. An antidote to the nightmares ambiguity was sure to spawn.

However, when he phoned the attorney to set up an appointment, the great man was consulting at the Tombs. In fact, the law clerk told Max appointments were hard to come by. Perhaps Howe would see him at the end of the summer. Max cajoled the clerk to no avail. Any audience with the solicitor would have to take place months in the future.

What else could he do? He'd have to ferret out Howe's daily itinerary and ambush him.

Parnell was waving him up to the throne. Max felt the eyes of the other space-raters on him as he wove his way through the tightly packed desks, ducked under a copy wire, and leaped onto the platform. The metro editor knew the effect of his gestures, he knew that the hungry space men kept their eyes on him constantly for signs of approval. Now Max had been summoned twice in a single day. No one would fail to notice his good fortune.

"Anything on the Negro?"

"Not a peep."

"Ahh, don't worry. We probably wasted enough ink on that one. Wait right there."

The editor ran his eye over a story on his desk, slashing at it several times while Max, straight-faced but barely able to contain his joy, waited for his next assignment. "They picked up your friend last night on East 126th. Caught her in the act," Parnell barked. "Get up to the arraignment. Harlem Police Court. You may be able to talk to her before she posts bail."

"Who?"

"Mrs. Edwards. Savior of the feline species. She went on a spree last night. The arresting officer said she gave him a lecture about her influence with Henry Bergh and the ASPCA. She's got a nice badge, he says."

"Didn't Bergh die five years ago?"

"You're a sharpie, Greengrass." Parnell tapped his forehead. "That's why we're hiring you. Now get out of here."

Hiring him! Giddy, Max ran halfway to the train before a stitch in his side stopped him in his tracks. *Hiring him.* He'd been so dizzy he hadn't asked any questions, but he assumed he would start drawing a regular salary right away. *Hiring him.* What a miracle. His years of scraping together stories about two-bit domestic disputes and horseblanket heists were over.

He had reached a turning point in his life, and all because a bunch of reforming biddies were running rampant with their smothering rags. Yet he still found their campaign, with its strange mixture of altruism and savagery, completely incomprehensible. Wouldn't he have to explain their motivation to the *Herald*'s readers at some point? Wouldn't he have to explain it to himself?

chapter fourteen

Draped in black, her hands in her lap, Mrs. Edwards waited patiently for her case to be called. Next to her, a working girl and a dip Max recognized chatted amiably. A wisp of gray hair had escaped Mrs. Edwards's hat, falling onto her high, smooth forehead. A somewhat younger, more attractive woman than Mrs. Warner, whose work with cats he'd observed close-hand, Mrs. Edwards seemed indistinguishable from any number of fashionable, active widows. A spare, distinguished-looking man leaned down to speak to her. His bearing, his tailored suit, and especially his complete lack of jewelry separated him from the other legal talent in attendance.

Chaim "Chad" Bernstein, a Tammany appointee, presided. The magistrate's credentials included two years in the practice of law, and the delivery of an entire congregation, B'nai Israel of Suffolk Street, to district boss Big Tim Sullivan. In gratitude, Sullivan had wrangled Bernstein a position uptown in Harlem. The jurist's pinched face and high, whining voice suggested the schoolmarm more than the judge.

With astonishing speed, he dispensed with cases involving a stolen horseblanket, a panel-house operation, three disputed pairs of pants, a dismembered pushcart, and a milk dealer alleged to have kept his cow in a dank alley. It took an average of three minutes for Magistrate Bernstein to dispense justice.

Finally Mrs. Edwards's case was called. The judge waved at the lawyer and his client to approach the bench. "Mr. Maple? You represent?"

The good, gray lawyer nodded. Satisfied, the magistrate turned his glare on the defendant.

"You have been charged with cruelty to animals, Mrs. Edwards, to wit, the suffocating of five cats on East 126th Street. Do you understand the charges?"

With elaborate dignity, Mrs. Edwards replied: "We are a benevolent society. The city is full of sick, starving animals, so we do our best to attend to their needs. I found the cats out after eight last night, and they haven't any right to be. Besides, the Henry Bergh Society has authorized us to kill cats."

Why did the Band insist on an eight o'clock curfew for the feline population? There existed no law to that effect. What sort of activity did they imagine they were preventing, Max wondered.

"Officer Connolly tells me you committed these acts at various locations."

Her lawyer began whispering in her ear, but she brushed his hand away. "I started on Cornelia Street and took two cats up with me to the El platform."

"Excuse me, your honor," the elegant lawyer interceded.

"Do you wish to speak, Mrs. Edwards?" the judge interjected.

"Yes, your honor. I've nothing to hide."

The lawyer murmured to his client, but Mrs. Edwards shook her head.

The magistrate didn't waste time. "Did you know that it is illegal to transport dead animals inside the city limits?"

Ignoring his question, Mrs. Edwards looked up at the judge with barely concealed contempt. "If you would like, I'll show you how quickly it's done. I'll bring a cat into court and dispatch it in ten seconds. You've never seen anything more charitable. I know my business."

Her emotionless demeanor struck an odd note, Max thought. Was that a key to her strange behavior? If so, distinguishing it from ladylike restraint was difficult. He sat on the edge of his seat, fascinated by Mrs. Edwards's utter stillness. Perhaps killing cats engendered inner peace.

"You won't murder any animals in my courtroom," the judge snapped.

"Your honor, may I have a word with my client?" the horrified lawyer cut in. Once again Mrs. Edwards shook him off. Folding his arms, he stared at the floor. This was not the type of law he was used to practicing.

"Rich witch!" a weathered mab shouted out from the side bench.

A bird in a mask of powder that didn't quite hide the pox hooted, "They oughta break her neck! What'd we ever do?"

A court officer plunged in to quiet them down, but a chorus of raspberries rose from all corners.

"It's that simple," Mrs. Edwards said, shrugging.

"Quiet! I know my business too!" Judge Bernstein shot back, losing patience. "You are the president of the Midnight Band of Mercy, is that correct?"

"Henry Bergh chartered our organization originally, and we have members doing good works on a regular basis."

"I fail to see how this wholesale slaughter amounts to a good deed. You say you eliminate these animals indiscriminately?"

By now the court officers had silenced the worst offenders, though a low, mean murmur still ran through the assembly.

"No, I did not say that at all. We go after the worst infestations."

"And where might *they* be?" the judge asked sourly.

"Many times near police stations."

A buzz ran through the flyblown congregation. A court officer with a scarlet face muttered under his breath. His friend, a boat-sized bondsman, burst out laughing. A moon-faced madame cupped her hands and shouted, "She's an agent!"

Judge Bernstein couldn't hold back the uproar.

Max laughed too, but he also wondered. Was the Midnight Band some strange permutation of the Reverend Dr. Parkhurst's crusade against the buttons? Parkhurst was busy stirring up the temperance hags against Tammany and the police bigwigs. He had plenty of ammunition too, though Max believed it would come to nothing because the police protection racket was an ancient rite of tribute that would never be rooted out. Meanwhile, the fiery minister might have inspired Christian ladies with their own peculiar ideas about civic salvation.

"She's a wild hair, ain't she?" a streetwalker called out.

In the eye of the storm, Mrs. Edwards stared straight ahead, a picture of equanimity. She probably didn't need any outside inspiration, he decided, the Reverend Parkhurst's or anyone else's.

Laughter and applause shook the dreary courtroom.

"We are not joking here, lady," the judge snapped. "This is a serious offense!"

Mrs. Edwards barely reacted. Instead, she continued speaking with conviction. "Then you should open your eyes. Everyplace you look, they're licking some sore. They get crushed by wagons. They get run over by cable cars. People throw bottles at them. They limp around more dead than alive." Now Max began to sense the woman's power. With the practiced ease of an orator, she turned to the crowded courtroom pews. "I guarantee, when you leave this place, you'll see them everywhere. Even if you close your eyes!"

"Your honor. My client obviously has no record, isn't a threat. . . ."

"Released in your recognizance, Mr. Maple. Get a date! Next!"

A weak smile clinging to his face, the lawyer let Mrs. Edwards pass down the aisle. Max followed close behind her, eager to put a dozen questions to the Midnight Band's leader. He finally caught up with her on the Police Court's steps.

Trotting fast to the bottom step, he blocked Mrs. Edwards's way. "Excuse me. Max Greengrass, *New York Herald.* Would you mind saying a word about the charges against you?"

Standing close to her, he noted Mrs. Edwards's small, delicate hands, the faint wrinkles radiating from the corners of her eyes, her mild smile. It was difficult to imagine those fingers smothering a powerful, struggling animal. Recalling Mrs. Warner's savage technique, though, his stomach sank.

Mrs. Edwards drew her head back and gazed at him intently. For a moment she fiddled with her elbow-length white glove. Had she seen the *Herald*'s coverage of her cause? He hoped not. If his instincts were right, she took the *Trib,* religious-society periodicals, and nothing more.

She didn't shrink from him. Instead, in measured tones, she launched into her own defense. "This affair is an outrage, and when the case comes up I will show that it is so. Here I set out in answer to a request made to me by a respectable resident of the city, and because I chose to stop on the way to perform an act of kindness, I am arrested and locked up in prison overnight. It's a shame."

He offered his sympathy, inspiring her to go on.

"Some time ago I was notified that there were fourteen stray cats in the yard of 32 Cornelia Street. Thursday night I started to get some of them, but succeeded in dispatching only two, as the others were too wild and would not come near me."

"You went uptown then?"

"I got on the El car headed for Mrs. Smock's house on One Hundred Thirty-Sixth Street. I saw a poor little starving kitten running along a hedgerow on an open lot near the house where I was going. I stopped and did what under the circumstances was the most humane thing to do."

"I understand."

"After that, I placed it in my basket. The attitude the general public takes toward a work which is productive of such good results is really remarkable."

"Actually, we've received a number of letters supporting your cause. Did you deposit the cat somewhere?"

The cords in her neck grew taut. "Where we take them and where we put them is our own affair. We make decisions based on modern science."

Mystified by this reference, he returned to a more concrete question. "Are you gaining public support?"

"Dozens of people have volunteered to join us lately, but our membership secretary, Miss Van Siclen, tells me most are entirely unsuitable."

"How so?"

"Well, they weren't quite the right sort for doing good works."

"Not everyone has the proper character for reform," he agreed, offering his practiced neutral face. "Would you mind giving me your membership secretary's address?"

She turned the question aside smoothly. "I couldn't impose on her. She's a very private person."

"I just need to ask her one or two questions."

"Certainly not," she snapped. As she drew her head back, her lips compressed and her nostrils flared as if she had smelled something foul.

He had pushed too hard. Before she could flee, he shifted to a more congenial subject. "What inspired you to perform these charitable acts?"

"The Henry Bergh Association is supposed to look out for all stray animals in New York, but they are neglecting their business. I have taken 122 homeless cats from the churchyard of St. Brigid's at Avenue B and Eleventh Street in the last year. In the yard of 217 West Forty-Ninth Street, there are seventeen half-wild cats I have as yet been unable to capture. Go look at the vacant lot at 430 Columbus Avenue. There are a dozen more starving there. Not to speak of the ones still running wild around the yard of 32 Cornelia Street. The ASPCA is euthanizing abandoned dogs, but they are derelict when it comes to suffering cats."

Despite some of her cryptic remarks, Mrs. Edwards appeared far more rational than Mrs. Warner, who seemed totally unhinged. Now he dropped in the question that had been plaguing him, watching her intently to see if she reacted. "Would you happen to know Martin Mourtone?"

Mrs. Edwards barely blinked. "No. Who is he?"

"Oh, probably nothing to do with you. What about an establishment called Stephenson's?"

She failed to react to this wild stab either. "No, I never heard of it. But why don't you go to those locations I mentioned? See for yourself. We have the resources to carry on this fight indefinitely. Put that in your paper."

"I'll pay a visit to Cornelia Street."

"Mr. Greengrass. I am aware that because we are women and choose to depart from conventional methods, we are ridiculed and funny stories are written about us." She gave him a penetrating glance. Nervously, he shifted his weight from one foot to the other.

"I see."

"I find among the poorer classes a disposition to harbor half-fed cats that are compelled for want of food to seek the streets, where they eventually die. In the cellars of tenements I sometimes find dozens of cats in all stages of disease."

He was struck dumb. Mrs. Edwards went hunting in tenement basements. The depth of her compulsion shook him. Why would this goo-goo with her fine diction and apparent social position crawl around in reeking cellars? What about sloshing around ankle-deep in standing sewage? How did she know a water rat wouldn't creep into her drawers? All of his attempts to penetrate her thinking were useless. Mrs. Edwards, however decorous, was in the grips of a mania that had nothing to do with reform.

"You actually go into the cellars?" he asked cautiously.

She went on serenely, a subtle shift in her tone suggesting spiritual exaltation.

"We have to make these sacrifices. These are the places to go if one wishes to see the misery cats are forced to undergo, and these are the places where the Bergh officials do not go. In the last two years I've been compelled to do away with over three thousand strays. Do you think I like doing it?"

She drew her shoulders back and stared at him defiantly.

Her eerie calm rattled him. Perhaps what she denied was at the core of her compulsion. Did she derive pleasure from killing cats? Why else would a person seek out these repugnant and dangerous places night after night? And why would she claim so many victims, unless she thought the sheer numbers would cast glory on her name? Stranger still, her following was growing, as the letters to the *Herald* demonstrated. He might think she was a dangerous crank, but to some *Herald* readers she was Joan of Arc.

"I'm certain you don't. That's quite a large number of cats you say you've killed. Do you think it's accurate?"

"We keep extensive records." For the first time he noticed the ends of raw scratches high on her forearms. Her elbow-length white gloves didn't totally cover the evidence of some recent skirmish.

"It occurs to me that the tenement cats are doing a service, aren't they?"

"I can't imagine what."

"Well, they keep down the rodents."

"We have a saying: 'A house full of cats is a house full of sores.'" She chanted these lines. "You and your newspaper should brush up on modern thinking, Mr. Greengrass."

Hopping rapidly up the courthouse steps, a shrunken man in a pearl-colored derby practically bowled Max over. Barely five feet tall, he wore narrow, high-heeled shoes. His black, darting eyes and his close-cropped black mustache gave him the air of a confidence man. A pink wart clung to the tip of his nose.

"Sorry, sonny," he apologized as he bounded past Max and took hold of Mrs. Edwards's elbow. Despite his odd appearance, the man exuded self-assurance.

"Mrs. Edwards? May I have a word with you?"

Now Max recognized him. It was Abe Hummel. Fascinated, he watched the lawyer consult his death's-head watch. Compared to his extravagant partner William H. Howe, Abe Hummel sported a mere three diamond rings and was otherwise the picture of sartorial restraint.

The gimlet-eyed attorney spoke rapidly. For once, Mrs. Edwards seemed to lose her composure. Her even features contracted in a look of furious concentration. Hummel was working her over fast.

Max stood there gaping. What attraction could the Midnight Band's case hold for Howe and Hummel? The Band's entire operation, however bizarre, bore goo-gooism's distinct odor. Mrs. Edwards would fit right into Mr. Comstock's Society for the Suppression of Vice, not exactly Abe Hummel's natural habitat. Yet Martin Mourtone had earned a bullet in the head after claiming knowledge of the Midnight Band. When his remains disappeared, William H. Howe had materialized. Hummel's interest in Mrs. Edwards seemed natural in that light. If the firm also represented

Stephenson's, as Max suspected, Howe and Hummel were cradling every possible conflicting interest in their gentle hands.

His mission completed, Hummel made a toy soldier's bow and clicked away in his shiny "tooth-pick" shoes. Max took a step toward Mrs. Edwards, but, scowling, she waved him off.

chapter fifteen

Under the Third Avenue El, an endless shower of iron dust had turned awnings on either side of the avenue rust-red. Max bounded up the stairs to the station two at a time. In a minute, a Forney steam engine roared in, he leaped aboard, and he was on his way to 32 Cornelia Street.

Gazing around the half-empty car, Max observed a Syrian reading an Arabic newspaper, a proper church lady, a pair of yarmulke-wearing observant Jews, a Chinese, a Bohemian peasant woman in fantastic garb, and an unconscious tramp, his fish-white stomach winking into view as he snored away. A Negro in a lemon-yellow suit and a pigeon's-blood cravat sat perfectly upright, hands gripping his knees.

Max loved these exotic tableaus and had to remind himself to tear his gaze away from the odd foreigners. He knew they were just human beings who craved a decent meal, someone to love, and a dry place to sleep, but they appeared so utterly alien that he couldn't stop staring. Yet he had been born abroad too, and he could summon up scraps of memories. He recalled Viennese boulevards, a garden with an ivy-covered wall, and a rusty iron ring on a worm-eaten door. He remembered a village with puddles for streets, a man with a beard that covered his chest trundling by. His mother said mice lived inside that greenish beard and shook with laughter when he hid under her skirts.

When his family landed in New York in 1873, he had been almost five, but he learned English in a few months and now spoke with a pure New York accent. Only in a technical sense was he an immigrant, he believed. It was the others, the recent arrivals, so strange and destitute, who were the *real* aliens. True, his family's original name was Visneshevski, a moniker reeking of the Pale. On the boat from

Hamburg, his father had heard about a fabulously wealthy German-Jewish family named Greengrass and managed to convince the immigration officer that Visneshevski meant Greengrass in Polish. Max had always known his new last name was an invention. His pedigree amounted to a petty fraud.

On his walk through Greenwich Village, cats trotted along with bits of fish in their mouths, cats got their backs up, hissed, limped, and tore at their fur. Cats lounged in the sun, cats sniffed around the back doors of restaurants. It took some groping to find the right alley, but he finally penetrated the 32 Cornelia Street courtyard. In the walled enclosure, a woman in a baggy dress was working the outdoor water pump that served the entire rear tenement. Two toms were chasing each other in dizzying circles. The first one had a fresh fish head in its jaws. In the shadows, a gray with a white chest was digging into a mass of slops. A wiry black cat darted into the appetizing swill and made off with a chunk of gristle.

That was all Max needed to see. He had his angle. His editor would eat this one up, he was sure.

Back in the newsroom, he asked Parnell whether he should see the paymaster and received a blank look in return. Worse, in the deep furrows of his editor's forehead, Max read the onset of a black, Parnellian mood.

"You said I was on full-time? Do I have to sign some papers? Don't I have to tell the paymaster when I started?"

"What the hell're you talking about, Greengrass?"

Was the door slamming in his face again? He could barely believe it. Then a familiar sensation took hold. Filled with shame, he was plunging down a black hole of his own invention. Once again his blind optimism had gotten the better of him. Angry, embarrassed, he could barely stammer out the words. "Before I went out, you said you were hiring me."

"For that story! That's all. Christ! How long have you been a space man?

Haven't you ever heard a figure of speech? If I want you on staff, you'll know, don't worry."

Stunned, he fought to keep his balance. The words rattled out of him. "Right. I'll knock out the Midnight Band piece. I caught an interview with the queen assassin. You'll like this angle. . . ."

"No rush on it. We're jammed up already. There's a decent fire on King Street. Want it?"

Jammed up? His stomach went into freefall. Parnell was losing interest in the Midnight Band just when the story was getting more intricate. "She had some blueblood lawyer. There was damn near a riot. That judge, Bernstein, was tearing his hair out."

"You want the address?"

"Sure."

The editor scribbled out the number, emitted a low noise resembling a growl, then spun away. Opening and closing his fists, Max stood there staring at the back of Parnell's scrawny neck, a fresh-shaved, paper-white neck that never saw the sun.

Singed curtains and blackened bedding. The fire turned out to be a bust.

Despite his black mood, he rode the El back to the *Herald* and went through the motions. He commandeered a messenger and sent a note to Howe asking for an emergency audience. He assumed the lawyer would dodge him again, but he wanted to be sure.

To kill time, he spread his notes out and started to reconstruct Mrs. Edwards's arraignment. He tried three different leads, but they sounded too flat. Disgusted, he yanked the sheet from the typewriter's barrel and started again. Slowly, his mind returned to the courtroom. He recalled a cabby's booze-seared face, the hissing gallery, the snickers, the jeers, the legal gobbledygook, the bubble and squeak of justice. On his smeared notebook page, he reread a sentence he'd written in capital letters. The courtyard angle. Only a couple of hours ago, he'd been sky-high about it. Now he wasn't sure he could pull it off.

Numb to his surroundings, he picked at his nails, took two trips to the john, pecked out another few grafs. Every word seemed questionable, every sentence a house of cards. Yet here and there a phrase lived, a quote sounded like the street's mouth.

He'd missed his deadline, but Parnell was going to get the story whether he liked it or not.

All the while, Howe and Hummel maintained an Olympian silence.

Max had a bender in mind, but he needed to drag Danny along.

Mrs. DeVogt's sitting room smelled of wax and varnish. Muttering furiously, Swarms sat squirming on the sofa, snapping the pages of his newspaper.

"Come on out, I'm buying," Max said. He could already feel the first spine-melting drink.

Darkened by sweat, Danny's thinning hair looked like a nest of wires. When he saw Max, he began reading newspaper ads aloud. "Sarah Jacob's Blood Thickener. Dr. Oresetes Fainting Powder. Firbanks Nerve Tonic. Do people throw money at these things?"

"They'll throw money away on Corbett and Mitchell."

Unable to contain himself, Danny shook the pages. "I'm not talking about some two-bit heavyweights. Dr. Minsky's Electric Belt! Christ! A perfectly good company seizes up, and all people can think of doing is throwing away every dollar on quackery. If people would just do the right thing, save a little, we wouldn't be in the shape we're in."

Since Swarms never saved a dime, Max found his tirade incomprehensible. After his own disasters, he didn't have much patience left either. A jittery, overtired sensation drove him on. "What're you raving about? Let's take the cure; come on."

"You probably don't know what's going on, do you? You're just standing there and grinning like an ape."

Danny looked so bereft, Max let up. "What happened? Did you lose your spot at Tony Pastor's?"

"Might as well have. Equitable went belly-up. They can't peddle a bond to a blind man."

"What does that have to do with you?"

"Nothing too drastic. Yesterday they approved my loan, that's all."

"The business loan?"

Max knew that Danny had been counting on the money to bail out his music-publishing venture. Without it, the actor would have trouble making next month's rent on his spartan office. Well, all the more reason to tear up the Rialto together tonight.

"Credit's tighter than a witch's sphincter."

"What about some other bank?"

"The banks are falling like tenpins. You got your head in the sand, or what?"

"C'mon. A few farmers' banks in the Midwest. Not here. New York's got all the gold."

"We were ready to put out this tune, 'Lorelei, I'll Remember to Recall.' It's kind of 'A Mansion of Aching Hearts,' without the dragging tempo. Lah lalah lalala, lah lalah la lee, you hear it once, it screws right into your head. Now. Pfft."

"How much are you into Sim for?"

"That bloodsucker? Don't even ask me."

"Yeah, well, I got hired and fired in the same day."

Distracted from his own misery, Swarms brightened. "That's a new one. How'd you pull that off?"

"Talent. You have to be born with it. How about a nice fresh one? You know what they look like, with the foam on top?"

He didn't hear her come in. Under the archway that separated the sitting room from the dining room, Gretta stood glaring at both of them.

"Ah, hello, Gretta," Max said, at a loss. Was he imagining it, or did she look like murder? "Want to join us?"

Her jaw set, she examined him with a long, cold stare, then turned on her heel.

"What was that all about?" Swarms asked, his tirade now at an end.

"Damned if I know."

"Well, I hope she wasn't holding any Equitable paper. Penny on the dollar if you're lucky." Danny riffled his newspaper. "The Reverend Weems is at it again! Just because there are half a dozen brothels across the street from his church, he takes offense."

"You think you'll have to close your office?"

"I've got to scramble." Abruptly, he changed the subject. "Did you see Faye's show yet?"

"No, I've been running around like a chicken without a head."

"You'll bust a gut, I promise. She's wondering whether you'll show up."

First she steals him, and now she's turning him into her mouthpiece. There was a time when he had felt more like himself with Danny than anybody else. Now Faye had them negotiating with each other. She was an evil genius, his sister.

"In my own sweet time. Come on." He snapped his fingers. "Chop-chop. Are we doing the Rialto crawl, or what?"

"Can't. I've got a rehearsal later."

Defeated, Max wandered up to his room and lay down. His triumphs at the *Herald*, his budding romance with Gretta. How many other tall tales had he been telling himself? He hustled like crazy, sure. He knew the score as well as the next guy, but finding out the score about himself was another game entirely. If he never got hired full-time, he wasn't a real reporter. If he never won the woman he craved, he wasn't a real man. He wasn't about to puff himself up about his paid conquests at the House of All Nations.

Now he'd attached himself to this wretched cat story, and it wouldn't go away. Perhaps when his latest article came off the press—if it did—things would change. He'd done his best to make one thing clear: this Mrs. Edwards, the reformer, spent her days in tenement courtyards and basements murdering poor people's pets. If he knew anything, he knew the *Herald*'s readers: they would want to knock her down and press a big chloroformed rag over her face.

Dinner was excruciating.

Mrs. DeVogt questioned Swarms closely about the Equitable collapse—evidently he'd been moaning to everybody about it earlier. Now he affected the long view. "Business runs in streaks, Mrs. DeVogt. It'll bounce back."

"I am not an infant, Mr. Swarms. I lived through the 1873 Panic. They were building railroads to nowhere, and nothing bounced back for a dozen years."

Swarms offered a tight smile. "Yeah, maybe; but from what I've been reading, when England starts scooping up our wheat again, the stock market will turn around."

Max could barely keep a straight face. When a soft-shoe artist started sounding like the financial pages, the country was in real trouble. What did Swarms know about the markets? What did anybody know? One day Wall Street was all fair skies and summer breezes; then out of nowhere came the typhoon.

Dismissing Danny's soothing words, Mrs. DeVogt addressed the table at large. "Railroads were going to solve everything. If they said the Northern Pacific was going to transport the moon to San Francisco, the public bought even more."

Mrs. DeVogt's mouth pinched in at the end of this brief speech, and Max wondered whether she hadn't lost more than a few dollars back in 1873.

"Danny, what's the bit you're doing at Tony Pastor's?" Max asked, deftly shifting the subject. He had enough doom and gloom on his own watch.

"Ahh, I've got a pretty funny song we just published, it's about a family with twenty kids. . . ."

Soon they were chattering away again. Only Gretta maintained her rigid silence. When she was the first to leave the table, Max waited a few minutes and then followed her upstairs. He was about to knock on her door, but then he started wondering. What made him think she was angry with him? She had plenty of reasons to be moody: her mother's health; her job; Martin's murder, of course. Why assume she was cross with him? Better to see how she was doing, be sympathetic and ignore her earlier icy slight.

He tapped on her door. She greeted him with an emotionless expression. "Don't come here and try to talk to me."

Sticking his foot over the threshold, he kept her from slamming the door in his face. "What? The last time we saw each other—"

"Why did you tell me that tall story? Why did you lie to me?"

"What? I didn't—"

"Then how do you suppose they can have a funeral?" She kept her voice low, but her anger was palpable. She looked at him with fresh eyes. Why had he made up such a wild tale, she was thinking. Was he out of his mind? Considering his jittery mannerisms, who could tell?

Now he knew what she was talking about, but he wanted to hear her say it. "What funeral?"

"For Martin, of course. I suppose you're one of those warped people who get pleasure out of nasty practical jokes." She had to take it out on someone. Why not a little man who wouldn't hit back?

He was floored. How had they found Mourtone so fast? Police Superintendent Byrnes could dig up a stolen brooch in a day or two by tapping his underground telegraph of dips and second-story men, but was it as easy to find a body? Perhaps, if the corpse came from the right family. "Wait, wait, let me absorb this. They're having a funeral for him? When? How did you find out?"

"The announcement is in your wretched newspaper. Don't you read anything except your own articles?" She knew she wasn't being fair, but so what?

Her barb stung, but somehow he had to convince her that he'd been telling the truth. Thoughtlessly, he tried to take her hand, but she quickly brushed him off. Her mouth twisted up in disgust.

Doggedly, he went on. "I swear I'd never lie to you. Especially about something like that! Why would I?" As he spoke, he gave her a searching, naked look, hoping his expression, stripped of any artifice, would convince her where words failed. "I'd have to be some sort of crank. What would I gain? Look how easily you found out about the funeral."

Mute, she stared back at him, her face masklike. Captured in her indifferent gaze, he felt like a specimen on a slide. Her eyes said he was insignificant, not worth hating. A countercurrent of anger flashed through him. What gave her the right to punish him? Who else was doing a damned thing to help her?

He bit his lower lip. "When are the services? We might learn something."

In a barren whisper, she said, "I haven't been invited. They didn't bother to contact me." She recoiled at her own admission, but there it was, her little hurt out in the open. How disgusting she was. Worse, she hadn't stopped hoping against hope that she would get something out of the family. She daydreamed about it. An allowance. A small house in honor of her devotion.

She thought of Martin's sunburned forearm on her lap. Why that? A dry, papery sensation closed her throat. Now she had nothing to look forward to but twelve-hour days slaving away for Gertrude and silent dinners with her prune-faced mother. How was she ever going to escape?

Now Max understood. Her rage had other roots as well. Still, he didn't much care for the way she'd lashed out at him. So bitter and thwarted. "Where are they holding the ceremony?"

"Holy Trinity," she said wearily.

"Do you know what time?"

"Why? What's the point?"

"Well, if it would make you feel better, I'll go with you. They don't post armed guards at funerals."

"I don't know. What good would it do?" Perhaps she *should* show up this one time. Asking for nothing. How they would blanch if she sailed into that showplace of a church with Max Greengrass on her arm.

His anger dissipating, he fell back on his professional manner. "These things are unpredictable. We could listen, keep our eyes peeled."

"I suppose."

His nerves quieted down. All he had to do was treat her like any other interview. Then he looked at her pained mouth, her lips sucked in, almost invisible, and the heebie-jeebies seized him again. Steeling himself, he concentrated on the practical matters. Gretta would provide a perfect cover for his own appearance at the services. What would the Reverend Weems say about the cause of Martin's death? Why had such a young, healthy, and privileged young man suddenly withered away?

"It's entirely up to you. All I can say is I'm as shocked as you are. If you think I'm some sort of madman, there's nothing I can do about it."

She sensed his temper flaring. Her face felt as if it were on fire. "Of course not."

"Then ask yourself, truthfully, did you think of me that way two days ago?"

"No," she conceded. She had thought he was earnest, rather nice, but decidedly rough around the edges. His directness chilled her. She didn't know whether to admire his candor, or attribute it to a lack of diplomacy.

"Then give me some time to find out what happened. Obviously, the family's keeping things quiet. Why shouldn't they? What good can come out of broadcasting that their son was shot through the head in a dive?" When he saw her flinch, he rushed to add: "I'm sorry. It's in their interest to put on a respectable show, isn't it?"

"Perhaps." Still wary, she ran her cool eye over him.

He cursed himself for telling her the truth. "We can't mention it to anyone, either. How he died. Especially now, when it will be even harder to prove."

"Who would I tell? I don't know anybody."

"Until we can get some evidence. We have to be very discreet . . . I can't conceive of the shock, to lose someone so close to you."

His sympathy felt palpable, like rough silk. "There's one thing I want to tell you, Mr. Greengrass." She used his last name pointedly. "Martin and I were very close, but his family . . . I met his mother once, but there was no compelling reason for his family to invite me." A wounded expression flickered on her face. Then it was gone.

"I see. I'm sorry you're so disturbed."

"I'm more disturbed than you can possibly imagine." She pronounced these words slowly, imparting weight to every syllable. She had loved Mourtone. There was no doubt.

For a moment he saw the world through the lens of her loss. He had hoped her grief wasn't so deep-rooted, and that eventually his attentions wouldn't appear in bad taste. Now he had to act with complete restraint. He could sense how easily the wrong gesture, the wrong expression might offend her.

"Will you go to the services with me?" he offered again.

"Come into my room for a minute," she responded.

Over her bed, Gretta had hung one of her street photographs. Several grinning barefoot boys were building a bonfire, and one guttersnipe, naked from the waist up, was virtually winking as he sucked on a bottle of blue ruin. The sharp focus, the sentiment-stripped quality of the shot startled him. Instead of insisting—as pictures like Riis's did—that the viewer pity the wild street arabs, Gretta's photograph showed the boys having a grand time.

Max didn't really know what to make of it. The photograph wasn't making a case for any particular social policy. It seemed almost perverse in its neutrality. "Very realistic. They're in their glory, aren't they?"

That was it, he realized. She had captured a wild, forbidden joy. The street arabs were supposed to be suffering, but they defied pity. Gretta had a brilliant and daring eye.

She shrugged. "Well, that's what I saw. I hate pictures with points."

"He—I mean Martin, he really admired your work. He told me all about it one night. He was head over heels—"

"He did, didn't he?" Martin had showered her with praise, he had taken her pictures to galleries; and when the dealers, mystified, shook their heads, he had raged against the money-grubbing philistines. She felt like weeping, but held herself in check. Wouldn't her tears be for herself alone? It was kind of Max to tell her this, generous in a way. Why was she tormenting him? She knew he was blameless. "Would you do something for me?"

"Anything."

"I want you to swear to me that you've told me everything you know about the way Martin died. Put your hand on your heart and swear."

"I swear to you that I didn't lie."

"And you've told me everything."

The matter of the five hundred dollars didn't pertain, he was certain. He would keep that secret forever. "I've told you everything I know."

"All right. I'll tell Gertrude I have to go to a funeral. She'll have to let me off for an hour or two. Reverend Weems is speaking at one o'clock. We should get there by twelve-thirty to get a seat. You know, I can understand why they'd want to avoid a scandal, but can't they keep looking for the creature who did this?"

"We don't know what the police are doing. So you do believe me?"

"Yes. Go, go now."

He almost asked her another question, but he checked himself. What should he wear to an upper-crust Protestant funeral? A business suit? Evening dress? He didn't have a cutaway, but he could always rent.

chapter sixteen

On Saturday night, Simon's Avenue B Theatre—Temple of Amusement! Around the Clock Frolics!—was offering The French Twins, Zapinsky and Newton, Professor Von Nigglehagen, Dutch Swanberg and Irish Annie Conlon. Flaking gold-leaf pillars framed the box office. In the lobby a sign proclaimed "AFTER BREAKFAST, SIMON'S! AFTER SIMON'S, BACK TO BED!" Max grabbed a beer and a shot at the crescent-shaped bar in the lobby, and then wove through the half-filled orchestra.

He was already well-oiled. Schooners and whiskey at a saloon on Fourth Avenue. The booze ran warm and sweet through his veins.

He took a spicy sausage sandwich wrapped in butcher paper to his seat. Underfoot, the floor was soft and sticky with melted candy, half-eaten apples, corn cobs, scraps of newspaper, and circulars. Men wandered in and out puffing cigars, pointing at the stage, poking their buddies. When they fell into their seats, they undid the top buttons of their pants. Max settled into the buzzing darkness.

If Martin Mourtone wanted to resurrect himself and climb into a coffin, fine. If Stan Parnell, that weaselly sonofabitch, wanted to tie him to the space-raters' bench, screw him and his monkey-faced mother. There was such a thing as having a good time.

Onstage, Zapinsky and Newton were settling their differences. Zapinsky wore a screaming yellow jacket down to his knees and a top hat an extra story high. Newton was decked out in a purple frock coat and a floppy red tie. Donning boxing gloves made of inflated pig bladders, the pair fought a battle of ferocious poses. Finally Zapinsky wound up and threw a haymaker, missing his partner by a foot. Newton fell flat on his back, examined himself in an elaborate pantomime, and, finding himself whole, bounced up and bopped Newton on the head. Then the pig bladders really started flying. The partners yowled, grunted, bellowed, and screeched with every jab and hook, they staggered like drunks, clung to the curtains and knocked heads.

A patron reeled down to the stage's apron, pounded it with his fist and shouted, "Kill the sonofabitch!"

"Nah, kiss him!" another man in his cups shouted.

Scattered laughter echoed through the hall.

"Zis is one tough customer," Zapinsky confided to the audience, jabbing his thumb in the direction of his critic.

Confused, the bloodthirsty commentator plopped down in the first row.

Newton stopped in his tracks, his greasepaint eyebrows bobbing. "You selling something?"

Zapinsky winked and pulled a rubber chicken from the depths of his checked pants. "Chickens, cheap."

Newton shrugged. "Just a second. I buy." He opened his jacket with a boxing glove, but handicapped by his huge mitts, couldn't get inside his own pocket.

Zapinsky hid his right hand behind his back. "Lemme help you." He cast a friendly paw over Newton's shoulder, mugging to the crowd. Newton dropped his arms to his side, stuck his chin out and froze. Stretching time to the edge of pain, the duo waited and waited.

The audience, unable to stand it, peppered Newton with advice.

"The right hand, you dope!"

"Behind his back! Sucker punch!"

Finally, almost as an afterthought, Zapinsky socked his pal right in the kisser, and they were at it again, flailing away, fighting and soft-shoeing it simultaneously as they glided to the wings.

When they trooped out for a curtain call, they were rewarded with tepid applause. Max took a healthy bite of his sandwich, the grease dribbling onto his chin.

Before the audience could catch its breath, a mob of chorines dressed as schoolgirls minced onto the stage. Each one held a slate to her chest. On second glance, their costumes didn't seem quite right for young scholars. Their flashy blouses were shades too loud, and their skirts crossed the line between outerwear and giant bloomers.

Faye was the last one to trip into the light. She stumbled, skidded, almost fell, but righted herself into a knock-kneed, pigeon-toed stance.

Her curly black hair shooting out in all directions, she bit her lip and peered cross-eyed into the darkness.

The Professor jerked a thumb her way and shook his head in sadness. His hands behind his back, he circled Faye, looking her up and down, winking. Polite people called Faye's type full-figured, which meant she hadn't lost the twenty pounds she'd put on before Leon was born.

Filing her nails, Faye feigned nonchalance. Pearl buttons flashed on her red satin shirtwaist.

"Oooohhh, it's Grasshopper!" another student cried, and the girls clustered around her in adulation.

Then Professor Von Nigglehaggen took control. The act was simple. The Professor asked the girls their ABC's. One reached F. Another made it all the way to J before losing the thread. Busy gossiping, Grasshopper couldn't recall the letter A. Despite his misgivings, the Professor was forced to roll out his Giant Spanking Machine, a device consisting of a chair on an axle, ridiculously large wooden gears, and a monstrous crank. He strapped Faye into the contraption, yanked the handle, and turned her upside down, her skirt flying over her head. Cascading, lacy drawers followed suit.

Faye whooped and wriggled in distress as one layer of underthings after another fell over her head. An evil grin on his face, the Professor held the Giant Crank in both hands, keeping Faye's head aimed at the floorboards. Clad in black tights, her legs wriggled. A titter ran through the assembly.

Max squirmed in his seat, gritted his teeth, crossing and recrossing his legs.

Circling his pupil, the Professor pulled out his Giant Paddle, an instrument shaped like a human hand. Foot-long fingers whooshed through the air as the pedagogue practiced his stroke.

"Ooooeeee!" his sister cried. Max knew it was an all an act, but he winced anyway. Could this be her star turn? The surprise Danny kept talking about? Maybe they'd both been in the business so long they couldn't distinguish between success and humiliation.

The Professor sauntered to the lip of the stage and consulted the audience, "Do you think she learned her lesson?"

The balcony shouted advice. "She's too thick!" "Teach her a good one!"

A more refined man in the orchestra chimed in. "She don't know her A's from her elbow!" This witticism almost brought the house down.

Her fellow students mobbed Faye, trying to protect her. Naturally, Max understood that it was all play-acting, he assumed the Giant Paddle was pasteboard and that Faye was smirking under her frilly shroud, but he wanted to vault onto the stage to rescue her anyway. He felt so embarrassed and sad for her, he almost bolted from the theatre.

He wanted to drop that twenty on her, though. Anyway, backstage, her mortification would all seem like a joke. Just another turn for another dollar. Faye wasn't exactly a shrinking violet.

A working girl in the fourth row leaped to her feet. "Spank her pants off!"

A rhythmic chanting and clapping took hold. "Spank! Spank! Spank!"

The frenzy for punishment rose. Feet stamped. Men who had been slumping in their seats, beaten by a day's work or a day's unemployment, came back to life. They whistled and howled for amusement, for punishment, for a little of both.

The Giant Paddle struck Faye's bottom, and she let loose an earsplitting howl.

The girls twittered, but the Professor cranked the Spanking Machine one more time. Then Faye started slipping from her chair. When she went flying, Max held his breath. Like the rest of the audience, he didn't know whether vaulting into the air was part of the act or a dangerous mistake.

But it was all planned. Hitting the stage on her toes, Faye executed two neat cartwheels, then bounced to her feet. A violin sawed in the pit. A piano struck a chord. The cracked orchestra hesitated, groping its way through the introduction. The stage went dark except for a simple spotlight. In its glare Faye threw her shoulders back, cocked her head and swayed. Her simple movements settled the muttering crowd.

When her voice rang out, a solid, rueful alto, Max felt all his all love for her rushing back. It wasn't her voice, rich and deep as it was, but her inflections, warm, wry, and world-weary all at once, that mesmerized him. Fayefaye, with all her whims and phony excuses, never lied when she sang a tune.

One night my sweetheart came to woo
When I was left and lonely.
He looked so kind and handsome too,
I lov'd him and him only.

The village chime told supper time.
What could I do, dear misses?

For as I live, I'd naught to give
But bread and cheese and kisses.

By the time she rounded into the closing verses, Simon's Avenue B Theatre, that Temple of Amusement, had fallen into a reverent silence. Faye's dark-timbred voice, so direct and plain it was almost unbearable, rose to fill the hall. Just an anonymous groundling, Max felt oddly close to her as she swayed in the cone of light. It was easy to love Faye at a distance.

Next morning we exchang'd our vows;
I prize his golden present
Which seems like magic to disclose,
But 'tis in fact like heaven

His cheerful smiles each care beguiles.
Believe me, dearest misses,
'Tis bliss to share with him our fare
Though bread and cheese and kisses.

Suddenly the stage lights burst on and one of the schoolgirls pulled a tiny American flag from her cleavage. A drum roll sounded. The next leggy scholar produced a larger flag, and the next a striped banner greater still. The Professor slapped a tall hat on his head, donned a stars-and-stripes cutaway, and grabbed a baton. High-stepping, the chorines fell in behind him and burst into a patriotic air.

Oh, see the boys in blue;
Their hearts are good and true.

After Faye's intimate performance, the brassy march jarred in Max's ear. It came on too fast, and made little sense, but the audience didn't seem to mind. They clapped, whistled, and stomped their feet to the booming drum.

He had to get backstage. In the wings he almost ran over Leon, who was crawling in his nightdress through the stage dust. Before Max could grab him, Zapinsky scooped the boy up and tossed him in the air. Close-up, the comic's putty nose covered half his face.

"Harry, give him here," Faye demanded. As soon as she started rocking the boy in her arms, he showed his gums in a wet smile.

Max sneaked up behind her and pulled her ear. Her back to him, she said, "Maxie, you showed up."

"Great turn, sis. I don't know about the spanking part, though."

"Listen to this. Show Uncle Max, honeybunch." She sang a soft scale. In a wispy voice, Leon hit the notes one after the other. "Isn't that something? I swear he knows middle C."

"Fantastic." You never knew. This kid could turn into something. "Anywhere we can talk?"

"Sure, I don't got another show for a while."

"How many left?"

"Just four." Nodding toward Leon, she said, "Mrs. Darling was full up."

She led him through the backstage labyrinth, past the bullpen dressing rooms, one for the male acts, one for the female, and into a quiet corner. When they were finally alone, Max slipped Faye the bill.

"You're on a streak?"

"Nah, nothing like that. I wasn't kidding. You really put that song across."

She pecked his cheek. He would have been happy to follow her home and sit on her bed all night. Now that the booze was wearing off, he felt the heebie-jeebies rushing back. Shooting the breeze with Faye would keep the dry-mouthed nightmares at bay. He wanted to tell her how he was going crazy down at the paper, with Parnell blowing smoke up his skirt one minute and pretending he didn't exist the next. He wanted to ask her about Gretta, too. Faye was shrewd about the female animal. Did he have a snowball's chance in hell with the woman?

Instead, he blurted, "Hey, remember that slummer Martin? Danny took him to see you that night?"

"I don't know. Leon, stop already. Look at him," she said, showing Max the child's sniffling face. "How can you say no to that?"

Max took the boy in his arms and brushed his face with his mustache.

"Unca Max! Tickley."

"Sniff his head," Faye said.

"Smells fresh." The boy wriggled in his grasp. How could such a small bag of flesh and bones turn into a full-grown human being? He felt a twinge of melancholy. Would Danny really look out for the kid? He couldn't count on it. Like it or not, Leon was his nephew and more. "Martin Mourtone. Very well-dressed, tall guy. Kind of pretty. Lots of cash."

"Oh, him. He came over to Sullivan Street one day. Out of the blue."

"Your flat? What for?"

"Don't have a coronary. He was just in the neighborhood," she said blandly. "It wasn't that, so wipe that look off your face."

"What did he say?"

"Oh, he liked the show, he was thinking of producing. That routine."

"A philanthropist, I get it." Imagining Mourtone sniffing around his sister, he began to form a different picture of the fey swell. "I had a few with him, and he was giving me a load of malarkey about starting some new rag."

"Yeah, I guess he wants to hire both of us." She rolled her eyes to indicate how much she believed Martin Mourtone's promises. "Danny says he's loaded."

"What else did Martin say? Was he visiting anybody else in the neighborhood?"

"What's the big deal? I told you."

"Did he say anything about Gretta?"

"You mean the picture queen? Not when he was talking to me, he didn't. Danny said you were mooning over her."

Irritated, he blurted the thing out. "Mourtone's dead. He just died." Then he caught himself. If he told Faye much of anything, in twenty-four hours every booking agent and song-and-dance man in the Rialto would be repeating the story. He might as well sell it to Fox at the *Police Gazette*.

"That's awful. How could he die? Just like that? *Ucchhh*. That spooks me."

"People do it every day. I hear it's easy. How long was he up in the flat?"

"Ten minutes. Less. I had to drop the baby off. He was so young. He had nice eyes."

"Yeah, well. Lemme go. I need my beauty sleep." He pecked her on the cheek. She smelled of powder and cheap perfume and milk, faintly sour.

chapter seventeen

Standing at the newsstand on Sixth Avenue and Fourteenth on Monday morning, Max devoured his article whole, then reread it slowly for mistakes. Nothing too bad, just a dropped comma and a broken capital T. Parnell had left his copy largely intact, and the headline man had displayed a glorious lack of restraint. He shook the change in his pocket. He was still in the game.

Glowing inwardly, he held the paper at arm's length and took in the head again. Then, uneasy, he began to rethink it. Wasn't it misleading? Didn't it mix up Mrs. Edwards's contentions and his own? Didn't it sound as if the *Herald* believed her claims?

POORER CLASSES STARVE CATS

Mrs. Edwards Charges Intentional Brutality
Says Pets Better Off Dead

The subhead clarified who was claiming that the poor were inhumane, but readers still might be misled by the upper-case headline. The contradiction made him squirm.

> Mrs. Edwards, the purported leader of the Midnight Band of Mercy, was arraigned Friday in Harlem Police Court. After closely questioning the prisoner, the magistrate, Chaim Bernstein, released her on the recognizance of Mr. Maple, her lawyer, until such day as she stands trial for

> chloroforming cats in Harlem, Chelsea, and Greenwich Village.
>
> In an interview after her court appearance, Mrs. Edwards contended that the poorer classes had a tendency to keep half-fed animals as pets, only to allow them to die in droves. She cited particular addresses, courtyards, and even basements into which she has crawled in order to put her prey out of their alleged misery.
>
> It was a distinctly unsettling experience to listen to Mrs. Edwards crow about her campaign of feline carnage. She asserted, apparently with pride, that she had done away with over three thousand cats in her ghoulish career.

Parnell had swallowed the angle whole, and for good reason. The piece was bound to elicit a tidal wave of outrage from the *Herald*'s faithful. Some readers wept over stories about hamsters with weak kidneys. How would they react to Mrs. Edwards's massacres? How much longer could Parnell keep him down?

When he took his place on the space-raters' bench, Parnell motioned to him immediately. Max did his best to keep a straight face as he ambled past the other space men who had been waiting for hours before he arrived.

"Someone wants to make your acquaintance," Parnell said dryly.

To Max's delight, the city editor led him to the Managing Editor's glassed-in office where two men, leaning back in their chairs, were chatting away. Managing Editor Garvey, a man with a thin pink face and ginger-colored muttonchops, turned to Max as if he actually recognized him.

"Greengrass?"

"In the flesh," Parnell agreed.

"Mr. Bennett wanted to take a look at you."

Max had never laid eyes on James Gordon Bennett, Jr. The son of the *Herald*'s original publisher lived principally in Paris, often sailing the Mediterranean in his steam yacht. Max did know that, long ago, Bennett, Jr., known for his disdain for propriety, had been exiled from New York society for having urinated into his fiancée's marble fireplace in mixed company. Society had never forgiven him.

"Not much to look at," Max managed. Before he could stop himself, he touched his swollen eye.

The bony-faced publisher tweaked the upturned tip of his Hussar's mustache. "So you're the cat man?" Bennett let go a full-throated laugh. "Nice work, Greengrass. The leads are a little spongy, though."

His face flushing, Max wondered whether he had been praised or chastised. Bennett had been reading his articles, perhaps in some Parisian café; Bennett had noticed him. On the other hand, what did "spongy leads" mean?

He had to make the most of his audience, though. "I do human beings, too, Mr. Bennett."

"Well, we may have something for you. Wait. I want you to take a look at this. Come on over here." The publisher led Garvey and Max out of the office to his high corner desk. From this perch above Ann Street and Broadway, he could see all the way down Park Row.

"Listen, Greengrass." Bennett picked up a few sheets of paper and scanned the type. "Here it is. 'We may have seen the last kick of the Tammany anaconda.' What do you think?"

Immediately Max noted—to himself—that snakes didn't kick in the natural world. What was he supposed to say? On the one hand, Bennett might have written the line. If Max criticized it, he'd never escape the spacers' bench. On the other hand, if he didn't point out the metaphor's weakness, he might end up a space man the rest of his life. "It's fine, but shouldn't it be 'squirm' or something like that?"

"As I said," Garvey commented softly.

Disregarding his editor, Bennett glared at the sheet once more. "The hell with it! I like kicking anacondas. That's the idea! Set the whole thing in fourteen-point, Garvey, and lead with it too."

Max's heart sank. When Bennett wrote his occasional editorials, he always demanded larger type so the public would know who had composed them. Max stood frozen, a pale smile on his lips. He'd gambled and lost.

Noticing his reporter's pained expression, Bennett clapped him on the shoulder. "Our cat man! So you think you can do two-legged beasts too?"

Max squared his shoulders. "Without a doubt. They swim in the same water, don't they?"

"That they do," Bennett muttered, his chilly blue eyes staring off into space. Then he whirled around to Garvey and cackled. "I hear that cowboy nabbed another feature man from the *World*."

"Hearst? The sidewalk's getting thin between those two," Garvey cracked.

"What do you think? He's bleeding greenbacks, I hear."

The managing editor twined his fingers over his stomach. "The banks aren't giving transfusions, either. The *Journal* goes belly-up in two, three months, tops."

Max had no interest in William Randolph Hearst and his raid on Pulitzer's stars; he lived far below that firmament. Garvey and Bennett no longer seemed to recognize his existence. "Back to work," he muttered.

Garvey waved an indifferent hand.

Had he made another misstep? All morning he sat on the hard bench. Not a single story came his way. Was he already paying for pointing out that anacondas lacked extremities? Yet Bennett had still seemed friendly enough. With nothing else to do, Max chewed over the publisher's every word, his tone, his gestures. Who could tell? Bennett might have fired him already. All Parnell had to do was let him rot with the rest of the space men until he finally got the message.

His mouth went dry. An internal itch seized him. He couldn't sit still. If he was going to squeeze one more drop of juice out of the Midnight Band story, he'd have to find the membership secretary Mrs. Edwards had mentioned, Miss Van Siclen. He didn't have much hope that this other biddy would offer fresh revelations, but he was curious about the women who, according to Mrs. Edwards, had been inspired to join up recently. What qualities did a fresh recruit need? Who were these new acolytes? What motivated them? If the Midnight Band had rejected them, that was a story in itself.

The book dealer wasn't happy to see him. Max had to follow the jumpy man around the store as he shelved new volumes. "Just tell me if you've heard of Van Siclen. Does she pick up the mail?"

"The purpose of a postal box, Mr. Greengrass, is to maintain a level of discretion. That is the service I'm selling, and I won't violate it."

"How's business?"

"The book business is in its death throes, if you want to know the truth."

"Why's that?"

"After they throw their money away on shows, they take a boat to Coney and burn the rest on some cheap distraction. Ouija boards, velocipedes, gramophones, dirty postcards, penny arcades. Publishing will be dead in a year."

"Maybe you need a boost." He unbuttoned his purse and pulled out a fresh greenback.

The dealer stopped fussing over his shelves. "Do you know what our profit margin is? Some fool cooks up a few pasteboard diamonds and makes a thousand percent. We're working on two or three."

Max worked another bill out of its leather nest. "Miss Van Siclen? She picks up the mail?"

The shopkeeper found a way around his moral objections.

The Midnight Band's secretary lived on Irving Place.

A spiked iron fence ran around Van Siclen's brick house. Its mansard roof had shed some tiles, and the chimneypot tilted at a precarious angle. The bay window, its frame peeling, was shrouded by threadbare curtains.

In truth, he was just going through the motions. The residence looked less than promising. Still, he tapped the Gorgon-headed brass knocker several times. He shuffled his feet, forcing himself to wait, but the house appeared dead to the world. Veiled, the windows revealed no signs of activity, but finally he noticed a handwritten note directing tradesmen to the back. He trotted down the stairs and followed a graveled walkway that ran to a stable in the back. Sensing Max's approach, a horse snorted and stamped behind the barn doors.

The house's rear looked shabbier still. A covered wooden staircase that ran all the way to the third story retained traces of paint but had otherwise turned that nameless shade of weatherbeaten clapboard. The whole rickety structure seemed to be separating from the brick. The shutters were sealed tight. At first he couldn't find the entrance, but then he discovered steps leading to the basement. In the shadows below, he made out a half-open door.

Before he took another step, he worried. If he was taken for a burglar, would James Gordon Bennett, Jr. protect him? A decent publisher wouldn't hesitate, but Max had doubts about Bennett, especially after their earlier ambiguous exchange. Finally, sheer curiosity drove him forward. He rapped on the door and, when no response was forthcoming, stepped inside.

The basement kitchen was long, low, and dark. A window admitted a dull light. Max thought he heard someone breathing, then the sound stopped short. Slowly, his eyes started adjusting to the light in the large cooking quarters. A clumsy table dominated the room, rough chairs pressed to it. From the ceiling hung dusty pots and pans. He made out the dumbwaiter that carried meals to the dining room above. The stink of rodent droppings, greasy cooking smells, astringent cleansers melted into the timeless aroma of sealed windows and close quarters.

Hesitating, he took small steps into the gloomy interior. To the right of the back wall, an archway indicated an alcove of some sort, but he couldn't see its interior. Grit scattered underfoot. Had the breathing resumed? He couldn't tell. Perhaps it had been a hallucination. No, someone was there, maybe a cook rummaging in the darkness.

Then he saw her. A mousy woman was stirring soup on a coal stove. A tight-sleeved dress peeked out from beneath her apron.

"I'm looking for Miss Van Siclen."

"I am she." She put down her wooden spoon and wiped her hands.

"Our friend Mrs. Edwards suggested I look you up." He held his breath, waiting to see if this convenient lie would fly.

"Oh, you know Julia?"

"I spoke to her at her arraignment."

She screwed up her pointy features. "What a horrible mix-up. The world hates an idealist."

"Yes, I agree. She told me your organization had attracted some new applicants?"

"You might call them that. A very unfortunate lot. One took in wash. Another worked in some sort of asylum, but I suspected she was an inmate. Another one had boils. . . . We don't take just anybody off the street, of course."

"Of course not. Mrs. Edwards said they were unsuitable. She said you would know more about them. We're getting quite a bit of mail supporting your group, you know. Our readers are eager to learn more about your good works."

He offered his most innocent face.

"Readers?"

"I'm sorry, here's my card. Max Greengrass. *New York Herald*." Now he took the plunge. If she had read a word of the *Herald*'s coverage, he was doomed anyway. "My editor thinks your organization is a remarkable phenomenon. He wants to give you the opportunity to explain your philosophy."

"Oh, I don't know. That's more in Julia's line." Her pinched features contracted. Was Edwards her superior? He sensed in her an ingrained compliance.

"Well, I've already interviewed Mrs. Edwards. Perhaps I could just have a few words with you."

"Well, we could sit in the parlor," she said uncertainly. "I don't know what I could tell you. . . ."

She led him up a dim staircase and into an airless sitting room dominated by a horsehair sofa with carved feet. He had the impression of hulking furniture, crowded shelves, and clashing floral motifs. The wallpaper featured lilies; the pictures, tooled frames jammed together, offered lilacs and daffodils; the rugs were crowded with threadbare roses.

"You're very kind. I was wondering about the women who tried to join. They admire your work. I'd like to get their thoughts. Would you have their names and addresses?"

"Perhaps. . . ." She opened a delicate mahogany writing desk, produced a leather-bound ledger, and studied it for a moment. Suddenly she snapped it shut. "I don't think I wrote anything down. They made me so uncomfortable."

"Are you familiar with the Mourtone family?"

"No, I don't think so. Who are they? Why do you ask?"

"No reason. Just wondering. Can you describe any of these women for me? Where they came from, what they did?"

"I'm so nervous now, Mr. Greengrass. I'm not certain we want all this publicity." A key rattled in the lock. Alarmed, Miss Van Siclen started for the door. "That must be Julia now. She went for the veal."

"Is that Julia?" another woman's voice called. Shuffling into the living room, clutching the neck of her loose dressing gown, Mrs. Warner stopped dead in her tracks. “Who let this man in?”

Her hair loose, her features blurred by sleep, she appeared to have just risen from bed. She narrowed her eyes, scrutinizing Max as if she were trying to recall who he was.

“Yes. What are you doing here, Mr. Greengrass?” Mrs. Edwards’s voice was pure ice. Carrot tops peeked out of the bag she held to her tight bodice.

Did they live together? According to the bookseller, the Irving Place address belonged to Miss Van Siclen. Yet Mrs. Warner had been napping in her nightie while Mrs. Edwards had been out gathering food for dinner. Were they communards, utopians, an obscure sisterhood?

“He said you invited him,” Miss Van Siclen offered querulously, wringing her hands.

Max smiled benignly. “You mentioned new converts, Mrs. Edwards. I was curious about them.”

“Would you mind leaving the premises?”

“I was telling Miss Van Siclen that many of our readers are very much on your side. You could help your cause by giving me some more background. Do you ladies live together?”

Edwards put her bags down and advanced on him. “Our domestic arrangements are none of your business, Mr. Greengrass. A decent publication wouldn’t conjecture about private matters.”

“Conjecture? Certainly not. We always put the facts in the best possible light.”

Implacable, Edwards led him down a narrow hallway. Before they reached the stairs leading up to the front door, he noticed a large room, rather barren, scattered with straight-back red chairs turned toward a lectern. Did they give lectures on the premises as well?

“Please don’t call again.”

Light with excitement, he wended his way toward Fourteenth Street. He’d stumbled onto a whole new aspect of the Midnight Band, and he hungered to know more. How many women lived at the Irving Place address? Was it some sort of headquarters? Did they indoctrinate new recruits there?

Was Mrs. Edwards their leader and boss? What he wouldn't give to get his hands on Miss Van Siclen's record book.

There was no cry of "Rrrrags! Bo-ones!" Instead, the wagon rolled by silently, a floating ark of final things. Only at the last second did he catch sight of the driver, a mab with a gash of red for a mouth and the forearms of a stevedore. A woman running rags and bones? No, of course not. It was the same wise guy in a different faddish mask. The smear of a mouth leered. Then the wheels jumped the curb.

Mesmerized, Max was slow to react. Had the gray nag gone batty? Had the driver lost control? He edged away, but the wagon followed him, pressing him to the stoops, cutting him off. Before he saw the weapon, he heard it whoosh through the air.

The driver lumbered off his seat. In his hand, a stick barbed with a long nail whistled through the air. Max had seen this instrument a thousand times. The Junkman's Needle. It picked, it probed, it examined, it speared.

"Chickie, chickie," the heavy man muttered, swishing his implement at the reporter's throat. "Chickie, chickie."

He took a quick step toward the street, but the Needle singed his shoulder. Dancing away, he started in the direction of the wagon itself, thinking he could scuttle under the wheels and escape to the other side. A malevolent wand, the Needle sliced across his path. Backing away, he almost fell flat across a refuse barrel. Regaining his balance, he grabbed the leaky container in both hands and hurled it at his assailant. A shower of ash poured over both of them.

In the blinding grit, Max came in low and fast. Big men never frightened him. It was the light guys with their buzzsaw hands and quick footwork who could kill you. When Vinnie Avenoso cut him up at Harry Hill's, he never saw where the punches were coming from. The junkman was a plodding target. Ducking, Max pounded him in the gut with both hands, sinking a hard left hook into his assailant's underbelly. The heavy man sagged. Max planted and roundhoused one right into the junkman's kidneys.

With both hands he seized the Needle. Grappling, the two men fell to the sidewalk. Max held on for dear life, the junkard's bulk threatening to crush him flat. He heaved, pushed, and somehow slithered out from under the man's flabby weight. Rolling across the pavement, he felt the Needle tear into his coat. Momentarily he was pinned. In desperation he shed his jacket and managed to gain his footing again. The time for niceties had long passed. Putting his head down, he bulled inside under the whistling stick and delivered a well-placed low blow. Doubling over in pain, the junkard loosened his grip. Surging up, Max seized the weapon and jerked it out of his tormenter's hands.

Gasping, Max staggered back, unsure what to do next. Could he stab a defenseless man? Could he herd the hulking bastard to the nearest precinct house? How? Hunched and bearlike, the junkman scurried back to the wagon.

"I'll take your eyes out, you sonofabitch," Max swore.

But somehow both men knew he wasn't up to the killing game. The reins snapped. The tilted wagon rocked off the curb, built up speed, and clattered away. Without realizing it, Max had begun touching himself all over. He was still whole. Just barely. But the next junkard might do a better job. The next pack of street arabs might swarm him under for good. He had to protect himself, and his fists were a feeble solution.

Then a strange idea gripped him. He'd have to get his own name in the papers.

chapter eighteen

Perched on the edge of his desk, Police Superintendent Byrnes held a book at arm's length. He wore a salt-and-pepper suit and salmon gloves.

"Last page," he said, holding up a gloved index finger. Shifting on his feet, Max squinted to see the book's spine. *Dead Eye Dick in Coney Island* by someone named Wheeler. Byrnes kept a vast library of dime novels and loved to talk about their clever heroes.

Cooling his heels, he watched the police superintendent's bobbing mustache, an enormous affair that curtained his entire mouth. Invisible lips formed invisible words beneath Byrnes's twitching whiskers.

Max had seen the famed policeman dozens of times, though he'd never before penetrated Mulberry Street's inner sanctum. But, as he'd hoped, Bennett was outraged that a *Herald* man had been assaulted. Evidently Max's recent audience with the publisher had helped: at least Bennett knew who he was now. As soon as Max had spilled his story to Parnell, the publisher began burning up the wire to Byrnes's office.

The superintendent especially liked visitors to see him perusing Julian Hawthorne's potboilers. In these racy stories, a character named Chief Inspector Byrnes thrilled readers with his brilliance and bravery. With all due modesty, the real Inspector Byrnes always pointed out that Julian was the son of that other Hawthorne.

Then there was Old Cap Collier, the potboiler master, who described in *The Thugs of the Tenderloin* how a fictional character named Chief Inspector Byrnes had kept the crooked lawyer Flash Jack out of New York. Collier was, of course, another Byrnes favorite.

Every reporter in town knew the practical purpose of Byrnes's scholarship. Aside from basking in fiction's free publicity, Byrnes also lifted stratagems from these imaginary detectives, and to the naïve delight of his Wall Street patrons retold the invented cases, attributing to himself their dazzling insights. In fact, he strongly implied that the dime novelists fed off his actual experiences. How could second-rate scribblers imagine such intricate scenarios without help from the police inspector himself?

Finally Byrnes deigned to look up. "You're the reporter? What's your name, boyo?"

"Max Greengrass."

"Bennett's all bent out of shape, eh? Well, go ahead. Give me the rundown."

Quickly, Max recounted the attack, and for evidence produced the Junkman's Needle. Byrnes turned the implement over in his hands.

"Screwed in. Nice job. But there's ten thousand of these blasted things in town. What else?"

"He was wearing one of those rubber masks. You've seen them?"

"It's a damn plague. What the hell's the matter with people? Their own heads ain't good enough for them? Which one?"

"The streetwalker. The one with the yellow hair and the big red mouth? He was a heavy guy, about five-seven. Big forearms. Saggy gut on him."

Byrnes shifted in his chair like a man with a hidden itch. The inspector's dark eyebrows worked furiously, but Max didn't feel as intimidated as he'd expected. The papers had invented Byrnes the mastermind, the artist of the third degree. Max sensed something else, a small but vicious intelligence.

"So who has it in for you, boyo?"

Max had more than one theory, but he wasn't about to go off half-cocked, especially to the superintendent. "Beats me."

"Who do you owe? C'mon. I can find out anyway."

"Just a few bucks to Sim Addem. That's about it."

"Addem plays it straight. Ain't him. Will Bennett play this on his front page?"

Max was about to say the story might run on page five, but checked himself. Byrnes was testing the reporter's pull before he surrendered a single gilded quotation. "If you give our readers the benefit of your thinking, there's no doubt."

Byrnes made a show of examining the junkard's weapon. "Say this for me, boyo, these exact words. 'It is intolerable for a member of the press to be attacked in this unspeakable fashion. We will hold every rag-and-bone man in this city to account. But this is a complicated case. An extensive investigation will be necessary.'"

"I'd think so."

Byrnes coughed into his fist. "Max was scribbling notes in his shorthand. "'This isn't Chicago. We don't let cranks and anarchists run riot in our city. Reporters have a job to do, and we intend to offer them every protection in our power.'"

Concealing his satisfaction, Max carefully took down the inspector's every word. "Much appreciated."

"Well, between you, me, and the lampost, we don't have the manpower to follow you around, you understand that? You have something in your pocket, boyo?"

"What do you mean?"

"Protection, you greenhorn. There's somebody'd like to take your head off, it looks like."

"Sure. I've still got my mitts."

"Your mitts! That's rich. Put this in too. 'The Police Superintendent advocates a new ordinance against selling false faces. A man shouldn't be allowed to parade around the streets pretending he's somebody else.'"

"Sucking up to Byrnes, are you?" Stan Parnell cracked, running his bleary eyes over Max's notes.

"Did I lay it on too thick?"

"Not necessarily. So, this character jumped you out of the blue?"

"I don't think so. He didn't bother going for my money."

"Bennett's in a twist. Takes it personally. Well, you can't write the thing yourself. I'll put it together. This one might have legs. Can you get yourself beat up again?"

The thinnest of smiles played on Parnell's lips. For the first time Max felt his editor's chilly affection. Inspired, he replied, "I'll do my damnedest."

"I'll bet you will. Okay, this is what I need from you."

He submitted to the interview, all the while observing Parnell's crisp, clinical approach.

"By the way, Nick Biddle's covering the Edwards trial, but Bennett wants you to work the crowd for color."

He was about to protest that *he* had developed the Midnight Band story and that Biddle would miss the nuances, but he bit his tongue. Nick Biddle always covered Howe's trials.

"Sure. I'll talk to him."

How could Biddle do the trial justice? Max knew how the women walked and talked, the shape of their smothering baskets and the way they justified their crusade. He'd seen their haunts and listened to their rants. He wondered if he could talk the old reporter out of the assignment or buy him off with some good whiskey.

He needed some air. It wasn't until he had done a complete turn in City Hall Park that he remembered Martin's funeral. It must have ended hours ago, he realized. What could he possibly say to Gretta? The truth ought to suffice. How could he have escaped the rush of events or his duty to the paper? She would have to understand.

Before supper, while Mrs. DeVogt was busy in the kitchen, Gretta dragged him into her room. "Where were you? How could you leave me high and dry like that?"

"I couldn't help—"

Her anger flashing, she cut him off. "I had to sit there by myself, listening to a bunch of platitudes and lies. It was disgusting!"

He tried to explain himself. "I'm sorry, but I was covering—"

Lost in her own world, she didn't hear him. "You should have heard Reverend Weems going on about Martin's vocation. Why did they have to say how much he cared for his job, and babble about his good works?"

"I was down at headquarters—"

"Why should I ever believe you again?"

She had good reason to lash out at him, she thought, but he looked so bereft, she wished she could take her words back. But he was also staring at her in that hungry way. What was she? A tasty piece of pork sausage? She wasn't above reveling in her beauty, but she didn't have a dime, or any prospects for that matter now that Martin was gone. Yet sometimes she wished she were as plain as a schoolmarm and free of the men who always buzzed about her.

She hated the unbending tone of her own voice. Didn't she sound exactly like her mother?

He groped for a small exaggeration. "I was almost killed, today . . ."

His words finally broke through to her. "What? How . . . oh, that's awful. How do you feel? I could get you something."

"No, not at all . . . It turned out to be a nice item. Might be page one."

His attempt to make light of the attack fell flat.

She bristled. "Is that all you care about? You were almost murdered, and you're babbling about page this and page that?"

He hated to keep apologizing to her. What could she possibly know? How could she understand that his life-and-death struggle was with words? "Sorry, it's an occupational disease. What do you mean about Martin's good works?"

"It was all mixed up. The Reverend Weems seems to believe that insurance companies are altruistic institutions and that by selling policies Martin was a sort of missionary. I suppose the family put the words in his mouth."

"What sort of insurance was Martin selling? I mean, his clientele could barely afford to feed themselves."

"That's what I always wondered. It had something to do with burial costs, I think. He told me that the poorest of the poor would do anything to keep out of the Potter's Field. Isn't that awful? I mean, to take advantage of people's fears and pocket their last pennies? I think that's why he was so repelled."

"There must be more than pennies in it."

He was so persistent, she could have strangled him. Yet he could be useful, couldn't he? Didn't their respective interests dovetail? He wanted to dig up his grubby story; she wanted to attend the execution of the monster who had taken Martin away from her. Was it true that one could hear the neck crack if the crowd stayed quiet? She could make plates of the condemned man climbing the scaffold; the executioner's expression; the crowd's reaction, face by gleeful face. What sort of woman had these thoughts? How could she ever reveal her savage side to a man?

She collected herself. "Oh, evidently. Mr. Mourtone thought the whole thing up. That's how he became president of the company to begin with. Martin always said it was too boring to explain, but his father found a way to increase profits quite a bit by selling this sort of policy."

It was all he could do to keep his mind on the discussion. If he could just reach out and stroke her cheek. . . .

"What is there to smile about?"

"Nothing, nothing. . . ." He flushed, but chattered on. "What exactly did Weems say about Martin's charity?"

"That was what kept bothering me. Why did they have to make a point of lying about how much Martin liked what he was doing or that it was some kind of noble calling, when Martin always told me the exact opposite?"

"They were selling—"

She cut him off. "That's exactly what it felt like. An advertising campaign. Not a funeral at all. He claimed Martin helped out at some sort of church mission."

"You knew about that?"

"Martin had a good heart, but it didn't include settlement houses. The eulogy wasn't about Martin. Not really."

"There are ghostwriters for these preachers. I once knew a reporter who picked up some extra coin every weekend."

"How charming." She opened her door for him to leave.

In some obscure way he'd offended her again, but for the life of him he couldn't put his finger on it. She might manipulate him to satisfy her morbid curiosity about Martin, she might even think of him as a friend in a bloodless sort of way. But the idea of a Hebrew lover was probably beyond her. Why was he banging his head against a stone wall? The city was swarming with gorgeous birds who would appreciate him. He was doing her favor after favor, and she was still condescending to him. No, it was more complicated than that. Out in Staten Island she'd been so different, simple and responsive. In the city she became all manners.

But how fair was he being to her? Mourtone wasn't even dust yet. Why shouldn't she protect herself? Didn't she have reason to be irritated with him? He'd left her high and dry at the funeral. Still, in his prickly heart of hearts, he resented her dismissive tone. He longed for her, but he wanted to retaliate too.

He lay on his bed, staring at the ceiling, making himself go as blank as the sweep of plaster above him, but he couldn't blind his mind's eye. He thought of her full mouth, her delicate throat, her body freed from whalebone and laces. He dreamed the shock of her lips. He ached for her.

He had to get out of the house.

His nose in the *Police Gazette,* Officer Schreiber was lounging in Mrs. Jabonne's vestibule.

"How's tricks, Maxie?" Schreiber brightened, tossing the pink pages aside. "Moonlighting, huh?"

"When you got six kids, you'll need the extra chink, too."

Max knew the setup. "Well, keep the pantata out of this one."

Schreiber folded the *Gazette* and yawned. "What, are you kidding? The captain put me in the way of this thing. Watch out. Minnie's in a lousy mood."

With its stuffed silk pillows, its gilded mirrors and electric lamps, Mrs. Jabonne's could have been mistaken for an upper-middle-class drawing room. The clientele included a jowly man in a new sack suit, a hayseed with a wispy fringe of a beard, and a pale man whose popping eyes suggested a thyroid condition.

Mrs. Jabonne's girls clustered on straight-backed chairs that faced the expectant clients. A tall woman in a filmy peignoir crossed her legs and dangled a gold shoe from her toe. Next to her, a mab in a highly modified Mother Hubbard caught Max's eye. A barely pubescent Italian with unmarked smooth skin had pinned a giant blue bow in her hair. The effect was unfortunate. All desire drained out of him.

A salmon-colored derby on the back of his head, a song plugger pounded on the upright piano. The women whispered in each other's ears, casting contemptuous looks at the night's pickings. The sack suit tried a smile, but it faded fast enough. Legs pumping, a cigar mashed in his mouth, the piano player sang in a good-natured growl.

Where'd you get that hat?
Where'd you get that tile?
Isn't it a dandy one?
And just the latest style.
How'd you like to have one
Just the same as that?
When I go out
The boys all shout
"Where'd you get that hat?"

Minnie Jabonne wandered through the room, pecking one customer on the forehead, issuing sub-rosa orders to the working girls, kneading the plugger's shoulders. Despite some extra pounds, she swung her hips like a woman used to being admired.

"Max, where've you been hiding?" She took his arm and led him to her bottles. "How 'bout a sour?" Before he could answer, she stood on tiptoes and whispered in his ear. "Mum about your newspaper. My customers, they get nerves."

"Sure, Minnie. Got any rye?"

Then his eye fell on a woman in the corner who appeared to be hiding. For a moment his heart stopped. Could it be? An Irish girl with an appealing open face and straw-colored hair, she looked just like his first girlfriend, Nora. But it was impossible. Nora would be years older than this slip of a girl.

"What's your name," he asked, just to hear her voice.

"C'mon, Maggie, show yourself to the gentleman," Minnie said.

"Margaret," she replied, turning in a full circle to show off her trim body.

Her diffident, familiar voice shook him. In the bedroom, whose amenities included a bed, a table, and a light globe, the illusion persisted. She had small breasts, one larger than the other, and hips wider than he'd expected. So much like Nora's. He tried not to be too coarse. In the end, he was carried away more by the memory of desire than passion itself.

The tiny apartment he and Nora had shared for two months. The sweet, unbearable secrecy. What else did he recall? Mad walks along the East River. Breakfasts at the greasy Suffolk Street café. Day-old bread, eggs cooked in bacon grease, plum blossoms in a beer bottle. Quick, moody Nora with her washed-out blue eyes. He used to lie on his back beneath the yellow shower of her hair.

A drunken teamster lurched out of a corner bar. Iron wheels rattled over paving stones. A dank mist blew in off the river. The heehawing of the last drink, the weary strains of the last tune leaked out into the streets.

Max hunched forward into the wind. His throat felt raw. Without breaking stride, he coughed up the evening's joys and spit them out onto the sidewalk. Booze. Smoke. Digestive juices. Fickle passion. Already forgotten.

Up close, the girl had looked nothing like Nora, but the illusion had persisted long enough for memory to hollow him out. He was twenty-five now, a quarter of a century old. His heart clenched at the number. What was time? A substance? An idea? A force? Speed itself? He could sense nothing but its utter indifference. Under the sheets in his own bed, dry-mouthed and dizzy, he felt himself hurtling into the darkness. When he reached out across the bed, he shaped Gretta out of empty air.

chapter nineteen

On his way to work Max picked up the *Herald* from a newsboy, and there it was, second column, upper left. With Bennett urging him on, Parnell had really gone to town. Scooting through the dark brigade of commuters, Max leaned against a peeling sign that demanded BUY FELS NAPHTHA. Though he barely recognized the figure at the center of the article, he smiled in satisfaction at the paper's baroque exaggerations. Bennett must have had a hand in crafting the prose.

HERALD REPORTER ASSAULTED

Cruel Attack by Junkard
Suspect Still at Large
***Herald* Man Puts Up Game Fight**

An unprovoked attack on a *Herald* reporter took place yesterday in broad daylight on Irving Place just north of East Fourteenth Street. Max Greengrass related to the paper's management that a junk wagon cornered him on the sidewalk, and the driver attempted to spear him with a weapon known in low circles as the Junkman's Needle. Quite a tussle ensued, giving the doughty Greengrass ample opportunity to display his fistic talents.

A former lightweight boxer with numerous notches in his belt, Greengrass managed to disarm his much larger attacker and pummel him into

> submission. Recondite scholars of the manly art still recall Greengrass's lightning handiwork, which he put on display more than once in exhibitions at Harry Hill's boxing emporium.

Max was laughing so hard, he had to lean against a wall. He had taken pains to point out how brief and disastrous his pugilistic career had been and how easy it was to deflate a slow-moving gasbag like the rag-and-bone man. Unfortunately, his real record wouldn't have redounded to the *Herald*'s greater glory. He read on.

> The *Herald*'s publisher, William Bennett, Jr., said, "We consider this cowardly attack an assault on freedom of speech itself. The *Herald* will not be intimidated or silenced, and we hope that Police Superintendent Byrnes will use every resource at his command to apprehend this vicious criminal."
>
> Greengrass was at a loss to explain the incident. "There have been no threats against my person until now, but I'm certainly going to be on my guard in the future."

The piece went on to quote Byrnes, then the outraged Bennett a second time. Max couldn't have asked for more. At least his assailants—he assumed the junkard had been acting on someone else's authority—would hear that he was under the police superintendent's wing. If nothing else, the illusion of Byrnes's omnipotence would provide some protection. He was also enough of a newsman to believe that placing his name in print had a mystical effect. The *Herald*'s typeface was his shield. Double-minded, he nursed this delusion to the hilt, never forgetting that it was pure self-deception. Every knot of street arabs stopped his heart; every rag-and-bone wagon closed his throat. But a countercurrent ran through him too. Damn the bastards if they thought he'd show an ounce of fear.

He took in the rest of the news on the ride downtown.

President Cleveland's doctor was putting him on a diet of mutton and beef and exhorting him to cease his daily exercises. Mayor Gilroy asserted that New York was wealthier than ever because it owed less than ever before. Credit was growing ever tighter, putting Wall Street in a sour mood.

The Reverend Weems had given a sensational sermon entitled "Rulers of Tomorrow?" in which he claimed that brothels were causing a plague of illegitimacy. "While white slaves often turn to abortion, many of these crude procedures fail. Others are rightly afraid of the barbaric methods available to them and carry to term. The issue of these desperate creatures are the citizens of the future. Considering that we each receive at birth our national character and intellect, and our physical attributes as well, I fear for our city. The legions of pinheads and epileptics are growing day by day. Open your eyes. The day will come when all the saving societies of all the churches will be as nothing before the tide."

The *Herald* had already called the Reverend Weems "morbidly obsessed with lurid subjects." The *World* speculated that the minister had a taste for smut himself. But as an ally of the Reverend Parkhurst, who claimed that his crusade against sporting resorts was a way of exposing police corruption, Weems had a respectable following. He also sold newspapers.

Max smiled. Evidently the good minister had not studied the economic advantages of operating a parlor house with steady business. Sim Addem had once laid out the figures for him. A Tenderloin landlord could realize over $40,000 a year from a single brothel, a considerable sum despite the protection fee—fifty dollars a day—that went into Captain Clubber Williams's pocket. The will to evict the ancient evil wilted before such fine returns.

Climbing the stairs to the newsroom, he ran smack into the departing Biddle. "Sleeping one off, Greengrass?"

"That obvious?"

"We've got a date in court, remember?" The reporter tapped Max on the head with his cane and smiled. "You've never seen Willy in action, have you?"

"Willy?"

"Howe and Hummel took the case. You didn't know that?"

"Not for sure, but I did see Hummel talking to Edwards at the courthouse. . . . I feel like a third wheel, actually. Parnell wants me to tag along with you and do color."

"Fine! You can sit on your hands and watch the show."

"This case isn't exactly Howe and Hummel's meat, is it?"

"Not only that. They're appearing *pro bono*. Who knows? It won't be too arduous. They usually break early for lunch."

Max wondered whether he had made a grave error in treating Biddle that first time. Now the old roué expected him to fork over every time they met. Still, he'd be able to confront Howe at the courthouse and ask him how he had manufactured one corpse and retrieved another out of thin air. Not to speak of his possible connections to enemies of the free press.

Despite his age, Biddle wove in and out of the sidewalk traffic at a mad pace. Max scurried to keep up. "It doesn't make sense, does it? I mean, reform ladies aren't their usual clientele, are they?"

Biddle stopped in his tracks and gave Max the once-over. "Don't make assumptions. Little Abie may have figured out a way to make charity pay." A violent cough seized Biddle, who produced a stained handkerchief to wipe his mouth. "I'll catch the white lung soon . . . We'll keep a close eye on them."

"They'll both appear?"

"I understand Willy will do the opening and closing statements, but Abie will cross-examine. Working from their strengths, you see?"

"It seems like a small case to spend so many resources on."

"It does, it does," Biddle reflected.

At least Howe couldn't dodge him any more. Why had he sent Max to the brewery to begin with? To intimidate him? No doubt the lawyer would claim ignorance about misleading him, and bafflement as to who in the world might want to do Max harm; but as a reporter he wanted to hear Howe's denials with his own ears.

Max had only seen William H. Howe in his office. In the courtroom, the attorney cut a much grander figure, his leonine head, his inflamed complexion, his piercing eyes, his copious gray walrus mustache, his lightly carried girth all suggesting an opera star more than a lawyer. Mrs. Edwards sat quietly, folded hands resting on the defense table. Seated behind her, gripping the rail that separated them, the subservient Miss Van Siclen stared straight ahead.

Also close by, a pair of scrubbed children, a boy in a brass-buttoned sailor suit and a girl in a high-waisted dress, swung their legs. Bored, the boy called out "Momma," but Howe flashed an avuncular smile and quieted him down. For some reason Max had assumed Mrs. Edwards was a childless widow. Perhaps her husband was looking on in the crowded chamber. That she might be sharing quarters with Miss Van Siclen and Mrs. Warner suddenly seemed less likely.

In deference to the court, and perhaps to harmonize with his austere client, Howe wore a rich brown suit and only a few diamonds on his chubby fingers. As the jury pool filed in, he kept up a light patter with the judge, the court officers, the gallery, creating a warm response from every corner of the chamber.

A rickety but sharp-tongued jurist, the Honorable Harry Thompson, presided.

Max amused himself by trying to guess each juror's vocation. One might be a mechanic, another a city bureaucrat, a third a commercial clerk. He wondered if Howe would dismiss a dark Syrian in a threadbare suit, or the plump Jew. One man's long, narrow Scandinavian face had a hangman's aspect. Did all the fashionable talk about national character affect the lawyer's thinking? Did he prefer one race to another to sit in judgment? Or did he focus on which ones had the best suits of clothes, which displayed the mannerisms of religious zealotry, which had ties to Tammany?

Howe's pacing focused all eyes on him, and Max felt a rising sense of anticipation. Once the jury box had been filled, the lawyer wandered over to the defense table and picked up a newspaper. With elaborate care, he rolled it up so that no one could read its headlines, or even tell which daily he held in his hand. The courtroom fell silent as he slapped the paper over and over against his leg.

Turning to address the prospective jurors, he smiled, his warmth embracing them, gathering them into his confidence. "I am sure that you intend to discharge your duty with open minds, but in our society these days we are constantly assailed by pernicious influences."

Fearing what was coming next, Max strained to make out the rolled-up daily's masthead.

"A person of the highest respectability may be blackened," Howe continued, slapping the newspaper rhythmically now, "smeared, mocked, held up to scorn, his reputation torn to shreds, libeled with impunity. Imagine that your name was suddenly printed in tall letters on the front page of a scandal sheet that millions relished with their coffee and hotcakes every morning? You with your hard-working spouse, your devoted children. How could you fight back against such a tremendous force? The answer is, you couldn't. You'd be shunned by your neighbors, ostracized at work, ruffians would taunt your little boy at school every day. There would be no escape, no defense."

With agonized care he unrolled the *Herald* he had been clutching and then slowly, holding it up, paraded back and forth before the jury box. Pausing, he set his massive jaw and stared furiously at Max, who did his best to remain frozen, fearing that his slightest reaction would reveal his identity to everyone.

Quoting from "POORER CLASSES STARVE CATS," Howe's tone dripped with sarcasm. "The reporter refers to my client's so-called 'ghoulish career.' She has spent a lifetime in philanthropy, and he sniggers that she crawls around in basements. What sort of vile, bottom-feeding crab would poison the public mind like this? So I ask only one question. Have any of you prospective jurors seen this newspaper headline?"

Max's head was spinning. Howe's attack was so forceful he wondered if he'd committed some heinous crime without quite knowing it. Of course the attorney's charges were ridiculous. He'd been reporting a story and had gotten his facts straight, too. Yet, wasn't there a kernel of truth in Howe's indictment?

Max could sense, in his own moral vertigo, William H. Howe's genius.

Several hands shot up. Howe shook his head in deep sadness. "Your Honor, may I approach the bench?"

Quickly, the judge dismissed Howe's intended targets. Each time the jury box refilled, Howe held up the offending headlines and weeded out the *Herald*'s faithful. Each time he glared furiously at Max, who would have been happy to slink out of the courtroom and disappear forever. By the time Howe had exhausted his challenges, he had built a jury filled with *Tribune, Times,* or *World* readers, or those who read nothing at all. Even Pulitzer's rag had shown more sympathy for Mrs. Edwards than the *Herald.*

"He's manipulated their minds nicely, don't you think?" Biddle whispered.

"You mean the ones who are left?" Keeping an eye on Howe, Max rose from his seat, determined to cut him off before he escaped the courtroom.

"Exactly. They think you've crucified her, you heartless bastard."

Max never felt entirely comfortable when crucifixion came up, especially when he was accused of pounding the nails. He managed a strained laugh.

"Well, let's fly. Time for lunch!" Nick announced.

Max already saw Biddle scavenging the menu for the most expensive wines, the milk-fed veal, the rum-soaked cakes. How could he say no? It was impossible. Why didn't the old operator just turn him upside-down and shake the coins out of his pocket? He could filch all of Max's money that way and skip the preliminaries.

"Do you have a fever? Let's go! Willy's taking us to Pontin's. He always pays!"

chapter twenty

In William H. Howe's wake, the party threaded through Pontin's crowded tables of judges, lawyers, well-connected felons, and the rest of the legal system's upper echelons. Of course, Howe and Hummel only dined in their back-room domain. This chamber contained two tables, one always reserved for the partners. There, between courses, the two lawyers split cash receipts for which they kept no records.

A group of distinguished-looking men in high collars filled the second table. The buoyant Howe greeted them as he passed by.

"Judge, judge, judge, judge," Howe called out gaily.

"Judge, judge, judge," the more reserved Hummel lisped.

"How's your back, Harry?" Howe inquired.

The Honorable Harry Thompson craned his neck, looked over at the boat-sized Howe and cackled. "As nasty as yours, Bill. But no worse."

Howe snatched a bottle of wine from the old jurist's table and squinted at its label. "A good grape. I've had it." He patted Thompson on the back, returned the bottle and sailed on.

After the four men sat down, Howe leaned over to his guests and whispered, "Remarkable. The entire Second Circuit, plus Harry. Usually a few are missing."

"Very handy," the poker-faced Hummel added. Seated next to Howe, his shoulders impossibly narrow, Hummel looked like a child with a middle-aged-man's head.

How could Max fail to be impressed? He had penetrated the inner sanctum. What inside deals had been orchestrated right at this table? Tammany masters Kelly and Croker must have consulted here over hors d'oeuvres. Howe may have wined and dined Bennett or Barrymore in this very room.

Both men, it was rumored, had received Howe and Hummel subpoenas in defense of chorus-girl honor, and each continued to employ the firm anyway. Nick Biddle insisted that Hummel always acted with perfect honor in these cases, never suing the same victim twice. That the firm preyed on its own clients was one thing, but the lawyers' sense of fun in the act spoke to their genius. That the clients stayed loyal to their extortionists only added to Howe and Hummel's glory.

Certainly, Howe had entertained Police Superintendent Byrnes regularly at Pontin's. Think of the tips, the secretive chats, the riches of gossip, stories, and piquant details Howe might offer up if Max gained his good graces. William H. Howe wasn't *a* source, he was *the* ultimate source: instigator, defender, and raw appetite combined. His labored breathing reminded Max of a steam engine chugging into an El station. His shrewd eyes, set in pockets of fat, recalled a faro dealer's. His gentle smiles brought to mind the settlement-house idealist. His faint Cockney accent suggested his murky past.

Max couldn't take his eyes off the man's endlessly shifting features. What he wouldn't give to discover the real story of William H. Howe. Had he been a doctor in England, as rumor had it? Was he a former convict? Or were his British inflections an affectation covering low domestic origins?

A flunky in a cutaway came by offering fine cigars. Biddle snatched two. Long-toothed, his limp gray hair yellowing, the old reporter looked more unhealthy than ever.

Howe snapped his fingers and quickly ordered two bottles of Rhine wine. "Send Judge Thompson another bottle too, eh?" Without missing a beat, he went on. "Ah, Norwegian anchovies, very nice for an appetizer. Abie, they've got your Broiled Kingfish. I recommend the Timbal of Blackcock, comes with a chestnut puree. Ohhh, Spring Lamb with mint sauce. Hard to turn that down, eh? Keep an eye on Abie, make sure he doesn't stuff himself."

After their first glass, Biddle said, "You may have been too clever by half in there, Willy."

Max, who had been surrendering to the sweet vintage, snapped to attention.

"How so?" Howe propped his bull's head up on his fist and waited attentively.

"Well, for one thing, one or two of our faithful *Herald* readers might have slipped into the jury anyway, but they weren't going to admit it. You left a mick there who's a nice bet. Face like the map of Ireland. Now that he's on the jury, he's got it in for you because he thinks you're talking down to him. He likes our headlines, and he doesn't want some bloviating lawyer preaching him the gospel."

"You may have a point," Howe mused. "But I think you're mistaken. Whoever saw my client so unjustly pilloried in your paper," he argued, offering Max a conspiratorial smile, "will want to prove how unbiased he is, and therefore bend over backwards in favor of Mrs. Edwards."

"We'll turn 'em," Hummel added.

"Wait for Abie's cross-examination. He's a rat catcher if there ever was one. By the way, Mr. Greengrass, I'd like to apologize for being so inaccessible. I did get your notes. We're just drowning in cases, and I like to go home and see my little daughter once in a blue moon. My family is my religion."

Max hadn't considered Howe's sacred family life. "I know how busy you are."

"Nick says you're a comer."

Was that why he'd been invited? So that the lawyers could weigh his potential? Howe's inflated face floated before him, filling his field of vision. Max flushed. "Nick's the authority."

From the attorney's perspective, he imagined, he'd already demonstrated his receptivity. He'd taken the money from Mourtone, and he'd followed Howe's directions and found the Negro in the barrel. He probably looked like a good investment. Was he? Did he know himself?

Ashes streaked the rheumy-eyed Biddle's lapels. Was Max gazing at his own future? A wash of bile scorched the back of his throat. At the same time, Howe mesmerized him. If he penetrated the lawyer's secrets, wouldn't he gain some special, almost mystical knowledge of the city's soul? This corrupt, life-loving, murderous, charming, deceptive monster, comic and tragedian rolled into one, was New York itself.

"Willy has a cottage in the country," Biddle put in.

"When the Metropolitan extends the line to the wilds of Yonkers, I may be able to get home at night."

Taken aback, Max wrestled with the idea of the ruddy-faced Howe, who was built for roaring in concert saloons, being attached to a wife and child.

The lawyer continued with thick sincerity. "At any rate, I'm sorry my contact gave you such poor information. I'm sure you know the matter's settled now."

Max assumed that "the matter' included Martin's funeral. This was the way it was done. Howe could blow him off for the price of a meal. How could he interrogate the attorney in public, especially while accepting his largesse? What could he say, anyway? Martin had died somewhere or other, and been buried a plaster saint. And Max had banked Mourtone's five hundred, however queasy it made him feel. Still, he didn't want to surrender so easily.

"I heard the eulogy was a big hit."

Howe shot Max an avid look. "The Reverend Weems is a talented man."

"It's a big town. Was it so easy to turn up the lost article?"

Howe's eyes were shining now. He was thoroughly enjoying the interrogation. "I hear Superintendent Byrnes can find a pearl in an outhouse."

"There was the matter of the barrel. I don't suppose Byrnes is pursuing that, is he?"

Tacitly, Howe accepted Max's assumption. "What can he do when he has so little to work with?"

At least they'd settled that matter. Byrnes wouldn't investigate, which made the Negro's murder all the more compelling. "And he's busy with Junior Gould's tips, too." Byrnes had been close to the Goulds, arch stock manipulators, for years.

The lawyer was beaming openly at him now, and he couldn't help feeling that he'd passed some obscure examination.

Howe's Lobster Victoria arrived, and he fell to it. Cutlery flashed and for a while the lawyer forgot philosophy. Biddle ate with his face close to the plate, while Hummel demonstrated a slashing attack, putting away far more of his kingfish than Max had expected.

During a pause between courses, Biddle said, "I never saw you work both sides of the street like this, Willy."

"How do you mean?"

"Nick means," Hummel interjected, aiming a fork at Biddle's throat, "that we don't usually represent his sort of people."

Biddle turned pale. In a placating tone, he said, "Not at all, Abe. Just making a joke."

Could Hummel, with his slight body and immobile features, be the firm's true power? As a nine-year-old boy, he had made his first dollar selling water to Union Army soldiers bivouacked in Tompkins Square Park. He had hawked potatoes, oranges, and neckties to stay alive before Howe took him in as an office boy. Yet in a few years he was practicing law, and in no time he had become a full partner.

"I may employ a few sharp practices," Hummel allowed, pulling up his sleeves to display brilliant shirt cuffs. "But I'm a clean sonofabitch."

Hummel's white line of a mouth gave nothing away. He could be joking, he could be making a threat.

"The street has no sides, Nick," Howe interceded. "That's strictly an illusion. Christian love binds us all."

They cruised through the entrees, the legumes, the rotis—Max chose a delicious roast capon—and finished off with entremets, Baba Au Rhum, Genoises Glacees, and Amandine Souvenirs. Cheese, fruit, and demitasse rounded out the fare.

By the time Howe announced their departure, even Max, with his ferocious appetite, could barely move. His host demonstrated far more stamina, however. Sprinkling water on his face, then patting his high flush down with a cloth napkin, Howe led the way down the sidewalk.

"Opening statements, gentlemen!"

chapter twenty-one

Howe began by talking about horses.

"Ladies and gentlemen of the jury, once upon a time on the streets of our city, day after day, we witnessed cruelty in the person of helpless beasts that were whipped, beaten, overloaded, and left out all night in the elements. More often than not, their owners, brutes of the lowest order, neglected to feed and water their animals. These tormented creatures hauled thousands of pounds of our goods and carried us around without complaint, but when they died on their feet, when their corpses grew fat at our curbsides, we barely noticed. We didn't know how to see them." Howe paused.

"What the hell is he talking about?" Max whispered to Biddle.

"He'll get there, don't worry."

During the long pause, several jurors shifted to the edges of their seats.

"We didn't know how to see them, and we felt no shame until a single man came along to open our eyes. You've heard of that man, Henry Bergh, a well-off gentleman who might have spent his life clipping coupons and drinking champagne. Instead, he looked around him and saw dumb beasts in a world of pain. And from that moment on, for twenty-five years, he gave them a voice." Howe's voice fell to a theatrical whisper. "And what did these inarticulate creatures say?"

Pausing, the attorney scanned the jury. Immobile, eyes wide, they gaped at him.

"They said, 'We are cold, give us shelter.' They said, 'We are hungry, give us clean food.' They said, 'We are sick, give us doctors.' They said, 'We are old, let us rest.' Henry Bergh didn't rest. He wrote letters to the great publications. He gave speeches. He raised funds. He went up to Albany to argue with legislators. He founded a great organization we take for granted nowadays, the ASPCA."

Though Max knew quite well that Howe was giving a performance, he was moved anyway. In fact, he could barely stand looking at the straining crosstown horsecar teams himself. Their bulging eyes, their sucking, desperate breathing transfixed him.

"In Mr. Bergh's waning years," Howe went on ruefully, "my client, Mrs. Edwards, worked at his side."

Biddle nudged Max with his cane.

"And now she stands charged with committing the same acts of humanity that made Mr. Bergh so revered in our city. He is gone now, but Mrs. Edwards and her friends have taken up his tattered banner. For this, the authorities have cast this dedicated, respectable woman into the Tombs."

Flinging his arm out in a sudden, violent gesture, Howe cast his client into that celebrated torture chamber. Her chin lifted, Mrs. Edwards didn't move a muscle. Howe had already carved her statue. Max gazed around the courtroom. Several women—cat lovers, no doubt—were crying softly. How could a man who believed so little make his audience care so much?

Assistant District Attorney Williams, a husky young man in steel-rimmed glasses, rose to parry Howe's remarks. His modest demeanor stood in such stark contrast to the lawyer's melodramatic performance that it acted as a silent rebuke.

"Counsel has made a brilliant beginning. No doubt he has tugged at your heartstrings, a skill for which he is highly compensated. What is fascinating about his presentation, however, is everything he left out. Conveniently, he overlooked his client's three thousand crimes."

Williams paused, fiddled with his glasses, stared down at the floorboards, his distaste palpable. "You look shocked, but the number is by her own admission. Relentless and unfeeling, she has waged a campaign to snuff out the lives of innocent animals all over town. Particularly the cats of citizens least able to defend them. Mrs. Edwards has the funds to hire expensive lawyers. The people have only their public servants, but I intend to show highly documented cases of this woman's illegal actions and wanton cruelty."

"He's got some talent," Biddle commented after Williams completed his opening statement.

Howe, who had shaken his head sadly several times during his adversary's argument, rose to make a request.

"Your Honor, if the court pleases, I would like to add the Reverend Weems to my list of character witnesses."

"Any objection, Mr. Williams?"

Evidently already apprised of Howe's move, Williams parried. "Mrs. Edwards's cousin? None, Your Honor. If I may introduce my first witness?"

"*That* Weems?" Max asked Biddle.

The old reporter's laughter turned into a fit of coughing.

"Are you all right?"

"It's nothing, nothing. What do you say? These damn goo-goos are all related!"

Assistant District Attorney Williams presented a straightforward case. First, he called Officer Connolly, the arresting officer. A bluff man with hazel eyes and a golden brown moustache, he appeared in a freshly ironed uniform, shirt and tie. A courtroom veteran, he marched to the witness box and arranged himself in a military posture.

The district attorney quickly established the facts.

"Officer, is it your understanding that it is unlawful and unjustifiable to kill dumb animals without provocation?"

"It is, sir."

"And when did you first see the accused on the night in question?"

"I seen her at the corner of Eighth and 136th Street pickin' up a cat."

"And what did you observe?"

"She grabbed this cat by the scruff of the neck, and she went and smothered it with a rag. Then she—"

Hummel shot to his feet. "Speculation by the witness, Your Honor."

"How so, counselor?" the judge inquired.

In a penetrating nasal voice, Hummel argued: "From that distance, the witness could not have known the animal was being smothered. Cats get colds. My client might have been wiping its nose."

A juror burst out laughing, then covered his mouth.

"Sustained. Rephrase your question, Mr. Williams."

"Yes, Your Honor," Williams said, with a curt bow. "After the accused picked the cat up, she covered its face with a rag, did she not?"

"Yes, sir."

"And she held the rag over the animal's face for some time?"

"A minute, maybe."

"And would you show the jury what she did with her hands then?"

"Yes. What she did, see, is she snapped the head back like that." Connolly mimed the neck-wringing to great effect. Several jurors turned their faces away.

"Did you question her?"

"Yes, sir. I followed her around the corner, and I saw her go into this alley here, so I stood there, and when she comes out I asks her what she thinks she's doing, don't she know it's against the law."

"Did she reply?"

"Yes, sir. She said she was the member of some kind of society, but I never heard of it, so she says I'm slow."

"Slow?"

"Yeah, thick. She can have her opinion. She says she knows her business and to leave her alone. So I asks her what's in her basket, and she shows me three more dead animals, and it stinks to high heaven in there. Some kinda gas. Chloro . . . chloroform, I think."

A clumsy actor, Connolly couldn't hide the DA's coaching.

Hummel raised himself to his full five feet, one inch again. "Objection! Calls for a conclusion by the witness, Your Honor."

"I'll lay the foundation, Your Honor," Williams replied.

"Proceed."

"Officer Connolly, would you please tell the jury when you previously smelled chloroform?"

"The other day, my wife was going through her medicine chest. She broke a bottle in the sink."

"And she showed you the label?"

"Yes, sir."

"Did Mrs. Edwards's rag smell the same way?"

"Yes, sir."

This convenient coincidence lowered Max's opinion of Williams a bit, but he doubted the jurors would question it.

Opening his cross-examination, Hummel stood before the witness and gazed up and down, appraising him. Then he pounced. "Officer Connolly, are you a doctor?"

"No, sir."

"A pharmacist?"

"No, sir."

"A medical student?"

"No, sir."

"An undertaker?"

The jury tittered.

"No, sir."

"Can you smell my cologne?" The gnomish Hummel stepped within sniffing distance.

"Objection, Your Honor! Counsel's question has no relevance."

"His direction is quite apparent, Mr. Williams," the judge replied. "Proceed."

"I repeat, can you smell my cologne? I am only three paces from you, Officer Connolly."

"A little," the policeman admitted grudgingly.

"A little? What sort of bloodhound are you? For the record, Your Honor, for medical reasons I am unable to use any of the French water. I break out in blisters."

From the back of the chamber came muffled laughter.

"I'm sorry to hear that, Mr. Hummel," the jurist remarked sympathetically.

"Thank you, Your Honor. Now, Officer Connolly, was the cat Mrs. Edwards handled emaciated?"

"I don't know."

"Do you understand what I mean?"

"No, sir."

"Well, was it thin, like a vagrant?"

"It was a good-sized cat." A belligerent note crept into Officer Connolly's voice.

"You have seen a good many vagrant cats?"

Eyes narrowing, Connolly shifted to the edge of his seat. "Yes, but this one was not like that. They're thin and starved."

"What color was it?"

"White, with black spots."

"Was it a wet night?"

Pausing, the policeman looked at Hummel with an irritated expression. "Well, there was some rain."

"Dry rain, I suppose. Dismissed."

Glaring at the tiny lawyer, Connolly stepped down.

"Destroyed him, eh?" Biddle commented when the witness withdrew.

"I don't know about that." Hummel's sarcastic questions had made Max more sympathetic to the cop, but Biddle had more experience critiquing lawyers. Still, Max thought the lawyer's approach had been trivial and argumentative.

The next witness, a timid man who manufactured felt flowers, testified that he had seen Mrs. Edwards pick up a fat black cat with white spots and put it in her basket. Hummel, on cross, made him repeat which part was black and which white.

"Did you hear the previous witness testify that the animal was white with black spots?"

"No, sir."

Though the point remained obscure to Max, Hummel looked at the jury, nodded his head emphatically, and adopted a satisfied expression.

The city's Veterinary Surgeon, Samuel J. Johnson, bore the brunt of Hummel's attack. The slight, bespectacled Johnson testified that he could not tell if the cat was homeless, but that an autopsy produced a stomach stuffed with potatoes. After consulting a large tome at the defense table, Hummel approached the doctor.

"Is it not a fact that cats only eat potatoes when on the verge of starvation?"

"No, I have fed cats many potatoes."

"I mean cats born in this country."

The doctor paused, eyeing Hummel with open distaste. "I refer to good American cats."

"Ahh, bloodlines are involved. How can you tell the American from the continental cat? What are the differences?"

Johnson glanced briefly at the judge for help. Finally, he admitted, "As far as I know there are none."

"Yet a minute ago you were testifying to the widely known qualities of the American animal. Have you been confused lately?"

"Objection!"

"I am only demonstrating, Your Honor, the limitations of this witness's experience. But if the district attorney is unhappy, I'll withdraw the question."

Max thought Hummel's obsequiousness utterly transparent. Was this the best the sharper could do? So far, he wasn't impressed.

Howe handled the direct examination for the defense. He had much to repair, but he made a start with Mrs. Edwards herself. Unlike Hummel, who picked and carped like any clever shyster, Howe glowed with humanity. Even as he took his client lightly by the arm and led her to the witness box, he seemed to radiate sympathy for all sides.

"Before I begin my direct examination, Your Honor, I'd like to clear up a misstatement, no doubt inadvertent, of the district attorney's. Defense counsel is appearing *pro bono*, that is, without payment in this case. We don't like to advertise the compassionate work we do, but the district attorney has put a misleading construction on our motives."

"Is that correct, Mrs. Edwards?" the judge asked. The high flush on his cheeks suggested an extra glass at Pontin's.

"Yes."

"The jury will be instructed to set aside the district attorney's remarks about defense counsel's compensation. Proceed, Mr. Howe."

If Howe and Hummel were working for nothing, Max wondered, what were they getting in return? Why would Mrs. Edwards choose *these* attorneys, given her connections to polite society?

He consulted Biddle.

The reporter offered a common-sense explanation. "That night in jail probably scared the living hell out of her. Rough girls."

"She wants a guarantee?"

"These are the boys to give it."

"I think it's something more complicated," Max replied. Biddle's analysis seemed too glib. Who knew? The protean Howe *might* be nursing a sincere impulse.

"You're turning into a philosopher, Greengrass." Biddle patted him on the back. "Beware. Ideas are bad for business."

In buttery tones, Howe launched into his questions. "Mrs. Edwards, would you tell the court who started you on your mission?"

"Henry Bergh. I worked at his side for several months." Mrs. Edwards spoke in a soft and cultured voice.

"In fact, it was Henry Bergh who taught you to euthanize stray dogs with chloroform, did he not?"

"Yes."

"To your knowledge, was Mr. Bergh considered a friend to the city's beasts?"

Mrs. Edwards squared her small shoulders. "I believe if they could speak, they would sing his praises."

"You consider your activities a form of ministry, as I understand it. Is that correct?"

"I believe we are doing good Christian work in the streets."

Biddle leaned over and whispered, "Kill a cat for Christ, eh?"

Howe led his client on. "And when you handle an unfortunate animal, does it ever suffer?"

"Never. We place them in airtight baskets filled with chloroform. They are stunned instantly and go off quite peacefully."

"And citizens write to you and ask you to help them?"

"Yes. Just yesterday, Mrs. Semenski in Harlem had to move and couldn't take her five cats. She asked me to stop by and do the merciful thing."

Howe was drawing a benevolent portrait of his client, and she was playing the part beautifully. If Max hadn't seen Mrs. Warner snap a healthy cat's neck, he might have viewed the Midnight Band as a group of high-minded Christian ladies too.

The jury might see it otherwise, though.

If Edwards boasted that she had committed thousands of catricides, didn't it follow that she loved her work? What sort of pleasure did the Band's faithful derive when they held a desperate animal in their practiced hands? And wasn't Christian piety at best a rationalization and at worst a convenient cloak for their activities? Yet he couldn't quite grasp their true motives, he couldn't penetrate Mrs. Edwards' real thinking, and it was beginning to drive him mad.

Under Howe's gentle questioning, Mrs. Edwards spoke of her late hours at work, her dangerous missions, her unstinting courage, her selfless sacrifice to her fellow citizens. Slowly, the lawyer transformed her from a marginal crank into an alleyway St. Francis.

"So in the early years of your vocation you were strictly interested in cats?"

"Yes."

"But there came a time when you began to notice particular infestations?"

"Most definitely."

"And where were these nasty nests?"

Mrs. Edwards blushed, cleared her throat and answered in the lowest possible whisper. "Where the men were lining up."

"I am sorry if this part of your testimony is so difficult, Mrs. Edwards, but I'm sure the jury would like to understand your contribution to public decency. I won't linger over it except to ask: Were these men who were out late at night?"

Biddle suddenly gripped Max's forearm. "Listen to this!"

"Yes," came the answer from Mrs. Edwards.

"I thought it was the cats out late," Max said softly.

"What're you talking about?" Nick whispered.

"Nothing. . . ."

"And did you recognize some of these men?" Howe went on.

"Yes."

A low rumble swept the courtroom, nervous laughter and whispered curses rising in a wave.

"Order! Or I'll clear the room!" Judge Thompson shouted above the din.

Howe, the avenging angel, scowled at the buzzing assembly. Max marveled at the way the lawyer conveyed moral outrage. The lines in his forehead grew deeper, especially the furrows between his eyebrows. Cheeks, dewlaps, nostrils and mouth performed a dance of disgust. His glare was black fire.

Beaten, the sullen audience fell quiet.

"And these establishments where men were lining up, they were offering illicit liaisons?"

"Yes."

"How do you know?"

"Because I overheard many references, many conversations. And I saw women . . . displaying themselves in the windows."

"You dried-up twat!" an anonymous male voice called out from the back of the courtroom. A fresh wave of tittering coursed through the assembly.

"Silence!" the judge thundered.

Howe drew out the ensuing hush. "You overheard what the men on line in front of these establishments were saying to each other?"

"Yes."

"Peeping bitch!" another voice bellowed.

Thompson pounded his gavel. Howe wrapped himself in quiet dignity. At the center of the storm, Mrs. Edwards presented her tormentors with a composed mask. Only her lower lip trembled.

All honeyed regret, Howe pushed forward. "I am sorry to press you on this matter, Mrs. Edwards, but unfortunately I must. Were these men talking about the prices they would pay for their illicit pleasures?"

"They were."

"And the *ages* of the girls being held in this wretched trade?" Howe's voice caressed his client. Speaking in ever-softer tones, he forced his audience to strain to catch every word.

Max couldn't help recalling Mrs. Jabonne's Italian girl with the sad blue bow in her hair. Well, he hadn't used the poor thing. Still, Howe's line of questioning made him distinctly uncomfortable. Then there was the girl who might have been Nora, who ended up looking nothing like her. . . . At any rate, he rarely sought Mrs. Jabonne's services. He wasn't at all like the men who lined up in the smutty darkness. Gazing at the jury, men in celluloid collars and four-in-hand ties, men with small potbellies that strained their vests, he could almost hear his own thoughts repeated in their minds. How could they fail to exonerate the crusading Mrs. Edwards without implicating themselves?

William H. Howe had turned his client into a scourge for decency itself.

"Yes."

"Did they say they hoped the girls were . . . young?"

"Yes."

Max could barely hear Howe now. "How young?"

Mrs. Edwards's reply was almost inaudible. "Twelve or thirteen."

"And you recognized many of the men? You saw them quite clearly?"

"Many, yes."

"And you returned sometimes to the same establishments with euthanized cats, at great risk to yourself, I might add, and you placed them at the doors of these brothels?"

"Yes. So they'd think about what they were doing. The consequences. We have a saying: a house full of cats is a house full of sores."

The corner of her mouth twitched in a secret smile, but she kept her chin up, her gaze level. Max marveled at how calm she appeared. But what did this Midnight Band aphorism mean? On some elemental level, did Mrs. Edwards confuse cats and straying sportsmen?

"You were trying to discourage the trade?"

Max suddenly recalled that first feline killing field in front of Mrs. Jabonne's, and the disgust on her customer's face. Perhaps Mrs. Edwards's campaign did have some practical effect.

"And the procurers too?"

"They might worry that they were being observed. They're a superstitious lot," she added.

"He's going for a corner," Biddle said urgently.

"What corner?"

"Objection," Williams boomed out, suddenly agitated. "What is the relevance—"

"Yes, Mr. Howe, where are you going with this?"

"Your Honor, it is not our intention to embarrass any particular gentleman, but simply to show another benevolent aspect of our client's activities."

"He's overreaching, if you ask me," Nick went on, not without a note of admiration. "What a strategy! He's trying to corner the market."

"What market?"

"She's been giving Willie their names, don't you see? The sportsmen going in and out. He doesn't have to announce them in court. He's cornering vice, don't you see? What nerve!"

Quickly, Max grasped the shape of the thing. Masters of the breach-of-promise subpoena, Howe and Hummel now knew, thanks to Mrs. Edwards, the identities of dozens of sporting gentlemen in her upper-class sphere. Who else would she recognize but men in her circle? And who else would have the rumored five to ten thousand it took to convince Abe Hummel to toss his subpoenas in the fire? No wonder the lawyers were appearing *pro bono* in her case.

Howe and Hummel in a *de facto* alliance with the Reverends Parkhurst and Weems? The perversity of it gave him chills. Nick Biddle grasped the mechanics of blackmail fast enough, but Max was starting to discern a shadow world beyond the exchange of dollars and cents, a place where contradictions made sense, where opposites melted into each other and vertigo was king.

The courtroom broke out in a round of fierce whispering. Delighted, Biddle tapped his cane on the floor. Evidently, other onlookers had reached the old reporter's dark conclusion as well. Flings with professional women fresh in their minds, many of the court's observers were already hoping they could negotiate Hummel's price down.

"One thing about Abie. He always makes a clean split with the girls, too. You can ask them. A real shyster would leave them with peanuts," Nick pointed out.

"I suppose the firm won't have to troll for cases now."

"You've got it, young man. It's brilliant! This Edwards creature's dumped a year's worth right in their laps."

By the time Howe completed Mrs. Edwards's examination, he had completely remade her. What the jury now saw was a crusader who had been active in the temperance cause, as well as Henry Bergh's Society for the Prevention of Cruelty to Animals, Anthony Comstock's Society for the Suppression of Vice, the Society for the Relief of Poor Widows, and the Society for Supporting the Gospel Among the Poor of the City of New York.

The assistant district attorney handled this paragon of virtue with care. He asked Mrs. Edwards if she had a license for her activities, and, when she snapped that dogcatchers didn't have licenses either, he tried another tack.

"The anarchist Emma Goldman doesn't have a license to kill judges. Do you think society has no right to restrain her?"

Edwards wasn't at all intimidated. "Are you saying you don't know the difference between a cat and a judge?"

In despair, Williams let her step down.

During a break in the proceedings, Max and Biddle strolled outside for cigars.

"That's a lot of societies," Max said, blowing sun-shot snakes of smoke.

"I have my own society," Biddle said, "and the way you're going, you'll get in."

"I'll bite."

"I call it the Society for the Suppression of Benevolence."

"I like it. I suspect there are dues."

"Not at all. We're all volunteers, like our counterparts in the morality dodge. Of course, we have to work for our crust."

Biddle showed his long yellow teeth. In the sunshine, his face also took on a yellow cast. Max feared that the old reporter's visage, with its dry, transparent skin, might suddenly tear like old paper.

His thoughts drifted back to the trial. While he had the chance, he peppered Biddle with questions. "Isn't Howe endangering his own people?"

"How so?"

"Well, isn't he exposing where his friends in the skin trade are doing business?"

"We'll see, but I doubt it. He'll avoid specifics. There are two words I predict will never pass his lips: 'police' and 'Tammany.' Willy will be outraged, but he won't go overboard. You're just starting out; you may not see the beauty of it, but you're witnessing something unprecedented." Biddle said, lowering his voice out of respect. "It's the perfect unholy alliance."

The Reverend Weems turned out to be a clean-shaven man who looked too young for the pulpit. When he smiled, he exhibited a set of rabbit teeth; and he smiled often, a disconcerting habit for a man of the cloth. Three carefully arranged strands of black hair curled down over his high, prematurely bald forehead.

Howe began leading his character witness through his paces. "Reverend Weems, your cousin Mrs. Edwards has assisted you at the Society for the Suppression of Vice?"

"Yes, she's gathered information for us during the course of her work."

"Gathered information?" he asked in mock surprise. He paused, waiting for this revelation to sink in. The church itself sanctioned Mrs. Edwards's work. "How exactly did she do this?"

"At night, when she saw vile resorts doing business, she left cats there to brand them." The Reverend Weems grew solemn. "The city is swarming with these establishments, and we must do our best to discourage them."

"Ahh. . . . So the Midnight Band of Mercy points the way for you to do your good work?"

"Yes. They have been a great help." Weems's tic of a smile broke out again.

"How did they accomplish this?"

"When they have the opportunity, they line the cats up with their tails pointing in the right direction. If they can make out an address, they inform us, but it is often impossible in the dark. And these panderers often tear the numbers right off their own buildings. We come by in the morning and knock on their doors."

"Until you identify these despicable enterprises?"

"Yes."

"And what do you find inside?"

"The purveyors try to hide them, of course, but we find young girls in there. Children forced into white slavery. Some are as young as ten or eleven years old."

A subdued, nervous chattering swept the courtroom.

In a rush, Max recalled another one of Mrs. Jabonne's young charges. He'd met her the previous year, but he could still hear her childish prattling, he could still see her sickly skin, her flat chest, he could still feel the hard knot in his stomach. When she had demonstrated her casual knowledge of sexual mechanics, he had fled. To his shock, he couldn't help sympathizing with Weems.

Did Biddle have it all wrong? Was Max's own instinctive distaste for goo-goos misguided? Was he harboring blue-nosed impulses himself? Was the shadow world within, as well as all around? Was there a place where paradox became Natural Law? Evanescent contradictions drifted just out of his grasp.

Howe turned and with a stern glance silenced the crowd. "Some of us have innocent children of that age. Then he asked the witness, "After you locate one of these houses of ill fame, what do you do?"

Weems didn't bother to hide his glee. "We add it to our map."

The court fell dead silent. Howe turned and scanned the onlookers' anxious faces one by one. Beneath the tense quiet, Max sensed a collective terror rising.

Now the lawyer let his voice boom out. "You have a *map* of the city's brothels?"

"And, now, so does Willy," Nick pointed out.

"Yes. So far it includes three hundred and ten houses."

"And what do you do with this map?"

"We show it to Mr. Comstock."

Now the dam burst, voices rising against the Reverend Weems's indecent snooping.

"Who gets *your* end wet, mister?" an onlooker shouted.

Hisses and catcalls rained down on the minister, who alternated a stony expression with spasmodic grins. Now Max, who moments before had felt surprisingly warm toward Weems, was brimming with disgust.

"You shake down the girls too?" another outraged citizen called out.

"Gets his gash for nothing. That's what!"

Hisses and catcalls rose in a cracked chorus. Weems couldn't seem to control his tic-like smirk. What an ally—Postal Inspector Comstock, who used a telescope to spy on the Academy of Music's French Ball? The same Mr. Comstock who wanted to dress Greek statues and who bragged about how many tons of erotic literature and racy postcards he had burned as United States Government Special Agent?

Wasn't he also the Comstock whom William H. Howe had previously dismantled in the Victoria Woodhull case? Comstock and Howe on the same side? There were no sides. What did a world without sides look like?

"The Midnight Band was particularly helpful because they often visited undesirable neighborhoods?" Howe prodded Weems.

"Yes, and they went out after dark to pursue their charitable business. Evidently, the lechery trade is doing quite well. Most of our poor city's deviants are conceived in these brothels."

The district attorney bolted to his feet. "Objection! With all due respect, the Reverend Weems has no standing in this field." He paused to ripples of laughter. "Unless he's made an intimate study of the problem."

"Peepin's his profession!" an anonymous voice called out.

Judge Thompson slammed his gavel down, bringing the crowd to heel. "Yes, what is the witness's expertise, Mr. Howe?"

Howe offered a ceremonious bow. "Yes, of course. I shall lay the groundwork, Your Honor. Reverend Weems, you are a frequent correspondent with the Academy of Sciences, are you not?"

"Yes, I have a deep interest in biology. I studied with Professor Cardozo at Yale before I went to divinity school."

"Excellent. Is it your opinion that my client is harming the American cat?"

The question jarred Max. They had drifted so deep into two-legged territory that he'd forgotten the four-legged beasts entirely.

"To the contrary, Mr. Howe. Nature, as Mr. Spencer and Mr. Darwin have pointed out, exercises a savage form of benevolence."

"She's weeding out the bad stock? Improving the breed?"

"To put it in a simple way, yes."

"One more question: how long has Mrs. Edwards been working with you on your campaign?"

"She's been risking life and limb for us for over two years."

"She's dedicated to rooting out this scourge?"

"We do not have a more dedicated collaborator."

Moments later, Howe wound up his direct examination. Showing no stomach for impeaching the clergyman, Williams allowed Weems to step down without cross-examining him.

Howe's closing statement, a full two hours and twelve minutes, numbed the senses. He appealed to the jurors' more delicate sensibilities. Would they really send a defenseless woman like Mrs. Edwards back to the Tombs? Could they imagine what would happen to a lady of her refinement when she was tossed into a pit full of dips, grifters, kleptomaniacs, and hardened ladies of the town? He quoted the Bible, Shakespeare, and the Civil Code. When he began to evoke poor Mrs. Edwards, weak, bent, and broken on the day of her release, he couldn't contain his tears.

Her children behind the defense table burst out crying.

Max found Howe's old-fashioned, ham-fisted performance repugnant. Who would be convinced by these transparent manipulations? Then he saw two jurors on opposite sides of the box openly weeping. The lawyer had made no attempt to disprove the charges against his client. Instead, for the third time, he touched on Mrs. Edwards's attempts to fight the white-slave trade and how she had risked life and limb in the most dangerous districts to protect innocent children from vicious procurers.

Max wasn't so sure Mrs. Edwards killed cats simply to help the Reverend Weems's crusade, though. By her own testimony, the cat killings had come first. Mrs. Edwards had taken too much pride in the catricides to be Weems's pawn. She'd turned the witness stand into her own pulpit.

Howe's voice played a full scale of agony; his expansive face performed a complete repertoire of outrage. Unashamed, he brayed, he moaned, he groaned, his great body shuddered.

"Reminds me of your Adler, Max," Biddle whispered.

Nick had never alluded to Max's racial origins before, but his comparison had merit. Max had seen the famed Adler perform Macbeth in Yiddish and had been similarly put off. At the time, he had chalked up the actor's hyperbolic mannerisms to an overwrought Eastern European Jewish sensibility. Perhaps Biddle was wrong, though. In his antiquated way, Howe seemed to be drawing from an ancient blood-and-thunder tradition that had nothing to do with keening Jews from the Pale.

"I hesitate to draw too graphic a picture for you," the lawyer boomed out to the jury. "But what won't these slave masters do to squeeze an extra coin out of these defenseless girls? And if my client risked life and limb to retrieve one poor soul, are we then to fling her into prison to rot with the rest of the lost? I don't think you have it in your hearts to commit such a crime against a purity crusader whom we ought to get down on our knees to thank from the bottom of our hearts."

Another juror honked into his handkerchief. How did the baggy old charlatan do it? Perhaps he believed every word he said, if only for a heartbeat.

When the jury began deliberating, Biddle checked his pocket watch. "They'd best get back before our deadline. Want to put something on it?"

"Sure. A dollar says she's acquitted. What difference does the law make?"

"Smart boy. Hardly worth it. Will you give me four to one?"

Even those odds sounded safe.

chapter twenty-two

"Who would have guessed it? Guilty with a suspended sentence," Biddle chuckled, graciously accepting Max's crumpled bills. "The jury paid attention to the law after all."

Convicted, Mrs. Edwards walked free. Howe and Hummel had proven their client culpable of an admirable offense. Max had lost on a technicality, but it would cost him real money.

"Not exactly," Max muttered. Losing a sure bet always stung. Before he knew it, he was going to have to make a withdrawal from the Madison Savings Bank.

"They convict your girl, but they demonstrate wisdom at the same time," Biddle continued, turning the knife. "I thought the foreman was eloquent, didn't you? Asking the judge for leniency like that."

"And Howe barely knew this judge, too." He had to laugh when he recalled the bottle of German wine Howe had sent over to Judge Thomspon's table. Didn't the judiciary cost more than a mediocre grape?

"Well, I'd say you do a squib on the Reverend Weems, and I'll knock out the lead story. Shouldn't be too tiring."

Max thought the Weems angle was more than a squib, but he kept that to himself. He'd work it up and let Parnell decide.

"Did you like the way Willy tugged at their heartstrings?"

Max stuck his finger down his throat. "Gag-worthy, if you ask me."

"Ahh, you might have a visceral response, but you see the truth now, don't you?"

"What's that?"

"People love it."

"I suppose so."

"I'm going to tell you something else, my young friend. At the same time, Willy was working for his own pocket. Do you see how?"

"I'd say a few sportsmen will be getting subpoenas soon."

"On the ball. Think of this, though. Even the ones who don't will be more malleable in other embarrassing circumstances, eh? Abie Hummel on one side, the church on the other. What a squeeze play!"

Why was Biddle taking such a huge delight in the impending misfortune of his fellow clubmen? Max was almost certain he knew. Having settled his own Howe and Hummel subpoena long ago, and therefore immune from persecution, the old reporter felt free to enjoy the carnival.

First Max tried City Hall, but the mayor didn't care to comment on Reverend Weems's charges. However, Max knew he could get a good quote out of Superintendent Byrnes if he wormed his way into his office. He had to wait two hours, but finally Byrnes granted him an audience.

Without looking up from his paperwork, Byrnes asked, "Did they throw your little biddy in the black hole, boyo?"

"Actually, she got a ten-dollar fine and a suspended sentence."

"That seems about right. They had Howe and Hummel?"

Now Byrnes fixed his small dark eyes on the wiry reporter. The detective probably knew how the trial had turned out already, but Max played along. "Both at the same time. Something else came up, though, that I thought you might want to comment on."

Carefully observing the stone-faced Byrnes, he explained how the Midnight Band had been helping the Reverend Weems in his crusade.

Byrnes greeted Max's revelations about Weems with a shrug. "It may come as a surprise to certain members of society that these establishments are so widespread," he said, adopting his most elevated vocabulary, "but I assure you they're like any other business. They have rent to pay and have goods to sell, and they sometimes operate in the most refined neighborhoods. When you shut one down, it only opens up the next day in a different location that charges a higher rent. Of course, the prices go up to compensate."

"So there's no point chasing them from one location to the next."

"What's the result? The city pays more, the procurer pays more, the clientele pay more, but in the end, they all come up with the dollar. Who gets it in the neck? The taxpayer, that's who."

Evidently, inflation had to be kept out of the brothel business for the good of society. Byrnes seemed perfectly earnest, though he left out the fact that at every fresh place of business the madame had to pay a new initiation fee to the local pantata. Whether Byrnes himself got a piece of the action was an open question, but Police Commissioner Jimmy Martin had somehow managed on a modest public servant's salary to hire a retinue of servants and buy a brownstone next to the Rockefellers.

"Is this on the record?" Max asked, struggling to keep a straight face. If he played Byrnes's comments up top, the Weems squib might be worth as much as Biddle's lead piece.

"I've said as much in the past."

"What about his charges regarding the young girls?"

Byrnes worked his jaw, coughed, and then put on a dignified air. "Appertaining to that allegation, we stick to the letter of the law. The age of consent is sixteen now. Maybe for some it ought to be never, but that isn't practical."

Smiling inwardly, Max scrawled Byrnes's comment on his pad, and circled the word "we."

With a deadline hanging over his head, he arranged his notes in a neat pile next to his upright typewriter and ripped off four grafs. By morning, the Reverend Weems would be famous—and infamous as well. If the story had legs, Sim Addem would soon be telling Weems jokes at the Hoffman House bar. Max could already hear Sim's gravelly delivery. "So the Reverend Weems goes to catch the Busy Flea show at the Slide, only he don't know what's a flea."

Looking across the newsroom, he picked out Nick Biddle in shirtsleeves and soft felt hat, scrawling away with abandon. Before he knew it, the old freeloader would be putting the bite on him for supper. Tearing the Weems story out of his typewriter, Max slipped through the maze of desks, climbed to the throne, and made his offering. Parnell produced an indecipherable growl. He had to get outside.

The next thing he knew, he was stalking north on Park Row. Mind blank, legs pumping, he forged his way uptown. He was a speed-walking machine, free of Howes, Hummels, Biddles, cat ladies, and philosophy of any stripe. His body bounded along, reveling in escape. Better to do handstands and somersaults for nickels. A light drizzle fell in the failing light. Sharp and clean, cold drops spattered his hair, trickling down his cheeks. He held his course, heading for home.

Belle flung open the front door. "Max! Danny's playing tonight. Are you going?"

She radiated excitement, her cheeks, despite a dusting of rice powder, visibly flushed. Bare inches from her, Max caught his breath. Her dress, cinched with a wide striped belt, wasn't at all revealing, but it clung to her figure in intimate pleats and folds. A fine watch chain hung down below her tiny waist.

Pinpricks of heat and cold broke out on his neck. His tongue was thick in his mouth.

Sensing his confusion, she went on. "I just have to get my jacket. You're soaked."

"I'll dry up."

He watched her up-to-date, diminished bustle ticktock down the hall. Only a few years ago, you could balance a dinner plate on these protrusions; now they had shrunk to vestigial pads. Surprisingly, despite her fine-boned frame, Belle didn't need artificial enhancements.

He hunted down Mrs. DeVogt in the parlor. A half-drained glass of sherry rested on an end table. "Was Gretta home for dinner?"

The landlady snapped her newspaper shut. "No, and neither were you. You'll have to send notice from now on. I'm wasting enough food to feed China."

"Sorry, you're right. Is she around?"

"She sent word from that horrible laboratory she works in. They'll kill her if she lets them."

"Oh, she's working late?"

"You seem rather dull tonight, Mr. Greengrass. Yes, I'm keeping a dish for her. You'll have to fend for yourself."

Belle tripped lightly down the stairs. She had thrown on a cloak in one of those new chemical-dye colors somewhere between purple and red. On her head perched a velvet hat bristling with feathers. He'd never seen her look so smashing. Should he accompany her? Why not? He couldn't be unfaithful to Gretta if they weren't even attached.

"A quick splash. I'll be right there," he said, taking the stairs two at a time.

A minute later, outside on the stoop, he unfurled his umbrella, she took his arm, and they strolled toward Union Square. "You look beautiful tonight," he said in a husky voice.

"I shouldn't wear this in the rain," she replied, touching her black velvet hat. Tightening her grip, her fingers made out his hard bicep. Jake, her longtime beau, had a pale scholar's body, curly black hair on his soft chest. A knowing smirk flared on Max's lips. Caught in his sidelong glance, she felt a sizzling sensation run through her.

"Watch out for puddles!" he cried.

Laughing, they timed their leaps over the muddy pools.

Smiling to herself, she readjusted her dress. He'd never dream how she had picked it up at Siegel-Cooper's, secreting it under her navy blue coat while the store's all-female orchestra sawed out a Strauss waltz. An atomizer was spraying a dizzying scent, the song played faster and faster, the mobs of women pressed up against each other at the counter piled high with smooth and silky things, and she'd lost her head. Before she knew it, she was floating past glass cases offering leather goods, perfumes, gloves, handkerchiefs, and watches, drifting among cawing tropical birds, wandering in and out of the photo gallery and past the pink tea room, her heart in her mouth, waiting to get pinched.

Then she was out on the street, swearing she would never do it again. What had possessed her? She was a visiting nurse, the daughter of a shop steward in the Cigar Makers Union, her father was a kind man who worshipped Joseph Barondess. After that she avoided Macy's, B. Altman & Company, and Abraham & Strauss until the day her patient, Mrs. Cohen, twenty-seven years old and the mother of five, died of typhoid in a rear Essex Street tenement. Her daughters had been hiding their infected mother from the authorities.

Mrs. Cohen, all ninety-four pounds of her, had surrendered to the fever, and then the velvet hat swam into view. First Belle was in an airless apartment, and then she was standing before a tree of feathered and flowered creations. In a dream, she tried on the plush number. Other women were snatching other hats off their hooks, the salesgirls were giggling to each other, so she just wandered away, the price tag hidden beneath her hair. This time she marched straight for the grand doors and no one said boo. She had an honest face.

She *was* honest. She just didn't have a trust or some uncle on Wall Street like the Gretta Sealys of the world. The woman's closet was probably ready to explode. Why shouldn't *she* have some nice things for herself? She spent her days picking nits and battling the white lung. Shouldn't she taste life, too?

They walked along, chatting so easily about nothing at all. Max didn't have to know about Jake, who was afflicted with a permanent erection and revolutionary ideals. She could only imagine his curses if he knew she was keeping company with a *petit bourgeois* like Max. An animal bent on his own pleasure, Jake would have said. The hypocrite. So why did she stay with him? Why didn't she have the will to break away? Was she so afraid of being alone?

Why was it a crime to have a good time? She was so weary of Jake's Schwabian arias on the virtues of syndicalism, and his arguments for a general strike. Since most of the Jewish boys at Schwab's bar were barely working, Belle thought their big talk was ridiculous. Sometimes Jake's friends muttered about a few well-placed bombs, but it was impossible to take them seriously.

She cared for him most when he was quiet, when they were touching, and she could trace the shape of his smooth face. His buttery skin told a different tale than his bellicose ideas.

Located in Tammany's building on Fourteenth Street between Irving Place and Third Avenue, Tony Pastor's theater was a world away from Simon's Avenue B Temple of Amusement. Aiming for a wider audience, Pastor had banned alcohol, smoking, and blue material in his vaudeville hall. Middle-class women and shopgirls occupied comfortable seats alongside the male element, which in Pastor's wholesome environment was less likely to unbutton a tight pair of pants or stand on its hind legs and shout abuse for the sheer fun of it. Pastor did maintain a well-oiled door to the saloon next door, and he did sprinkle his audience with elegantly dressed professional ladies from time to time, but in public he was four-square for clean entertainment, the family, and bigger profits.

Craning his neck, Max took in the crowd. "This is some break for Danny."

Belle wondered at the sweeping, curtained stage. "How could he get up there in front of all these people?"

"Danny? To him, this is like falling off a log."

They took orchestra seats in the heart of the bubbling crowd. Touching Belle's hand, he waited; when she didn't withdraw it, he wove his fingers in hers. Simply squeezing her hand loosed streaming sensations, light electricity running through his whole body.

He threw his arm across the back of her seat. He wasn't getting anywhere with Gretta. What business of hers was it anyway? Belle's shining eyes, her febrile excitement, her naïve delight were a tonic. And he'd thought she was one of those bloodless socialist bores. How could he have been so wrong?

A Dutch act, Golden and Waller, opened the bill. They were neither Dutch nor much of an act, but their hoary routine drew a few scattered laughs. Phillip St. Louis, Juggler Extraordinaire, tossed around a few colored balls and fiery sticks. The mixed crowd of shopgirls, middle-class ladies just off a spin down the Ladies' Mile, merchants, drummers, shoulder hitters, and Democratic Party potentates barely reacted.

Then, in patent leather boots laced to the knee, Tony Pastor minced onto the stage, swaying, his steps barely achieving dance. Swaggering, he snapped off his opera hat before planting himself to sing. In a nasal warble, he put over his favorites, "Yum Yum Yum," "I'll Give You a Pointer on That," "Lula, The Beautiful Hebrew Girl," and "The Strawberry Blonde." Despite his keg-shaped body, he managed a few jaunty steps in between numbers. Finally he launched into his signature song, "Sarah's Young Man."

My first love was Sarah,
Oh, none could be fairer.
The fact is indeed
I've ne'er seen one so fair.
On her I grew lovesick,
She was a domestic,
And lived in a mansion
On Washington Square

Belle stood and clapped. "He's so old-fashioned, but it's hard not to love him," she said, flush-faced, her face powder studded with sweat.

Then, in a striped suit and boater, Danny Swarms soft-shoed onto the boards. The blowzy band struck up a tune. Twirling his cane expertly, he knocked his hat at a rakish angle, did a quick pirouette, and danced toward the wings.

"It's him, it's Danny!" Belle gasped.

Leaning at an insouciant angle, Swarms tapped his way back to center stage and launched into a song.

Ida, Ida, I'm so glad I spied her,
Ida, Ida, she's my Coney-oney queen,
Ida, Ida, I'm so glad I spied her,
Ida, Ida, she's my one and only dream.

Danny worked hard to put Izzy Ballin's song over, but the response was tepid. Perhaps the melody sounded too much like a hundred others. Perhaps Izzy Ballin was not going to make it in the songwriting business. But Max suspected that Danny was selling the tune too hard, using every funny face, every tricky step, every one of a dozen deliveries all at once. The whole performance, as professional as it was, had an edge of hysteria to it. As a singer and dancer, Swarms didn't seem quite human. He moved more like a Swiss wind-up toy.

Then out of the wings spun a woman in a shimmering pink wrap and matching parasol. On her wide-brimmed hat clung a pile of wax fruit. As the band pounded out the simple theme, she fluttered just out of Danny's reach, her intricate, natural steps pouring life into the act. Vamping without shame, she drew a leer from Danny, who took her hand as they broke into a bounding waltz.

Max's jaw dropped. The tight-lipped, sly bastards had kept it from him all this time.

"She's great, isn't she?" Belle whispered.

"That's my sister I told you about!"

As Danny stepped aside, Faye seized center stage. A barely concealed wildness infused her gestures. She tossed off her hat and cloak, the lights went down, and she shimmied in a strapless gown.

There are some who see an angel
When I stroll down Division Street,
And some who see a devil
When they gaze at my flying feet.

I don't hear what they are saying
When the violins start to play,
Music's my lord and master
I can't help it, I swing and sway.

Faye's singing seemed to inspire Danny, who worked the break in a frenzy of elbows and knees. As he played the moth to her flame, Faye, assuming a demure expression, bent over to display a rosy décolletage. Exhausted from his labors, Danny stepped back, tapping his cane in time. Max had seen Faye perform a hundred times, but the way she lit into the chorus here gave him chills.

Who cares what they're thinking
Who cares if they turn away?
I was born to sing songs,
Who cares if they're sad or gay?

Gripping his sleeve, Belle said, "She's fantastic . . . like a powerhouse . . . and he's so cute . . . imagine. . . ."

He took her backstage, where they found his sister still huffing and puffing from her performance. His face a greasepaint-streaked mask, Danny beamed, his arm around Faye's naked shoulder.

Max made the introductions. "Fresh stuff, sis. Faye, this is Belle. I told you about her."

The white lie cued his sister, who batted her eyes at Belle. "Oh, sure. All about."

"I couldn't take my eyes off you up there," Belle said, glowing herself.

"Like a dancing bear, huh?" Faye joked.

"We had to come out after those fish, too. House was dead as a doornail," Danny pointed out.

"Is this a one-shot, or what?" Max asked.

"Tell him, Danny." Faye poked Swarms in the chest.

"I'll whip her into shape soon," Danny responded, slapping Faye's hip. "We caught on a tour. Keith. Nine cities. Boston. Hartford. Philly."

"We're looking for a place near the Square, too," Faye blurted. All their secrets were pouring out now.

"Yeah, we want to be close to Panic City," Danny put in, referring to the booking agents and theaters that ringed Union Square.

"So you're moving out?" Belle asked.

"Faye wants one of those little dogs," Danny responded. "The ones that travel."

Max cut in. "Don't talk to me about dogs, you S.O.B. Grab a quick one?"

"Go, go," Faye agreed, shooing the men away.

When they repaired to the bustling saloon, Max bought the first round. "Marry her or I'll stab you to death, you sonofabitch," he suggested.

It was all in good humor, except that he meant every word. Danny's amorous record included a brief marriage at seventeen to a minister's daughter in the wasteland of Roxbury, New York, a long affair with the wife of a ticket manager, a fling with a chorine named Maxine St. James, and steady attendance at Mrs. Jabonne's and the House of All Nations. In other words, he was no better than Max himself.

"It ain't you I'm worried about," Danny declared, sucking the foam off his beer.

Max slapped him on the back. "You're right. Faye'll shoot you in your sleep." He stayed away from the Leon question, figuring they could work that one out themselves. "I don't believe in mixing the races, you mick bastard, but you'll have to go down to City Hall, I guess."

"How many times I gotta tell you? Scotch-Irish! Presbyterians, for Jesus' sake," Danny protested.

"I can't tell you heathens apart," Max growled.

By the time the men listed back into the dressing rooms, Belle and Faye were laughing and whispering in each other's ears. It was about the last thing Max expected. "Thick as thieves, huh?" Max observed.

This comment sent the women into fresh gales of laughter.

Outside in the night air, Belle dragged deeply on a cigarette.

"You're a tobacco fiend?" he asked, surprised.

"It bothers you?"

"Are you kidding?" He lit up a Cairo cigar. "You're giving me an excuse."

Soon they were wandering through the seething Rialto. Sports in striped suits and bowlers ogled Belle. Drunks careened in and out of the crowd. Dips worked the excited and careless, the rubes from Columbus, Ohio and Albany. Inside Fleischmann's Dairy Restaurant, the humming conversation, the clash of dishes, the tinkle of silverware blended into a single buzzing sound. The tiled floor reflected the brilliant electric lights.

Gazing at Belle across the freshly wiped table, Max's spirits rose.

In his mania to chase down one more good story, he'd been forgetting to live. Fleischmann's house band played a light melody. The coffee and strudel tasted wonderful. He drank in the eager look on Belle's face, her large brown eyes, the way she fidgeted on the plain wooden chair.

"You liked it, huh?"

"I could have split. They're such a couple. Don't they just go together?"

"Yeah, like nitro and glycerine."

"You think it's a bad idea?"

"Nah, it's perfect. I get rid of both of them but keep them in the family."

"The two of you, it must have been wonderful growing up together."

"More like the Battle of Chickamauga."

"You fought?"

"Each other? Like cats and dogs. But mostly we had an alliance against the old man. Faye would save up hair balls and stick them in his soup."

"Your family's close?"

"Are you kidding? My father said the mumbo-jumbo over me years ago. You know the one, Blessed art Thou, Oh God, King of the Universe, do me a little favor and strike my son dead. I'm one of those dead sons you see walking around.

"So, you and Faye were gabbing it up back there."

"She has some sense of humor, your sister. Such nerve."

Why shouldn't they become friends? Belle could examine Leon and talk sense to Faye into the bargain. He wasn't about to reveal his nephew's existence behind Faye's back, but Belle would take it in stride, he felt certain. "What're you talking about? You plow through Mulberry Bend every day by yourself. All she does is get up on a stage and flounce around."

His compliment made her face burn. "In front of all those strangers, I'd be tongue-tied."

He ordered one more strudel. She put the plate in the center of the table, and they ate quietly, cutting smaller and smaller pieces, each making sure, wordlessly, that the other got a fair portion.

"You know what? You might be able to help me."

"How?" Her quick tongue licked crumbs from her lips. Then, more decorously, she used a napkin.

"Never mind." Couldn't he think of anything but his stories? "Let's talk about something else."

"No, now you made me curious."

Didn't she know the tenement terrain far better than he did? Why not ask? "Well, this may sound funny, but I was just wondering if any of your patients—the poor ones—if they took out insurance."

"I have rich ones? Insurance, I can think of one. She said she didn't want to be thrown in a hole in the ground. The insurance promised to buy her a stone."

"The rest couldn't afford it, huh?"

"Some of them belong to burial societies, but then the societies go broke and they don't pay. Plenty of them have nothing."

On the slow, looping walk home, they stepped into a warehouse doorway. STRASSER'S LAMPS AND CHANDELIERS read the legend on the wall. Tilting her head back and standing on her toes, she kissed him frankly. What was wrong with trying him out? He looked so healthy and strong. Sometimes she thought Jake was going to burn himself up from the inside out.

Just to hold her close, not quite knowing what he was doing, he lifted her off her feet, and they bumped awkwardly against the door. Their front teeth scraped together, he staggered back, flailing, and her hat went flying.

When they finally reached Mrs. DeVogt's boarding house, they slipped around the side of the stoop and down the basement stairwell. Opening his coat, enfolding her, he made a warm cocoon. There she matched him, hungry kiss for hungry kiss. This time they kept their balance.

chapter twenty-three

"What a turn Danny did," Belle informed Mrs. DeVogt's breakfast table. She danced her fingers between the rolls and the marmalade.

"You went to the show, you two?" Mrs. DeVogt asked.

"Somebody was holding Danny up," Max put in.

Max and Belle exchanged significant glances, but Danny didn't bite. Instead, he arranged and rearranged his wispy red hair, but his shiny scalp still showed through. "How'd 'Ida' go over?" he asked eagerly.

"Great, Danny. You should see him, Mrs. DeVogt. He dances like a wind-up toy," Max explained, miffed that Swarms hadn't breathed a word about Faye. She was the natural, for crissakes. In fact, he knew why Danny hadn't mentioned her. The contrast between their respective talents was all too painful.

Swarms kept flogging Izzy Ballin's song. "We printed a thousand copies. That's where the real mazuma is, in publishing. If I had the dough to pay a dozen pluggers and the *padrones* like the big boys do, then we' d have something."

"The *padrones*? What do they have to do with it?" Max asked.

Danny looked agog. "Who tells the guinea with the squeezebox and the monkey what to play? The chimp?"

"Oh, you're exaggerating," Gretta said. "They play what you ask them to."

"Doesn't Danny know his business?" Belle shot back. "The *padrones* own them in the old country, and they own them here, too."

Max tried to cut off any further polemics. "That's why I hear the same damn tune all over town sometimes? On the ferry too?"

Danny went on serenely. "Sure, it's all sewed up. People start humming a tune, they don't even know why. Before you know it, they're running out and buying the sheet music."

"Tell them, Danny. He has a new partner," Belle announced.

Now Swarms came clean. "And she can put over one helluva a song, too. Makes me look like an amateur. You oughta hear the lungs on this girl."

"He's telling the truth for once," Max conceded. If Belle hadn't wormed it out of Swarms, though, would he have said a word?

"Oh, be quiet, you two! It's Faye, Max's sister. She sings . . . it gives you goose bumps," Belle explained.

"Yeah, well. Pastor booked us again." Danny tried to sound casual, but his wide smile betrayed him.

"Look at him, he's in seventh heaven," Max said. True, Swarms's voice was a little thin, and his steps none too fresh, but he was a pro. You had to admire him. "Nice job, kiddo."

"Thanks, bud."

Max basked in his friend's reflected glory, but he couldn't repress a twinge of annoyance. If Swarms was doing so well, why had he put the touch on him before breakfast? Was the five-spot going straight to Sim Addem? Or to that curb broker who had all the inside dope?

After coffee, Danny spread out the Wednesday edition on the breakfast table. "Which one's yours, Maxie?"

"Let me see the heads." His eye fell on Biddle's lead piece first.

CAT KILLER CONVICTED

Light Fine; Jury Sympathetic
Her Remarkable Tenderloin Odyssey
The Rev. Weems a Character Witness

William H. Howe, the Nestor of the Criminal Bar, effected a narrow escape for a deeply distressed client yesterday. Mrs. Edwards, on trial for illegally executing five cats, obviously improved her chances considerably when she employed Mr. Howe. It was clear from the outset that Mrs. Edwards had vio-

> lated municipal ordinances, but by the end of the proceedings the jury was requesting leniency for Mr. Howe's client, who revealed some remarkable secrets during her testimony.

Max couldn't believe this puffery. Was Biddle a reporter or a press agent for Howe and Hummel? "That one's not my doing! What a joke! She was convicted and Biddle's turned it into an advert for the lawyers."

He almost said, I'd hate to see what Howe has on Biddle. Instead, he gritted his teeth and read on.

> Mrs. Edwards, of 212 West Thirty-Second Street, was tried in the Court of Special Sessions on the charge of "unlawfully, unjustifiably and willfully killing five dumb animals—to wit, cats." She was found guilty and fined $2 for each cat murder.

Swarms snatched the paper back from him. "What's the scoop? Ooh, listen to this. With all due respect, Mrs. DeVogt. 'On her errands of mercy, Mrs. Edwards noticed numerous houses of ill-fame doing roaring business. She testified that cat nests proliferated around these establishments and felt it was her duty to inform the Reverend Weems, who is also her cousin, of their locations.'"

Mrs. DeVogt took up the challenge. "Oh, what do *you* know? It used to be much worse. On Broome Street, they used to stand in the windows in chemises and show their boobies. Who is Biddle?"

Max didn't have the heart to tell her that that particular time-honored practice was still in fashion. "Just a reporter."

"Well, Mr. Howe must have done something for Mr. Biddle or your publisher."

"They can't get anything by you, Mrs. DeVogt," Max said.

"That's because they're trying to get the same things by us all over again."

"Exactly. They're giving us circuses to take our minds off how they're stealing," Belle put in.

"Emma Goldman has spoken," Swarms said, waving his fork. "Oh, this must be yours! 'Weems Charges Brothel Boom.' Is that you, Max? 'Has Created Map of Vice,' That's a hot one!"

"I'd poke out your eyes, Danny, but we're in polite company. Everyone knows I don't write the headlines."

"You see, he does love me," Swarms retorted. "Ahh, did the reverend say this? 'Most of our poor city's deviants are conceived in these brothels.' How does he know unless hc has personal experience?"

"They say it, I write it down."

"Maybe they'll give you a better thing to write about next time," Belle offered in his defense. She kicked him playfully under the table. Pain had never felt so sweet.

"You're red as a beet, Greengrass," Swarms observed.

Max threw a murderous glance at his friend, who whistled a few taunting notes.

"I read that we should probably give up all wheat products," Mrs. DeVogt remarked. "In a natural state we lived on nuts and fruit. Now we're racing around on bicycles. I suppose you haven't heard of bicycle kidney, Gretta?"

"My kidneys are in perfect working order, Mrs. DeVogt." Fresh color rose on her sculpted cheeks, in the hollow of her throat. One look at her and a prickly sensation, hot and cold at once, ran down Max's spine. Her beauty was shocking.

Without looking, he could sense Belle gazing at him. Shifting uneasily in his chair, he worked up a weak smile. "Well, the rest of you can lounge around, but I've got to get to the office."

"Run, run. The city can't burn without you," Swarms said.

"I *set* all the fires, Danny."

Outside, he marched to the corner. If he lingered there, he might catch sight of Gretta and intercept her, although to what end he didn't quite know. Just to stand close to her, to let his eyes run over her body, to feel that melting sensation. What harm was there in that? Belle didn't own him. Why did he feel so guilty?

Leaning against a building, he lit his morning cigar and puffed smoke rings. Mrs. DeVogt's door remained sealed. Time froze. Edgy from the tobacco, he paced up and back, craning his neck, biting his lip.

A rag crooked inside his elbow, a bootblack sat at a nearby stand. Two chairs stood empty on the raised platform. To distract himself, Max looked at his scuffed shoes and considered a quick once-over.

FIRST CLASS SHINE
5 Cents
Oil Shine 10
Pat Leather
Pillow Shoes

A good shine always lifted his spirits.

Then Gretta emerged. He watched her take a few quick steps, swing onto her bicycle, and launch herself down West 16th Street. Pedaling smoothly, she headed straight toward him. The ribbons on her sailor hat fluttered.

"Max, I'm glad I caught you," she said, braking, her ankles peeking out from under her skirt. Rolling to a stop, she fixed her natty gray shirtwaist and cocked her hip, the balloon-tired bike tilted and hidden between her invisible legs. He could feel those long, muscular legs holding the machine in place. "Do you have a minute?"

No wonder so many sermons had been preached against the shrouded motions of thigh, calf, and ankle that went into a woman bicycling. No wonder lead weights were sewn into the hems of riding costumes.

"Sure. Union Square?"

As they walked, she eyed him sidelong. He was solid. Single-minded. He couldn't have been more different than Martin. For him, a kiss would be a straightforward act of lips pressing lips, not the complicated, lingering affair Martin had made of it. How could she expect delicacy from a grasping Hebrew, her mother would ask, but she didn't think that way. At the camera club she had met several Jews, and though every one of them had foreign mannerisms, even a distinct smell, one or two had fine, polished manners.

A chilly wind blew down Fourteenth Street, swirling dust into the park. Gretta rearranged the strap around her neck, pushing the Kodak box camera into her lap. For a moment she stared off into space, absentmindedly biting her cuticles.

"I thought you hated those things."

She patted the camera like an adored pet. "Well, that's one of the things I wanted to tell you. I had a theory. If I carried one of these, and I dressed like the creatures who use them, nobody would see me."

"I don't understand."

"If I haul all my usual equipment around with me, and I set up the tripod and handle the plates, I always attract a mob. If they see a Kodak girl dressed like this, they think I'm harmless." She didn't want to get too technical, but the Kodak negatives would probably lack all detail. Still, to snap away, unencumbered, on the fly, held a seductive charm.

"You're an undercover Kodak girl?"

"Exactly. Completely invisible. Shirtwaist and everything. The pictures I take won't be worth a thing as far as their quality. This is what I wanted to tell you. What I've been doing is following Martin's old route, at least the parts he told me about. I wanted to see what he went through."

Perform an act of cleansing, capture his ghost in her lens. How could she explain how she wanted to kill Martin's afterimage? Plain prints might murder his memory and let her live again.

"Did you see anything?" He wondered if her cool persistence hid an irreducible love for Mourtone.

"I'm not exactly sure, but I should get the prints back from Rochester in a week or two. You can't open these little things. You've got to mail the whole camera back. Would you come out to Staten Island again sometime? I'll tell my mother to behave herself."

His throat tightened. As they crossed the trolley track circuit south of the park, he could barely keep from grinning like an ape.

"Don't put yourself out," he mumbled. All she had to do was play her fingers lightly on his forearm, and he was lost. Belle's appealing, open face flashed through his mind. He had felt so natural with her. And in no time she'd fallen in with Faye. Was he going to betray Belle so easily?

Gretta took a skipping step and mounted her bicycle before his lips could shape another word.

He forced himself to stop imagining her sheer skin, to stop thinking of the way her breasts would feel against his chest or how he would lose his mind when she arched her back and raised herself up to him. He forced himself to stop thinking of the tip of her tongue, her rich mouth, the complicated terrain of her kisses. He forced himself to stop thinking about waking and watching her rise from the bed naked, watching her lift her hair to expose the nape of her neck, watching her slip into a silk robe. He forced himself—and failed.

He could barely walk. Taking to the doorway of a cast-iron loft building, he lit a cigar and blew masses of smoke, praying his aching hard-on would subside. Was there anything more pathetic than the corkscrew walk of a man with an erection? He was attracted to Belle, and he felt so free and easy with her, but she didn't destroy him like this. No woman but Gretta ever had. She turned the backs of his knees to water.

He had to drive her out of his mind. Puffing away, he tried to think about work. Fourteen Irving Place wasn't that far away. Why not take another look at Van Siclen's rundown mansion? He was fascinated by the Midnight Band's living arrangements. Did Mrs. Edwards reside there with her acolytes? Was the Irving Place house a sort of nunnery? Did the women practice purifying rituals peculiar to their sect? Were they unrepentant? Were they about to embark on a fresh spree of catricides?

The case cried out for a post-mortem, especially since Nick Biddle's article had turned the whole thing into another Howe and Hummel carnival, draining all the strangeness out of the Midnight Band's crusade. Why let Biddle have the last word? It was Max's story, Max's right to say when it had ended.

He took up a station across from 14 Irving Place, just under the bay window of Stanford White's sprawling digs, but the Midnight Band's headquarters remained sealed. Not a soul stirred. An hour passed. He wandered around the block and found a new surveillance post under a shady elm. Still there was no activity.

What if they were all out?

Curious, he hopped up the stairs of No. 14 and pounded on the door. Nothing. He leaned over and caught a glimpse of the shrouded parlor. The horsehair sofa stood empty. Not a single lamp had been lit. He rapped again, checked the upper floors for signs of life, but the house remained mute. His heart racing, he took the gravel path around to the back. Again he pounded, but the building might as well have been abandoned.

Then again, Mrs. Edwards might be lying down with a cold compress on her head and a pistol in her hand. Who could predict what she might do to protect herself now?

He knew exactly where Miss Van Siclen kept the membership book. Wouldn't he love to get his hands on that? What other refined ladies had signed on to the campaign? Let William H. Howe corner vice; Max would plumb the depths of the virtue business. The last time he had stood in Miss Van Siclen's parlor, she had consulted the volume right before his eyes.

Then he noticed the window next to the back door. Cracked open a foot and a half or so, it made a tempting target. If he didn't make a decision quickly, some neighbor might see him prowling around. His fear of being caught warred with his fear of the Midnight Band story drying up. If it died, how much life was left for him at the *Herald*?

Looking around, he pressed his body close to the building and stuck his arm through the opening. If he could find the handle, the hook, the latch, he could let himself in. His hand groped blindly, then he found the iron bar. Gripping it was awkward, and using only his wrist, he couldn't move it an inch. How much longer could he stand there? Flop sweats drenched his shirt. A hard lump rose in his throat. Could anybody see what he was doing? He was going to get caught for sure.

He had to give up. He was no housebreaker.

Dejected, he wandered a block uptown. Behind Gramercy Park's locked wrought-iron fence, Famous O'Leary stood on a bench, surveying his domain. A bronze water-nymph gazed back at the boy. That Famous had defeated the padlock and the spiked barrier didn't surprise Max in the least. If anything, the street arab looked scrawnier, paler. The way he kept scratching himself suggested a case of lice, too. Before he approached, Max looked over his shoulder. It was a reflex by now. Was there another gang of miscreants hiding in the bushes? Behind that dustbin? But Famous appeared to be alone.

"Famous, how's tricks?"

Eyes darting up and back, the boy tensed for flight. "I didn't do nothin'."

"It's me, Max. The reporter. Remember, I gave you some money?"

Famous squinted. Were his eyes bad too? "Oh, yeah."

"Want to make some more?"

"Fifty cents?"

Famous had the gall of a real estate speculator. Max knew he would lose the street arab's respect if he knuckled under too soon. "Twenty-five."

"Nah."

"And a hot meal. You like beefsteak?"

"Sure, who don't? Forty."

"Thirty-five and supper."

"Got a quarter now?"

"Climb over."

Famous scaled the fence, easily avoiding the spikes. Extending his hand, Max dropped a dime into the street rat's palm.

"The rest after the job."

Gazing at the cracked window, Famous said "Nothin' to it."

He snaked through the opening as if he had no spine. In a moment, he opened the back door.

Together they climbed a dark stairway and padded into the living quarters.

Max had never broken into a building in his life. Dread mixed with exhilaration as he penetrated the shrouded dining room and made his way into the parlor. The crowded room pressed in on him. There were shelves of painted china, Meissen porcelain, commemorative plates, and imitation Fabergé eggs. Famous stuck a few eggs in his pants pockets. An overstuffed chair pressed against the horsehair sofa, the latter rubbing against a scarlet divan. Lace antimacassars draped the furniture. Hooked rugs covered every inch of floor space. Muddy landscapes filled the walls. The room gave him a headache.

He knew where Miss Van Siclen kept the membership book. The exact drawer. He groped for the bound volume, but he came up with two books instead, ledgers of some sort. Then he heard voices. He had no time to scan their pages. Where was the conversation coming from? Outside? Downstairs? In the next room? His stomach seized up in a single hard cramp. Famous rushed to the front window.

"Bulls out there," he whispered.

Scraping sounds penetrated the parlor.

"And downstairs, too," Max said in horror. He slipped one of the ledgers into his pants and tightened his belt. The others wouldn't fit. He stood frozen, gripping the other volumes, trying to compose a plausible explanation for his presence. He didn't see Famous lift the brass floor lamp, but he heard the glass shattering. Without wasting a shred of attention on Max's plight, the boy was making his escape, shinnying down a drainpipe. Above the gravel path that ran alongside the house, Famous, skinny arms flapping, let go. Max was certain he couldn't follow. To get through the window he'd have to break out more glass. He was twice Famous's weight.

Would the flimsy pipe give way? Then he'd have to jump. Famous had sailed down like a flying squirrel, but Max might break his neck.

But when he heard a door opening, sheer terror drove him on. In a blur, he dropped the ledgers in his hands, kicked out more window glass, stuck a leg out into empty space, gripped the cold metal, slid down, and tumbled head over heels before finding his feet. His legs churning, he rode a rapids of adrenaline. An ancient thrill took hold of him—he was an animal fleeing for his life.

Bounding, he caught up to Famous. Together they raced through an ornamental garden, then scrambled over a fence. A beaten dirt yard. Crawling mounds of refuse. A chained hound started barking his brains out. A voice shouted "Blackie, shut yer pie hole!"

They were trapped. A great, choking muscle, his heart scuttled up his throat. A window shot open. Famous pounded fence boards with his pointy fists. Before he knew what he was doing, Max was clawing at the old planks until he found one that was rotten as an old tooth. It gave in his hands and they squeezed through.

He could have whooped for joy. Shifting course, Famous faded into an alley. His legs growing heavier and heavier, Max struggled to keep up. Staggering, he knocked over an ash barrel, fell, tore his pants, but scrambled to his feet. Famous didn't look back. Then at the alley's mouth he stood stock-still. Max almost bowled the boy over. Smoothing his fantastic outfit, Famous poked his head out onto Fourteenth Street.

chapter twenty-four

Bending over, Max let his head fall between his knees. When he stood up again, the earth rushed away. Giddy, he balanced himself against a moist wall.

"Act like you ain't done nothin'," Famous instructed, brushing himself off and blending into the sidewalk traffic. Max bit his tongue. What choice did he have? They walked briskly for several blocks. Famous came to a dead stop in front of a drygoods store. He's like a dog on point, Max thought in wonder. Was he sniffing the air for the police?

Max gave himself over to the boy's instincts. "Are we okay?"

His shoulders slumping, Famous seemed to relax. At least he started scratching again. "Gimme the rest."

"How about that beefsteak?"

"I can get my own hash. Gimme the coin."

Then it dawned on Max. He couldn't take Famous to a horse stall the way the boy looked, much less a restaurant. He'd have to get him a fresh suit of clothes. Half rag, Famous's shirt hung open halfway to his navel. Of an indeterminate color, it might have been a curtain or a skirt in an earlier incarnation. His voluminous gabardine pants had been cut down a few inches below the knee. A knotted cord held them up. As colorless as his shirt, his hair lay limp on his narrow skull.

Famous fidgeted, hiking the adult-sized pants halfway to his chest.

"How about some new duds, too? Just for the favor you did me?" Max offered.

"Nah, I'll keep these. Gimme my money."

"No clothes, no steak, kiddo. I'm gonna blow you to a fancy spread." As he spoke, he gazed up and down Fourteenth, searching for a likely shop.

At the corner, but closing fast, Mrs. Edwards advanced before a trio of hulking buttons. Had she recognized him?

"Drop the eggs, Famous," Max warned.

Famous dashed away down the sidewalk before Max could take a step. Only half a block away, Mrs. Edwards and her police escort were charging in his direction. He had to hotfoot it. Backing up, he stumbled into a sidewalk knife sharpener, upsetting the man's grinding wheel. The vendor unleashed a torrent of curses. Ignoring him, Max whirled, scanning the street for Famous, but the boy had disappeared into the roiling crowd. His blood pounding in his head, he skittered around a pushcart piled with peanuts and gumdrops and a peddler hawking pocket watches. A high-wheeled baby buggy cut him off, but he danced around it, then broke into a run.

On the next corner he darted into a storefront. Children screeched and scattered. A counterman waved a spoon. On a mirror behind the soda fountain ran the legend EAT HORTON'S ICE CREAM. Peering through the candy-store window, Max watched as his pursuers changed direction and bolted downtown.

In the middle of the block he launched himself into the stream of wagons and carriages, picking his way to the uptown side. At the curb his boots sank into a stew of soft cabbage, rotten eggs, potatoes, chicken bones, pigs' knuckles, and horseshit.

Cursing to himself, he scraped off the muck as best he could.

If the kid didn't want his beefsteak, the hell with him. Why lay out another nickel? Maybe he could grab a bite himself and take a look at the Midnight Band's ledger, still secure under his belt.

Over on West Fifteenth and Ninth there was a hash house that wasn't too bad. Schneider's. He just had to remind Oscar to cut away the fat. He wouldn't mind wetting his whistle either.

In succession, a boy selling toothpicks, a girl peddling cigars, and another kid selling pocketbook straps accosted him. An army of black-clad customers snaked in and out of the shops. A boy in a flat cap bounced on a cellar door.

Lacy white hats relieved the eye. A woman in a bottle-green satin dress hustled past him. Tight at the hips, the garment rippled in the sun. A pair of Italian children played violins, but no one paid much attention. A better attraction, a glassy-eyed monkey, hopped to an organ grinder's tune.

Threading his way through the tangle of bodies, Max reached the corner of Sixth Avenue and Fourteenth Street.

A crowd had gathered in front of a plumbing-supply house. A businessman craned his neck. A girl hopped up and down to get a better look. Two lady shoppers stopped dead in their tracks and were drawn in, as if by some invisible gravity. The small mob tightened around its hidden pearl. Max suspected a novel act was being born. Street performers mesmerized him. Why not take a quick look? He edged his way in to catch the show.

Famous O'Leary lay there, passed out on the cobblestones.

A middle-aged lady clucked her tongue. "One too many, I'll bet."

Another added her disapproval. "They drink like there's no tomorrow."

"Shut up, you animals! Look at the poor thing!" a woman in a black shawl snapped as she bent and poked the prostrate street arab.

"Watch out, honey, they bite!" a suit puller shouted from his storefront. Derisive laughter bubbled through the knot of onlookers.

"I know him," Max called out.

"He's yours? You should be ashamed of yourself," the Good Samaritan scolded.

"Excuse me, I just inherited him," Max shot back, lifting the frail Famous with both arms. The boy was light as a feather. What was he made of? Air?

Slack, his legs draped over Max's left arm, his narrow head pressed against the reporter's chest, the kid didn't stir. His face was gray, his body skin and bones. Mrs. DeVogt's boarding house was only two blocks away. Praying Belle was home, he headed uptown. She'd know what to do or where to take the boy.

All of a sudden Famous buried a pointy fist in his neck. In disbelief, Max hung on to him, but, by bucking and kicking his legs wildly, Famous slithered free.

"Hey, you're sick. Calm down."

When the kid hit the pavement, the imitation Fabergé eggs slid down his pants leg. Hollow wood, they wobbled along the ground. "You won't get much for those," Max laughed.

In a rush Famous scooped up his booty. "Who asked you? How 'bout coughing up, huh? Forget the steak and gimme a buck."

"What was all that back there?"

Famous gave him a haughty look. "Stop gettin' in my way, is all."

Then it dawned on Max. The old faint-and-cry routine. He'd interrupted Famous's act before its climax. A street arab with practiced fingers could skin a half dozen sympathetic citizens while they petted and stroked him. It was long past time to unload Famous O'Leary. Give him some coin and get rid of him.

He groped inside his jacket for his purse, but all he found was a slit pocket. All that cash! In a panic he dug deeper, but there was nothing inside the lining but bits of lint.

Max spun around, a sickening sensation flooding through him. All that scratch! Famous too. Vanished into thin air. The little sonofabitch had buzzed him good and proper. How much had he lost? Over twenty dollars.

Max raced down the street to get a look around the corner, but a van and a horsecar blocked his view. Placidly, a woman examined a pushcart cabbage. A lush in a slouch hat veered off the sidewalk and plopped down onto the curb.

Max was mad enough to snap Famous' skinny neck, but the sly little dip had already melted into the traffic.

He had exactly one dollar and twenty-three cents in pocket change left. What was the point of even searching for the damned sneak thief? If Famous O'Leary wanted to disappear, there was no hope. He could be laying up in any nook or cranny. On a hay barge. In a sewer pipe. What was Max supposed to do, report the little sonofabitch to the police? Your Honor, I was just breaking and entering when my partner in crime went and pinched my purse.

At least he had a few dollars stashed in his dresser, as well as that most effective palliative, his deposit at the Madison Square Bank. Not to speak of the Midnight Band's ledger.

For safety's sake, he cut uptown to Fifteenth Street. Finally he took out the leather-covered book. Sitting on a brownstone stoop, he flipped through it. Instead of names, he found pages and pages of numbers arranged in neatly ruled columns. In his scattered state, it took a moment for him to understand what he was staring at. At the top of the first page, penciled in the left corner in a haphazard way, was the legend "Our Properties." At the top of each column ran street names: Houston, Varick, Clinton, Cherry, Fulton, Clarke, Dominick, Canal, Grand, King, Sullivan, Bleecker, Greenwich, Christopher, Charlton, Clarkson, Spring, Broome, Hudson, Desbrosses, Watts, and others spread out across the Eighth and Ninth Wards. Below each name, the lines of numbers represented separate addresses. Fifteen buildings on Houston, a dozen on Vandam, another nine on Sullivan.

As he turned the pages, he did the mental arithmetic. The Midnight Band's holdings were breathtaking, over four hundred buildings in all. Did the group's leader, Mrs. Edwards, control the far-flung properties, just as she ran the Midnight Band itself? Recalling the faded Irving Place manse, its missing shingles and flaking walls, he had to laugh. Some nunnery. More like a real estate corporation in mufti.

Stuck loosely inside the back cover were several newspaper articles. Max recognized the *Trib*'s typeface. He scanned one quickly. The first quoted Yale biologist Samuel Garner, on "disharmonious unions." In a guest lecture at New York University, Professor Garner explained that the internal organs of each race were adapted to their relative frames. He pointed out that a union between "a tall Scot and a stubby Italian" would produce children with "large frames and inadequate viscera." Similarly, mixing large-jawed and small-jawed species led to "irregular dentition." The other pieces also quoted leading scientists.

On the ledger's back pages, someone had recorded another list of more obscure numbers. 202H-M1432; 11S-M1764; 141K-P19863. He didn't have time to puzzle them out. When he raised his eyes, Mrs. Edwards was marching down Fifteenth Street, a phalanx of buttons in her wake. Tipping his hat over his eyes, he slipped into a nearby alley. Refuse lapped at his ankles. He could barely keep from choking. He'd blundered into one of the city's leading pissoirs. As soon as his pursuers trotted past, he burst out of the alley and headed east again. After racing downtown along Sixth Avenue, he veered toward Washington Square Park, wandering past fine Federal houses that had been broken up into flats. Only on the north end of the park had the Coopers and Rhinelanders held on in their marble-trimmed red-brick mansions.

The sun broke out, streaming through the budding shade trees. Beds of daffodils had already started blooming. Italian immigrants strolled along the paths, mixing with students, merchants, laborers, and a smattering of older Negroes left behind after most blacks had migrated to the West Thirties and San Juan Hill. Flocks of children flew across the pavement. A piercing hunger seized him. The aroma of roasted chestnuts made him feel faint. In his right pants pocket he still clutched a few coins. He sat on a bench near Garibaldi's statue and devoured the treats.

He flipped through the Midnight Band's ledger again. He couldn't stop wondering who had amassed so much property. Mrs. Edwards? One of her followers? Some unseen magnate?

Still ravenous, he bought two ears of corn. The delicate vendor, a girl of about ten, might have been Famous O'Leary's sister. Dabbed on her cheeks were two unlikely moons of rouge.

Sated, he hauled himself to his feet and headed south toward Thompson Street. On the steps of the Judson Memorial Church, a black minister stood gazing out at the park.

Inspiration seized him. Who knew? You just had to keep talking to people. As the clergyman descended the steps, Max cut across his path.

"Excuse me, may I ask you a question?"

A tall man with pure white hair, the minister regarded Max suspiciously. "What might that be?"

Max noted the man's New York accent. Native-born. That was good. "I'm a reporter from the *Herald*. You may have seen the article about the Negro who was found."

"Refresh my memory. We get so much attention from your paper," the minister said with unmistakable sarcasm.

"Decapitated behind a brewery? That one?"

"I haven't the slightest idea. All you report about Negroes is who slashed whom in Minetta Alley. Why don't you go peddle your scandal in the barbershops?"

Brushing past Max, the clergyman stalked away. Still, he had given Max an idea. Barbershops. Why not? He recalled one near the corner of Thompson and Bleecker. Several men were playing cards inside the establishment. One light-skinned black had reddish hair and freckles. Another wore a silk jockey's cap. The third looked older, bleary and beat-up. One by one they eyed Max with slow-eyed resentment.

"Watcha wan'?" the barber asked. A wiry man with an alert expression, he looked Max over.

"I need a quick trim."

"Right there." He aimed a pair of scissors at a broken-down chair. The card game resumed.

Max sensed that the shop didn't do too many haircuts. "Not too much off the sides."

Clipping away, the barber made small talk. "Not too many respectable peoples comes down the Village no more."

"You said a mouthful," the redhead called out. Max couldn't place his accent.

"Oh, yeah, we have some nice families here in the old days. Families with six, seven servants and that was nothin'," the older man put in.

"Didn't I work for the Conklins? And the Van Dykes?" the barber replied.

"You take a little policy?" Max probed. He didn't really want to place a bet, but he needed to gain the barber's confidence.

"Depend."

"How about the gig?" Three numbers—the simplest combination.

"Awright. How much?" the barber asked.

"Fifty cents."

"Give me 227." He always played his birthday.

"Ernie, you takin' that down?" The redhead took out a pencil and pad. The tense atmosphere eased. "You wan' buy one of them dream books, mister?"

"Nah, leave that to the women. I can pick my own numbers."

"Yeah, jus' pick 'em outta the air. The numbers don't know nothin'."

Max let the scissors clip away for a while. "Listen, fellas, I'm from the *Herald*, you know that paper?"

The scissors froze.

"You the police? Cap'n Frank take care of me," the barber said. Max could hear the catch in his voice.

"No, I'm just working on a story. Did you hear about it? Colored fella was found all cut up in a barrel?"

"Ain't heard nothin' 'bout that."

"Ain't heard nothin'."

"Nope."

The scissors came to life.

"Okay, I just thought you might have heard some scuttlebutt on the street."

"Don't know that one."

Up until that moment, Max hadn't looked in the mirror. Now he saw the skinning he'd taken in all its glory. "Hey, wait. You're mowing it all off."

"Wha'ever you say, mister," the barber said, straight-faced. "Hair oil?"

"No, thanks," he said, controlling himself. "That's enough. Here."

The barber took the coins and dropped them into a cigar box. "Suit youself."

Just for the hell of it, he felt them out one more time. "So, anybody know anything?"

The mute trio just shook their heads.

He was halfway down the block when the freckled card player caught up with him. "Mister."

"Yeah?"

"That man's wife, I know her. That's all I do know. She lives around here." Again Max picked up the trace of an accent. What was it exactly?

"What's her name?"

"I have a sick baby. How about giving me a hand?"

"Every joker's got his hand out." Max dug into his pocket and came up with a pair of dimes. "That's all I can do."

The redhead shrugged and took the change. "Marianne Granger. She's at 207 on this block. In the back."

"What's your name?"

"Don't put it in your paper."

"Just for the record."

The redhead hesitated. "Wally. Wally Moskowitz. Yeah, I know. My father, he's from Warsaw."

A Polish Negro. Maybe a half-Jew to boot. Parnell would think he'd made it up, but there were more like Wally than people realized. The black-and-tans weren't doing a roaring business in Little Africa for nothing. Life, that polyglot stew, kept simmering. Yale professors sitting up on their tuffets, the Reverend Weems decrying fresh-minted imbeciles—nobody could stop it.

Hell, considering that his father had crept into Vienna from far-flung Galicia, and his mother was a native-born Austrian, he was practically a mongrel himself.

Maybe it was the warming May day, or maybe it was the fluttering white wash hanging on the line, but Mrs. Granger's courtyard didn't look too bad. Two skinny girls were jumping rope. A young mutt circled them, barking. Someone had pushed the refuse into a neat pile against the rough plank wall. Of course, there was only one privy for the whole building, but it looked like a two-seater. In the pitch-black hallway, Max bumped into something warm and soft.

Recoiling, he couldn't see what—or who—he had stepped on, but the dark mound was snoring. Cooking cabbage, burning garlic, and odors unidentifiable drenched the darkness. Covering his face with his handkerchief, he climbed higher, steeling himself.

An iron in her hand, Marianne Granger opened the door. A husky woman in her thirties, pinpricks of sweat studded her forehead. Her shrewd eyes appraised him.

"You need washin'?" she asked.

"May I come in?"

"M'mm . . ."

Her apartment looked far better than Max had expected. In the center of a large, bright room stood an imposing brass bed. Over a coal-burning fireplace hung a pair of engravings. A tub full of wash, an ironing board, and a stack of folded linen crowded together against the far wall. Several children were playing quietly on the floor, and a white-haired granny rocked next to the window.

"I'm sorry to bother you, Mrs. Granger, but I wanted to ask you about your husband."

"What? Why you askin' me question? I already tell the police everything I know, which is I don't know what happen or who he been fussin' with."

Max was taken aback. As far as he'd been told, the police had no idea who the decapitated Negro was.

"I'm a reporter for the *Herald*. Maybe I can help you with the cops."

"How you gonna help? They do as they please, and you can't tell me nothin' different."

"Well, what was your husband's first name?"

"Harry. And we was married at the African Zion Baptist church on the second of May, 1885. Put that in your paper."

"Would you tell me what the police said?"

"I go down to the police lookin' for Harry, and they shows me . . . he in a big drawer . . . they asks me if this be him, all broken up like that." She turned her face away, suddenly sobbing softly.

He waited. "It was a terrible thing to happen."

She patted her face with a rag. "Four kid, and he work so hard. Anythin', everythin', he do."

"Did they say they were investigating?"

"What they gonna investigate, a nigger get kill?" Her weary eyes looked at him with contempt. Didn't he know anything about the way of the world?

"Wha's a'matter, honey?" the granny asked.

"Everything okay, Momma. You want more tea?"

He looked toward the wrinkled old lady. How old was she? Seventy? A hundred? "No, ah'm fine."

"Did you get the officer's name?"

"Why? You think I ever see him again?"

"Did you ever hear of Martin Mourtone?"

"Mr. Martin? He a good man. They pay me full price, at least."

Jolted, Max struggled to keep a straight face. Mourtone and Harry Granger. *They knew each other.* Granger hadn't been a random Stephenson's barfly. Had Martin brought him along? Had Granger been killed because of what he knew, not just what he'd seen at Stephenson's?

"For what?"

"For the gravestone."

"So your husband knew Martin?"

"They work together. Harry find him colored peoples, you know, for the insurance. At ten cent, ain't too many, Lord knows."

"Was your husband worried about the business? Was there anything wrong with it?"

"Nah. Jes' too few colored. He always say don't put me in no Potter Field. You wanna be stuck in the ground like that, mister, no cross, no mark, no soul to comfort you?"

"Wha's a matter?" Granny drawled again.

"Nothin', Momma. She hard of hearing. In South Carolina they sell me when I were only two, but she come up north later. She *say* she my mother." Marianne Granger looked doubtfully at the woman in the rocking chair. "'Course I can't never be sure."

Slavery. The War. It sounded as distant as King Arthur, yet the subject was too coarse to discuss in polite society. What it meant to be a slave, Max couldn't begin to fathom. What it meant to be torn apart by the Gatling gun was beyond his comprehension. A financial reporter once told him that after the carnage ended, one quarter of Tennessee's budget went for artificial limbs. "Of course, that boom went bust a long time ago," the business analyst had remarked ruefully.

"So the company did pay for your husband's gravestone?"

"They pay full price. The carving man make that finger that point straight to heaven."

"I'm sorry. Where is Harry's marker?"

"African Methodist bury him."

"By the way, your husband couldn't speak, could he?"

"What you talkin' 'bout? Harry, he talk to everybody."

"He wasn't deaf and dumb?"

Her voice grew shrill. "Who you talkin' to? Harry, he can talk a blue streak. Talk to any man."

"You'd know best."

"Don' listen to no lyin' dogs. Harry work from the minute he wake up. He make a good livin', too."

Stephenson's rag, Joseph MacNamara, had lied from the start. Marianne Granger's rage spoke the truth.

Bone-tired, but unwilling to head home, Max threw himself down on a Washington Square Park bench. Why had he fallen for MacNamara's lie? It just seemed to fit. In his tattered overalls, Harry Granger had looked like damaged goods. How many times had Max read in the papers that blacks were more prone to idiocy? But Harry Granger hadn't faded away on his own. He'd been cut to pieces by somebody who believed he could speak only too well.

Parnell wouldn't give the story much space—he'd already featured the decapitated Negro once—but if the buttons coughed up Granger's name, it was worth a squib. Max couldn't get over it. Granger and Martin, partners. He traced the suggestive outline of it in his mind. What did they gain? For Harry Granger, a few finder's fees meant a great deal; for Martin, the sheer novelty of having a Negro partner might have been the lure. Harry Granger gave him a contact inside the shrouded African world. What did the Negro tell him?

Who had identified Granger's remains? Which cop had interviewed Granger's wife? Was the case still active? Or had Police Superintendent Byrnes killed it for good?

chapter twenty-five

Detective Stout was sharing a cigar with Max's old friend, Officer Schreiber outside police headquarters.

"The big man home?" Max asked.

Schreiber looked at him with amusement. "Byrnes? He's down at City Hall. Who mowed you, Maxie?"

He ran his hand over his shorn head. "It's the latest, boys."

"Hey, whatever gets the quim," Stout put in.

"Yeah, that's what I figured. But while I've got you, Stout, can I ask you a few questions?"

"No," Stout deadpanned.

"What do you mean?"

Schreiber rubbed his thumb in his palm. Was this a new refinement? The buttons had never put a cash value on quotes before. "How come Byrnes'll whisper in my ear for free?"

"That's Byrnes. I don't give it away for two bits neither."

The three men exchanged expressionless looks. In the tense silence, Max tried to find his footing. Finally, he just started laughing. "C'mon, Stout. You always gave it up before."

Stout poked Schreiber. "I had him going, did you see that? He was pissin' in his pants."

"Sometimes I worry about you, Maxie. You might fold under questioning," Schreiber speculated.

The button's ambiguous joke gave them all a laugh. "No, what I wanted to know is when you identified Harry Granger."

Max observed Stout's sunken features closely, but the detective covered any flicker of recognition. "Who's that?"

"That Negro they found in pieces."

"Which nigger?" Stout laughed.

"Which pieces?" Schrciber inquired.

"It was in the papers. Behind the brewery. He was dismembered."

Stout's hedgerow eyebrows rose. "Yeah, I heard about it, but they got somebody else on the case."

"Maybe nobody else. I've got to file the story. You think anybody in there wants to make a statement?"

"You can make that shit up on your own, can't you?"

"Sure, but Byrnes likes to appear in the right light, doesn't he?"

Dropping the forced bonhomie, Stout looked Max up and down. "Wait here, sonny. I'll go and see."

The detective disappeared through the tall side doors. Schreiber coughed into his fist. "He's got his own troubles."

"Why does he take them out on me?"

Schreiber's face split into an expansive grin. "'Cause he hates you, Maxie. You didn't know that?"

The Police Department offered up a single sentence. "The remains of the Negro Harry Granger of 207 Thompson Street have been identified." It was almost nothing, but now Max had corroboration. At the *Herald* office, he started toward his corner when he noticed something strange: Parnell was missing from the throne. In his place, a harried assistant editor was trying to keep up with the piles of copy building up on his desk. Parnell was like an office fixture. He never took a day off. Max wondered if the editor had fallen ill, but he didn't have time to ask around. His deadline loomed.

Unfortunately, he had to leave almost everything out. He couldn't talk about Granger's relationship with Martin Mourtone. He didn't know enough about it, and he didn't want it to get out. Nor did he want to mention the "paid-in-full gravestone." In the end, he came up with two skinny grafs, dropped them off, and headed for the door. Then he saw Biddle leaning close over his copy, scrawling away.

"Biddle, got a minute?"

The reporter tossed his pen across the desk. "My young savior."

"Where's Parnell?"

"Ahh, that's not for public consumption. However, as you are intimate with the principals, I'll confide in you. Refreshments?"

"I'm short, Nick. Your treat." Few words had ever given him more satisfaction.

"M'mm . . . well, my finances are a bit tight too. . . ."

Inadvertently, he'd cornered the old roué. "Your call."

Biddle's call turned out to be the Plucked Hen, a basement dive on Nassau Street. The establishment featured barrels fitted out with rubber tubes. "They take a good deep breath," Biddle explained, "and suck 'til their eyes pop out."

"All you can drink?"

Two disheveled men were sucking, without end.

"That's the attraction. Plus free snails."

One tube jockey fell to the floor in slow sections.

"But I think we ought to take the conventional path," Biddle went on.

The flat beer had a strange, metallic taste. Max cursed Famous O'Leary for putting him at Biddle's mercy. Without breathing, he drained half a glass. "What's in this piss?"

"Mystery ingredients. One day it's a dash of mercury. Another day it's a spot of shellac. That's part of the fun, don't you think?"

Biddle offered an evil grin. Even when he was treating, he got the upper hand.

"It ain't Hoffman's, huh? Where's Parnell? I thought he lived in the office."

Biddle sipped thoughtfully. "It's not that bad. I draw the line at turpentine."

"Parnell? Remember?"

"Yes, it might surprise you to know that our Mr. Parnell has a wife and three little Parnells. You look astonished. It's true he never leaves his post, or almost never, but he has a very respectable wife and goes to a very respectable church. Of course, that sort of life creates obligations."

A self-satisfied smile played on Biddle's bloodless mouth. He had taken a wiser path leading to no obligations whatsoever.

"So?"

"How much do you think Abie Hummel's subpoenas cost? Take a guess, a wild guess."

"Parnell?"

"He got off his desk long enough to climb onto something else, I suppose. And the innocent woman had no choice but to seek legal counsel. Actually, our Parnell's in a nasty spot. A summons like that could break him."

"How much? A thousand? Two?"

Biddle jabbed a thumb heavenward.

"Four?"

"On average, Abe will settle for between five and ten. Usually, though, he's dealing with clients who can afford it, so I think he'll be lenient with our leader. Abie has a heart."

"You think they got his name from Weems?"

"Possibly. What you have to realize, my young friend, is that since that trial, H&H have every sportsman and every married man of means in this city in a panic. Is there a single man who hasn't visited a resort now and then? Now these same sports are sitting there thinking, they have a *map,* they know *my name*. Think of it. Only one man ever stood up to them."

"Who was that?"

"Barrymore. You know what he said to Abie? He said 'Give it to the papers! All of it! It will just add to my reputation.' Johnny's a visionary, if you ask me."

"What did Hummel do?"

"He burned that summons on the spot. And then he negotiated a new theatrical contract for Johnny that beat the band."

"So he blackmailed Barrymore, then he kept him as a client?"

"That's the kind of man Abe Hummel is," Biddle said, beaming.

A tingling sensation ran up Max's spine. Was it the Plucked Hen's mystery brew? Or the realization that Howe and Hummel reigned over a shadow world beyond ouija boards and table knocking?

"Hey, Nick. I've got to check some real-estate stuff. What's the name of that hack at the Buildings Department?"

Biddle put a skeletal hand over his eyes and groped through the darkness. "Candle? Joseph T. Candle. A human slug if there ever was one."

"What does he cost?"

"Two or three dollars is enough to inspire him."

Max put his hand out. "You can spare it."

Biddle sighed, peeled off a few bills and gazed at them with nostalgia. "You mind if I search you first?"

Max snatched the greenbacks. "For the greater glory."

Nick lifted his glass. "To the *Herald*."

"The *Herald*," Max agreed. He shot to his feet, but a queer gravity took hold. The Plucked Hen turned on its axis, the bar shifted at a forty-five-degree angle, tables and chairs orbiting merry-go-round about his head. Listing left and then right, he stumbled up the steps into the braying city.

Slowly shaking off the Plucked Hen's needled brew, he set out to examine the Midnight Band's empire. One-Forty-One Varick Street, a two-story frame house with an outdoor staircase and a swaybacked roof, held a cobbler's and an abandoned saddler shop. A few shards of glass graced the first-floor windows. Stepping over a fetid puddle, he climbed the steps to the apartment. A white dumpling of a face peered out at him.

"My husband's out. Can't let nobody in," the woman grumbled, cracking the hooked door. A bleary eye gazed at him.

"That's all right. I just want some information. I'm from the *Herald*."

"Sho' what?" Her thick speech hinted at a fresh growler.

"I just want to know who you pay your rent to."

"Who wants to know?" she repeated.

"The *Herald*. The paper wants to know. Here's my card." He slipped the scrap of cardboard through the opening.

"We pay Moriarity. Now scat. Go, go."

"Not Mrs. Edwards? Or Miss Van Siclen?"

"Moriarity what got the goiter. Thirty-five dollars he sucks out of this palace. Put that in your paper, mister."

With that, she slammed the door shut. He knocked again, but she just glared at him through the wavy window glass.

Weaving his way uptown, he examined the next Varick Street address on the list. Tilting out of plumb, a three-story frame building seemed to be sinking before his eyes. Its muddy yard was composed of fermenting vegetable matter and mounds of human waste. Max decided against crossing it. He consulted the ledger and found some other nearby residences in the Midnight Band portfolio.

One, at 22 Spring Street, turned out to be a remarkable rookery. A chamberpot festival was in full swing, several tenants in succession pouring excrement from the higher floors. Stinging liquids rained down. Soft missiles struck the sidewalk and stuck there, quickly devoured by the effluvial sea that ran over the curb all the way to the front steps. An outdoor staircase dripped with children. They swung from railings, skittered up and down unpainted steps, shouted, issued threats, sang scraps of song, leaped and fell into the muck below. A knot of men huddled before the tenement's black mouth of a doorway.

Max went straight for them. "Say, Mac, who owns this temple?"

A beetle-browed resident looked Max up and down. "Who wants to know?"

"Max Greengrass, *Herald*." He stood toe to toe with the man, refusing to blink.

"He ain't no reporter. He's an agent," a man with a cherry-red birthmark on his cheek sneered.

This made no sense, but more accusations percolated up from the assembly. Max balled his fists.

"Nah, he's the fucking landlord."

"You kidding? His lordship don't wanna dirty his socks."

"Here's my card," Max said, extracting his paper totem and waving it in the air.

"Less see it," the birthmark-stained resident said.

Max doubted any of them could read, but he let them pass it around. The official-looking typeface had a magical effect. The men drew their chins back. From under a coat, a brown glass jug appeared, the fat-necked bottle passing from mouth to mouth.

"We pay through the nose, I'll tell you that. T'ree or four onna bed. How d'you like that stink?" The dark-browed man flattened his nostrils and sniffed the air.

Gravelly laughter mixed with hoots and shouts. The fun was starting again. Max didn't hesitate when the jug materialized in his hands. He threw his head back and sucked down the burning juice. "I showed you mine, now what's your names?"

Whitey. Johnny. Tim. Waxey. Meyer, the one with the birthmark-stained cheek. They shook hands all around.

"So who do you pay for this dump?"

"When we pay!" Whitey put in.

A wineskin came out, and a bottle wrapped in burlap.

"Let 'em suck blood outta somebody else's neck," Waxey threatened.

"Well, c'mon, when they finally get ahold of you," Max joined in, "who sticks his hand in your pocket?"

"Suckass landlord, who the hell else?" Whitey said.

"His name, her name, who is it?" Max persisted.

"Corky picks our pocket. Name's Corky," Meyer explained.

"You know his first name? And where his office is?"

"Mike Corchoran. Next to the Chink laundry on Hudson." Meyer looked at Max askance, as if he didn't know where the center of the universe was located.

"You ever hear of a Mrs. Edwards? Or Miss Van Siclen?"

"The Edwards takes it lying down, or the one takes it off the wall?" Johnny inquired.

"Nah, he's just chewing your ear. Mikey Corchoran's the one," Whitey assured him.

"What's your name again, mister? You wanna see one for the books?" Meyer asked.

Max dug out his last few coins and slapped them in Meyer's palm. "Sure, I'm game."

"Foller me. Touch yer fingers to the walls when we get there," he added, cryptically.

Meyer led him through an alley and out into a flooded courtyard. A lively girl was yanking at the pump. Max took a good look at the brown water that was spurting into her pail.

"No water in this building?"

"We're just on the second floor," she said, a shy smile on her face.

"This way," Meyer urged him, disappearing down the cellar stairs.

He sloshed after his guide, tensing in case the man tried to roll him. A character like Meyer was as weak as a kitten, he figured. He'd go down fast if you caught him with one good uppercut.

Following close, he stepped into pure darkness. Wobbling, he groped for the wall. His hand found moist stone. An ancient chill pervaded the pitch-black basement.

"I gotta save the candle. This way," Meyer urged him.

Now he wasn't so sure he could defend himself. Who knew which direction the shot-weighted sap was coming from? Then he heard the snoring. There were multiple notes. Low wheezes. Musical sinuses. Trumpet blares from slack throats. Full chords on organs of fleshy pipes.

He smelled the musk of human beings in close quarters. Gagging, he dug into his pocket for a handkerchief.

Meyer lit his nub of a candle. "These is only sleepin' it off. At night there's a dozen, easy, in here."

At best, the chamber was no more than six by ten.

In the guttering flame Max beheld the human pile. Lying across one another on deflated mattress ticking, the sleeping men formed a single wheezing body. A bearded face was embedded in an anonymous thigh, a hand sprouted between tangled legs, bare feet seemed to grow from a throat. In a rattle of phlegm, the mound exhaled as one. He had seen derelicts frozen to death, their features skinned with ice, and watched floaters hooked from the Hudson by the harbor police, but there was something about this many-armed, many-legged heap of human beings that outdid those horrors. Perhaps because it was still alive.

"So how much do they have to cough up?" he inquired.

"Nickel a night. Beats Happy Jack's Canvas Palace."

"By two cents, last I looked."

"Yeah, but most of the times Mike the Cork keeps it dry in here," Meyer observed before killing the candle with his thumb.

chapter twenty-six

Max was no stranger to the tenements. He'd grown up in one, and his mother, that whirling dervish, was still cleaning another out and dreaming of owning it one day. Fifth Avenue reformers might have regarded Max's childhood home as a slum, but it wasn't that bad at all. He didn't have to haul water upstairs from a pump, there was a toilet on his floor, and the halls were scrubbed down every other day. Mr. Brodsky, the owner, prided himself on whitewashing every three years, and he looked down on those cockroach landlords who resorted to three-month paint, a flaking concoction that had a habit of bursting into flames while still wet. Max's family of four shared three rooms while his friends were jammed into identical apartments with five or six brothers and sisters, and a boarder to boot. As a boy, he believed he was from a better class.

Tenement life seemed normal to him. More than half of Manhattan was jam-packed with apartment buildings. The worst, usually rear tenements, often had nothing but a single outdoor privy and a single water pump to serve all the tenants. On his own block, apartment houses of this lower order were scattered among the more habitable dwellings.

The Burnt Pot, for instance, had been condemned in 1864 but continued to thrive. It couldn't burn down, the story ran, because its walls were nothing but dirt itself. Then there was the Shipwreck, a listing three-story rookery that housed a baker, a fishmonger, and twelve families. A single sink in the basement served for wetting down dough, scaling cod, and urinating. Max knew all about it because his Shipwreck buddies loved to let loose in this sink as a form of recreation and revenge. The adults who relieved themselves in it had more prosaic needs.

On his block, some buildings hadn't been painted in decades; others were slathered rust-red every five years. Some stayed stone-cold all winter; others kept their furnaces just warm enough. When he walked down a block, he habitually picked out the pariahs, the half-gutted, the teeming hives, and the piles of sticks so far gone even vagrants avoided them. But these disasters stood out among, by his standards, the other more or less habitable dwellings.

Where the unpracticed eye might see identical run-down shops, Max could discern which store sold rotten vegetables and which one had a better stock; he could tell where to buy a fresh chicken and where the milk swarmed with too much life; he could sniff out which joint tapped a decent beer, and which dive served the drippings from a hundred barrels.

Mrs. Edwards's property—or Moriarity's or Mikey Corchoran's—reminded him of the Burnt Pot. Her buildings loomed like Untouchables on the Hindoo continent. Max had no beef with landlords in general, and he had mixed feelings about the derelicts in the human pile—how could anybody let himself sink that low?—but no one deserved to live in complete ruins. There were complicated political theories that explained these things, but he sensed without putting it into words that there was a line, however unclear, between making a dollar and committing a crime.

He was slightly embarrassed to find that he had such feelings, and he certainly intended to keep them to himself. But whoever owned the hundreds of properties listed in the Midnight Band's ledger ought to be dragged into the light of day. It would make a pretty story. Why shouldn't he be the one to tell it?

On Thursday morning, he battled the light. When it struck him flush on the eyelids, he mashed a pillow over his face. When it reflected off the mirror, he dove deep down under the covers. When he emerged from his hiding place later on, tangled in his bedclothes, his mouth agape, the terrible brightness was too much, and he scuttled back into his cave. He had to get to work, but he'd never been so worn out. He heard someone calling his name, heels tapping on the stairs, breakfast's clatter, but he blocked it all out, sinking back into a delicious swoon.

When he crawled back to consciousness, Mrs. DeVogt's boarding house was shrouded in silence. He lay there a long time, luxuriating in a warm daze.

"Are you decent?" Belle shouted from the other side of his door.

Her penetrating voice shook him awake. "That's a matter of opinion," he called back. "What time is it?"

Backing into the room with a tray in her arms, she said, "Cover yourself. It's eleven-thirty."

The office! Hell, he wasn't on deadline. Sitting up, still bleary-eyed, he took in the way her hair curled at the nape of her neck, her slender back, her elegant figure. Her crisp skirts rustled as she came around his bed. "It's so quiet. Where's the rest of the zoo?"

"They all flew the coop. Here, coffee and rolls. Mrs. DeVogt fed your eggs to the cat."

He sipped the coffee, wondering where she would sit down. The edge of the bed would make her handy. His hopes were dashed when she turned and chose the Morris chair. Her feet barely touched the ground. He was so busy trying to catch a glimpse of her ankles that her pallor and her red-rimmed eyes barely registered.

"This is smashing, thanks. Ahh, you remembered the jam too."

"Mrs. DeVogt's preserves," she said in a constricted voice.

He smeared the sweet fruit all over his roll. "Peach?"

"Something happened," she began.

Her blood-drained face struck him now, and he realized she'd been crying. "What's going on?"

"I have a confession to make."

"Let me grab my collar."

"It's not funny. I stayed home from work. Faye's in jail."

"What?" He leaped out of bed, his legs shooting out from beneath his nightshirt. "What? What for?"

"We were shopping. . . ." She averted her eyes from his exposed knees, but not before noticing how sturdy they looked.

Quickly, his terror subsided. He knew exactly what his sister had been up to again. "She got pinched? Where? Macy's? McCreery's?"

"Stern's, but it was my fault entirely—"

"I doubt it. Faye had the light fingers long before she ever laid on eyes on you." Along with a few more questionable habits best left unmentioned. He was irritated but relieved all at once. At least his sister hadn't stuck a fork in some stage manager's eye. Damn her! She didn't care if she ate up his only day off.

"It was my idea, I was showing her. . . ." If her father ever found out, she'd die of shame. Jake would use it like a lash against her. And didn't she deserve it? Who could be a bigger hypocrite? She always swore to herself she'd never succumb again, but the scarf's fabric was so rich, and the store was spraying that perfume that made her head spin, and the Stern Brothers were swimming in gelt and who was watching anyway?

"Since she was about six," he went on, shaking his head and laughing out loud. "Just tell me which jug she's in, and I'll go get her. They've probably stashed her over at the Jefferson Courthouse, huh?"

Belle's face grew hot. Thoughtlessly, she twirled a strand of hair around her index finger. "You're not listening! It was my idea to show her the gloves and . . . anyway, she's the one who got caught."

Finally, he grasped the whole situation. Belle the crusader had a dash of thievery in her, too. The difference between her and Faye was obvious, though. Belle was in agony. Faye, in the clink, would be cursing herself for getting caught.

"You've got the fever, too? That's a shocker."

Straightening her back, she stiffened, and a new note crept into her voice. "Well, you read every day about doctor so-and-so's wife and how she didn't know what she was doing or she has a woman's disease. The ladies have kleptomania. The shopgirls they send to jail."

She knew what she was talking about. Faye needed the white lace gloves for her wedding, they looked darling, but how could an actress afford them? She didn't have money to burn like some people; but with all her talent, didn't she deserve a few nice things? Then that miserable store detective with booze on his breath and pot-roast stains on his vest, he should have been ashamed of himself.

Her own shame was a chill, a spasm that radiated from her stomach down her legs. She pressed her knees together.

"You're right about that. Oh, damn it. I'm short. You wouldn't have ten dollars on you 'til tomorrow, would you?" Max asked.

"Ten dollars? What for?" Jake might berate her, but he wouldn't take a cent from her. With Max, she was a little wary. Anyway, ten dollars was a fortune. Where did he get off asking for so much?

"You don't want her to rot over at Jefferson, do you? We've got to spring her now." Whistling under his breath, he poured water into the porcelain basin and soaped his hands.

She couldn't get over it. He seemed positively cheerful. In fact, he hadn't lectured her. He didn't seem to take her humiliation seriously. She thought less of him than ever, and liked him more. Look at the way he was showing off his legs in his skimpy nightshirt, proud of his muscular calves and tapering ankles, casual and brazen all at once.

"I'll see what I have," she agreed. On the one hand, she didn't want to face Faye; on the other, she didn't want Max to go off on his own and make too free with her money. "I'll go with you."

Stretching, he arched his back and yawned. From under his sleeves his whipcord forearms slid out. "Why not?"

He splashed cold water on his face and rubbed it with a fresh towel. The terrycloth smelled clean, the soft material soothing against his skin. He was coming back to life. Looking up, he caught her staring. For a heartbeat she held his gaze before catching her breath and glancing away.

Her waist was so tiny. He could feel his fingers unlacing her, the smooth silk panels of her corset, the sweet thrill of her breasts pressed against his naked chest.

"I'll get my purse," she said, starting for the door.

When he held out his arm she curled into him and they were kissing, breathless, in a blur. Her tongue darted into his mouth, and he realized that she knew more than he had expected. Without thinking, he lifted her, stroking her hair, nuzzling her ear, kissing her throat. He was lost now, more mindless electricity than man. When she slipped her hands under his shirt, he thought he might die. Her fingers stroked his chest and then, to his amazement, worked their way down his taut body.

He was thicker than Jake. Pulsing in her palm, his erection felt hard yet strangely delicate. His whiskers rubbed her cheeks raw. She felt her courage surging back, the nerve to surrender to heat and nothingness. She snaked out of his arms and turned her back. "Quick, help me," she whispered. His dumb fingers tugged at the buttons, finally freeing one, then the next and the next until she could bend down and draw the silk dress straight over her head.

Unable to speak, he groped to hook the door. He felt drunk as he freed her, eyehole by eyehole, from her restraining garment, intoxicated in the flooding light. When she stepped out of her corset, sunlight penetrated her white camisole, and he could see the outline of her whole body, his heart beating madly against his ribs. Then she was holding his gaze, steady and defiant as he lifted the hem of her chemise and pulled it up to reveal her slender legs, her black-haired crotch, her outflowering hips, her dark-nippled breasts in the plain sunlight.

An obsidian necklace, her single adornment, gleamed dark around her throat. He cupped her breasts gently in his hands. Leaning over, he kissed the velvety mole on her face.

In a rush, he tore off his nightshirt and stood naked before her. A white knotted scar stood out on his shoulder. His swelling chest was covered with wiry hair, but not too much, she thought; and the way he stood, his square chin up, his legs apart, his erection quivering, engorged, made her feel faint. She pressed herself against his flat-muscled body. Her fingers, not her own, ran down his back and traced the shape of his buttocks. Deep in his throat he groaned, and she could feel the great muscles clenching in her hands, she could feel him shuddering in her arms.

When she folded her legs and drew him in with her hand, it was light. When he began to move in her, it was light. Light washed the bedclothes and lifted them up. Lost in light, they passed through each other, and then they were light itself.

"You think anybody heard us?" he gasped, coming to his senses.

"You sound like a steam engine," she laughed, slapping his chest. "Don't worry, they're all out." She fit herself into his arms and they lay there a long time, not speaking, but she knew what he was thinking. "You're shocked?"

"No, why should I be?" he lied without conviction.

"Because I'm not the type you think. Well," she went on, taking a deep breath to steady her voice, "I'm not. You're only the second one. But I'm not sorry. Are you?"

She was making a point, he understood. She might be a socialist, but that didn't make her into some crazy Free-Lover. "Are you kidding? Did I sound like I was sorry?"

What had made her do such a thing? She felt worse than sorry, but dizzy and exhilarated, too. Making love to him was like slipping a silk blouse into her coatsleeve, the sheer excitement of getting away with it, and the fear that she would do it again. Against her better judgment, against her will, against her principles. In a fever, principles melted so easily, didn't they?

"Next time we'll use a sheepskin," she added, the efficient nurse coming to the surface.

"Who's the first?"

She put her hand on his wilted penis and yanked it softly. "That's my business. You want to tell *me* everyplace *he's* been? H'mm?"

"I don't think so," he laughed. She was prickly, blunt. He liked her, but she made him nervous, too. Now that they were so intimate, what did she expect from him? And who *was* the first? One of her scruffy anarchist friends? He could have her again, she'd said it plain as day, but was she intending to keep two lovers? Or was it all a ruse to lure him in deeper? He didn't believe in love, but he felt so comfortable talking to her. She had a good head on her shoulders, and a profession too. He didn't believe in romance, but she fit herself into his arms so sweet and tasty that he ached for her again. If a craving didn't die, what was its name?

It only cost seven dollars to get Assistant Warden Vandersee to drop the charges against Faye and release her into Max's custody. Although he didn't know Vandersee personally, they both held Sim Addem in high regard. In the course of explaining the painful operation Faye had endured, a medical procedure Max invented on the spot, and her unfortunate recourse to Mrs. Winslow's Syrup, Max also mentioned his warm feelings for Clubber Williams, the Tenderloin pantata, and Max Hochstim, king of the Essex Street Courthouse.

Faye had dark pouches under her eyes, but was in good spirits otherwise. "What a break, the two of you showing up. Got a cig, Maxie? No? Rats! I thought I'd be cooped up in that sewer 'til the hearing on Friday."

"You owe Belle seven simoleons for this show."

Faye seemed oblivious to this remark. Strolling up Sixth Avenue, he steered the two women, one on each arm.

"I'll squeeze it out of one of you," Belle swore. She made a joke of it, but she wasn't letting them off the hook so easy. Didn't she sweat blood for seven dollars?

Faye leaned over and whispered into his ear. "Lookit who got stung!"

Was it so obvious? His face turned scarlet, and for once he couldn't find a quick comeback.

Then she let go and started skipping down the street, heads turning as she flounced past. Breathless at the next corner, she twirled around a lamppost and bowed. "I know a cozy spot," she informed them when they caught up.

Linking her arm through Max's, she led the way to a basement rathskeller on Fourteenth Street. A mouse skittered through the sawdust on the floor, but otherwise the Raven made a good impression. Clean glasses hung upside down over the bar, and the brass rail was polished to perfection. Faye produced a five-dollar bill from a secret hiding place.

"Usually, the screws won't go through your drawers," she advised Belle.

"You don't want to go making a good impression all at once," Max said, wishing she'd button her lip for once.

"Tell him. Was it my fault?" she appealed to Belle. "I was already out on the sidewalk scot-free. They're not supposed to drag you back into the store like that."

"He was a louse," Belle commiserated. "But I think my shoplifting career is over." She couldn't help being fond of Faye, but she didn't trust her either. She made drinking in the middle of the day seem like a lark.

Faye gave her an evil smile. "Reformed already, cookie? There's a costume-jewelry sale at Macy's, I heard."

"Leave her alone, Faye," Max interceded.

"Oh, don't bother her, Max. Look at what she just went through," Belle said. Under the table she rubbed her shoe against his ankle. She knew she should be wary of Max too, but she wasn't in the mood, not while she could still savor his energy rushing through her.

Her touch made him so hard so fast, there was nothing to do but surrender. "Yeah, you're right. One more round?"

"Only one," Faye declared. "I've got to pick up Leon."

"Oh, shit: Leon! Who's taking care of him?" Max blurted.

"Mrs. Darling, don't worry. She's a wonder. Leon loves her. God, I must look horrid. It was just crawling in there!"

She rested her head on Belle's shoulder and let her friend pet her.

Together they walked Faye over to Sullivan Street and waited for her to bring the baby downstairs. Mrs. Darling lived practically next door to his sister in a two-story frame house whose windows, set barely higher than Max's head, suggested pre–Civil War origins. Traces of colorless paint clung to its batten-board siding. The angle of the roofline implied a sinking foundation, but the windowpanes were in place, the front door opened and closed, and a thin line of smoke rose from the chimneypot.

Leon had a woozy look on his face, but Faye held both of his hands over his head until he managed a few shaky steps on the sidewalk. Max picked his nephew up and searched his face. His skin was splotched red and white. Did the kid have a fever? He kissed the boy's forehead. Warm, but not burning hot. Holding Leon at arm's length, he examined the child's face. For the hundredth time, Max wondered who Leon's father was, but he'd stopped asking long ago. His sister was right, it wasn't anybody else's business.

"Look at those chipmunk cheeks!" Faye declared, taking the boy and passing him to Belle.

"I think he's hot," Max said. "Check his temperature when you get home."

"Unca Max. Come back," Leon suggested, ducking his head, then popping up again and laughing, showing off his glistening gums.

"Are you hot, chubs?" Faye asked, screwing her face up at the boy until he gave her a wobbly smile.

Max seized his nephew again, bouncing the kid onto his shoulders. There were no two ways around it. Danny Swarms might come and go, but Leon was his nephew forever. Who else was going to look out for the kid, come hell or high water? That was the real dope, and it made him as nervous as that dancing chicken in Chinatown.

"Leon, Leon," Faye said, inciting the boy. "Say it, you know, un. . . ."

In his piping voice, Leon obliged. "Un . . . hand me, you cad."

"Like in the plays!" Belle said, clapping.

"Sings scales, too," Max added. "Leon can do anything, right, Leon?"

When his sister disappeared up the stairs, he took Belle's hand. "I'll get to the bank tomorrow, don't worry."

"I'm not worried. Otherwise, I'll strangle you," she promised. He went to kiss her right there on the sidewalk, but she pushed him away. "Not here, not now," she said, gripping his wrists.

chapter twenty-seven

Max was already waiting when the doors to the Buildings Department swung open on Monday morning. Behind him a horde of lawyers, financiers, cockroach landlords, and more august property owners surged into the offices, bearing him along on the tide. Working his way through the marbled corridor, he slipped into the Deeds Office, a high-ceilinged chamber whose great record books were packed vertically on deep shelves against opposing walls. In these volumes were hidden the true mysteries of New York City, the hieroglyphics of ownership and easements, the obscure financial acts of faith and deception that told the stories of great fortunes and of lives passed in subdivided rooms.

He had decided to avoid Joseph T. Candle at all costs. Why let a Tammany hack get wind of his investigation? Nick Biddle swam in that water, but Max was developing a different way of doing things. On one wall hung a map revealing the city's sinew and bone. All Manhattan was broken into numbered blocks in this plan. On it he found the 141 Varick and 22 Spring blocks. He hauled a record book off the wall and turned its venerable pages—sheets covered with minute handwriting above, below, and around certain lots, and in the margins around individual blocks.

A small map was folded into the property book containing the Varick Street address. With care, he turned back its stiff folds. Broken down into numbered lots, the plan displayed every building site on the block. And there it was, 141 Varick, a bland rectangle on an ink-stained sheet of paper. To his surprise, the deed did belong to Clarence Moriarity. The same Moriarity "what got the goiter," he supposed. The structure, originally a single-family dwelling, had gone up in 1857. Owners included Cornelius Schenevus, who sold it to Benjamin Sloan on September 12, 1862, who turned it over to Andrew Lavender on

August 7, 1874. An O'Fallon, a Greenberg, and a Hirshenfang also played landlord in the ensuing decades. Finally, the hulk had fallen to Clarence Moriarity, who had held it tight for the last dozen years.

Max had been hoping to find simple connections—documents that would, for instance, make Mrs. Edwards's hidden interest plain. But if she didn't own any of the buildings—and he couldn't link Miss Van Siclen or Mrs. Warner or any of the Midnight Band's faithful to the property—he was lost. Was Mrs. Edwards a mere factotum? Did the Midnight Band have little or nothing to do with the tenements?

Disappointed, Max pulled down another heavy volume and tracked down 22 Spring Street. To his irritation, Michael Corchoran did in fact hold the deed to that fantastic warren. He pressed his nose close to the yellow sheet of paper, squinting to make out every odd notation, scribbling down the moniker of every owner ever attached to the rookery, but Mrs. Edwards's name was nowhere to be found.

Stymied, he fell into a hard municipal chair. He cursed himself for not bringing more of the Midnight Band's listings with him. Now he would have to comb the streets and interrogate more tenants, and he'd have to return to the Buildings Department with more locations of more ramshackle holdings.

He'd been hoping to spring the case on Parnell and, with the editor's backing, work up a sprawling series on the Edwards empire. His instincts told him that the tale was hidden in the addresses, but until he could make the numbers speak, he had nothing at all. On his way out, he paused and stared at the real-estate map, the underlying skeleton of the shifting city: rigid, quantified, mute. Gritting his teeth, he wove through the real-estate bazaar, dodging agents, *padrones*, contractors, and wizards of the unsecured loan until he finally burst out into the street.

Outside in the warm sunlight, he fished in his pocket and came up with twenty-seven cents. He already knew where his purse had gone. By his calculations, Famous O'Leary had filched twenty-two dollars from him. He could only imagine what a fabulous sum it had seemed to Famous. What would he do with it? Max wanted to wring the street arab's neck, but he couldn't help smiling when he imagined Famous stuffing himself with hot chestnuts and ice cream. Maybe he was blowing his friends to clams and fried potatoes and hauling overflowing growlers to Grove Street Park. No doubt he was having the time of his life.

He had twenty-seven cents in his pocket and a debt to Belle that couldn't wait. His best bet would be to go to the bank, grab lunch at Logan's, and forget that Mrs. Edwards and her wretched list had ever existed. Instead of worrying about his slashed pocket, he incited his imagination with visions of Belle, her delicate mouth, her brave and unashamed eyes. Her dark hair, dark skin, dark nipples, the silken thrill, so sweet and obliterating. Let Famous run wild. Let all the foundations in Manhattan sink. Let all the basements flood. Let all the deeds in the municipal archives burn in holy hell.

Armed with fresh cash, he'd take Belle to a musical show at Koster and Bial's, or if she wanted something more high-class he could scare up tickets to Daly's. Afterward, they could take a car uptown to the Metropole. The three-sided bistro was loaded with Broadway types, dancers, song-pluggers, fire-eaters, and talent scouts, and he'd heard a rumor that Maude Adams showed up around midnight sometimes, all wound up after her show.

The El whisked him to Madison Square in no time. Out in the center of the traffic, a broad-shouldered button gravely motioned to the converging streams of traffic from Broadway, Fifth Avenue, and 23rd Street. Carriages with plush interiors rolled by. Black-lacquered victorias flashed nickel-and-gilt harnesses. Like proud hussars, mounted police rode down Broadway, their stallions' hooves ringing on the paving stone.

High up on Madison Square Garden's campanile, St. Gauden's copper-sheathed Diana, balanced on her toe, drew her bow. Once the province of nannies and children, Madison Square Park now filled with clubmen and tourists from the great hotels. The buff brick-and-terra-cotta Madison Square Garden building had been a great success when it opened in 1890, hosting the annual horse show and a string of mediocre melodramas. However, Anthony Comstock had raised questions about the Diana's shocking nudity and its effect on public morals, despite the fact that the statue stood a full eight stories above the street. Heeding Comstock's warnings, mothers had withdrawn their small children from beneath the goddess's corrupting form, giving free rein to the sportsmen who gathered with their binoculars below.

In a light-hearted mood, Max approached the Madison Square Bank. For some reason, a dense crowd was blocking his way. He wondered if someone was having a heart attack or if a horse had spooked and trampled pedestrians. Up ahead, people started shoving one another. The jittery mob seemed to be muttering under its breath. Far from the bank's entrance, and unable to see above the sea of hats, Max started asking around.

"Oh, its bad business up there," a gray-faced businessman said. "You didn't hear?"

"No, what?"

"They shut the doors."

Still the man's point didn't register. What was he talking about? One of the stores? Why would that cause such a frenzy?

"Who? Who closed?"

"What're you, daffy? The bank. There's a run."

"The Madison Square Bank?"

"No, the Royal Bank of Persia. Sure, the Madison Square Bank. Do you see any others?"

His money, all the money he had in the world, lay behind the bank's coffered doors. In blind reflex, he tried to push his way closer, as if by getting nearer to his deposit he might magically free it from dissolution. The crowd quickly hurled him back. A man climbed on a mailbox, another shinnied up a lamppost.

"There he is! He's coming out!"

Now Max didn't have to push forward. From behind, a crush of bodies slammed into him, and he lurched forward. His hat flew off, but the mob imprisoned his arms. Depositors bellowed at the top of their lungs. Just out of reach, his derby toppled down and disappeared, crushed under stamping feet. He flinched.

"Thieving sonofabitch! Where's my money!"

"You filthy crook. We want our money!"

"High-hat bastard!"

The whole mass took up the chant. "We want our money! We want our money!"

Max twisted around to scan his neighbors. A red-faced man with veins bulging in his neck, a scrawny biddy, a pale clerk, a young woman clutching a bunch of carrots—they all joined in the incantation. "We want our money! We want our money!"

In a panic he saw his four hundred dollars vaporizing, too. When would he ever accumulate that much again? Four hundred dollars. Always in the back of his mind, it had cushioned every blow. So what if he hadn't earned it? It was his anyway. Now he was exposed raw to the elements again. Did the paper owe him for space? A few dollars, anyway. What about that last touch Swarms had put on him? In the chaos he couldn't remember how much Danny had plucked him for.

A queer spasm ran through the crowd. Helpless, Max fell back, barely righting himself before falling bodies smashed him onto the sidewalk. Then he looked up. On a chestnut whose eyes bulged with terror, a mounted button galloped through the panic-stricken mob. Max heard the sickening thwack of wood on bone, grunts of pain, the cop's curses, the report of hooves on stone. Knocked flat by the retreating crowd, he scrambled to his knees in time to see the great chestnut rear up above him. Instinctively, he fell to the ground, rolled and scrambled away on all fours.

The horse's hooves rang on the pavement, barely missing his skull. Out of control, it was rearing again. On his hands and knees he scuttled through a maze of legs, an animal fear driving him. His pants tore at the knee. Shards of stone ripped his palms. His mind turned solid, an unthinking ball of dread. He didn't want to die. Like soldiers in a battle, an entire line of depositors fell back before the raging beast. Staggering to his feet, Max whirled around, trying to find an escape route.

Behind the flailing cop, three more mounted buttons were charging the crowd. From the north another cavalry squad bore down. Stepping high, shying, the horses looked ready to bolt. Savage expressions on their faces, the police smacked their long nightsticks against the flanks of their mounts. Warming up, Max thought. Desperate, he turned west where ranks of foot patrolmen marched shoulder to shoulder right at him. A woman went down, flat on her face. A man in a sack suit lunged toward a massive bay, as if to grab its reins, but the mounted cop bent over and swatted him once in the center of his skull. The man wobbled, touched his bleeding head, and stumbled back.

Max took off toward the marching platoons, waving, shouting over and over. "Reporter! From the *Herald*! Reporter! From the *Herald*!"

When he reached the line, it parted for him. He couldn't believe his luck. Then as an afterthought, from behind, a cop clubbed him on the back of his neck. Instantly, a blinding headache blossomed up from the root of his brain, but he pushed on, still calling out for safe passage. Behind the lines he paused, gathering his wits. His head throbbed and he had to spread his legs to get his balance.

From a safe distance the rout looked like a series of small skirmishes. The smack of nightstick on flesh and bone had a muted, distant quality. To his woozy eye the clashes became animated tableaus, flashes of color and gesture and speed. Then a hatless man, his loose-woven shirt torn at the collar, trotted past, his eyes white with terror. In a lazy motion, a foot patrolman wound up and caught the laborer flush in the windpipe. Clutching his throat, the man gagged and fell to his knees. Three buttons leaped on him then, flailing away from every angle. Crumpled on the sidewalk, covering his head, the man coughed up blood and bits of his front teeth.

"You want summa the same?" an agitated cop proposed, pointing the business end of his nightstick at Max's skull.

"Reporter. The *Herald,*" he croaked.

Drawing back, he watched the rout, the police squeezing the mob, nudging it this way and that, breaking it up into smaller and smaller pieces, tossing rioters, seemingly at random, into Black Marias.

Blocks from the action, on West 21st Street, he hunted down escapees.

"They came out of nowhere, beat us all to hell," one limping man claimed.

"It's not like we're a bunch of pinks. We had deposits in here," another gasping victim complained.

"Did you see the police strike people?"

"You got eyes in your head?"

"They'll be lucky they don't kill nobody," an indignant woman cried out.

Working his way back toward the Madison Square Bank, he found Captain Robinson, the commander, sitting calmly on his mount, surveying the littered landscape before him. A broad-shouldered, tall man, he was made more magnificent by his perch on his gorgeous black stallion.

"He looks ready for Saratoga," Max said, stroking the animal's glistening flank. "Max Greengrass, the *Herald.*"

"Forget about it, Jack."

"I just need a few words. Was your operation a success?"

"Yeah, a complete success," he replied laconically. Gazing down at Max, the captain spit a healthy gob of tobacco-laced phlegm right over the reporter's head. With a sharp yank of the reins, he guided his horse onto the sidewalk.

"You don't say?" Parnell responded after Max poured out his story. "Did you talk to Sanderson?"

Lawrence Sanderson, who reportedly feasted on gilt-edged tips, wrote the financial column. Max had never spoken to him, but now he threaded his way to the business section. An elegant, proper man, Sanderson looked more like a banker than a reporter. He had a long, aristocratic nose and a prissy little mouth. While Max spilled out the story of the Madison Square Bank fiasco, the columnist leaned back and made a tent of his long, tapered fingers.

"Yes, I understand there have been improprieties."

"How so?"

Sanderson gave Max a long look, considering whether to share information with him. Grudgingly, he added, "Well, the D.A. has been whispering in my ear. You'll have to wait for my column."

"Oh, sure. Parnell asked me to write up the riot."

"Yes, you go ahead and do that."

Max bristled. Sensing Sanderson's distaste for him, he stayed on a bit longer. "People were trampled. It was quite a scene."

"I imagine."

"Depositors. It was a real run." With a pang of despair he recalled that his own money had evaporated too.

"These things happen." Sanderson may as well have been talking about a distressed ant colony.

With the financial reporter's chilly attitude in mind, Max wrote up a precise account of the police assault, quoting extensively from the most respectable shopkeepers, teachers, and housewives who had been terrorized by the mounted police. Then he slipped in the buttons' attack on the defenseless laborer. In juxtaposition to these cries against injustice, he placed Captain Robinson's claim of success. It made a pretty article, seven inches, page five maybe.

His losses weighed on him now. What was he down to? The five dollars he'd squirreled away in his dresser? When was he getting paid? On Friday? He wondered how long it would take Famous O'Leary to spend twenty-two dollars. It was a huge sum for a street arab who never wasted more than a few cents for a night in a lodging house. Had he gone back to his Hudson Street gang and thrown a party? Max wondered if he could ferret the little thief out near Grove Street Park. For a few coins Cham-peen or The Basher might finger Famous, and Max could get ahold of him and turn him upside down.

It was a satisfying thought. Street arabs stayed in their territories, too, simply for self-preservation. Why didn't he take a look around the park, or see if anybody at the White Stag could help him. Then there was that stablehand, John Buri. To prevent his building from burning down, Buri had to keep track of every guttersnipe in the neighborhood.

Shame gnawed at him. Why had he put all the cash in one bank? Why hadn't he kept more on hand? He knew quite well that he hadn't earned the money, but it didn't matter. While he had that pile behind him, he thought more of himself. All those dollars were dreams, security, inner peace. Now he'd fall back into a life of crumbs and column-inches. What was he supposed to say to Belle? That he couldn't scare up her seven dollars? That the bank was to blame? That nameless forces had turned him into a deadbeat? He squirmed with humiliation.

He examined the tear in his pants. Now he knew why they always sold two pairs with the jacket. To go home and face Belle with a mouthful of feeble excuses was out of the question. Instead, he canvassed the secretaries until he found a needle and thread, and sewed up the tear with a bunch of fat stitches. Damn! It would have to do. It was time to scramble.

chapter twenty-eight

Grove Street Park was empty, except for a tramp who was nursing a bottle of blue ruin. Oblivious to the crash of the bank, Hudson Street sunned itself in the warm afternoon. Its humble shops stood open, its pushcarts offered vegetables, eggs, and flyblown meats, and its housewives toddled along with market baskets under their arms. Max stopped by the White Stag, but the bartender, who knew Cham-peen and Famous, said they'd made themselves scarce lately.

A thoughtful artist with the bar rag, he went on. "They nick their own bottle and get pie-eyed who knows where."

"I was just over in Grove Street Park. Anyplace else they might be making trouble?"

"Well, there's always the docks. Good thieving over there."

Standing outside his Hudson Street stable, John Buri sucked on his inevitable skinny cigar. "No, no see 'em nowhere. I break their neck they come here."

"Are they still around the neighborhood?"

"Oh, sure. On Perry Street, they sleep in cellar."

"Just around the corner?"

"Yeah, Perry. House have a broken window. They putta tape. Like this." Buri demonstrated the angle of the repair. "They no come here no more. They ascare now."

On Perry Street near the corner of Hudson, the three-story building displayed its wounded window. Behind a wrought-iron fence, several steps led down to a shuttered basement. Cautiously, Max peered down the stairs. Curled up on a bed of newspapers, Famous O'Leary was taking a snooze. Three empty gin bottles were lined up neatly on a nearby ledge.

It must have been some party.

Max's blood surged. When he thought of the way he had groped through his jacket, so desperate to find his missing purse, his rage rushed back. Not to speak of the crooked bank that had really picked his pocket. His anger at the Madison Square Bank mixed with his fury at the boy—and shame about his intentions. Look at what he had been reduced to, creeping down basement stairs to pick a pocket himself. But the money was his, damn it. His. This time he'd get the better of the thieving little bastard.

Still, Famous was quicksilver itself. He'd already vanished into thin air more than once. If Max wanted to get his hands around the street arab's neck, he had to attack hard and fast.

Skipping down the last two stairs, he flung himself on the boy. It was like landing on a pile of broken sticks.

Max met no resistance. Famous simply held firm in his fetus-like position, fighting back by keeping his chin down, his arms curled up, and his legs pressed against his bony chest. For a moment Max's ire flared at this clever strategy. When was the kid going to strike out at him and bolt? Was he hiding the knife he used to slash pockets and purses? Max had to be wary. Utterly still, Famous was probably scheming like crazy. The consummate little actor feigned fits for a living. Why not feign sleep? The boy lay under Max's bulk without making a sound.

Experimenting, Max rose slightly to see if Famous would stir, but the bony kid refused to move a muscle. Max admired the boy's discipline. Think of all the beautiful tricks he had acquired in a lifetime on the streets. Considering his performance at the Midnight Band's headquarters, Famous could probably break into a warehouse, pry loose dock goods, or wriggle into a jewelry store with similar ease. All the gangs used these kids for their slender frames and fearlessness. If Famous avoided the white lung, starvation, fevers, beatings, poxes, and the police, he might eventually rise into the ranks of the Hudson Dusters, the Fashion Plates, or the Whyos. He had that sort of talent and nerve.

While Famous clung to his foxy strategy, Max wondered what to do with him. At the very least, he could grab the street arab by the scruff of his neck and march him over to the precinct house, barely a block away. Raising himself up another inch, he waited for Famous to make his play, but the boy stayed frozen, giving nothing away. Thoughtfully, Max pressed down on him again without getting the slightest reaction. No, it wasn't possible. Still wary, he circled his arms underneath Famous and lifted him from the stone floor. If this was playing dead, it was the greatest act of all time.

In fact, rigor mortis had set in. His heart sinking, Max set Famous down again, crouched over the body, and tried to pry the limbs apart, but the scrawny arms and legs wouldn't give. Rolling the corpse with his toe, Max exposed the other side of Famous's face. A blue bruise high on his forehead and a crust of blood revealed why he had departed. Cradling the boy in his arms, Max lifted him and straightened up. Bird-boned Famous O'Leary rose into the air.

Shifting the dead body in his grasp and pressing its face against his chest, Max made sure to hide the child's wound. Famous's pointy knees poked his stomach. Stunned by the turn of events, the reporter wandered toward the precinct house, picking up a few stragglers along the way. Sensing some disaster, a small boy ran up, touched Famous's bare, blackened foot, giggled and raced away.

"He sick?" a lady in a black shawl asked. She waved over another dolorosa, who was carrying a laundry basket.

Max nodded. The women swayed and clucked their tongues. The first boy raced back with his friends, who pulled at Famous's stiff toes and then ducked away, giggling and whooping. Max must have growled because they retreated to a respectful distance. John Buri emerged from his stable. Working his cigar, he approached and took a look.

"He steal the fruit. Nobody catch him. I get doctor, eh?"

Broken words choking in his throat, Max just shook his head. Words seemed to be piling up down there, words covered with stickers and thorns. How could he cough them up? His throat felt paralyzed. Had he killed the boy himself when he jumped on him? He didn't think so. The wound wasn't fresh, and, after all, Famous had been picked clean.

Still, in horror, he saw himself pouncing on the curled-up body and ransacking the dead kid's pockets, and he wondered how close he had come to murder. One blow against that thin skull might have been enough.

A ragged procession followed him: guttersnipes, the black-shawled housewife, her laundress friend. All they needed was a gilded Madonna on a raft, a cornet, and a drum. Across the street, Cham-peen and The Basher appeared, watching uneasily. Did they know? Did they have anything to do with it? Cham-peen dipped his foot into the street, thought better of it and returned to the opposite sidewalk. The Basher stepped in and out, too. For a while they shadowed the procession as it grew. More children joined, a curious shoemaker took a quick look, a round-faced greengrocer offered his assistance.

A gray veil seemed to hang between Max and the world around him. He blinked, but it wouldn't go away. The kids' chatter sounded muffled. Mouths made noises he couldn't decipher. He walked so smoothly he might have been sailing. He felt altogether too calm.

"Found him dead?" the greengrocer asked.

That was it. The standard headline, FOUND DEAD had myriad uses. Suicides were always FOUND DEAD. Cataleptics and epileptics sometimes. Lovers could be FOUND DEAD UNDER QUESTIONABLE CIRCUMSTANCES. Aged husbands were FOUND DEAD IN BED. The destitute were FOUND DEAD IN SQUALOR, but even a loving parent could be FOUND DEAD IN AN ABANDONED COTTAGE. Famous's chances of getting a headline were equal to FLEA FOUND DEAD.

His busted nutter hat clutched in his hands, Cham-peen suddenly materialized next to Max and walked along, gravely examining his old friend. The Basher brought along a hard-looking girl with ash-colored eyes.

"Oh, him," she said.

"He got kilt?" Cham-peen inquired. "That's lousy."

Max nodded. Something about the street arab's tone, cool yet laced with a dash of feeling, exonerated him in Max's eyes. Adults might slaughter their friends, but not Cham-peen. A woman hanging out a second-story window waved her handkerchief. A rolling garbage scow slowed down to pay its respects. When Max turned toward the station house, the cortege followed. Droning, gossiping voices cloaked the procession in a shapeless dirge.

Max didn't know the officers who lounged in front of the station house, but one of them, a stately veteran, leaned over to make out Max's bundle. "Ahh, Jeez, I know this one. He's a dock rat. Hey, Mike, c'mere, what'shisname?"

Max couldn't let the boy go unnamed. Clearing his throat, he finally managed to croak, "O'Leary. Famous O'Leary."

"Seamus?"

"No, Famous."

"They love the big names, don't they," the cop said, lifting the boy's hair from his forehead. Famous's sky-blue eyes had grown a dull skin. "No bigger'n a cat, eh? Take him to the sergeant. He'll show you the drill."

Inside, several officers gathered around. One brought a blanket and wrapped the stiff body gently on his knee. Another took out a flask and passed it to Max. The booze warmed his parched throat.

Jimmy Ennis, a local beat cop, tapped him on the shoulder. "Lousy luck, hey, bud?"

"He was a pisser, I'll tell you that," Max said, his voice another man's, his dread someone else's.

"I guess he don't got no parents?" the sergeant asked.

"None I knew of. I just used to see him around the neighborhood," Max replied.

"Where'd you find him?'

"Perry Street. Down a stairwell. I thought he was asleep." An idea for his story struck him. Max played with the wording in his head. It would have to be succinct, because Parnell would never give him more than a single graf.

"Goddamn shame," Ennis, said, shaking his head and passing the flask.

"Every day it's another one," the cop said.

Dead guttersnipes washed up at the precinct doors all the time, yet the buttons' tenderness was palpable. Most of them had children, Max knew, and the sight of Famous lying there filled them with the worst dread of all.

"Ahh, Gus, call the dead wagon for me, would ya'?" the sergeant cried out.

The idea had possibilities. Maybe he could sell it to Parnell, and with a little cajoling Donnie Walsh, the headline man, would do him a favor.

He caught a break. An ad for a miracle corn remover was cancelled. In its place the city editor slotted the single graf.

FOUND DEAD IN STAIRWELL

> A West Side boy named Famous O'Leary, widely known for his clever thievery from the docks and the pushcarts of Hudson Street, was found dead yesterday at the bottom of a Perry Street stairwell. Admiring friends said that had he lived beyond his

> estimated twelve years of age, he could have had a career with the local Hudson Dusters or perhaps Tammany itself. "He was pinching my goods since I can't remember when," a local grocer reported.

Parnell appreciated an inside joke. Famous O'Leary's death notice was the first *Herald* obit to tell the unvarnished truth. It wasn't much—it was barren, in fact—but it would have to do in place of a stone.

chapter twenty-nine

Before dinner, Max cornered Danny in the parlor and shook three dollars out of him. "You're bleeding me dry," Swarms protested.

"Yeah, well, open your veins. You still owe me," he snapped.

"Whoa, don't lose your sense of humor, Jackie." Swarms tapped out a nervous beat with his right foot. His filament-thin red hair stood up on end. At times Danny looked like a stranger to Max, and he wondered what he really knew about the actor who, according to Belle, was making noises about tying the knot with Faye.

"What're you living in, a bubble? Madison Square went belly-up today."

"No crap? You?"

"Every cent I've got. Used to have. Four hundred simoleons." The fractured hours whirled in his mind. The mad crowd. The mounted police charge. How was it possible that greenbacks could sicken and die? A queasy sensation came over him. He might as well have taken a swan dive off the Singer Building.

"*Oooeeee*. That smarts. No wonder money's so damn tight. I tried nine banks, did I tell you? Flit. Zilch."

"You had to shut down?"

"Forget the publishing business. All's I got now's sheet music in a trunk."

There was no way to dance around it. He was too washed out to try. "Listen, Danny. When do you and Faye get paid? The paper owes me for a dozen sticks, but I'm flat busted 'til Friday."

"Faye?" He bobbed his eyebrows. Max knew what that meant. If Faye found a haystack of money, she'd turn it into a bonfire.

"Yeah, I know. Well, you'll see her before me. Tell her she owes Belle seven bucks. She'll know what I'm talking about."

Danny tugged his sleeve. "You did a good thing, kiddo, springing her so fast. I gave her a talking-to."

It was perfect. Now they could both fail to keep Faye in line. The beauty of it was that Swarms understood why she went off the rails and why she was worth it; he was half-cracked himself.

"So, a birdie's been whispering in my ear. When's the big date?"

He expected Danny to flinch, but Swarms handled the question smooth as silk. "We're thinking pretty soon. Before we go on tour. Did I tell you Albee wants to change our name? Whadda you think of The Credenzas? Danny and Faye."

"What're you, some kinda furniture?"

"Yeah, that's what I said. Tell your sister. She thinks it's classy. Anyway, she says she won't let nobody call her Faye Swarms. Sounds like a bunch of bees, she says. Four hundred? *Oooffff*."

"Yeah. Listen, keep this Madison Square thing under your hat, right?"

A few minutes later, Mrs. DeVogt was passing the snap beans around the dinner table. Max had already piled pot roast and fried potatoes in a pyramid on his plate.

Imagine not being able to pay back a miserable seven dollars. Why had he confided in Danny, anyway? Going broke was like the French pox: a man ought to keep his trap shut about it. He rammed some stringy pot roast into his mouth. The dry, half-masticated meat went down in a lump.

"Excellent, delicious," he declared, winking at Belle.

Staring off into space, she didn't respond. He tried to conjure up the sun-shot chemise, the shape of her beneath the glowing cloth, but it was hard to square the serious-looking creature across the table with the woman who had stood before him, so defiant and unashamed in the light.

"Did you hear about the bank today, children?" Mrs. DeVogt asked.

Max froze. Hadn't he sworn Danny to secrecy a heartbeat ago? He knew he should have kept his misfortune to himself.

All innocence, Swarms intervened. "Not a word, Mrs. DeVogt. We were rehearsing all day."

Belle came to life. "My friend Maria was over there," she said in an acid tone. "They just slammed the doors in her face. She lost her whole savings she broke her neck for, working." She poured the Yiddish-inflected words out in a jumble.

So she knew all about the bank run. That explained her opaque mood. How would she act when she found out Madison Square had picked his pocket, too? Faro banks wouldn't stoop so low.

"How terrible!" Mrs. DeVogt patted her mouth with a napkin. "The poor thing."

He shot Danny a killing glance. "Rotten luck," he put in.

Swarms picked up the ball. "Well, it's been coming for a year now. All those Kansas banks. Ohio. These farmers are so jumpy, somebody says boo, they'll start a run. 'Free silver.' Malarkey. They don't understand the money is tied up in bonds. Mortgages and such."

Danny Swarms, economist. Max bit his tongue.

Mrs. DeVogt's voice reached a nervous pitch. "Of course, the Canal Street Bank isn't J. P. Morgan, but these things are contagious. Beans, Mr. Greengrass?"

Canal Street? *Another* fine institution with empty pockets? He almost fell out of his chair. Was it possible that Belle, Gretta, and Mrs. DeVogt didn't know about Madison Square yet? What a fortunate disaster. In a wholesale calamity, Belle would have to excuse his personal misfortune.

"The Canal Street Bank?" Recovering, he spooned khaki-colored beans onto his plate. "Did they shut the doors?"

"Sure. The bigwigs had to pay themselves first," Belle snapped.

"That's terrible. She lost all her money?" Gretta asked, as if she finally comprehended the conversation.

Belle could barely keep the contempt out of her voice. "Oh, they'll give her two cents on the dollar when they open again. Excuse me, when they *reorganize*." Her sarcasm came out bitter and undisguised. "It's a cozy system, isn't it? They take your money, they lose your money, they say *whoopsiedoodle*, we made a little mistake. Then they declare bankruptcy, and they *reorganize*."

Max didn't care for this side of Belle. He agreed with her, sure, but did she have to sound so harsh? Here she was, Lady Light-Fingers, preaching to the world. Then, recalling her generosity, he softened. If it weren't for Belle, Faye might still be stewing in the Jefferson Market lockup.

Mrs. DeVogt's voice quavered. "I saw it all in the '70s. They were building railroads to the moon and everybody went money-mad. All of a sudden, somebody noticed there were too many tracks going in the same direction and the banks lost their shirts."

"Other people's shirts," Belle pointed out.

"Quite right," Mrs. DeVogt agreed, patting Belle's hand.

"I saw something so strange yesterday," Gretta continued, oblivious to Belle's antipathy. "Near St. Marks Place. These men were marching without saying a word. Just plain men. They didn't have banners, they didn't say who they were, but they were parading right along. Their faces . . . they looked hypnotized."

"What were you doing down there?" Mrs. DeVogt inquired.

Max knew what she meant—St. Marks Place with its seething immigrant tenements wasn't Gretta's natural habitat—and he knew the answer too. She was hauling her bellows camera with the polished mahogany body, her tripod, and the rest of her equipment around the square.

"I was making a few plates," Gretta explained. "It was quite eerie. Hundreds and hundreds of them, so silent, like some sort of religious procession. It reminded me of a Renaissance painting I once saw."

Only Gretta would put it that way, he thought. Her way of seeing was so foreign, it appealed to him. All at once his fascination with her flashed to life again. "Did the pictures come out?" he asked.

"I haven't had time to make prints yet."

"The men look like that 'cause they're hungry," Belle said dryly.

Gretta couldn't ignore the jibe this time. "Of course I could tell they weren't well-off. Why would they be marching otherwise?"

"How about that Kodak? Did the company send the pictures back?" Max inquired innocently.

Gretta's face looked drawn, thinner, her skin stretched translucent over its sculpted structure, her eyes looking inward at a place he could barely imagine. His desire for her would never die, he knew it then, but he wondered at how her beauty had obscured her strangeness, her otherworldly eye.

"Oh, they take a century. I'm sorry I wasted so much time," she said.

"Do you think we should withdraw our funds? These things seem to be catching," Mrs. DeVogt worried. "What would happen to the house?"

Mrs. DeVogt's simple remark made dread palpable.

Instinctively, they all looked around at the dining room. Could the sideboard with the colonial plates be swept away? Could the high-backed chairs disintegrate beneath them? Could the rugs, the drapes, the Japanese knick-knacks, their entire cocoon fall away like last season's stage set?

Pleading exhaustion, Max escaped to his room, but an overtired energy kept his mind racing. Idly he sat on the bed and flipped through Mrs. Edwards's addresses, but the numbers refused to surrender their secrets. If he couldn't decipher their meaning, how could he grind out the column-inches? What a way to scratch out a living, scavenging dustbins for scraps of memory; sifting lies; stitching together whispers, wild guesses and half-truths into paragraphs worth pennies. But he had no choice. He had no other skills, no other inclination. Painstakingly he began copying every single address on a separate sheet of paper. Through some failure of imagination, he had closed off every other way of being. He had to write to stay alive.

chapter thirty

The ledger against his stomach, he woke up at dawn. In the dim light he turned its pages again. Canal. Charlton. Christopher. Clarke. Clarkson. Commerce. Desbrosses. Dominick. Fulton. Grand. Greenwich. Grove. Houston. Hudson. Barrow. Broome. King. Spring. His mouth tasted like coal dust. Squeezing his eyes shut, he stabbed at the page with his index finger, picking an address at random. Ten and a half Grove Street. He'd been up and down that route a hundred times, sniffing out Famous and his gang. He could almost visualize 10½ Grove in his mind's eye.

Fog was pouring in off the river. Groping his way down Seventh Avenue, he heard the slow clipclop of hooves, and the soft curses of a driver. Out of the mist, a fly cab drifted past. Blots of gaslight smeared in the haze. Wrapped in a shawl, a young woman skittered past. In full sail, a drunk burst out of nowhere, shouldering Max off the sidewalk. His shoes slathered with muck, he let go a few choice comments, but the reeling man had already disappeared, swallowed by gray capes of drizzle. At the corner of West Twelfth he ducked into a saloon for a cup of tea with a splash of rum.

In a curious trick, the rising sun seemed to illuminate the fog from within, the rolling mist luminescent now but no less blinding. Revivified, he plunged downtown, then veered west along Bleecker. The shops weren't open yet, but here and there domestic skirmishes were breaking out, unseen voices clashing in their morning rituals. A pair of shutters flew open and a chamberpot emptied onto the paving stones. Lamps glowed in a few windows. He smelled coffee, horsepiss, and rotting vegetables. Ten and a half Grove Street swam into view.

An outside staircase clung to the side of the dilapidated three-story building. Max ducked into a nearby doorway as a man in a plush overcoat and a homburg picked his way down the wooden slats. At the foot of the stairs, he paused to tap out his ivory pipe. A baby-faced man with an immature brush of a mustache, he stretched and sighed.

Max strolled up to him. "How's the pill upstairs?"

"Fook Yuen." The man smiled.

The Fountain of Happiness brand had a good reputation. Faye had bought some one time, and after she came out of her dream she sang a dozen verses of "Willie, the Weeper," the hophead dirge. Max wasn't averse to the cloying, rippling pleasure himself.

"High-hat, huh?"

"The best," the apparently satisfied customer testified. "Ask for Yung Fat. He'll fix you up."

Yung Fat turned out to be a black-haired entrepreneur in a snappy vest. Just to establish rapport, Max ordered up a gong and watched as Fat carved out a sticky opium pill with a pair of ritual scissors. Drapes kept out the morning light, but Max could make out other dreamers sleeping in bunk beds across the room. After a few hits on the yen tsiang, he drifted into a warm, curved place, and, for a while, in perfect bliss, he became golden syrup, liquid atoms.

Max rode the opiate waves to sweet surrender. Warm thrills broke on an internal shore, showering him with agonizing delight. In time's slow dance, his mouth went slack. A miniature sun burst in the back of his neck, soothing streams of light running down his arms and legs. Saliva banked under his tongue and trickled in rivulets down his throat. Working his jaw was a luxurious act. One more dollar, one more pill, and he floated on mild updrafts into dreamland.

When Yung Fat raked open the drapes, exposing a bright globe of pain high in the sky, Max threw his arm over his eyes and rolled over on his bunk. Fat rocked him gently. "Time go now, mister. Come back later."

Digging deep inside his being, Max roused himself. He knew he had to ask Fat an important question, but in his loopy state it kept eluding him.

"Time go now," Fat repeated, shaking him harder this time.

Max gathered himself again. A great green sea weighed down on him, but he began swimming to the surface. Then he was sitting up, brushing away glistening cobwebs. It all came back to him. Then on a fresh swell of delight, he again forgot what it was. Shaking his head, he groped for it.

"Ten and a half Grove Street. Right?" he blurted.

"Ya, get up, mister. Got to mop."

Some wire in his head suddenly lit up. Mrs. Edwards's empire. "So, who owns this wreck?"

Yung Fat stopped wrestling with him. His even, flat features froze as he gave Max the once-over. "No know, mister."

"Who do you pay your rent to? You don't own the building, do you?"

"No know. Go, get out. Bad time."

"You don't know if you own it or not?"

"No know."

Before Max could get another question out of his mouth, Yung Fat lifted him bodily and hurled him toward the door. The attack came so suddenly, Max stumbled, long enough for Fat to grab him by his collar and shove him out onto the staircase. Woozy, he rocked on the creaking structure, the door slamming in his face. Leaning over the railing, he peered inside, but Yung Fat raked his hand across the pigeon's-blood drapes, sealing his den from view.

Meandering through the neighborhood, Max slowly regained his senses. He had half a mind to barge back into Yung Fat's and give the man a lashing, but there was no percentage in it. Better to keep moving like a dumb beast from address to address until somebody spit up the goods. At 449 Greenwich, nobody would open a door to him. Four-Fifty-Five Greenwich might have once existed, but now it was a missing tooth in the street's crooked row. Fifty-Two Commerce Street consisted of a stable, a blacksmith's, and an upstairs apartment.

"Who's the landlord around here?" he asked the smith.

"Who's askin'?" A slight, rope-muscled man was nailing a shoe onto a skittish bay mare. "Stay still, you bitch bastard," he muttered.

"Max Greengrass. *New York Herald*."

When the horse tried to bolt, Max threw himself against the slatted wall.

"I'll hit you with this here!" the blacksmith warned, grabbing the horse's halter and waving his weapon between her eyes. "How the hell should I know who owns this bloody shack?" Turning back to the snorting mare, he shouted, "You there, I'll knock your teeth down your throat. Mind your p's and q's, lady."

Edging along the stable wall, his heart rattling against his ribs, Max crept back to the sidewalk. He wasn't sure he wanted to reconnoiter the rest of 52 Commerce. Then he saw how to get up to the second floor.

"Yeah, go up there, put your questions to Connie. She knows everybody's business," the smithy called out, his animal under control again.

Connie Flannagan came to the door with a baby at her breast. A harried look on her pointy features, she bounced the child on her shoulder. "Whatcher want?"

"Max Greengrass. *New York Herald.* We're doing a survey of the real estate around these parts."

"Ahh, don't go botherin' me. Can'tcha see what I got to put up with?"

Over her shoulder Max saw several cribs. An infant climbed up on unsteady feet, trumpeting discontent. In a rolling rebellion, the children sent up cries of distress. "I got my own and then these here. Tie me up and ship me to Bellevue, might as well."

"Do you know who owns this building? Who you pay your rent to"

"Sure. The beetle's got his hand out every month, don't worry." Now Max saw that Connie Flannagan was much younger than he first supposed. Her drawn skin still retained a trace of youthful glow, but the purple bruises under her eyes and her collapsed mouth implied what was to come.

"The beetle? Who's he?"

Her charges whimpered and mewled. "Shut up, the lot of you! The beadle, from the corporation."

"Sorry to be so dull, but what corporation are you talking about?"

"Holy Trinity's the landlord around here. My friend Eleanor, she pays 'em, and Suzie Watkins around the corner. She's got a room, plaster's all muck in the rain. Falls down and sticks to your head like bird crap."

He retained his bland mask; but at the mention of Reverend Weems's Holy Trinity Church, his blood started racing.

"What's your friend's address?" he asked, all mildness.

"Around the corner. You'll see. Chimneypot's falling down. The mothers go God knows where, and who has to feed 'em?"

"The exact address?" he persisted.

"You're a reporter, ain't you? Go find it yourself," she snapped.

He'd squeezed Connie Flannagan dry, but within ten minutes Suzie Watkins named the beadle, a Mr. Cunningham. Suzie showed him the melting plaster, too, an irregular three-by-five-foot patch shaped like South America on her ceiling.

His pencil flew as Suzie Watkins poured out her disgust.

"Ask him, do his vermin pay rent too?" A doughy-faced woman in a shapeless dress, Suzie Watkins had a New York sense of humor.

"Rodents?"

"They live under his roof too, don't they? Why don't they cough up too? I sleep with a corn broom, don'tcha know?" It was easy to imagine why she needed this weapon at night, but Watkins seemed to relish the details. "They run right over your face if you don't smash 'em," she told him.

Max had to repress the urge to race back to the office and start writing up these revelations, but he needed to build a firmer foundation. To clear his head, he took a hike downtown, planning his attack on the Buildings Department as the pavement disappeared beneath his flying feet. Mysteries of lot and block numbers, deeds, transfers, and obscure agents waited to be plumbed. He could already feel the thrill of ancient paper between his fingers, though his first foray into the old records had yielded nothing but blind alleys so far.

He needed a guide. In the Deeds Office, he surveyed the hive of lawyers, contractors, agents, managers, and cockroach landlords. These men seemed to come in twos and threes, their private colloquies conducted in bare whispers. When Max passed by, they turned their backs, and their voices fell to an inaudible register. In the hushed, suspicious atmosphere, great piles of bricks and mortar and human cargo were changing hands, undergoing the obscure surgery of clause and codicil, sundered partnership and hidden interest.

He felt a sense of awe. This simple municipal office with its dented spittoons, its murky official portraits and dusty light globes, was the epicenter of perpetual change.

In the far corner of the chamber, poring over a record book, a gawky waterbird of a man adjusted his pince-nez, then dipped his beak deep into a tattered volume. His lint-skinned suit hung limp on his skeleton. A hungry scavenger, Max surmised. It was too bad he was down to a single dollar again.

"Say, bub, mind if I ask you a question?"

"Depends." The voice resonated surprisingly deep.

"Well, I've been trying to track down who really owns some property, and I think they're using agents to cover their tracks."

"Did you check the mortgages?"

"No, I was looking at those books over there."

"Mortgages. Over there," the man said. "Match the lot numbers."

Max grasped the point at once. Discovering who owned the paper might be illuminating, although mortgages could be bought and sold until a bank in Chicago held the rights to a slum on Avenue C. On the other hand, if Mrs. Edwards's addresses represented the holdings of a single great entity like Holy Trinity, some of her property should be directly linked to the parent corporation. Or had the church conducted a systematic campaign to hide its hand?

In a few hours of hauling down heavy volumes and squinting at chicken-track notations, Max mapped the church's crazy-quilt empire. To start, he checked the mortgage for Moriarity's warren. The church had done nothing to cover its tracks. It held the mortgage on 141 Varick outright. On the other hand, the 22 Spring Street rookery's paper had been purchased by none other than the Canal Street Bank, but the latter had obtained its interest from Holy Trinity. Connie Flannagan's Commerce Street digs were owned directly by the church, as were dozens of other properties in the Midnight Band's portfolio.

Famished, his lungs sticky with dust, he made his way out of the Deeds Office, doing his best to keep an idiotic smile from cracking his face. He could barely believe his good fortune. Here was a story with deep roots and thick branches. No, it wasn't just a story; it was too complicated for that. Once he started interrogating church officials, and Weems himself, his revelations would flower into a series. Then a delicious idea flashed through his mind. The Health Department.

Why show his cards yet? Draw a few more from the deck first. But before that, he needed Parnell's benediction.

A perfectly morbid smile played on the metro editor's lips as he read Max's proposal. Irregular patches of color, faint but visible, stained his pallid cheeks. Then he sucked in his bloodless lips.

"Oh, we could raise holy hell with this. . . . It's a nice piece of work. But there may be a problem."

"What? Why? We could roast these stuffed shirts for weeks with this stuff," Max burst out, shaking his handwritten pages in his fist. "Wait 'til I dig into the Health Department records, Stan. I don't even have to look at them to know what's there, for godsakes!"

"What're you, Baby Riis? We'll have to go to Bennett. It's got potential, but it may be too dicey."

"Pulitzer would plaster this all over his front page. Dana would have a field day! We've got a scoop. Why should we wait?" He regretted the fine spray of spittle he was raining down on Parnell, but it was too late now.

The editor measured his young reporter with his gimlet eye. "Let me ask you a question, you damn hothead. Do you know where our publisher communes with his Maker?"

"No. Don't tell me."

"Pardon the expression, but our lord and master worships at Holy Trinity. Where else? We'll have to go see him."

His heart raced as they threaded their way to Bennett's corner office. The aristocratic publisher sat at his tall desk, a distracted look on his hollowed-out features. The tips of his mustache pointed perfectly in opposite directions. "Do you know what's happening in Rome now, Parnell?"

"Haven't a clue, sir."

"Leaves. The trees have leaves, and they've had them for weeks. What's the news here? Snow around Albany. Ice in the river in April. What fool said hell was hot?"

"I suppose the Mediterranean is looking rather agreeable about now," Parnell said, sensing the great man's mood.

Max bit his tongue while Bennett passed through his spiritual crisis.

"The Mediterranean? That pisshole puddle? Oh, it's warm, it's sunny all right, but where is the action? In Paris, in London? They're fossilized, if you want the bald truth. How many days of his life can a man spend in pleasant cafés?"

Skillfully, Parnell pushed Max forward. "Here's a bit of action, Mr. Bennett. Remember Greengrass?"

The publisher squinted at Max with a look of complete incomprehension.

"You called Byrnes on my behalf?" Max offered.

"Ahh, you're the one. Junkard stuck you, eh? Okay, I'm game. Spit it out!"

When Max explained what he'd found out about Holy Trinity's property, Bennett cut him off. "What of it? Of course they own some buildings. Every imbecile with a temperature knows that."

Placing a light hand on Max's elbow, Parnell interceded. "That's what I thought when he first came up with it. But I could see, if we handled this right, how we could give circulation a good shot in the arm."

"Garvey says we're flat as a pancake. But I don't see the point. Every church in town's got some real estate."

Parnell went on, though, in a cajoling tone. "Just give Greengrass a chance to lay it out. You might change your mind."

Bennett's eyes flicked from the view of St. Paul's spire to his editor's pale, seamed face. Parnell held the publisher's intent gaze, and Max realized for the first time that the editor was taking a risk for him. The sphinx had become his champion.

"Shoot," Bennett said.

Max set his feet wide and launched into the story.

"It's the scale of the thing that matters," he explained, turning page after page of addresses.

While Max spoke, the publisher seemed to drift away. His pale eyes rolled back, he whistled under his breath and smiled while Max pounded a dreadful point home.

When Max finished, Bennett asked Parnell a single question: "If we go with this, do you think they'll blackball me for good?"

"They may let you through the church door, but don't count on any conversation," the editor advised grimly.

"Ha-ha! That's rich! They already threw me out of Society once! They can't do it a second time! Go, go, Greengrass. What do we pay you for?"

chapter thirty-one

Stookey emerged from a shadowy aisle, an armful of folders clutched to his chest. A plump man whose cousin was married to a cousin of Big Tim Sullivan, he had purchased his Health Department clerkship at a discount. "You oughta get a load of this life sentence," he complained, jerking a thumb at his domain of overstuffed cabinets and shelves. "I get a snoot fulla dust," he went on, coughing into his fist, "somethin' awful."

"Maybe working in the Health Department's killing you," Max sympathized.

"In the winter I get the grippe." He stroked a his scraggly beard. "Here's the goods."

Bennett had come across with a decent advance, so Max put down a token of his esteem. Patting the mass of papers, he sighed. "I may need some more of these later."

With mounting excitement, he repaired to a high table and cracked the records for 22 Spring Street. At his right hand he placed his handwritten copy of the Midnight Band's ledger. Before he approached Colonel Fisk, the president of the Holy Trinity Corporation, or any of the vestrymen whose names Bennett had provided, he needed numbers. The white-bearded, spotless Fisk, who as a youth had served in Mexico with Cadwallader's regiment at the battle for the Churubusco convent, could dismiss any accusation with the time-honored question: Who was to blame for the destruction of the property but drunkards, their lax wives, and wild children?

He needed ammunition to counter the colonel's predictable fusillade.

Twenty-Two Spring Street, he hoped, would become the tip of his lance. First, the material seemed a jumble: reports, scraps of paper, a page from Hallorhan's Steak and Chops menu, correspondence between departments, and death certificates. In 1891, typhus had struck 22 Spring hard. Records showed that the disease had taken twelve lives, including five children. A memo referred to "standing water compromising the building's water supply," but the agency hadn't pursued the matter. A copy of a receipt for a pump handle dated January 12, 1892 surfaced, but he had no way of knowing whether it had been intended to combat the foul water.

One report observed: "Emanations from decomposing refuse surround this property and permeate its apartments."

A remark by one investigator intrigued him: on September 14, 1892, the Health Department estimated that 97 people were living at 22 Spring. For that same year, he added up the toll of cholera, typhoid, smallpox, and other plagues. Twenty-eight people had gone to their higher reward from 22 Spring, it turned out, fairly close to one out of three of its residents. Stunned, he reworked the figures, but came up with the same result.

One rookery wouldn't prove his case, though. Stookey handed over more stuffed folders. "These oughta hold you," he muttered.

Eight Macdougal Street consisted of one front and two rear tenements. "The north wall leaks in storms, and one water pump serves 18 families," an inspector noted on January 27, 1892. A catalogue of violations leaped out: leaky roofs, crumbling walls, filthy cellars, broken and uneven flagging in the yard, loose plaster, standing water, closets in the last stages of filth. Meticulously, Max went over every death certificate the 8 Macdougal file had disgorged.

The address had a talent for dysentery, but was no less proficient at scarlet fever and measles. The 1891 cholera outbreak had visited as well, and the white lung had claimed its usual toll. Dazed, he added up the numbers. A full thirty of 8 Macdougal's men, women, and children died every year. Based on the assumption that each apartment contained eight human beings, related or otherwise, he developed an average number of Macdougal corpses per year, between 1890 and 1892. According to his thumbnail estimate, close to four out of ten tenants were losing their lives every year.

Dimly, he became aware that he was grinding his teeth. He was a creature of the city; he knew Fifth Avenue and Bottle Alley, the Hoffman House and Stephenson's; but nevertheless he had been blind to this quiet plague. And though, from a newsman's point of view, hypocrisy was a quaint concept, he was disgusted by the way Holy Trinity was growing fat on sickness while the Reverend Weems campaigned for higher moral standards. He was horrified, disgusted, enraged.

He could hear Belle in his head now, the way he always heard Faye. She'd want to flay Colonel Fisk and his minister alive. Didn't she have a case? He realized something else, too. He was shocked. And stunned at his own naïveté.

Possessed now, he gathered more folders and worked out more calculations. Thirty-Eight Cherry Street, an ancient church property that had been cited for violations as long ago as 1864, contained 462 persons. Mutely, he checked off the Cherry Street casualties. One out of three residents, year after year, had expired in the old warren. In silence, in secret, the invisible war raged on. Sheet by sheet, Max ransacked the records. A ground-floor restaurant at 421 Canal Street was separated from living quarters "only by a skeletal partition. Raw sewage pours into basement." Two-Eleven Varick featured a roof "twisted into an outlandish shape." At 515 Greenwich Avenue, during the winter of 1891, six children under the age of five caught pneumonia and died within days of each other.

When Max was growing up, children had always been coming down with fevers and chills and poxes with exotic names. Sammy Solomon, his friend from first grade, spit blood on his desk, but stayed in school until he couldn't stand up. Theresa Sloane, an ethereal blonde girl he admired from afar, caught some nameless plague and disappeared one showery spring day. Before he was born, his mother had "lost"—a bland euphemism that made him think of misplaced purses and loose change—his brother Meyer, and a sister Lily, who had lived for eighteen days. Children died with the regularity of the seasons, a sad but immutable part of existence.

He forgot to eat. Stookey closed down for lunch, but Max hunkered down, mesmerized by the vision conjured by the numbers. His bill of particulars grew building by building. Death by death, he expanded his indictment. Fingering the old documents, he kept reminding himself that each one represented a human being who had once taken a dip in the Hudson or licked syrupy ices on a summer day.

Small details swam before his eyes: "Walls no more or less than the baseboards of a barn. . . . Roof in last stages of decay, warped and curled into hillocks and depressions . . . floor a patchwork of boards . . . newspapers and scraps of muslin tacked to the ceiling to hold plaster . . . $12 per month."

"Closing time!" Stookey called out.

Max barely heard him.

"This shop is closed!" the clerk boomed out again. "You, buddy. Time to skedaddle."

Max blinked. Spasms grabbed his lower back, and his neck was a single throbbing muscle. In a scrawled hand he'd filled dozens of pages with notes. Piling folders in a tall stack, he staggered to Stookey's counter.

"You want to join the department?" the clerk proposed.

"Huh?"

"What paper'd you say you're from?"

"*Herald.* Yeah, well, I guess this should choke 'em. Here's two bits for your trouble," he added, tipping Stookey a second time. "Publisher says keep this . . ." He made the timeless gesture, palms pressing down empty air.

"And you wouldn't know why?"

"I can see how a man can get the sticky lung in here." He coughed into his fist.

He sent his card in to Colonel Fisk's office with a note from Bennett himself. Sitting on the edge of a calfskin-covered chair, he arranged and rearranged his notes, attaching a question to each damning fact. He intended to start with a few innocuous queries, and then try to confront Fisk with the appalling conditions he'd uncovered, all in a bland, disinterested tone. Fisk was a tough nut, he knew. On staff with General Winfield Scott, he'd penetrated the fort at Chapultepec, though he denied the rumor that he was the one who stole Santa Ana's spare wooden leg. A few years later, he'd stormed the citadels of Manhattan and ended up managing property for the Astors and Van Rensselaers. His ascension to the Holy Trinity Corporation's presidency in 1887 had been like a coronation.

A high-ceilinged, spacious chamber, Fisk's office was carpeted with Persian rugs. Heavy mahogany furniture predominated. Prints with classical architectural themes hung on the walls, along with a water color of a Mexican café. A commotion of blazing candles, swirling red and white skirts, and sword-wielding hidalgos, the picture was the single reference to the military man's storied past.

At sixty-three years of age, the compact, barrel-chested Fisk still affected a bluff, soldierly manner. From behind his desk he gave Max a frank once-over. "What's this all about, young man? I can give you three minutes."

Fisk's face was carved soapstone. Not a single hair in his close-clipped white beard was out of place. He radiated force.

"Mr. Bennett sent me," Max stumbled.

"I received the note," Fisk snapped.

"Some complaints about church property have come to my attention," Max said, regaining his balance. He'd survived Byrnes and William H. Howe. Why let this martinet faze him? Still, he couldn't quite quell a fluttering sensation in his chest.

"The address?"

"Actually, I have dozens you might want to comment on."

"Leave them with my secretary. We investigate the slightest problem. It's our property, and we would be foolish to let it deteriorate, wouldn't we?" Fisk said in a crisp tone. "Tell Bennett we're guarding our investments. That should give him peace of mind." He took up a pen and dismissed Max with a curt nod.

The gesture got under Max's skin, and in an even voice he pressed on. "I understand the corporation's holdings are quite extensive. These issues," he said, shaking his sheaf of papers for emphasis, "may have escaped your attention."

"Doubt it. We run an exceedingly tight ship. However, as our friend Bennett sent you, you have my word that my secretary will look into the matter."

He had hoped to hold back his strong suit, but the interview was slipping away from him. "There's quite a bit of sickness in your buildings; were you aware of that?"

Wielding silence, Fisk held Max in an icy glare. For an endless moment, he wondered if Fisk would deign to reply at all. Hands folded in his lap, Max returned stillness for stillness.

Finally, realizing the reporter would not relent, the manager said: "Mr. Greenberg, I'm a property manager, not a physician. Call on the Health Department. They deal in this sort of thing."

"It's Greengrass. I've been to the Health Department."

"Whatever you call yourself." Fisk examined him with detached curiosity. "You don't intend to write something, do you?"

Incredulous, Max realized that the colonel had no comprehension of what an unfavorable article could do to the church's reputation. That such a piece might come into being was totally beyond Fisk's imagination. Twenty-Two Spring Street was grotesque enough, but Fisk's disinterested savagery struck him as even more deeply malformed. He suppressed his rage. Barely.

"I certainly do intend to write an article, but I want to give you a chance to disabuse me of certain notions I've developed. . . ."

"Such as?"

"Some details I came across at the Deeds Office, to begin with. Let's start with 22 Spring. . . ."

Not bothering to hide his irritation, Fisk fell back in his chair. "Make it short."

"Sure."

But halfway through Max's presentation, Fisk cut him off. "Tell your publisher you are poorly informed. Our records are open to him at any time."

"Are they open to the public?"

"These tenements you're talking about may be on our land, but we didn't put them up, and we don't own them." From his research, Max knew this was true only in part. Holy Trinity engaged in every real estate configuration known to man: it leased, it rented, it mortgaged, it owned directly, it used agents to collect rent, and it collected rent itself. Still, he let Fisk ramble on, scribbling shorthand notes in his lap without peering down. "We offer every inducement to our tenants to put up new buildings. If a tenant will do so, we will provide a twenty-one-year lease. The Holy Trinity Corporation is not responsible for buildings on its property that are owned by others. We cannot dictate to these owners any more than we can dictate to owners on land we don't own."

"When you say 'tenants,' you're referring to the builders who lease your land, correct?"

"Of course. Does Bennett have a business reporter I could talk to? I don't have time to educate you in these matters."

Max ignored the slight, his confidence growing in leaps and bounds. "All of your property is handled in this way?"

"Not all, of course. These transactions can become complicated."

"The church's corporation holds some tenement property directly, doesn't it?"

Fisk's mouth pursed in disgust. Without saying a word, he communicated that his distaste had become highly personal. "It is my job to protect the corporation's assets. Whether the Croton Reservoir's water is clean or not is a matter for the city. Good day, Mr. Greenberg."

Max didn't bother to counter the repeated slight. In his own increasingly cantankerous way, he took it as a sign of victory. He almost pitied the old soldier. Fisk didn't understand that he had made a noose of his own words. "By the way, has a Mrs. Edwards ever worked in your office?"

The colonel rose from his desk, strode to the door and held it open himself.

Outside, Max blinked in the torrent of sunlight. Had he been too aggressive? Had he tipped his hand too quickly? His carefully constructed attack had lost direction under Fisk's pressure, but he had regained his footing, hadn't he? The notes he'd scrawled, while keeping a straight face, proved his coolness under fire, didn't they? Leaning against the office building, he extracted the crumpled sheets to make sure he could make out his chicken-scrawl. He had to squint to decipher the penciled lines, but they were legible. He could breathe again.

Blindly, he hurtled toward the *Herald* office, going over the interview's every parry and thrust. Had Fisk reacted ever so slightly when he'd tossed out Edwards's name? From those stony features, it was impossible to read a thing. Still, Fisk's refusal to answer his question meant he'd hit a nerve. Or did it? Whole blocks disappeared as, fueled by his furious thinking, Max stalked toward the *Herald*. An over-wound spring, he couldn't bear being confined in a streetcar, not now.

The longer he walked, and the longer he thought, the better he felt. He had more ammunition than he could possibly use in a single article. Fisk had tried to intimidate him, but he'd forced the colonel into haughty denials. Pure gold.

Then he remembered 8 Macdougal and self-laceration flared again. Why hadn't he posed a single question about that pestilent pile? Fisk had rattled him right away. What else was that fluttering in his chest but fear? On the other hand, the colonel had spewed out enough contempt to paint a wicked self-portrait.

As he crossed Printing House Square, he gained confidence. The facts were unassailable. He had the story of a lifetime in his grasp. He had survived Fisk's withering silences, his sarcasm and slights, and he was still standing. What could the colonel do to him now? Instead of surrendering to his fears, he had to organize his material and write that first pointed line. He made a mental note to kick Fisk's rationalizations up top.

There was no point in eating or sleeping until he composed his opening salvo; but before he reached his desk, Parnell summoned him to the throne. "What the hell'd you do? Fisk's been burning my ear off on the telephone."

Panic flashed through him. "What'd he say?"

"He wants your head, that's all. He was squealing like a stuck pig. What the hell'd you stick him with?" Parnell's white-lipped smile was all the encouragement Max needed.

"I've got the goods, Stan. Health Department records. The hospitals are safer than Holy Trinity's shacks."

"Use that."

"What?"

"The hospitals. That'll grab them. But don't go overboard. Their lawyers will be sniffing out every word. This isn't some batty old biddies; this is Holy Trinity." The editor folded a sheet of paper and pushed it across his desk. "Use this. Straight from the colonel's mouth. Now get out of here. You're on deadline."

Piling his mountain of material next to his writing machine, he froze for a moment. His crabbed hand had scrawled out too many facts, too many quotes, too many ideas. In the margins, in unblotted ink, he had recorded secondary issues and tangential calculations. Unfolded sheets were sprayed with half-legible information. A tidal wave of particulars threatened to crest over his head. How could he keep from drowning?

It was one thing to collect facts, quite another to carve a simple line through the mass of material. Now, facing the terror of the blank page, he fought with the simplest question of all: What was the story about? The condition of the buildings? The suffering of the tenants? The smugness of the landlord? Holy Trinity's hypocrisy? (A follow-up interview with the Reverend Weems cried out to be written.) All of these and more?

He was no Sachs' Café socialist, he had no ax to grind against property owners, but Fisk's way of thinking burned him up. Part of it was personal, he had to admit. He didn't care for being called Greenberg twice in that arch, patronizing tone. But the colonel's rationalizations turned his stomach, too. A cold rage gripped him. Perhaps this fury had been bred into his bones all along, but he had never sensed its depths before.

He knew how an assassin must feel the moment the crowd parted and he could take a good clean shot at his tyrant. He also knew he would have to resist that temptation.

Then his fingers began playing the keys. "In 1864, a Holy Trinity Church property at 38 Cherry Street was cited by the Health Department for numerous violations, including a tainted water supply and 'emanations from decomposing refuse.' Today, almost thirty years later, the rambling tenement contains 438 persons who share a single water pump. As recently as January 8, 1893, Health Department investigators described the same pump as 'lacking a handle and being virtually inoperable.'

"An analysis of recent deaths at 38 Cherry Street reveals a death rate three times the city average. Eight Macdougal, another Holy Trinity property, has experienced a rate of four deaths for every ten residents, every year. Cholera, tuberculosis, typhus, and influenza have all found fertile ground at 8 Macdougal and many other church-owned tenements. They are much like old hospitals, whose infected wards take their toll every year."

Now he unfolded the quote Fisk had telephoned in to Parnell. "The idea that the church's corporation ought to act in any way contrary to its stockholders' interests is abhorrent. There are certain foreign doctrines that propose that business ought to build its own funeral pyre, but Holy Trinity's board does not subscribe to them. I have a fiduciary responsibility which I do not propose to shirk."

The colonel had outdone himself. Max worked up a transition and inserted Fisk's quote. Now he started hacking away at the rest of the piece. Time melted as he poured it out, checking and rechecking his dates and figures, firming up attributions, revising a phrase here and there, bumping this graf up and that one down. Shape-shifting, slowly settling, hardening in place, the article rolled out before his eyes. Tearing the last sheet from the platen, he raced across the office and delivered.

Parnell went light with his pencil. "Garvey's got his back up. Let's go."

"What's up?"

"He wants to kill it. C'mon."

Like disconnected spurts of electricity, his thoughts stuttered. They couldn't, not now . . . all that reporting, all that composing . . . what was Garvey's interest? Was he a Holy Trinity man himself? Numb, he stumbled behind Parnell into the glassed-in office.

A dyspeptic look on his face, Garvey stroked his soft doorknob of a chin. To Max's surprise, Bennett stood glowering behind the managing editor. Under the publisher's fierce gaze, he felt transparent. Stranger still, a bald working man in a linty jacket sat in the corner, rolling his cloth cap in his hands.

Garvey offered Max a curt nod. "Stan. Greengrass? I'll make it short. I don't give two figs about Fisk and his corporation, but he's got a point. Where do we get off making accusations when none of this is their responsibility? Did they go around infecting their own tenants? Did they tell them to make a pigsty inside four walls and spread the clap while they're at it? I don't see it. We're going off half-cocked, and we might end up in court."

Frowning, Bennett asked, "What do you think of that, Greengrass? It's my money you're playing with. Suppose Garvey's right, and I end up with some shyster choking me to death?"

"It's not libel if every word is true," Max shot back. A torrent of words swelled up in his throat, but he bit his tongue. The worst thing he could do was make a speech defending his work.

Bennett hooted. "Ha! What do you say to that, Garvey?"

"It's way out of left field. Do you think the church's trustees know a thing about this crap? I like to think twice before joining a lynching. What about the vestrymen? You're talking about some of the best people in this city, and you know how nasty they can be. This can turn around and bite us, I'm telling you."

Garvey was a celebrated infighter—he hadn't become managing editor by being a creampuff—and he had Bennett's confidence. Long ago he had damped down the publisher's infatuation with Henry George, and he maintained an intricate web of contacts with Tammany and the Reverend Parkhurst's goo-goos. After a lifetime serving the Bennetts, father and son, his word had a special weight.

Max's heart sank. If they murdered this story, he was flat out of ideas. Bone-deep exhaustion gripped him. Pins and needles pricked at his right foot.

Parnell didn't back down, though. "Those fellas read the *Trib*," he pointed out. "This thing's got my-how-the-mighty-have-fallen written all over it. What else do you want? And it's a beat, for godsakes. Who else's got it?"

"Exactly! That's my point!" Bennett said vehemently. "Tompkins, what did I ask you to do?"

Shifting uncomfortably in his chair, the working man coughed into his fist. A pattern of freckles stained his naked scalp. "Excuse me, I gotta toucha the congestion. What I did was, I walked the whole island, and I seen how we was doin' against the *World*."

"Tompkins has been delivering for us for how many years?" A conspiratorial smile crept over Bennett's sharp-etched features.

"Twenty-three, sir."

The pomaded tips of Bennett's mustache quivered. "No guesswork, right? I told you to find out the real figures, didn't I? Not those self-serving estimates the Circulation Department loves to feed me, eh?"

"That's right, sir. I went to every newsstand up and down and got an earful. Took me five weeks. The long and short of it is, we're dead as a doornail."

"The *World*'s boxing our ears, isn't it?" Bennett crowed.

"So they says."

The publisher spread his arms wide. "What else do we need to know, Mr. Garvey? Whip it! Ride it 'til it dies."

chapter thirty-two

Belle was sitting up in bed with Faye, stroking her hair with one hand and rocking Leon's cradle with the other.

"He's got a fever," she said, patting the mattress for Max to sit down. Her curly black hair hung loose on her shoulders, and her plain dress was unbuttoned at the throat.

He had tracked her to Sullivan Street after finding her note pinned to his door. This was not the rendezvous he had planned when he left the office, famished and longing for company. What he'd had in mind was a Blue Blazer at Jerry Thomas's on 22nd, maybe a Tom and Jerry for Belle, a chat about the depredations of Holy Trinity—he knew she would love his imitation of Colonel Fisk—and then a surreptitious visit to her room around midnight.

Faye lay her head on Belle's shoulder. "He was standing up and falling down," she said in a faraway voice.

Leaning over the child, he put his hand on the tiny forehead. Leon was burning up. "Jeez, he's hot as hell. You think he'll be okay?"

Belle calmed his fears. "His temperature's 103, but they run high at this age. We'll keep an eye on him."

He didn't like Leon's ashy complexion. Did he ever sleep?

"Pour yourself," Faye offered, pointing a languid finger at the gin on her dresser.

Max took the liquor neat. There was no savor to the stuff, you just poured it down your gullet like medicine. For some unfathomable reason, women seemed to like it, though. Equally mysterious was the intimate bond Belle and Faye had forged out of the blue. He had been planning to tell Belle in intricate detail about 22 Spring Street, but Faye's boudoir, with its astral lamp, its decorative screen and violet scents, didn't seem like the right place.

"You should have seen Faye at the show today. She topped herself," Belle said, an adoring note in her voice. She knew she sounded like a greenhorn to Faye and Max, but how could she help being entranced? Standing backstage, she'd seen Maggie Cline belt out "When Hogan Pays the Rent." The way she sauntered around the stage and joked about her nine-dollar fan—Belle got knots in her stomach laughing so hard.

"I was light as a fairy," Faye agreed.

"I watched from the wings," Belle went on. "Danny did a nice turn, too."

What amazed him was how easily she had insinuated herself into his cracked family. The way she was stretched out, her boots unlaced, rocking Leon, petting Faye, casting warm glances his way with those liquid brown eyes—it all seemed so natural that it frightened him.

"Mr. Swarms is nothing without me," Faye said, a sly smile on her painted mouth.

"No, he's something. I just don't know what," Max laughed, finally taking a seat on the edge of the bed. Everything was going so smoothly between Swarms and Faye, it made him itchy. He'd never given two thoughts to Danny's character in their pub-crawling days. Swarms needed Faye in his act, but was that it? She was such an easy mark when she was in love. So far Swarms had been an angel, even hinting that he might adopt Leon when the time came. In fact, he had been too damned generous for Max's taste. Danny Swarms, philanthropist, made his skin crawl.

"Is there a chicken leg or something in this dump?"

From somewhere under the covers Faye produced half a sandwich. "Polish sausage. Your favorite."

He tore into the soggy bread. The meat was tasty, but it did nothing to satisfy his raging hunger. Morelli's on Sixth Avenue grilled a nice T-bone steak. He wondered if their kitchen was still open. "So, Belle, are you camping out here or what? 'Cause I've got to get my beauty sleep."

Faye grabbed her friend's arm and batted her eyelashes. "She can't go. She's my prisoner."

Belle gave him a helpless look. "I have to keep an eye on Leon. If the fever spikes. . . ."

Faye puckered her lips and blew him a kiss. "You know what you can do, Maxie? On your way home, tell Mrs. Darling Leon's out for the next day or two."

Suppose he and Belle got serious? Would he have to fight Faye for Belle's attention? He would lose that battle every time.

"Let me borrow her," he replied, taking Belle's other wrist.

They wended their way through the crowded kitchen—Faye's roommates were giving a potluck dinner for some of the other chorines—and out into the hall. The gas fixture threw a yellow light onto the whitewashed wall. Doors slammed. Water gushed in a hall toilet down below. As soon as they were alone, she fell into his arms, her kisses ardent, probing, and his chest went weak. Encircling her tiny waist, he swept her off the floor and held her close. His pinkie traced the hollow of her delicate ear. She ran her fingernail down the back of his neck. The tips of their tongues met. A current bolted through him, and he went hot and faint and hard all at once.

Biting her earlobe, he pressed her again. "Why don't you come back with me? The kid's gonna be okay, isn't he?"

She wanted to more than anything, and she hadn't forgotten the sheepskins either. Who knew where any man had been, especially this one? She didn't answer until he set her down again. "Probably, maybe. I should keep an eye out."

"It can't be that serious, can it?"

"It's most likely nothing, but I want to watch out for meningitis. Faye's such a sweetheart, but between you, me, and the lampost, I don't think she can boil water."

Defeated, he leaned against the wall.

Her eyes fell on his pleated trousers. "You made a tent."

"I'm not the only talented one in this family." He pulled her against him again, kissed her and groaned. "Sorry, sorry, I couldn't help that one."

"Neither could I," she said, stroking his face, tugging his mustache. "It's so bushy."

"Does it scratch?"

"No, it's like a pillow on your face."

Her hair corkscrewed in three directions at once. He was puffing like a Forney engine. They both burst out laughing.

"When you go to this Mrs. Darling, I haven't seen her insides. . . ." As soon as the malaprop escaped her lips, she could feel her face burning. The things she said sometimes, he'd think she was an imbecile.

"Neither have I."

She placed her palms on his chest and pushed him away. "Stop, you know what I mean. These places . . . sometimes, you have to make sure about them."

"Did Faye say anything?" he asked, alarmed.

"Not exactly. It's just the way she *doesn't* talk about it."

"Another Fayefaye expert, huh?"

"I'm getting my certificate."

Three-day paint choked the numerals, but he could still make out the address, 217 Sullivan. Mrs. Darling turned out to be a jovial, three-chinned woman, and another Faye Greengrass acolyte to boot. Through the cracked door, she told him all about his sister's largesse. "Oh, Faye, she gives me a free ticket to Mr. Keith's when she can snag one."

"Mind if I get a glass of water? I'm parched."

Her eyes hardened, scrutinizing him. "You're not one of those gyps, are you?"

"Nah, I gave up forking years ago."

That got a laugh out of her. Her chins jiggled. "We have to be quiet. They're all asleep for once."

She led him to a sink and gave him a greasy glass. The kitchen was cheerful enough, the walls papered with chromos of Kathy O'Neill, Ruth St. Denis, and Eva Tanguay, as well as anonymous Gibson Girls torn from Sunday supplements. With her theatrical airs, Faye must have impressed Mrs. Darling no end.

A pot of frankincense smoked on a deal table. The thick, cloying fumes didn't quite cover another more complex stew of odors. Separating the kitchen from the inner chambers, a beaded curtain hung still in the dead air.

Before she could stop him, Max parted the clicking strands. In the shadows, he made out two large cribs. The room smelled of sour milk, mildew, and piss. Several infants were jammed into each crib. Mrs. Darling had stuffed at least seven or eight babies into the windowless room. He couldn't be sure, but he thought he could make out a door to an interior chamber. Were there more stacked in there, like chickens in a coop?

How could Faye leave Leon here? He knew only too well. Faye had constructed a mythical Mrs. Darling—so attentive, so sweet—for her own benefit, and no matter how hard you drummed the facts, she would stick to her fantasy now. The truth was that she could dump Leon off here on the run—it was only a few doors away from her own tenement—and Mrs. Darling's was probably dirt-cheap, too. Belle had sniffed out the truth right away.

"Oh, don't look in there: I keep Leon in *my* room," Mrs. Darling cooed, her hand on his shoulder.

"Oh, that's better," Max said. "It's a little tight in there, eh?"

"Faye's not like the ones that thinks I'm a hotel. Oh, they're sly, don't you believe 'em. They come to Mrs. Darling 'cause they hear I've got the heart, and they put a little down, and you know what? God as my witness, it's the last I see of 'em. Then what am I suppose ta' do?"

"Exactly. You have to live yourself, don't you?"

"When I was bringin' up my own, didn't I have to wet-nurse out, and that hurts a woman something terrible, givin' suck on Fifth Avenue while she's got to pay some other poor soul to feed her own. Oh, it's a merry-go-round, I tell you. But Faye, she's on time almost all the time, and when she ain't, she's a good girl, and I'm understanding."

"She misses her payments? How much are they?"

"I never take more than $1.50. You know who's in there? My sister Betty's little Morris, she's working for the Simpsons, a nice family. They sell the plate glass. And there's Christine, my friend Gloria's. I known Gloria years now, don't you know? The lady downstairs from Russia, I got her David. I got the heart, that's why they come to me. But when they stop paying, what am I supposed to do with my stock? I got rent, expenses. You don't see me with my puss in the growler like these others. Faye, she's got the insurance, and Betty too. So I rest easy with them."

He ambled over to the sink and turned on the tap. "Insurance?"

"Oh, sure. That's why I know she's one of the better ones. Ten cents a week the company wants, but you have peace of mind when all's said and done."

He kept the question casual. "It pays for everything, does it?"

"Oh, sure, all the expenses. Naturally, it's not what you want to put your mind on, but it's practical. I seen plenty, it's a sad thing, they go into the ground without a marker."

She was always up to something, Faye, always looking for the easy way out. How the hell could she stick Leon in a menagerie like that? Wait until Belle got a look at it. Now he was glad she'd gotten so tight with his sister. Maybe she could influence Faye, embarrass her into behaving herself. No, that wasn't possible. When it came to making herself comfortable, Faye didn't listen to anybody. And she had peculiar ideas about comfort too.

She'd trot along, day after day, doing her impression of a normal person, and then blooey, she'd veer off the reservation. She was six months gone before she mentioned she was pregnant, and the way she dropped it into the conversation, as if she'd picked up an annoying hangnail, still got his goat. And who the hell was the father? That booking agent with the brilliantined hair? The swami mind reader from Rutgers Street? The Irish clog dancer with the suspiciously Jewish mug? The song plugger who only played in two keys? In the back of his mind he was always worried. What would she do next? All his life, Faye had been a lump in his throat.

And what the hell was she doing buying insurance? What was that all about? Fayefaye, Fayefaye. Her name hammered in his head. Maybe it was the gust of cold river air, but his sinuses were swelling like bladders.

He took the horsecar uptown, determined to cap his labors with a Blue Blazer, but at Seventeenth Street the vehicle began to crawl and by Eighteenth it rocked to a dead stop. A mouse darted out of the straw and ran right between his feet. A man with a watchman's cap groaned and hauled himself down to the sidewalk. Two more passengers followed. Max heard the driver cursing, the whip's hiss, but the car remained stock-still. Finally, surrendering, Max climbed down, too.

The beast stamped and shied when he came close.

"Sonofabitch threw a shoe," the driver said.

Jerry Thomas mixed the cocktail himself. "Still burning up the newspaper business?" the proprietor inquired. A man with slicked-back hair, a needle nose, and a well-known aversion to sunlight, Jerry had the look of a sickly mole.

"Settin' a few fires," Max admitted. He took a sip. "You're a genius, Jerry."

"That's what they say," Thomas admitted, showing his pointy teeth.

A polished rail. A horseshoe-shaped bar reflecting droplets of light. The wood smooth and waxed under his palm. He was at home. The mixed drink placed strategically at his elbow, Max leaned over his notebook and began drawing a diagram of circles.

He tagged the primary circle Holy Trinity. The next, The Midnight Band, overlapped the church in the person of Mrs. Edwards, cousin to the Reverend Weems. Martin's sector, by virtue of his cat-lady fascination, his insurance sales territory, and his house of worship, impinged on both. Inside his sister Faye's zone he placed the word "Martin" and a question mark. Who else would have sold her a policy? Harry Granger's territory overlay Martin's, but covered Minetta Lane and the other remnants of Little Africa still alive in Greenwich Village.

Stephenson's connected Martin and Harry Granger and Martin's murderer. To represent this relationship, he penciled in a cigar-shaped area for the black-and-tan. Nestled inside of it he wrote "M's killer." Then he had an inspiration. Around these incestuous shapes he drew a ring in dashes, encompassing them all. This porous boundary he labeled Howe and Hummel. Hadn't they represented Mourtone Sr. and Mrs. Edwards, as well as being on the Liquor Dealers Association's permanent retainer? And wasn't Stephenson a power among the saloon barons? Willy Howe had played the prestidigitator in Martin's case as well. In its best tradition, the firm was on all sides of the affair. Just to be comprehensive, he sketched a floating bubble inside Howe and Hummel's territory and tagged it Parnell.

Didn't Holy Trinity own Sullivan Street property? He dug out his list and there it was, 217 Sullivan, Mrs. Darling's address. Dutifully, he inserted her domain.

In the intersection of these shapes, he tried to conjure up Mourtone's killer, but the tangle of lines blurred before his eyes. To understand why Martin ended up spattered on a tin wall, did he have to make sense of a pious Christian sect that gouged its tenants? To figure out why Harry Granger ended up with empty eye sockets, did he have to understand Mrs. Darling's peregrinations?

One thing was certain: Leon wouldn't be returning to Mrs. Darling's. Max was going to give Faye a piece of his mind as soon as he got ahold of her. And he'd find out every last detail about the damned insurance

Mourtone had sold her. How much were the premiums? What was the payout? He could still feel Leon's hot forehead in his palm, the boy's thin skin and delicate skull, and his heart sank. It was all too obvious why his sister had bought into an insurance proposition. It made perfect, awful sense.

His mouth dry, he tossed and turned and twisted himself into such original positions that his bedclothes ended up tangled around his ankles. A persistent itch climbed his left forearm, driving him mad. Sleep, that sweet oblivion, drifted just out of reach. Finally, he gave up and at the crack of dawn he hopped out of bed, poured some water into the enamel bowl, and splashed his face. Mrs. DeVogt's was still shrouded in darkness as he picked his way down the stairs and into the thin light of day. The papers would be out. Fitzgerald and Ives would be open for business.

He planned to spread the morning edition out on the bar, peel a hard-boiled egg, and take his sweet time before heading to work. He snagged the *Herald* from the newsie at Fourteenth and Sixth, tucked it under his arm, and sailed downtown. Despite his lack of sleep, he felt buoyant. His series would hit today, and he could envision the string of articles to come. The corporation would have to respond to the charges, the Reverend Weems would be forced to chime in, and the vestrymen, goo-goos to the core, would have to invent their own convoluted defenses. What a spectacle! Mayor Gilroy would be forced to make some mealy-mouthed statement, the Reverend Dr. Parkhurst would be drawn in, and Tammany would have to figure out whether it should make political hay or play dumb, as property was its life's blood too. Real estate's unseen arteries fed Fifth Avenue and Tammany braves alike. When he thought of that prig Colonel Fisk, he almost burst out laughing. The story was writing itself. The more he walked, and the more he thought about his coup, the more his self-regard grew.

To prolong the delicious moment, he sipped his first beer, separated shell from egg, showered the delicacy with salt, and rearranged his rear end on the bar stool. Only then did he unfold the paper. The front page featured a story about a bank run in Cleveland and a murder in Chicago: a Mrs. Edson's corpse had been found in a luxury hotel, along with a false beard. Not for the first time, the *Herald* observed that Chicago, that sprawling cowtown, so incongruously the site of a World's Fair, was in truth a "criminal's paradise."

In another article, the Reverend Dr. Parkhurst promised shocking revelations about Police Captain Devery and a bail bondsman Max knew well, Max Hochstim. In the main political feature, Tammany leader Richard Croker contended that rumors about his lavish racehorse farm in Ireland were grossly exaggerated. As for any new investigative committees coming down to the city, Croker said, "This is the best governed city in this country, and they won't find a thing. What about Senator Fassett's investigation four years ago? The whole thing was a fizzle."

Not a word about Holy Trinity and its miserable properties. He snapped through the pages, headlines flashing past. ANARCHIST PLOT IN BARCELONA. FEET KEY TO CHARACTER. RICH RESORTS SHY AWAY FROM WOODCOCK. MADISON SQUARE SURPLUS WIPED OUT.

He lingered over the last one. Apparently, certain Madison Square Bank officials had been borrowing against "large blocks of worthless stock." As the bank collapsed, these nameless executives had enriched themselves to the tune of tens of thousands of dollars. It was remarkable how the bankers managed to remain anonymous while the *Herald* reported the names of every Orchard Street vampire and horseblanket thief.

Had he torn through the paper too quickly? He turned every page and scanned every headline a second time. Not a peep about Colonel Fisk, his vestrymen, or the Reverend Weems. He tried to calm himself by recalling how he'd barely made his deadline—the piece was long, they could have held it until the next edition—but Garvey's words kept coming back to him: *You're talking about some of the best people in the city, and you know how nasty they can be.* He could see that tinpot dictator Fisk applying pressure, cajoling, making threats. On other hand, he had Parnell on his side, and, better still, Bennett, who wanted more than anything to nip at the *World*'s heels. Why kill a story that would sell thousands of papers?

chapter thirty-three

A few reporters bent over their desks, the electric globes pale in the early light. The eternal cigar smoke wound around slow fans, falling in a soft, acrid pall. Max's eye roamed over Graham, the spindly proofreader, chained to his desk since the days of Bennett, Senior. Over in Advertising, Stanley, a doughy father of seven, gazed blankly out at a rat's nest of electric wires. The grisly Kingsley, a clerk in Classifieds since the fall of Tweed, squinted through his thick glasses at hand-scrawled personals. Max loved to read these miniature tales of unrequited love; he could recite some of the finest by heart.

> A businessman, 35, desires acquaintance healthy, sensible pretty blond Protestant under 20: view, marriage; kindly describe appearance, height, weight; mercenaries, gum-chewers or bicycling noodles not wanted.

> Broadway cable car, yesterday morning, ten fifteen—will lady wearing astrakhan jacket, who noticed gentleman who got off at Court House, honor him with her acquaintance?

> If magnificent stout lady who left the Broadway car at Hilton, Hughes & Co. yesterday will walk down Broadway Thursday at noon from 23rd Street, the stout gentleman with full beard who sat opposite will try to meet her.

Parnell hadn't yet arrived, so Max busied himself with organizing his papers and planning the day's attack. His prime target was the Reverend Weems. The minister's predictable denials and pleas of ignorance would make good copy. When he looked up, Parnell had materialized on his throne.

Eternal, welded to his chair, the editor was already mowing through a stack of copy. Max hated to interrupt, but he had no choice.

Mounting the steps, he stood at a respectful distance until Parnell could no longer ignore his presence. "Greengrass?"

"Sorry to bother you, Stan, but I didn't see the Holy Trinity piece."

His eyes watery, Parnell looked past him. In a soft voice, he said, "Just stick to it. We'll see."

The phrase "we'll see" chilled him to the bone. Hadn't Bennett been calling for a whipping less than twenty-four hours ago? Still, he did his best to ignore the obvious implications. "I was thinking of interviewing our friend Weems today."

"Sure, sure. Makes sense."

Finally, he couldn't help himself. "Bennett's still on board with this one, isn't he?"

"Bennett's sailing today," Parnell replied gruffly. "Greek islands. Crete."

He was dumbstruck. Had Fisk forced Bennett's hand overnight? The publisher's flight left Max exposed, without his most powerful ally. Garvey would be in the saddle now. Bits of boiled egg and bile rose into the back of his throat. "Just like that? I mean, was he planning to go?"

"He comes, he goes." Parnell shrugged. Max understood the message in those bony shoulders. Bennett was a capricious storm. What could you do about nature?

He read every one of Parnell's signals, he heard every warning bell, but it was as if he'd lost his brakes. "I mean, if it doesn't run today, the *World*'ll get the beat, no two ways about it."

In truth this claim made little sense. The *World* had no reason to investigate Holy Trinity, or to swarm over Health Department records. It was his work, his idea, and now it was coming to nothing. Hot and cold flashes swept through him, and in their wake a bitter disappointment.

"That's my problem, not yours." Parnell fingered his copy pile, indicating that the audience had ended.

"I risked my neck for this one, dammit!" The words burst out before he could call them back, and the pencil flew from his hand. Transfixed, Max watched it spin through the air. The stick of wood bounced once on Parnell's desk, then struck the editor on the shoulder. "Sorry," he muttered.

Parnell's frigid look finally brought him to his senses. With a correct nod, Max withdrew to the newsroom floor, but his fury wouldn't abate. Garvey had murdered his story. It was probably lying in bits on the composing room floor—or, worse still, it was suffocating under a mass of trivial items still stacked on the managing editor's desk. He wanted to bolt, but that would be suicide. He had to make himself available, otherwise he'd slide right back to the end of the space-rater's bench. Steaming, he wedged himself back behind his battered desk and carved out meaningless designs with his pen until the nib flattened under his fist.

As the morning wore on, Parnell ignored him. Time turned thick until it froze and refused to pour. In a stupor he watched fan blades disturb the haze, new rivers of smoke streaming in fresh directions, braiding, giving birth to rushing tributaries. Hypnotized, he gazed at the churning substance until, dissolving, he became smoke itself.

A familiar voice drifted toward him. Belatedly, he rushed to heed Parnell's call.

"What're you, going deaf?" the editor snapped. "You look like hell in a handcart."

"Thanks."

"This shouldn't tax your abilities too much. A woman on Duane Street has a bitch."

"Yeah?" The editor was exacting his punishment now. Canine tales were the province of the lowliest cub.

"Don't interrupt me. This bitch has a litter, nine it says here, and they've all got six toes."

That was twenty-four toes per dog. Despite himself, the line popped into his head. "We could run it under 'Nine Dogs, Two Hundred Sixteen Toes.'"

The editor responded with a rare smile. "Stick your head in the sink before you go out."

"Bad night. Do you mind if I interview Weems? I think there's some meeting this evening."

"Why not?" Parnell put his hand on Max's shoulder and shook him. "Just have a little patience, kiddo."

For a brief moment he basked in the editor's chilly light, and his love for the shabby business revived. Biddle, Parnell, Stanley, Graham, Kingsley. They were all brothers in a six-toed world.

It took him forty-five minutes to discover that the wonder dog's litter consisted of one puppy with a vestigial claw, and that her owner, Mrs. Ianelli, had a hunger to see her name in the paper. Max obliged with two inches of type. Although he longed to assault Parnell's redoubt one more time, he chose the better part of valor and slunk out of the office. Out on Printing House Square, he rubbed the thin sticks of hope together. The editor had agreed to let him interview Weems, hadn't he? Didn't that mean the story was still alive? Just because Bennett was sailing to Crete didn't mean he was giving up the reins to Garvey, did it?

Holy Trinity's neo-gothic spire rose above Lower Broadway's brownstone and brick. Lacy and light, the church posed as a cathedral despite its diminutive proportions. Fashionable carriages lined the sidewalks on both sides of the avenue, and Max was surprised to see parishioners jostling their way through the elegant doors. He hadn't realized that the Reverend Weems was so popular. For a Thursday evening lecture, the outpouring was astonishing. Then he noticed the discreet sign announcing the Reverend Dr. Parkhurst.

Every Parkhurst appearance promised a whiff of scandal. The wily crusader had started by attacking the time-honored practice of police extortion, particularly the department's protection of brothels and dives. When the newspapers ridiculed him, he hired private detectives to gather evidence of what was in plain sight: saloons doing rip-roaring business on Sundays, gamblers operating roulette wheels in wide-open storefronts, and madames paying off local pantatas on the first and fifteenth of every month.

Like most newspapermen, Max regarded Parkhurst as a blue-nosed peeping tom, but he also had a certain grudging respect for the reformer. Police Superintendent Byrnes had set up Parkhurst's chief detective, Charlie Gardner, and had him thrown in jail for extortion, but Parkhurst had fought back, gathering affidavit after affidavit testifying to a system of bribery that knit together patrolman, bagman, police captain, and Tammany ward heeler alike. Corruption was like the waves at Coney, Max believed, an irresistible tide; but however naïve, the clergyman had guts.

Excited whispers ran through the congregation as Parkhurst ascended the Frenchified pulpit set, after the continental style, halfway into the nave. In rimless glasses, his graying brown hair falling limp to his neck, he cut a modest figure. Yet with his shoulders flung back and his beard trimmed to a Mephistophelean point, he exuded an animal energy. Off to the side, the Reverend Weems was showing his formidable teeth, basking in reflected glory. Max was prepared to pounce on the Holy Trinity minister and extract a statement as soon as Parkhurst finished his sermon. Taking out his pad, he sighed, ready to record the usual bombast.

The Reverend Dr. Parkhurst didn't disappoint. His piercing voice, abraded from roaring speeches day after day, still penetrated the soaring, gray stone vaults.

"Christ came into this world aflame with a purpose. His attempt, burning and all-engrossing, was to take this world as it was and make it into what it was not. To clean it, to beautify it, to make it over from a damnable world into a blessed world. And the first step Christ took in his career was to quit Heaven."

A buzz ran through the pews. When the Reverend Dr. Parkhurst quit heaven, he usually ended up in odious, thrilling places. "The world's salvation *costs*, and we are too comfortable to pay for it. It is expensive work, self-immolating work, it is Heaven-abandonment work, and there is no getting around it. Sometimes the fires of Hell penetrate humble places. For instance, a soda fountain on Ridge Street. Do you know where Ridge Street is? Not far from the Essex Street Courthouse."

Max scanned the uncomprehending faces. Parkhurst was right. None of them had seen the anthill of Ridge Street, or the cattle-pen courthouse where judges settled evictions in sixty seconds.

Parkhurst fussed with his clerical tie, pausing until every last whisper had died away.

"A widow named Celia Urchittel, with her three surviving children, opened a modest shop there. She had fruit gums, malt balls, and toffees in glass jars, she sold cigars, and she slept in the back of the store with her little ones. One day a ward detective from the Eldridge Street station came to this store and took a paper of tobacco. When he said he would pay sometime in the future, Mrs. Urchittel demanded he give back her goods. At midnight this reprobate of a detective returned, and not with the paltry nickel he owed, but with a warrant for her arrest. Mrs. Urchittel, who came from a country where the police were as powerful as gods, and who no longer enjoyed the protection of a husband, was terrified."

Surveying his rapt audience, the clergyman milked the nervous silence. Max marveled at the minister's talent. The man was a brilliant storyteller, and a genius of outrage to boot. Max was transfixed.

"But the detective was a merciful man. He offered to withdraw the warrant if she paid him fifty dollars. Despite her terror, Mrs. Urchittel mastered her fears and chased the scoundrel out with a broom. This, my dear friends, was the beginning of a nightmare that will illustrate exactly why bribery and police corruption are not material for satire, but the stuff of human tragedy. Our guardians of the public safety are not mere passive receptors of a benign system of tribute, but aggressive predators who seek to strip bare the most vulnerable among us. What happened to this immigrant woman, who cannot speak our language, who does not know our laws, who is used to being ground into the dust by the Cossack's bootheel?

"She was dragged two blocks from her store, where the detective introduced her to a man named Max Hochstim. For those of you not familiar with this reptile, he is a bail bondsman who holds the power of life and death at the Essex Street Courthouse. Mrs. Urchittel begged Hochstim, a fellow countryman, to save her, but he told her he had already helped her beyond measure, having reduced her payment from seventy-five dollars. These are crippling sums for a woman who can barely meet her rent obligations every month, but the two men browbeat her, threatened to toss her into a cell that night, and when she expressed fear for her children's safety, they told her the authorities would *take care* of her little ones."

Parkhurst's hoarse voice descended to hushed tones. In a rustle of crinoline, the parishioners shifted to the edge of their benches. "How would you feel if your home was invaded by armed marauders promising to 'protect' your children? And how would you feel if you didn't have the money to buy their freedom? How did this fairy tale turn out? Did some prince intercede, vanquish the wicked, and raise up the oppressed? Did our city fathers, our police commissioners, our Police Superintendent strike back in the name of justice? Or was this woman arrested, accused of soliciting and convicted by trumped-up, perjured testimony? Did she lose her children who are to this day, a year after this wretched affair began, still in the custody of an agency that refuses to surrender them? And in the course of these events, did Mr. Hochstim and his friend Captain Devery rise higher in the municipal firmament, did they enrich themselves, and are they still in power?"

Everyone in the vaulted chamber knew the answers to these bitter questions. Max wrote furiously in his private shorthand, taking down Parkhurst's accusations in fine detail. The Urchittel story turned his stomach. It was one thing for Mrs. Jabonne to buy a little peace of mind for her brothel. That seemed only natural: she and the police were in the same business. But the Urchittel affair was like rape by an occupying army, and Parkhurst was shrewd enough to seize upon it.

Despite his professional detachment, Max couldn't deny the power of the minister's oratory. Having witnessed the third degree in a half dozen precinct houses, he still flinched when a nightstick artist painted a skull blue. When his friend Schreiber slammed a drunk's mug with the back of his hand, Max always winced inwardly, yet he prided himself on keeping a straight face too. Usually, the buttons were dealing with creatures who only understood the language of knuckles and boots. Unorganized brutality had a human face.

But Parkhurst went on, evoking a crushing and cold machine, financial arrangements that had a life of their own, hungry and dead at the same time. This vision of underlying, unspoken rules, of choking forces and secret arrangements, was a part of the shadow world Max had always sensed just under the city's skin. Its eruption, in the Urchittel case, affected him. Weren't these the same pressures that kept him on the space-rater's bench and smothered the Holy Trinity story before it saw the light of day?

Lost in these speculations, Max was barely aware that the Reverend Weems had taken the pulpit. Weems thanked Parkhurst profusely, and when the crusading minister apologized about his pressing business elsewhere, Weems said, "We are eternally grateful that you found the time to address our humble assembly."

Light applause, and the tapping of walking sticks accompanied Parkhurst as he made his exit. Max found a seat closer to the younger clergyman who, all toothy smiles, launched into his own homily. The Reverend Weems held his own fascinations.

"I am sure we have all been touched by Dr. Parkhurst's exhortations. It is inspiring to see a Christian soldier so full of compassion and so dedicated to good works. But I don't think it was lost on us that the central actors in his tale came to us courtesy of foreign countries that could no longer endure them. Mrs. Urchittel landed here penniless and proceeded to produce three children she could not support. The execrable Mr. Hochstim, a Jew from the Pale who only preys on the weakest among us, found her a perfect target. The police captain, whose antecedents never mastered the mysteries of subsistence farming, found a good harvest of misery among our illiterate immigrants."

Max sat up. Weems's remarks made him squirm. Of course Max knew that he was himself an immigrant, but he didn't feel like a *foreigner*. His accent was perfect. He knew everything there was to know about the Giants, politics, and the latest shows and crazes. In point of fact, he was more up-to-date, and more American, than half of the dusty creatures in Weems's congregation.

Distracted, he had to remind himself of his original purpose, to extract a juicy quote from Weems about Holy Trinity's property. Let him ride his hobbyhorse.

Weems injected a quiet fury into his next remarks.

"Is this misery our fault? Or is it being imported in steerage every day? Did we create it, or are we the victims of rotten regimes that prefer to regurgitate their castoffs onto our shores? The philosopher Herbert Spencer teaches us that through God's beneficence, we are moving ever closer to His image. Yet when we see the struggle to survive, particularly in our suffering tenement wards, we wonder, how can we say God is good? How can we say God is charitable when we see our city filling daily with Europe's failed men and ruined races?"

An approving murmur swept through the pews. They had had enough of Dr. Parkhurst's hair shirt.

Max knew which failed men and which ruined races Weems was singling out. As much as he loathed his father's superstitious rituals, his rocking, prayer-shawled mutterings, he loathed this particular streak of reforming zeal more. A target of Weems's chilly disgust, he shrank to the hard pit of himself. He was barely a Jew, but the minister wanted to spit him out no matter what, and Max could think of nothing more satisfying than sticking in this goo-goo's throat. He flipped a page and strangled the pencil in his fist.

A satisfied smile played on Weems's lips. "Today, science is giving us the answer to this age-old question. It lies not in spurious philanthropy, which only succeeds in prolonging strains of weak blood, but in the understanding that God is making man more perfect every day by winnowing away the congenital criminal, the feeble-minded, the damaged issue of sin factories, and the dumb brute who cannot comprehend modern machinery. Spurious philanthropy saves the least equipped to survive, willing to our children a terrible burden and prolonging the misery of the weakest among us."

Max's eye strayed to the elegant crucifix mounted behind the altar. Agony distilled in his twisted body, a scrawny Jesus displayed his ribs. Did Christians ever wonder why they worshipped such a tortured symbol? Or how barbarous their fixation seemed to the Jews, inventors of a purified, immaterial God?

"However paradoxical it may sound, we must make ourselves hard to dispense compassion. Two thirds of Manhattan Island is now covered with tenements. I do not want to offend any delicate sensibilities, but our immigrant population is breeding out of control in these hovels. It behooves us to protect these unfortunate people by keeping them out, and this will protect the genius of Anglo-Saxon civilization as well. I do hope you will join with me in supporting our new Immigration Restriction League. I will be speaking more on this subject, and more frankly still, because if we do not face this disaster head on, we will be overrun."

He couldn't get over it. Parkhurst and Weems had drawn diametrically opposed lessons from the Urchittel affair. He had been moved by Parkhust's oration, affected despite his distaste for clergymen and reform. Without question Tammany was a rapacious tiger. Yet Weems's ideals repelled him even more. Howe's seductive formulation that there were no sides was too clever by half. Every side had sides.

While Weems was receiving thanks from his grateful parishioners, Max waited in the transept, biding his time. Finally, the minister made his way to the chancery, where Max caught up with him.

"Reverend Weems, Max Greengrass, *New York Herald*. May I have a word with you?"

The clergyman stopped dead in his tracks. A bony six-footer, he was more imposing than Max had realized. "You already spoke with Colonel Fisk, didn't you?"

"Yes, but I thought as minister—"

Weems cut him off. "The corporation must be the judge of its ability to do all that might be done," he said, his tone pure ice.

"What about conditions in church property? You don't condone them, do you?"

"That is for the corporation to decide, Mr. Greengrass. Colonel Fisk has my complete trust. If you'll excuse me."

Before he could fire another question, Max found himself staring at a heavy oak door.

Still, he'd extracted just enough. If the Holy Trinity story ever saw the light of day, Weems's mealy-mouthed answer would say more than any invective a reporter could muster. Meanwhile, he comforted himself with the fresh material he'd stumbled on.

Parkhurst's fiery accusations would make a pretty headline. Max knew exactly where to find Hochstim, too: at a saloon where the walls, the floors, and the ceiling flashed with silver dollars. Enterprising patrons had been trying to pry the coins free for years, but Silver Dollar Smith used plenty of solder.

Two hours later Max had transformed his notes into eight tight grafs.

"H'mm. Parkhurst versus Hochstim? Cute," Parnell muttered before calling for the copy boy.

Max bit his tongue. He stopped himself from pestering his editor about the Holy Trinity article, or where Bennett was sailing his steam yacht. He was back in the game. Rolling home, he directed his thoughts into more optimistic channels. Let the higher-ups fight over Holy Trinity. If they didn't want to let the story out, he could peddle it elsewhere. Who could stop him? Weren't there magazines? And what about the *World*? Wouldn't Pulitzer eat the real-estate scandal up? He could ring up that cowboy Hearst, too. Garvey wanted to step on his neck? The hell with him, and his playboy publisher too.

Mounting Mrs. DeVogt's front steps, he barely noticed the milkman lounging at the door above him. Then dimly it registered. What was a milkman delivering near midnight? Thrusting an envelope in Max's face, the man flashed a yellow grin before trotting back down to the sidewalk.

"Consider yourself served," the messenger hooted over his shoulder. Without even opening it, Max knew what lay inside.

chapter thirty-four

Pinned to the subpoena, a hand-written note read: "We are at your service in this matter. Late evenings best."

His insides in spasms, he stood frozen in the vestibule. Were Howe and Hummel simply practicing their usual trade, or were they trying to scare him off the story? They had represented Mrs. Edwards: why not Colonel Fisk and Holy Trinity's corporation? Worse still, they were squeezing Parnell. Perhaps, under pressure, the city editor, while playing the innocent, was gumming up the works along with Garvey, and suppressing the article against Bennett's wishes.

The legal document filled him with terror, but with a perverse pride as well. Branded by Howe and Hummel's most devious instrument, he had finally arrived. Then the sickness gripped him again. Weren't his arrival and departure taking place simultaneously? Stuffing the thick papers into his jacket pocket, he stumbled into the living room.

Her hands arranged in her lap, Gretta sat staring out the window. She looked so composed, so lovely in the soft gaslight. Her lavender gown's scalloped décolletage was modest, but still revealing enough to make him forget to breathe. She touched the hollow of her white throat. "You're so late," she said.

"You were waiting up for me?"

"*La Forza del Destino.*" Sensing his confusion, she added: "I can't stand opera."

The opera. How could he be so thick? Had she replaced Mourtone so quickly? Did she have another rich toff waiting in the wings? "Some people swear by it."

"My aunt is back, and she always makes a beeline for the Met."

She seemed to be reassuring him. Why did it matter so much? Didn't he already have Belle? The answer was right before him—Gretta's naked shoulders, her smoke-blue eyes, her lush mouth, her thrilling voice. He hadn't made any promises to Belle, had he? She was invading his life, getting mixed up with Faye's machinations. He hadn't invited her to join his demented family.

The blood rushed to his face. When Gretta patted the divan, he sat on her skirt. Embarrassed, he hopped back off the horsehair sofa and waited for her to gather the cascade of silk around her. Then he decorously took a spot a safe distance away.

"Sorry, my head's spinning."

"Hard day?"

"Big-time dog story." He meant it as a joke, but she didn't react. Why was it so hard to find the right words with her?

"Gertrude had me chained to the enlarger. Then I came home late, but I couldn't go up to my room." His eyes looked a bit mad to her. Since Martin had died, her craving to be by herself had intensified. To see no one, to stare out at the harbor, to escape the tyranny of speech—what bliss. She didn't dislike Max exactly. Far from it. But he was like some sort of grasshopper. Then she envisioned the weekend stretching out like a featureless landscape, days when she and her mother would barely exchange three words. "Oh, I have something funny for you. The Kodaks came back. Wait right there."

While she rustled up the stairs, he lit the stub of a cigar and pulled out his flask. A dram of brandy would smooth his nerves. He prayed she wouldn't wake Belle. Well, so what? Didn't he have a right to talk to another woman? As if Gretta could ever be just "another woman."

"Here they are!" she said, running her thumb over the stack of small prints. "What a failure. I must have wasted half the exposures. Either that, or this new process is a fraud. All I ended up with were a bunch of rusty old buildings. Except this one. Isn't that your sister? In the corner there? I didn't realize it when I was shooting. I only met her that once when she stopped by here to see you."

Faye was the last thing on his mind. Without much interest, he gazed at the crude image. Flattened into two dimensions, his sister's face had a smeared quality. Dusty white, her features lacked detail, but her thick-painted eyebrows and mouth were all he needed. She was talking to an older woman, an austere matron in a hat shaped exactly like an inverted flowerpot. Was it possible? He snatched the picture and squinted. "Where'd you take this?"

"Is there something the matter?"

"Do you remember?"

"Sullivan Street. Between Bleecker and Third. Martin's route. . . ."

"Do you know the other woman? Did you hear what they were saying?"

"Of course not. It was an accident. I barely knew they were in the shot. What are you so upset about?" His eyebrows bobbed, his eyes seemed to wink independently. Such unusual expressions raced across his face.

"No, no, I'm not upset. Just surprised. Never mind. I can hardly make it out." The more he stared, the less he was able to decipher the other woman's features. Black smudges for eyes, black dashes for nostrils, an almost invisible mouth. He would have to ask Faye, damn her! When was she going on tour? In a few days? If he didn't grab her right away, she'd be on the train to New Haven with Danny. The Credenzas. Ecch. How long would that act last?

Fayefaye, that well-worn groove in his brain—she insinuated herself into his life at the worst possible times. How did she do it?

"They were just chatting. Nothing special. Who is she?" She moved closer to get a better look at the snapshot. Reaching out, she steadied the picture in his hand.

He raised the photo, their fingers brushed, and he blanched. A tiny muscle twitched in his cheek. "Nobody. I'm getting buggy, that's all. Can I show it to Faye?" For so long, he had held back with Gretta. He had lectured himself on taste and timing. He had offered her comfort and nurtured their bond. Now he ruined everything by blurting, "I love seeing you."

Eyes widening, she drew her head back and withdrew her hand. His declaration filled her with terror. With this man, she could never have a moment's peace; he'd never leave her alone. He would stuff every room with words. "If you got to know me, you'd find me dull, Max. I'm very narrow."

With nothing to lose, he took her cool hand. His temples were pounding. She didn't resist. "I doubt that."

"All I can think about is taking pictures. My dreams are the stupidest things. I dream about tripods. I waste my time playing tennis for hours and hours. I don't read. I sit there mindlessly watching the harbor; I just want to be."

Her mother had been a great beauty too; but after Gretta's father disappeared into thin air, she had refused to see another man. Nothing could go wrong if you saw no one. Not a thing went wrong in her mother's life. Solitude was the perfect state, pristine and perfectly empty. Yet she struggled to give him a chance.

"There's less of you than meets the eye?" He had a mad vision—Gretta on his arm at Holy Trinity. He could shed his skin in the airy church. The Reverend Weems would preside. What sweet revenge.

She returned his satirical glance. "Definitely."

"All *I* can think about is chasing stories. I'm a monomaniac." What sleight of hand. He could become agnostic in two religions at once, and escape the ancient stain in one fell swoop. Why did the impulse fill him with such shame?

"We'd never see each other."

"Isn't that perfect? Who else would leave us alone like that?"

She laughed ruefully. "If it were only that easy. People pick at you with their stupid ideas." She wasn't going to say anything about his Hebrew origins, she wouldn't lower herself. Max wasn't the only clever foreigner she'd found amusing. There was that Italian engraver she'd met at the Art Students League, Arturo Natale. Of course, her uncle said the Mediterranean races would outbreed New England stock in a generation, and he knew all the mysteries of organic chemistry. It was such a confusing subject.

Anxiously, he glanced at the doorway, expecting Belle to materialize in her nightgown. She might be at the top of the stairway, taking in his every double-crossing word. Then he remembered—she was still at Faye's, keeping an eye on Leon—and he plunged ahead. "What about dinner in a real restaurant in a few days? Have you ever been to the Hoffman House?"

"Where they have all those racy paintings?"

"I didn't think you'd object."

"Do you know they have separate viewing hours for the ladies? I can see naked bodies at the Art Students League every day of the week. So what?"

The way she tossed off the word *naked* took away his breath.

"How about a lobster dinner? You can't work day and night."

If she kept resisting, he would drive her insane. She looked at his eager expression, his crooked nose, his square chin. At least there was no ambiguity about his masculinity. "Only if we have champagne too."

"Done."

He slid closer to kiss her, but she held him at arm's length. "Not now." She heard the promise in her own husky voice. She felt drawn to him, but she couldn't tell whether it was physical attraction or pure longing. Tentatively, she pressed his cheek with the flat of her palm. "I'm shy."

"I understand," he said, covering her hand with his own.

But that was what men never understood about her. They took her imperious expression, fear's mask, for confidence. They didn't know how the paws of strange men groped and poked and pinched her on packed trains, on horsecars, in shops, at proper dances, and on crowded streets, how these anonymous reptiles with their jiggling legs and hooded eyes terrified her, or how she secretly devoured penny dreadfuls that described, in horrific detail, the way pomaded brutes took women by force.

"If I don't get some rest. . . ." She removed her hand from his cheek.

He watched her take the stairs in her stately stride.

Max was ecstatic. Apparently she didn't consider his advances out of bounds. On the other hand, she treated him with a light, sisterly touch. It was so hard to know how to behave with a woman so desirable and so untouchable at the same time. No wonder men spent their last dollar at the House of all Nations.

Up in his room, he threw himself on top of the covers, hoping to take sleep by surprise. Flat on his back he lay there, his mind racing. Had she encouraged him, or kept him at bay? Did he feel guilty, or was he simply afraid of getting caught? Was he willing to cast Belle off? Not exactly. In fact, he was ready to lie through his teeth to get her into his bed again. It wasn't that he didn't care for her. She was quick, she was loyal, especially to Faye—and look at how he was going to pay her back. What a miserable weasel he was. And yet, and yet . . . Gretta opened another world. She was her Staten Island cottage, the shining bay, the sailing ships, a sanctuary from the sense-numbing city. Imagine unlacing her every night. How could he sleep now, or ever again?

Gretta stared at the ceiling. She had once drawn a model at the Art Students League, a Hebrew like Max with whipcord muscles, solid thighs, and a penis with a drooping head that reminded her of a sunflower. Martin had had a soft hairless chest and arms like white sausages. If he had lived, she would have had to hide her repugnance while rubbing up against his slack body. Her whole soul had been tensed against this violation. Now his death had freed her from that duty, and she couldn't, wouldn't deny her sense of relief. Didn't that make her a terrible person? Was she capable of forming any attachments at all?

She couldn't count the ways Max was unsuitable. For one thing, he didn't have a dime, and she was determined to escape Gertrude's studio before her hair turned gray. His low profession and his racial origins gave her pause too, she had to admit it. Her uncle said the Hebrew race was specialized for a parasitic existence. Max seemed like anything but a parasite, but her uncle had shown her a textbook thick with charts and graphs and talk of mutated germ plasma. How could she question Science?

She wanted a calm life, a life in which worries about money and family and children didn't intrude on her marriage to her camera. When she was framing a shot, she forgot she had a name or a sex or a body at all. That release into nothingness she craved more and more.

Still, she was thinking about Max. Martin had been so pliant. Max was all sharp angles. She imagined his sinewy muscles stretched over his thin frame. Under her hot lights, his blue-white skin wouldn't obscure its skeleton. Would he pose for her? From a clinical point of view, she wondered whether his circumcised penis looked like the Hebrew model's and whether it was true that all Jews possessed overdeveloped organs.

A vision of Martin's face came to her, but the details looked subtly distorted. His hair had been receding, but how high had it retreated? He had that delicate nose, almost like a woman's, but how small had it been? She knew his eyes, his cheekbones, his mouth, but not how they fit together any more. His voice, so quick to laugh at the smallest absurdity, was still alive in her ear. She missed his kindness and his triviality too. With him she could make the rest of the world disappear. No one was doing anything about his miserable death. Not his father, not the police. Only Max. Of course he had his own reasons, but even if he was climbing over corpses to make his name, he was doing something. Anything was preferable to the paralysis she felt as she sat on the edge of her chair for hours, alone in her room.

She changed into a black-and-white silk kimono her aunt had brought back from Japan. The smooth material soothed her senses, but she couldn't sit still. Taking her brush, she ran it through her hair in long, slow strokes until she found herself staring at the polished bone handle in her hand.

She could feel her mother's loathing of the outside world running through her veins. What could be more perfect than the cottage on the harbor? Other human beings created a mess, they upset your routine, they contrived obligations with their little cries for attention. She hoarded her detachment. Indifference sang its seductive song in her ear, yet it filled her with dread.

Her fist was tapping at his door. She barely knew how she'd arrived there. His eyes widening, he let her pass inside.

"You're not asleep either?" he asked.

"I forgot to give you the picture."

He took the snapshot from her and tossed it on his dresser. "Great. Thanks for remembering. Why don't you sit down for a minute?"

She never reached the chair. An inch too close to her, he couldn't resist desire's gravity. He told himself to step back, but his hands, falling lightly on her hips, wouldn't obey. She didn't want to push him away, she didn't want to think at all. Instead, she draped her arms around his neck and edged closer. All the blood drained from his face. She had never seen him look so afraid.

When she kissed him, she gave her whole body, her full breasts, hips, thighs pressing against him. What was she doing? Was it possible? At first, dry lips met dry lips, but then she let her mouth grow loose.

Tentatively, he touched the tip of his tongue to hers. The next kiss spiraled into another more intricate still, until he lost himself for a week or a month. He kissed her forehead, her cheeks, her throat and then her mouth again.

When they fell onto the bed, she felt him shudder. It was an odd sensation, as if he were in the throes of a death rattle. On top of her, his lean body felt stronger than she had imagined. There was a certain pleasure in rolling around with him; but when he struck her knee a glancing blow, a buzzing sensation ran right down to her foot. Not pleasant at all. Rubbed raw by his whiskers, her cheeks burned. What a peculiar wrestling match. He was squeezing all the air out of her, getting much too carried away. Her dressing gown slipped off her shoulder. One of his busy hands cupped her breast. She had to bring an end to it. Gripping his wrists, she held him while he shivered against her.

"No, not like this," she whispered, sliding out from underneath him.

He sat up, sweat plastering his hair to his skull, his face blotched pale and scarlet, his eyes half mad. Turning away, he gave her a moment to rearrange herself. "Yes, of course. Sorry."

She almost laughed at the way his lap came to a point. Why had God arranged things in such a ridiculous way? She wondered what his penis would feel like, pulsing in the palm of her hand. She had no one to talk to about him, no one to tell her she was being a fool. She almost wept at her own isolation.

"Are you still seeing Miss Rose?" she blurted. Now he'd think she was a jealous fool. Still, she wondered. Did Mrs. DeVogt's gossip contain a shred of truth?

Max's blood froze. Of course she had to have picked up something. They were all living in the same fishbowl. The question was, how much did she actually know? "Oh, we went to see Faye and Danny's act. She's great friends with my sister."

"Miss Rose thinks I'm a lost cause."

Was she buying his white lie? Maybe she wanted to believe him, maybe she was interested in him after all. "Why do you say that?"

"She thinks I'm a dangerous reactionary."

"Ahh. She passed judgment on me a long time ago."

Smoothing her wrinkled silk kimono, she rose to her feet. "You'll need your sleep." He went to kiss her again, but she turned away and his lips glanced off her cheek. "Don't, please. I'm so . . . I don't know what I'm doing, I'm sure."

She had come to him and fled, all in a matter of moments, leaving behind the perfumed smell of her hair, the taste of her lips, the impress of her luxuriant body against him. His longing for her felt more like a nervous condition than love.

chapter thirty-five

He waited for the newsie to cut open the fresh bundle of *Heralds*. A few earlybirds were climbing the covered stairs to the apple-green chalet of a station above. A giant soundingboard, the El's under-girding boomed out the roar of an approaching steam engine. Max stuck his fingers in his ears until the Forney rumbled away. This time he didn't wait for his hard-boiled egg at Fitzgerald and Ives. Standing on the sidewalk, he snapped the pages one after another, scanning every headline.

MAYNARD HISSED, DEPEW CHEERED. Chauncey Depew Calls Candidate a Criminal. WHERE DID THE MONEY GO? Madison Square Bank Was Plundered of Half a Million. WHIPPED IN THE STREET. Then at the Police Station Young Mrs. Neville Punched Janitor Farrar Between the Eyes. MISERIES FOR FLOATERS. Robert Stewart Says Warrants Are Ready for Tenth Ward Repeaters.

Not a word about Holy Trinity, Colonel Fisk, the Reverend Weems, or the church's property. Disgusted, he shoved the paper under his arm and stalked up to the train. In a stew, he almost missed his stop. Lunging, he threw his body between the closing doors, the car started rolling again, and for a moment he feared he was going to lose a leg. Then the train lurched to a halt and spat him, dazed and rubber-legged, out onto the platform.

What was the point of all his backbreaking, meticulous research? He would be better off inventing dogs with extra toes or giraffes in love triangles. Still steaming, he practically bowled Biddle over in the newspaper's lobby.

"Hey, Greengrass. Where's the fire?"

"Yeah, well, I'm burning up, I'll tell you that."

"I'd avoid the premises if I were you. You look like murder." Biddle threw an avuncular arm over his shoulder and led him outside. The presses in the basement blew warm air through the sidewalk grates. "Parnell's sitting on your story, eh?"

"How'd you know?"

"Why don't you take the morning off? Cool off."

"Who told you? Spill it, Biddle, c'mon. I broke my keister on this one."

Biddle looked around and over his shoulder, his love of conspiracy imprinted in his corner-of-the-mouth smile. "There's blood on the floor up there. Off the record, Garvey says he's resigning unless Bennett cuts off Stan's head."

"What's Parnell saying?"

"They'll need siege engines to pry him out."

"So Parnell's still fighting for the piece?"

"He's fighting for his life, if you ask me. And Bennett, you know where Our Savior is?"

"Yeah, somewhere near Corfu."

"Not yet. Steamships can't fly. It'll take him two weeks to get to Greece, maybe more. You and your little story seem to have caused this civil war, so if I were you, I'd dig a trench and put a pot over my head," he added. As the soul of altruism, Nick Biddle roused Max's suspicions, but his advice had the ring of truth.

"You didn't mention your sources."

"When I'm on my deathbed, Greengrass. When I hear the trumpets. Maybe."

"You dirty dog. Too early for a quick one?"

"Sorry. Some Bulgarian nobility put a bullet in his head at the Windsor. From what I hear, he kissed his wife and then he ruined some very expensive drapes."

Max could feel his self-immolating anger receding, but he still didn't trust himself to keep his trap shut. "Thanks, Nick. I'll take a hike. Keep me posted."

Biddle looked both ways, licked his finger and held it up to the wind.

Faye's trunk was flung open, her things tossed helter-skelter all over her room. A scarlet shirtwaist hung on a nail. A lacy chemise, a mound of stockings, costume jewelry, and a boned corset were piled high on her dresser. The trunk lid held crinolines, a hat featuring an entire bird of paradise, a majolica rooster, and several pots of cold cream. He had to talk to her back, but he could see her rouging her cheeks in the vanity mirror.

"Take a load off. I'm fixing my face."

She was laying it on with a trowel. "You slap on any more of that stuff, you'll get a reputation."

"I already have a reputation, sweetie. Did you see the *Clipper?*" She yanked open a few drawers and groped around to no avail. "Anyway, the notices said 'Miss Greengrass practices a kind of lunch-counter art, but art is vague and Miss Greengrass is quite real.' What the hell is that supposed to mean? Do you think I'm fat?"

She twirled around to face him. For a young woman, her incipient jowls were striking. He wished she wouldn't paint herself up like that either, but he had more important business with her. "Nah, you look fine."

"Yeah, well, listen to what else the *Clipper* said. 'She has the roly-poly appearance of all successful comediennes.' I have to oink to make them laugh?" Pouting, she tilted her head and flattened her nose with her index finger.

"Don't do that one in public."

"Too piggy for my own good, huh? Oh, well, it pays the rent. Did I tell you we got our first check from Keith? Thirty-five for the week, and forty when we go on the road. You know how much that tight bastard Simon on Avenue B was paying? Twenty! For five shows a day." She frowned. "Danny says Keith's turning into an octopus."

"I'll leave that to him. Hey, where's Leon?"

"Oh, my roommate Joanne got him out of my hair. They're over in Tompkins Square."

"The fever broke?"

"Belle said he was doing much better." This assertion had a tinny ring. "Danny's teaching me to clog. I'll be another Mike Rooney soon."

"Listen, Faye. I gave that Mrs. Darling your message like you asked me. . . ."

"Isn't she a sweetheart?"

"I went up to her place to look around."

"H'mm," she responded, twirling back to her mirror.

"You can't keep leaving Leon there. It stinks to high heaven. You've got to get someplace else."

"Oh, you're just not used to all those diapers," she said blithely. "Mrs.

Darling is a treasure. Besides, it's too late. Where can I find somebody else on such short notice?"

"You could ask Belle. She probably knows a decent setup."

"It's too late! Don't you get it? We're going on the road!"

He had to lay it on the line. He had no choice. "Sorry, that's not acceptable. You're putting the kid in jeopardy, leaving him in that pigsty."

Indignant, Faye leaped to her feet. "Who appointed you Jesus H. Christ? I don't see you knocking yourself out for him. You show up out of the blue and go kootchie-kootchie once in a while. You don't know what I go through!"

She had him back on his heels, but his temper flared too. "Okay, let's get it out in the open. Is it my fault you went and had a kid by some Champagne Charlie who won't cough up a nickel? And who is the sonofabitch, while we're at it? Why're you still protecting him?"

He regretted the words the moment they flew from his lips, but Faye didn't give an inch. "That's my own damn business! Where do you get off, coming from on high like that? You're drinking yourself to death, and then you come in here and get up on your hind legs with the sermons."

How the hell did she know how much he put away? Anyway, Biddle and the rest of the reporters could drink him under the table. He mustered up his dignity and shot back. "What're you talking about? I take care of myself fine and dandy."

"Danny says you need the hair of the dog every morning. How is that going to help you get ahead? You're getting a little long in the tooth to be a space-rater, you know." Faye was going for the jugular too, and she knew where his was located. Keith had waved his wand and made her big-time—and all of a sudden she was lording it over him.

"You get my goat," he fired back with all the fury of a man who knows he's been exposed. "Danny? He's got a hollow leg, for crissakes. Liquid lunch every day. And who're you to talk, with that bottle of Mrs. Winslow's Soothing Syrup in your drawer?"

She gave him a haughty look. "When you get the female problems, come and cry on my shoulder."

"Let me ask you something. Do you ever even look at my articles? I gave Danny all those clips for you. Do you know how many stories I've gotten into the paper the last few months?" As he mounted his defense, he couldn't help thinking about his series, suffocating under reams of copy on Parnell's desk. Who was he kidding? She was the one on the way up. He was flailing around in the same damn puddle.

"I looked at them . . . you know I don't have time to read. . . ." For the first time, she sounded defensive.

"Don't lie. You never read a word, did you? You're the center of the universe and that's that, right?"

"So you want to play the hero? You're making promises? So help."

What was he supposed to say? He couldn't back out now, but taking care of the kid was the last thing he wanted. Faye was no pushover. She'd twisted his argument around to suit her own purposes. She had a point too, and if he tried to wriggle out of his responsibility now, after shooting his mouth off, he'd look like the world's biggest heel.

He'd have to track down Belle, or he was cooked. What did he know about taking care of a sick kid? "Damn right I will. But don't get on that train 'til it's settled, either."

"How am I supposed to feed him if I don't work? You tell me that."

His best bet was to change the subject. And then he remembered Gretta's snapshot. What had that been all about? "Hey, I almost forgot. I wanted to show you something—"

"Take it back!" she burst out. "Take it all back!" Suddenly she was crying, her chubby shoulders quaking, rouge smearing her cheeks. Faye could fake a good cry at will, but these sobs, deep and gasping, were wrenched up from the depths. He knew the difference, and now he felt lousy. Why had he started up in the first place? To make himself feel high and mighty?

"What'd I say?"

She wiped her face with the back of her hand, smearing tears into her rouge and powder. "I don't know who his father is. How's that? Feel better? Wanna know the rest?"

She knew what she was doing. About this subject, he preferred knowing less than nothing. "Hey, like you said. It's your own business."

"Take it back then."

What was the point? He had to work things out with her, no matter what. Fayefaye. She was his flesh and blood. She lived under his skin. "Yeah, hey, Faye. Kiddo, I take it back. I shouldn't've opened my big mouth."

Mercurial, she plopped down on his lap and nuzzled his neck. She really had packed on a few fresh pounds. "I'm sorry, Maxie. Friends?"

"Sure. Who else have I got?"

"Will you really help with him while I'm gone?"

"Leon? Sure, sure. Don't worry." He groped in his pocket for Gretta's picture. "Listen, it almost slipped my mind. What about this?"

With thumb and forefinger, he dangled the snapshot before her eyes.

"Oh, God, I look awful. Don't show this to a soul!"

"I'm only showing it to you. Who's the old biddy you're talking to?"

"Oh, she's the one who collects the rent."

"Rent?" he asked sharply. "From who?"

"From Mrs. Darling's building. A few more on Sullivan, I think."

"What'd she want from you?"

"She buys the insurance. I don't know why she asked me. Maybe Mrs. Darling told her."

He was sure she'd gotten it backwards. "You mean she *sells* insurance?"

"No, no. She buys it back."

He could feel all the blood draining from his face. The shape of the thing rushed into focus, but he had to turn away. This was it. The way to make a killing on the most worthless thing in the world. He had to be wrong.

"What's the matter? You look funny."

"Do you know her name?"

"Mrs. Something-or-other. What's the big deal?"

"Mrs. Edwards?"

"H'mm . . . yeah, sure, that's it. Edwards."

Dread bred an ethereal calm. Logic was a form of serenity. "Martin sold you insurance on Leon?"

"Martin? Of course. Everybody buys it now. It's only ten cents a week."

Mourtone was selling, and the Midnight Band was buying back. It was a nasty joke, the one-liner Martin had been dying to tell. Max asked his questions without inflection. "And what does the policy pay?"

"Are you all right? I've got some gin."

"C'mon, Faye. Don't play dumb."

"Don't start up again. It's something like fifty, sixty dollars. If . . . something happens, it covers the costs. Do you know what they do otherwise? They throw him away in the Potter's Field, that's what. Like a dead chicken. I could get caught short, and then what would . . . ? I know three other girls who bought from him, too."

"And how much did the Edwards woman offer?

"Oh, I wasn't listening, something ridiculous. Ten dollars. Why would I sell it to her anyway? It didn't make any sense."

Step by step, the logic was inexorable. The desperate women turned to the Mrs. Darlings of the world, who were only a shade less desperate themselves. When the money ran out, acts of mercy were the only solution.

"Perfect sense to a goo-goo, Faye."

"I think you've got a screw loose," Faye said. "What the hell're you raving about?"

"Never mind. Did Belle go to work? Is she coming back here?"

"Leon's better, I told you. She didn't even have a change of clothes when she stayed over." She looked at him as if to say: Belle loves me. What about you?

"What'd you tell her? I'm the devil's right-hand man?"

"Why should I do that? You need somebody steady for once. You think you can run around forever?" There it was again. Faye, the voice of reason. The worst part was, she had a point.

"What does she say about me?"

"Let me see if I can get the exact words. . . ." She closed her eyes, pretending to dredge up the forgotten phrase. "She said 'He's got possibilities.'"

"That's it? 'Possibilities?'"

"Oh, shut up. She likes you, maybe she's crazy about you, I can't figure out why, but let me tell you something, Don Giovanni. You've got plenty of competition."

"Competition? Who? She's got a boyfriend on the side?"

"You don't get it, do you?"

"C'mon, Faye, don't play games."

"*You're* the one on the side, dummy."

He was thunderstruck. The way she came to him that night . . . that sweet obliteration . . . he took it for granted that he could have her whenever he wanted. How could Belle, Miss Idealism, be so underhanded? Was she taking some other blind fool for a ride too? Dimly he recalled his clinches with Gretta, but he still felt betrayed. One thing had nothing to do with the other, did it?

"Who is it?"

"What's the difference? Some spieler from the café. More of her own type."

"So why's she my big friend?"

"She likes you, Maxie. She's just afraid."

"Afraid of what?"

Faye covered his hand with her own. "She's worried you're going to pieces."

Somehow Faye had turned the world upside down. Wasn't she the one who was veering all over the lot? The one with the nameless boyfriends and the fatherless kid, the one who never knew where her next meal ticket was coming from? Wasn't it his job to keep her on the straight-and-narrow? He was solid as the Rock of Gibraltar. Didn't she know that?

How could he ask Belle for help now? He needed her to talk to Mrs. Darling, to find a place for Leon, but how could he look at her with a straight face any more? He couldn't sort out the complications. A tree of pain was pulsing in his brain. "Where'd she get . . . no, never mind. I never felt better. You tell her that."

chapter thirty-six

Howe and Hummel were open all night. Electric lights blared on their huge sign and over their simple doorway. A half dozen fine carriages were lined up at the curb. What were they doing there so late? A tail-docked stallion stamped the stones. In sympathy, a chestnut pounded his hooves, iron shoes echoing down the deserted street. Nearby, a gleaming victoria rocked in place.

Evidently the lawyers, concerned for their clients' reputations, conducted their more discreet business under cover of darkness.

Inside, in the stark waiting room, a man in evening dress sat stiffly on the edge of a bench. His long, pale face held a stoic expression, but the red wen on his nose had an angry look. Another client, whose peeled face reminded Max of a colicky baby's, sported pomaded hair and striped bankers' trousers. A third, whose senile aspect argued against erotic adventures, played with his tie. Next to him yawned a fork who picked pockets on the east side trains. Jackie Connors. Max had seen him arraigned three times.

Kicking his feet, a boy of about eleven sat on a stool smoking a cigar. His face tugged at Max's memory. Then it came to him: Mrs. Edwards's "son," the one who had bawled with so much conviction at her trial. Was the kid a member of Howe and Hummel's "stock company"? He almost laughed out loud.

Max had barely taken his seat when several exotic dancers bustled in. Their scant costumes suggested unspeakable Egyptian delights. The dwarfish Hummel raced out to greet the performers, who stood two heads taller than the diminutive lawyer.

"Abie, they locked up the Central Palace!"

"Ain't nowhere we can do our act!"

Raising his palms, Hummel tried to soothe them. "Zora, calm down."

A second dancer, whose accent was more Canarsie than Cairo, let loose her outrage. "Those preaching ponces! Dr. Prickhurst! Comesuck!"

In the uproar, the fork slipped his hand into his more elevated neighbor's pocket. Expressionless, he rapidly redistributed some wealth. Max kept a straight face, knowing that pickpockets had a fondness for razors.

Zora remained indignant. "Comesuck, I call him. He's probably ballin' off some bitch at Billy McGlory's when nobody's lookin'."

To keep the peace, Hummel led the Oriental artistes into his office for a private conference.

One client after another walked the plank. The longer Max sat on the hard bench, the more distraught he became. For one thing, he had no idea what cards the lawyers were holding. He wasn't in the habit of promising chorus girls holy matrimony, though he knew his innocence was of little use. The sums Howe and Hummel usually extorted, five to ten thousand dollars, were beyond comprehension. What did they want, half his column-inches every week? He'd starve.

Long after midnight, Hummel summoned Max to his inner sanctum. A tight smile on his lipless mouth, he was all nasal apologies. "A most unfortunate situation. We did our best to protect you from this sort of thing; but, as I always counsel, if a man stays close to the home fires, he'll never get in trouble."

"There's probably some mixup."

Hummel frowned and shook his head. "I wish that were the case, Mr. Greengrass. But, you see, we look into these matters with extreme care. If I may say so, sometimes we squander our resources looking for a way out before we bow to the inevitable. But when a woman is determined to bring suit, we must accede to her wishes. Mind you, most of them have been wronged."

Max took a deep breath and launched into his prepared argument. "You know I don't have a dime. I had my entire savings in the Madison Square Bank that just went belly-up. You'd just be flogging a pauper. Why waste your time?"

The bloodless smile disappeared from Hummel's lips. "George! Send Linda Lee in."

A door on the far side of the office flew open. On the gallant arm of Hummel's assistant, Linda Lee tiptoed in. A young woman with lustrous blonde hair, she fixed him in a limpid gaze. Her pale blue eyes tugged at his memory. In a white platter collar and jacket, and a long skirt that brushed against her boottops, she was the picture of respectability. Pressed to her chest, like a shield, she held a soft round hat.

Shrewdly, Hummel kept Linda Lee in a soft light. Even then, on second glance Max made out a spray of pox on her cheek. She was older than he had first thought.

"Do you recall what you promised this unfortunate girl?" Hummel intoned.

"I don't recognize her."

"You may recognize her child in about eight months. Isn't that right, Linda?"

Shifting her feet, the young woman nodded, the small gesture jogging his memory. The blonde girl from Mrs. Jabonne's. She had been light as a bird when he held her up against the wall. Light and willing. He had prepared himself for Hummel's manipulations, but not for the shame and sadness that swept through him. Standing there in Hummel's office, Linda Lee looked nothing like Nora, but it didn't matter. He remembered the way his heart stopped when he first saw her, the way she looked down and away from him, the way she shrugged her small shoulders, and the blue glow of her impossibly white skin. The briefest illusion of his first love had been enough.

A queasy sweat broke out under his arms. His shirt stuck to his back in moist moons. He had to cough to find his voice. "This woman is a professional. You can't possibly attach her to me."

"So you recognize her!"

He steeled himself to look straight into Hummel's eyes. "I didn't say that."

"First you seduced her, and she ended up at a certain establishment where you continued to take your pleasure. If you drove her into the life, all the more reason you ought to compensate my client."

"How can you prove it?" Once the words escaped his lips he knew how feeble they sounded. He was talking to a man who had mastered the badger game before he was born. Half the sportsmen in the city were praying they wouldn't find a Howe and Hummel subpoena in their soup.

"You can go, Linda," Hummel said, waving his hand in a paternal way. "Minnie?"

Her cape gathered around her ample girth, Mrs. Jabonne ambled in. She set herself squarely in Max's face, fingered her diamond choker, and shrugged. "Yeah, that's him. He was after that poor girl like nobody's business. Wouldn't leave the little thing alone."

"That's a damn lie."

Mrs. Jabonne looked him up and down in wonder. "So?"

"Thanks, Minnie. George has something nice for you." After the madame waddled out, Hummel said, "Cigar?"

Mechanically, Max accepted. The lawyer hopped over to give him a light. "Connecticut tobacco. There's nothing like it." Then he hoisted his tiny body up on his desk and clicked his narrow shoes together. "I'm sure you find this business unpleasant. Believe me, I'd rather be protecting an actor with an airtight contract than mucking around in these affairs. The producers are savages, you know. Slavin is excellent in *The Merry Wives*, by the way. Have you seen it?"

"You don't understand. I have absolutely nothing. What can you get out of this?"

"Usually ten thousand. In your case, I could prevail on Linda's better nature. Maybe we can cut it to five."

"You don't seem to understand. I don't—"

Rummaging around in a cabinet, Hummel plucked out a musty bottle. "Ahh, this is the one. Brandy?"

Dumbly, he accepted the burning liquor. Every appeal to logic, every argument in favor of Hummel's self-interest, fell apart before he could form the words. Every maneuver he dreamed up led to a brick wall. So often he had talked his way out of bad spots in card games and newsrooms. So often he had fought off his debts. Now his imagination simply froze up. It was like having a ball of ice for a brain.

Hummel sipped his drink. "Spanish. Willy gets cases of it. Not bad, eh? Let's see. How could we turn this around to your advantage?"

"Tastes fine. How about another?"

He held out his glass to his tormentor. Hummel poured and then returned to his perch, the click, click, click of his heels driving Max to distraction. He wanted to reach out and break the little feet off at their ankles.

"Now, I could take this subpoena and lock it away, perhaps forever. Of course that would cost the firm money, as the girl would have to be compensated out of our own pocket. But what would I want in return?"

"My firstborn child?"

"No need to get grim. There is a relatively painless way out: don't stick your nose in the wrong places."

"What are you talking about?"

"Stop asking questions of certain people, you know who I mean, and don't even think of writing any stories about it. You cooperate, and the firm will protect you. Not to speak of releasing you from this unfortunate breach-of-promise action. What do you say?"

"So you represent. . . . "

"It doesn't matter who we represent. For your purposes, just imagine that we represent everybody."

"Do I get some time to think about it?"

"Not a single second."

It was too late to wake Mrs. DeVogt, and he wouldn't be able to face Gretta and Belle in the morning either. With several of Hummel's cheap brandies under his belt, he began drifting west in a dream. Finally, veering south, he grabbed the Sixth Avenue line at Chambers Street and rode blindly uptown. In a second-story apartment he saw a scrawny woman in a chemise, her head resting on a kitchen table. In another cube of light, an insomniac waving a flyswatter seemed to stare right back at him. No one ever quite said it, but the lure of the Night Owl was the dream that just once, if you kept your eyes focused on the worn-out, gas-lit rooms flashing by, you would finally see the mythical couple lost in the act.

In fact, the denizens of second-story flats were indeed remarkably casual about exposing their lives to the bone-rattling trains that passed a few feet from their windows. They ate dinner in their underwear, they drank and argued and threw things at each other, they even embraced, but Max had never seen any lovemaking. Perhaps in these exposed cells, not much lovemaking was going on.

A man in overalls and a toolbox got on at Houston Street, along with a few bleary clerks and a worker with ink-spattered palms, stigmata of the printing trades. He'd never felt so low. All this time and he'd never realized it—Faye believed he was a bust and that he was coming apart at the seams to boot. When he thought about how he'd been stymied, his church exposé in limbo, his love affairs misshapen, his finances in ruins, Hummel fixed on his neck, he wondered why he hadn't gone to pieces before. Faye may have been changing the subject for her own benefit, but she knew him better than anybody else.

The Night Owl's wheels squealed, the Forney rained sparks on the streets below, and all of his carefully tended blind spots drifted into the light. He had done a brilliant job concealing the obvious. He had no prospects, no future. One day he would wake up and find himself a graybeard, glued to the same bench, writing the same stories for the same rate, a used-up ribbon printing fainter and fainter on the typewriter's platen. He'd end up like the hoary clerks in the Classified section, or the humpbacked proofreaders who lived in single rooms with a gas ring.

At Bleecker Street a man in a glittering gown tripped into the car, swinging his hips and batting his kohl-smeared eyes. In the past Max would have reacted with revulsion, but now he was riding the Night Owl too, and he wondered at the nancy's confidence, the way he sashayed down the aisle and blew kisses with his painted mouth. This brave soul didn't give a damn if he was going up, down, or sideways. All he cared about was whether his beard was showing through his powder.

As the train rushed further uptown, the lights grew fewer. Soon it was plunging through uptown's pure darkness. Max fitted the night around himself, surrendering to anonymity. He slept in short bursts as the Night Owl made circuit after circuit. Fitfully, he wondered if he could find a way around Hummel, but every scheme unraveled before his eyes. Why should he risk his skin, running down stories best left buried? Even Wall Street barons did flips when Abe Hummel whistled. Who was he to stand up to the brilliant extortionist?

Finally exiting where he had started, and after taking the hair of the dog at Logan's, he headed across City Hall Park to Newspaper Row.

His eyes dry as sand, he threw his overtired bones down on his chair. Didn't the scattered, beat-up typewriters tell the real tale? He was working in a word factory, but a factory nevertheless. He watched, numb, as Parnell picked his way through the packed desks and ascended to the throne.

Shoving himself to a standing position, Max walked on stiff legs across the newsroom. There was only one way to keep Abe Hummel from devouring him. Parnell raised his rheumy eyes. "You're starting in already, Greengrass?"

It was time to embrace defeat. The good stoic, he took a deep breath and squared his shoulders. "No, no, it's not that, Stan. I was thinking it would be best for all concerned, considering the . . . conflict over the article . . . that I withdraw it. I don't want you. . . ."

"Too late, kiddo," Parnell growled. "Morning edition, column three.

Jump to page six. You'll have to follow up, too, before Pulitzer gets on the bandwagon."

"There's no way you can yank . . . ?"

"Did you hear me? Column three. Follow up. You got wax in your ears?"

He didn't want this, not now. He was just beginning to relish despair. How had it happened? He couldn't get his mind around it. "What about Garvey? I heard. . . ."

"That cowboy from California picked him off. He's bought half the *World*'s staff too, from what I hear."

"Garvey went over to the *Journal*?"

"That amateur Hearst, yeah. McGowen says he's bleeding fifty thousand a month. These traitors are going to come running back with their tails between their legs."

Max stood there, stupefied. He couldn't hold back the tide. The hazards of good fortune would soon destroy him.

He spent the day in a daze, going over and over his predicament. The minute the Holy Trinity article hit the street, Hummel would set his court date. His name would appear in the papers; and when Bennett got wind that his reporter had been branded a deadbeat, the publisher would toss him out onto the sidewalk. It was one thing to carry an account with Sim Addem, but quite another to have a judge issue legal documents declaring a man a pauper and a liar. No publisher could trust a reporter who thumbed his nose at his financial obligations. A ruined man stayed ruined.

Howe and Hummel had snapped the spines of brokers, sportsmen, judges, industrialists, actors, producers, and, it was rumored, at least two senators. How could he defend himself against such polished predators? Despair was a form of freedom, though. He might be doomed, but if he could stitch together all of the fragments before his destruction. . . . The church. The Midnight Band. Insurance policies bought as a speculation. A hidden commodities market. The underground arteries that pumped blood between goo-goos and gangsters, preachers and ponces, a unifying theory that wiped away distinctions between saviors and their prey. . . .

chapter thirty-seven

He needed Belle; he would have to forget her double-dealing. He tried to re-create the simple soul she had once seemed to him, but he couldn't resurrect this vision of her. That she allowed two men to paw her at the same time revolted him. Did she lie down with both on the same day? Had she been making the same agonized noises in the back of her throat with some stinking refugee from the Pale? He saw the other man's fingernails, moons of dirt, smelled his sweat and the stewed onions on his breath.

And yet when he saw her sitting across the dinner table on Sunday, so lovely and austere, he still wanted her. How could she be so stained and yet appear so pure? Her cameo of a face looked exactly the same. Her hooded eyes, her delicate nose, her bud of a mouth hadn't changed. He could feel his hands closing around her tiny waist, stroking her flaring hips. He could still sense the shock of her kiss.

He had to pass the plate of snap beans to her. How could such a basic act be so difficult? So awkward? So freighted with clashing insinuations? Suddenly a hand intruded, he saw the flash of a checked cuff, and the plate was whisked away.

"Max, chop-chop. The lady's got an appetite. Lookit, he's in a dream world," Danny said.

"Thank you, Mr. Swarms," Belle replied, with mock politeness. "The newspaper business is driving him around the bend."

"He prowls around at all hours," Mrs. DeVogt observed.

Somewhere in the back of his brainpan a clever remark was sizzling. He just couldn't quite seize it.

"Hey, snap out of it. Presto!" Aping a stage mesmerist, Danny wriggled his fingers.

"Where's Gretta?" he blurted, looking around the table.

"That Van Rensselaer daughter is sitting for her portrait tonight. In buckskin, Gretta says," Mrs. DeVogt informed the table.

"Ahh. Well, I'm preoccupied, I suppose." He extended his leg, but Belle had withdrawn her ankles to a safe distance. He inclined his head slightly in the direction of the staircase, but she stared right through him.

After dinner, she swept up the stairs, but he trotted after her, catching up on the first landing. "Belle, wait. We've got to talk."

She whirled to face him, her jaw set. "Talk. . . ." Mrs. DeVogt certainly knew what was what, but Belle didn't want to believe Max would two-time her, especially under the same roof. Not after that night. But what did she expect from his type? At least Jake was faithful. Too faithful. With one side of his mouth he said he didn't believe in private property and with the other he wanted to own her. Now nobody owned her.

He lowered his voice to a whisper. "Would you come by my room?"

"Everybody goes to your room. It's a regular Madison Square Garden, I hear." She hated the caustic sound of her own voice, but he deserved it. A dog in a suit, that's all he was. She'd invented his kindness and melancholy out of her own romantic delusions. Love. Ha. A greasy sheepskin and endless regrets.

"What are you talking about?"

"I didn't believe it until you started mooning over her right at the table. You should show a little more taste."

He grabbed her wrist. "We need some privacy."

She wrenched her arm away. "The whole house knows your 'privacy.'"

He backed away, shaken by her fury. "Please. I need a favor. For Faye and the kid, too."

Her arms crossed over her chest, she glared at him. "You first," she said finally, shooing him towards his door.

She wouldn't sit down. Instead, she staked out a place near the window, as far away from him as possible. "So, talk," she said brusquely.

"I thought . . . I thought we were friends," he said, groping for neutral language.

"Was she or wasn't she?" How could he fall for those insipid looks, those fake Parisian fashions—knocked off in some loft on Henry Street, no doubt—not to speak of the woman's empty head. She wouldn't know de Maupassant from de Cock. It galled her.

"What?"

"That spoiled cow."

The way she was coming at him from on high was getting under his skin. Here she was posing like the Virgin Queen herself. Where the hell did she get off pulling this routine? "Look, for the record, nothing . . . untoward . . . happened between me and Gretta. And from what I hear, you have a few things to answer for yourself."

The accusation burst out, ugly and unadorned. Enraged, he had no desire to take it back.

Every drop of color drained from her face. "And who's telling tales?"

"Never mind. I know you're . . . keeping house . . . with somebody else. So our hands aren't so clean. Neither of us."

She was so mortified, she thought she would faint. She was living inside that dream she had over and over. The hooligan wolf-whistling. Union Square. Her sheer chemise fluttering around her knees. Shame that swallowed her whole. Somehow she remained on her feet, somehow she croaked a retort. "Sorry your sister can't keep a confidence. It doesn't mean I don't have certain feelings."

She looked so brave and wan that he wanted to take her into his arms right then, but his wounded pride still held the upper hand. "I was hoping we could be friendly."

"So, it's true, you're going with *her*? I'm sorry I don't have a mansion on Staten Island." He was running after the Sealy woman's money. Why should she be surprised? Ambition without substance. Why else would he work for that sensational rag of his? Oh, she was sick to her stomach.

"That's not fair. I don't know what I'm going to do."

A new spasm of shame gripped her. She had been hard on Jake, who at least had some ideals. She'd crumpled him up and tossed him aside, and now she was left with this one, who believed in nothing. "Send me a telegram."

"I was hoping we could work on something together. I'll probably get fired in the next few days. . . ."

"Why should they fire you? You're such a loyalist."

In her mouth the word sounded like *royalist*. She refused to bend, but still she lingered. A thick silence descended.

He cleared his throat. "Did you see today's paper?"

"No, I had so many calls. Who has time?"

He pulled a much-folded copy of the *Herald* from his inside pocket. "Just do me one favor. Read this. If you don't want to help me then, fine."

He cajoled her to sit in his Morris chair. Tight-lipped, she sat and spread the blanket-sized pages out on her lap. In the end, the headline man had gone for the throat.

HOLY TRINITY CORPORATION
RULES EMPIRE OF DECAY
Rookeries Bursting at the Seams
Buildings As Dangerous As Old Hospitals

He had arrayed his facts with inexorable logic. His reporting had a diamond-hard quality he'd never achieved before, but he was far from satisfied. If the church was connected to the Midnight Band's insurance game that story might, if he handled it right, transcend any tale of broken pump handles and the white lung's rampages. Riis had set off his flash powder in a world of darkness, but the shadow world had eluded his lens. Who could take pictures of a shrouded trade that turned the city's most worthless commodities into gold?

She read in great gulps, her intelligent eyes devouring the columns. He watched as her expression mutated from suspicion to absorption to disgust. When she was finished, she shook her head. "Crooks with their white collars; then they try to justify it, no less. This Colonel Fisk character. Have you ever noticed how when they steal, they turn it into some high and mighty principle? You wrote this?"

"I did. And take a look at this."

He dropped Miss Van Siclen's ledger into her hands and watched as she turned the pages, a quizzical look on her face. "These are the addresses? They own half the downtown?"

"Nah, only a fraction. A bigger fraction than anybody else, though. I want to ask you something. Yesterday I was over at that lady who takes care of Leon. Mrs. Darling. She had kids stacked up in there like chickens in a coop. Do you know anything about it?"

"Oh, she's probably running a baby farm," Belle said without hesitation. Alarmed, she added "Faye can't keep him there!"

"What's a baby farm?"

"These women, they're barely surviving themselves, they take on too many children. Before you know it, the mothers can't pay and the minders, they're giving the kids bottles full of water, or worse. Paregoric to keep the infant quiet. They can't afford milk."

"And if the mother disappears, what're the odds the kid will survive?"

She didn't flinch. A clinical note entered her voice. "Maybe if one of the charities takes the infant. That's maybe. Most, you're asking me? They starve to death. It takes ten days, two weeks at most. Skin and bones, that's what's left. I saw one of these businesses on Allen Street. Four died in one day, and who knows, that may be normal. I saw another one on Mott Street and another one on Elizabeth. They're all over town. Once in a blue moon the Health Department might come around. What do you think the inspector wants?" and she rubbed her thumb and forefinger together in the time-honored gesture.

"You make it sound like everyday business."

She gave him a look. "Are we living in the same city?"

Her casual response made the underground trade all the more unspeakable. Was there such a thing as mundane horror? How many of these farms operated on Holy Trinity property? Did they produce on a regular schedule? Why not? The tenements poured out velvet flowers, fresh macaroni, gabardine pants, feathers, beaded cords, and boxed nuts. Why not another product? You could slap a healthy mark-up on this one, and there was an endless supply.

He directed her back to the ledger. "Look at the back pages. See those numbers?"

"M'mm. . . . What are they supposed to mean?"

He sat on the edge of the mattress and coughed into his fist. His chest tightening, he wondered if she'd think he was half-cracked. "Insurance policies. They buy back insurance policies the mothers have bought on their kids. They're banking on them croaking. Or . . . or probably they're helping the sickest kids along. You think that sounds nuts, huh?"

He'd need to nail down every last detail. How were the policies transferred? Who signed the death certificates?

In a delayed reaction, her delicate features screwed up in distaste. "God, that's awful. Is that what they're doing? Who are *they*?"

"I think it's the Midnight Band of Mercy."

Now she did give him a fishy look. "Do you know what you're saying? It's monstrous. They do it for money?"

"Not for the money, not entirely. For the cause. The money's secondary."

By the time the Midnight Band came along, the damage had already been done. The mother had lost her husband, her lover, her job. She couldn't pay the baby farmer, whose own children were clinging to the precipice. The insurance policy represented hope and self-deception and sleight of hand. No one was more concerned than Mrs. Edwards. She would take care of things . . . if the worst came to pass. And when the time came for the final act of mercy, it was performed in a mist of perfumed lies.

Mrs. Edwards's savage compassion was connected to an inexorable chain of events. He understood the Midnight Band's ideals now. The campaign against the brothels and the campaign against what Reverend Weems called "the issue of sin" were one and the same. The insurance bait-and-switch was the dark side of the same impulse—one that paid the bills, too. There was nothing sweeter than making money doing good.

Insight didn't equal acceptance, though. His blood rebelled against the thought. He had always been in an uproar, in vague and general opposition, but he now had something to push against, and in his rage he felt at home in his skin.

He knew Martin's joke now, but not who had splattered his brains on the black-and-tan's wall. Or why Harry Granger had ended up with clam shells stuffed in his mouth. In their own ways, both men had threatened this trade; but how, precisely?

"Even crazy people have their reasons. But this? How do they justify themselves?"

"You don't get it? They think they're serving God Almighty."

In the morning, on their way to Faye's, Max and Belle groped toward neutral ground. Just under the surface, her resentment still throbbed, but it was muted now. She had been too harsh. Look at his concern for Faye and Leon. Look at what he was writing for his wretched paper. Then she thought of Gretta's watch, the one on the fine gold chain, and how it hung—as if she didn't know—so suggestively between her fat breasts. Spite poured from some hidden gland, and Belle shook inside.

Max drove the thought of Belle's other man from his mind, but he couldn't quite wipe the after-image away. Suddenly his heart would clench, and he would see Belle, her chemise off one shoulder, her face buried in an anonymous, matted chest. Then he was grinding his teeth, as if he could chew up his torment and spit it out for good.

She managed a stiff politeness as her impulse to sting retreated. He became all manners too, killing the desire to fire off one last crack and a simultaneous urge to seize her hand. In the jostling Fourteenth Street crowd, their shoulders bumped, but they each pretended they hadn't touched. Then a peddler spilled a whole case of braces in the middle of the sidewalk and, without thinking, he put his hand on her back. She didn't brush it off.

Faye's stairs ascended at an impossible angle; by the time they reached the sixth floor, they were both out of breath. In a loose robe, Joanne appeared at the door. "Oh, you just missed them. They went to catch the nine-eighteen."

"What're you talking about? I thought she was leaving tomorrow," Max said. His Faye-trained nerves told him what was coming next.

"I don't know. Danny was all hot and bothered to get out. He said Keith was going to dock them if they got to New Haven ten minutes late. I think he's kinda nervous, if you ask me."

Belle cut her off. "Where's Leon?"

"With that lady down the block."

"Damn it!" He couldn't contain himself "Typical. She does whatever the hell she pleases."

"When did she leave him?" Belle persisted.

"Oh, I think it was last night," Joanne yawned. "Yeah. Late last night after Danny came home."

"You see that! Right after she swore—"

Belle grabbed his sleeve to stop him. "Did she leave any instructions?"

"Beats me. Sorry, I'm all washed out."

"It's practically next door," Belle said, leading him down the stairs.

"I'm ready to blow my stack," he muttered.

"Don't. There's no time for that," she admonished him. "Let's just see what's what."

A junk wagon rattled to a stop near Mrs. Darling's doorway. The nag pulling it wasn't fit for a fly cab. A cloudy cataract skinned the mare's right eye, and her ribs formed a visible cage under her dull brown coat. In a felt hat that threw a shadow over his forehead, the junkard's face was only partially visible. Bits and pieces clawed at Max's memory. The heavy forearms. The flat profile. The cascading mustache.

"Rrrraaaagggs! Bo-ones!" the man called out.

Could it be? Out of the thousands of rag-and-bone men . . . and this one unmasked, disguised only in his own skin.

An oilcloth package pressed to her chest, Marianne Granger emerged from Mrs. Darling's tenement. Her face lacked all expression, but her yellow eyes darted up and down the street. Hunching her shoulders, she scurried across the sidewalk. Behind her, at a decorous distance, came Mrs. Edwards in mourning crepe, a long and deep basket swaying from one arm. In the other she cradled a muslin bundle tied with rough cord.

Max grabbed Belle's wrist and drew her to the doorway next door. Together they watched the two women mount the wagon and arrange themselves on the plank seat. Without uttering a word, Mrs. Edwards turned and lifted the tarp a few inches, allowing Marianne to deposit the parcel she'd carried from the tenement beneath it. Then Mrs. Edwards deposited her bundle. Max heard a soft thump. He could not say the word, not even inside his own skull. He must not imagine, he must not speculate . . . despite himself, he groaned.

The entire procedure took less than a minute.

"Would you go see Mrs. Darling?" he whispered, his heart scuttling up his throat.

"Is this . . . ?" She grabbed his arm, her fingernails raking his skin.

The ancient cry rang out again, a singsong ditty of dissolution and decay. "Raaaaags! Bo-ones!!!!"

When the reins snapped, the junk wagon jerked forward. It wasn't hard for Max to keep up with it.

chapter thirty-eight

He wiped his mind clean of terror. He knew what he feared, but he dreaded acknowledging it in words, even to himself. Simply to have fathomed the scheme made him feel tainted, queasy.

The city's traffic was his main ally now. The junk wagon bumped along until it hit West Houston, where it ran into dueling omnibuses. The junkard managed to trot his nag around the paralyzed vehicles and then down Grand Street a bit, before turning right and slamming smack into Canal Street's anarchy. A painted sunrise graced the side of a van stranded in a muddy trench. Blocking the carts and carriages seeking Lafayette Street's relief, the tilting conveyance threatened to tip over. A teamster in a plug hat blasted his whistle. Hitting a more piercing note, another driver joined the ear-splitting serenade. Packed tight, two opposing geldings stamped and snorted, rattling their traces.

Max caught up without much effort. His shoes pinched at the heel, though, and he could already feel the back of his foot blistering. Terror was a distant sensation now, dammed up by sweet amnesia. He could go on as long as the word Leon, two simple syllables, stayed silent in his mind's ear.

Standing half a block from the junker, he watched the wagon inch through the Canal Street melee. When it finally squeaked its way past the last vehicle, Max broke into a run. At 17 White Street the driver made a second stop. Marianne hopped off the plank seat, disappeared into a doorway, and then returned within minutes, a burlap sack in her arms. Mrs. Edwards held the tarp up, the African shoved her rough package underneath, and the nag lurched forward again.

Max's eye raced down his list of church property. There it was in his own crabbed scrawl. Holy Trinity owned two buildings on White Street, including number 17. His best bet was to keep his distance from the rambling wagon, take notes, and see where the route ended. They would have to unload. He could see this was a swift, practiced routine, but beyond that his imagination failed. He wanted it to fail.

Mrs. Darling wouldn't dare . . . Belle would see to her. There was nothing to worry about. So why did his own thoughts conspire against him? Why was it so hard to breathe? Faye had done it to him again. Would she still be a stone around his neck when he hit seventy? He could see her, toothless and hell-bent, careening over a cliff in her wheelchair, dragging him behind her.

Threading his way through the back streets, the junkard picked up speed. At times Max fell an entire block behind. Fearing he would lose sight of the wagon, he poured it on, bumping his way through the peddlers, spielers, horseradish grinders, and reeling sailors. Soon he was panting like a dog. Too many cigars. Too many barstools. Was it his clothes or his sweat that smelled like Fitzgerald and Ives? Damned if he wasn't raising a blood blister on his other foot now.

The pick-up wagon made another stop at 23 Desbrosses Street. Holy Trinity property too. With a sense of satisfaction, Max checked it off his inventory. Every fresh address, every new transaction, solidified his hypothesis. He would overwhelm Parnell with deal after deal, location after location. Baby farms honeycombed the corporation's holdings. Every time she picked up the rent, Mrs. Edwards had business opportunities galore.

Le-on. Two wretched puffs of air. The dam collapsed, dread pouring through the breach. He felt light-headed. His heart rattled in his chest. Pretending was his only defense, pretending he had not heard the word he'd whispered against his own will. He had to go cold so he could go on. Become an instrument, a barometer, a fine lens, an acid-etched plate.

This time, both women entered the tenement's dark mouth. In the brilliant sunlight, the driver pulled out a crumpled package of Sweet Caporals and lit up. A truck hauling beer barrels bounced over the humped stones. Observing meaningless action soothed his raw nerves. A bread delivery wagon followed hard by. A flatbed piled high with fresh lumber rolled to the corner. Above, the narrow slash of sky vibrated warm and blue. Max leaned against a nearby loading dock and caught his breath.

From underneath his seat the driver produced a pail and filled it at a nearby hydrant. Holding it up to the nag with one hand, he patted her head while she lapped away. Gnats swirled around her head. Her matted tail quivered, and she let go a few pats of horseshit.

This was no shadow world. It was broad daylight. The junk wagon was just one among thousands, delivering, picking up goods, moving them through the city's indifferent streets. Its cargo was like any other. There would be paperwork, payments at every point along the route. The milkman, the cheese man, the iceman did the same. Who knew if there weren't receipts? Every business needed to keep careful accounts. Perhaps there was no shadow world. Maybe the Midnight Band's trade puttered along right out in the open.

When the women emerged, Marianne was clutching a package wrapped in a checkered tablecloth. Mrs. Edwards held another coarse bundle under her arm, her basket swinging gently at her elbow. Who had gone under her smothering cloth? A pang of fear shot through him. No, not fear exactly. Intense discomfort. Not Leon, certainly not him. Faye had kept up her payments; Mrs. Darling had no incentive. Anyway, the baby farmer seemed to be in awe of his sister's renown.

His chest tightened. Doggedly, he tramped further east.

In the netherworld between Wall Street and the docks, sailors' boardinghouses came into view. Grog shops were doing brisk business on every corner. Max stalked past a crazy quilt of chandlers, clam houses, and tumbledown wooden structures that had been thrown up before the Civil War. Business bubbled and squeaked in every nook and cranny. Barter was the blood of the city, commerce its very soul. He was swept along, a molecule in the turbulent stream. Making his way up Front Street, he came upon a block of peak-roofed Georgian buildings.

Wagons full of imported goods rumbled by. Silks from Genoa, wines from Bordeaux, watch movements from Geneva, wools from Manchester. Dealers, sailors, brokers, and longshoremen crowded the street. Sweet's Restaurant occupied 2 Schermerhorn. Next to it stood a naval supply house, its soot-covered window obscuring the goods inside. Nearby, an old rope merchant, clay pipe in hand, sat on a barrel outside his door. Two seagulls fought bitterly over some tasty offal. The air stank of rotting fish.

Finally, at 8 Schermerhorn the wagon stopped. He didn't bother to consult his records. He knew who held title to the soot-streaked warehouse.

The women descended, but only Marianne Granger went inside. Taking her leave, Mrs. Edwards strolled toward a nearby excursion boat. Its thin black stacks spewing smoke, the side-wheeler *Thomas Starling* rocked at its slip. For a moment he considered following her, but the warehouse drew him back. Its mute walls attracted him, and repelled him too. Didn't he know enough? Did he have to witness the final transaction? As if to answer his own question, he crept closer.

The name came to him now. This was not only the junkard from a couple of weeks before. It was Joseph MacNamara, Stephenson's former rag. The junkard whistled through his teeth, the nag hesitated, and then the wagon wobbled toward the side of the building. He wasn't wearing the rubber mask now, but it had to be the same man.

The chipped gilt lettering on 8 Schermerhorn's window read DR. SLURRY, DISPENSARY. Still puffing on his clay pipe, the rope merchant remained on his barrel.

Like a trained dog, Max began doing reporter's tricks. Muffling his fears, he put the soothing routine in motion. "You know those ladies who went in there?"

The man's face looked like stained leather. "Nope."

"Ever seen them before?"

Meditating, he took a long pull on his pipe. "Nope."

"Any women like them?"

The old shopkeeper shrugged.

"Is the dispensary still in business?"

"Don't know."

Had he heard right? "The doctor's out of business?"

"Maybe yes, maybe no."

"Thanks a ton." A cart rattled past, a fresh flounder splatting onto the stones. "Can I ask you a question? Does anybody ever pick up the fish?"

"Nope."

He didn't bother to ask about the smell. He was already adjusting to the stench himself. At first he tapped on the dispensary's front door, and when there was no response he rapped hard with his knuckles. He tapped the dusty windows, too, but still no one appeared. Wiping some grime off the plate glass window, he peered inside. No desks. No chairs. No examining tables. No instrument cases or sinks. Just a long, narrow space. Finally, he grabbed the doorknob and twisted it, but to no avail. He headed around to the back of the building.

At the rear dock, the wagon stood empty. MacNamara had made his delivery.

Max had no choice. He was a seeing machine. He had to name the thing in the oilcloth, even as he prayed it had no name at all.

Of course, the rear loading door was bolted too. Standing on the deserted dock, he craned his neck to look up. A second-floor window was open a crack. An exterior stairway hung from the wall at a sickening angle; the first four steps had rotted away. From directly underneath the structure, he could see the rusty bolts that had once held them to the brick.

Rolled on their sides, a few sprung barrels lay empty at the dock's lip. Positioning one under the staircase, he used it for a stepstool. Stretching, he lifted his weight up to the first intact slat above his head. Under his weight, the worm-eaten strip of wood screeched. Bits of grit and stone showered down on his head. His heart in his throat, Max waited for the entire stairway to peel from its moorings, but the creaking construction held. Satisfied, he started climbing.

When the window wouldn't open farther, he gripped it tight and yanked as hard as he could. Grudgingly, the frame slid up a few notches. Now he bent his body low, scraped through the narrow opening and onto the floor. When he landed, his ankle bent sideways, pain searing through it. Groping in the pure blackness, he touched a cold, hard object. Lighting a match, he illuminated the few feet around him. Immense anchor chains lay rolled, curled and piled about him.

He rubbed his ankle, tested it for a step or two. It ached but seemed sound. Lighting another match, he crept deeper into the darkness. The low, beamed ceiling pressed down on him. Torn sails, pulleys, rope, pots and pans littered the floor. The airless loft smelled of dust and dead mice. Max stopped and considered whether to creep back to the window, but another adventure on the rotting staircase didn't appeal to him. In the dense silence he turned slowly, trying to sense the slightest flaw in the darkness. At the far end of the loft, faint stripes of light leaked through the planks, forming a rough square.

Holding his breath, he made his way toward the glowing outline, taking care not to trip over the ship supplies. He stubbed his toe once, and he stumbled over a large metal object, but he kept his balance. As he approached the trapdoor, he paused several times to listen, but the stillness remained unbroken. The loudest noise was his own breathing, amplified by the utter silence around him. Bending down, he grasped the trap's frame, lifting it ever so slightly. Lit by gaslight, a sliver of floor below became visible.

He stopped and waited a long moment, his blood pounding in his ears, but when the quiet persisted he shifted the trap a few more inches, revealing a narrow aisle between crude shelving. He made out a wooden box jumbled with hardware and a peeling wall streaked with dirt. The floor below seemed barely seven feet away. He dragged the trap away, this time exposing the entire opening. Crouching, he bounced on his toes a few times. His ankle didn't feel too bad. Keeping his knees bent, he took the leap.

He hit the floor harder than he expected, the jolt turning his ankle a second time. Before he could catch himself, he muttered "Sonofabitch!"

Biting his lip, he pressed himself against the shelves, waiting to be discovered. Frozen, he let one minute pass, two, three. Where were they? Why didn't they come after him? When he finally felt safe, he tiptoed down the aisle, examining the goods: screws, knives, tar, lamp wax, and inventions he couldn't quite identify. The first floor was another storehouse for the shipping trade, though the blanket of filth suggested that the equipment had long since been abandoned.

In the front room, a dispensary, covered with dust, stood empty. A torn curtain hung limp next to an enamel table. Arrayed on a towel gray with silt lay instruments of the trade. Ancient, stained linens. A reflector on a long handle. A selection of knives and bandages.

He was almost relieved when he heard human voices rise from the basement. Down there, talking among themselves, they hadn't heard him. Creeping step by step, he reached a second, up-flung trap door. A ladder led straight down into the darkness. Barely breathing, he took a few tentative steps down and hung there, listening intently. A harsh whisper. A woman's voice. Coming at even intervals, a chuffing noise he couldn't quite identify.

"He pay you fo' the las' time?" It was Marianne Granger.

"Ahh, shut your pie hole," a man's voice snapped. MacNamara? "We got work."

Intermingled with a grunting sound, the chuffing resumed.

As quietly as he could, he descended the raw slats. Halfway down, he stopped, suspended, and narrowed his eyes. Torchlight threw shadows onto the dry foundation. A lattice of chickenwire hung slack above the man and woman.

His sweat-stained back to Max, Joseph MacNamara was digging a trench. Humped mounds of dirt, previous plantings, ran parallel into the darkness. Under the low ceiling, the cloying odor of decay clotted the close space. Half-illuminated by the torchlight, the fresh ditch looked moist. At Marianne's feet lay a small pile of bundles. Would she unwrap them first? His stomach seized up, and he gagged. Covering his mouth he fought the spasms, hard contractions that rippled up from his gut, his throat burning with acid.

Leon? No, no, he wouldn't, couldn't allow himself to believe it. Leon wasn't yet two, and he could sing a scale, prattle like a kid twice his age. Leon could do anything.

Marianne screwed up her mouth. "I ain't doin' nothin' for her no more. I know how her game work. See how many she find without me."

"Ahh, bullshit. She'll find another nigger scout."

"Who else gonna do it? I knows which little mamma jazzin'. We oughta get her to pay us double."

Hadn't he seen enough? Prickly cold sweat broke out on the back of his neck. He could scuttle up the ladder and rush out into the street, swallow fishy air; but hooked on the ladder he couldn't seem to move a muscle. Instead, he seemed to separate from himself, entering a curious state of mind, at once hyper-aware and distant.

There was no word for this thing they were doing—it was as forbidden as the name of God. He thought of the way the Jews said "Adoshem," a euphemism less terrible than the real symbol etched onto Torah parchment. To make the true sound of His name was an unspeakable sin. What then for this word that did not exist? He felt preternaturally calm. His skin had no pores. The horror could not penetrate.

"What she give you and me? He think I can't count?" Marianne droned on.

"Like to see that witch dig a decent hole."

Shrugging her shoulders, she dug into her dress pocket, produced a cigarette, lit it and blew a derisive blast of smoke. "Ask me, she skim the cream."

"Gimme here," Joseph said, putting two fingers to his lips. Knee-deep in the trench, he lit up and took a few puffs. "Ahh, this is deep enough."

"Never hear no trumpet. You got the lime fo' the smell?"

"In this stink market? Street's paved with cod. You think Tammany gives a royal shit about sanitation? Give 'em here, c'mon."

When she lifted the first oilcloth-wrapped parcel, Max's gorge rose. Then she tossed it into the dark gash in the earth. The bundle struck the carved ground with a barely audible splat. That was the end of it. A splash in the mud, and the world ended.

A crazy idea gripped him. He was being cheated. They weren't going to let him see. . . . What could he tell Faye?

"What's that?" Joseph asked, hearing a noise, climbing out of the pit.

His thoughts raced in disconnected circles. Leon was too big to fit . . . Mrs. Darling wouldn't dare . . . then his body decided. First he was clinging to the slats, and then, without transition, he was climbing, hurling himself up the ladder.

Up on the ground floor, disoriented, he whirled around, searching for the door. He could hear MacNamara cursing as he quickly hauled himself up from below. Before Max could bolt, the bartender cut him off. With a feint, Max tried to get around the low-slung man, but MacNamara, brandishing his shovel, threw himself in the way.

Winding up, the bartender took a swipe at Max's head, the spade spraying mud and stinging pebbles. His mouth open, Max tasted dirt on his tongue. His eyes burned with grit. The two men circled each other, MacNamara holding the shovel across his chest, Max dancing just out of reach, going cold with the rage to live. All the fear drained out of him. If he could just land one shot on the man's soft chin, one solid uppercut, he could knock him back on his heels.

Out of nowhere came a hissing sound, and a blow that felt like a stone crashing into his temple. Reeling, he identified the sensation. That time outside the Haymarket. Rolled good and proper. A slung shot. Rubbery legs led him this way and that. Boxers called it Queer Street, didn't they? Marianne Granger wound up again. He threw his forearm up to protect his face, but the heavy bag thudded into his stomach instead. Doubled over, he staggered, but powerful hands gripped his shoulder and flung him to the floor.

From a great distance he heard MacNamara gasping. "He's that sonofabitch reporter. What if he goes blabbing?"

The answer came in one more stunning blow to the side of Max's head.

By the time he regained consciousness, smoke was filling the room. He could smell the stench of kerosene. How long had he been out? A few minutes? An hour? A long time, long enough for a fire to get a good start. An oily stink saturated the atmosphere. Barely a flame was visible in the black haze, but he could hear the conflagration spitting in the darkness. The ceiling rained down cinders.

Rolling away from the blast of heat, he tried to get up on all fours, but his hands and feet had been bound tight. In a sidewinding crawl, on his elbows and knees, he inched toward the door. Crawling was better anyway. Always stay low, under the fire, firemen had told him a hundred times. The heat intensified, scalding his face, his hands, every scrap of exposed skin. What was left of the air seared his lungs. With a deep sucking sound, the fire was devouring the last scraps of oxygen. A swooning sensation flowered within him, a call to luxurious surrender.

There was a window. A plate glass window with chipped gilt lettering.

His clothes, his hair, his skin were turning tinderbox-dry. Inside his body, the temperature skyrocketed. He didn't need the fire; he'd go off like a Roman candle all by himself. Then he butted the wall. Barely able to balance himself, he clawed his way up and felt for a smooth surface. When he found it, he hurled his body through the darkness.

Glass shattered, hot pinpricks in his face. Rolling on the cool paving stones, he could feel the whoosh of fresh air rushing over him, oxygen racing to feed the flames. Turning over and over, he tried to put out the fire inside his skin. Pieces of glass bit through his clothes. The stink of burning hair filled his nostrils. Dark smoke poured over him. Saturated with fumes, his lungs clotted. Every gasp for breath felt like a dry heave. Expanding his chest faster and faster seemed to do no good. His sticky lungs wouldn't inflate. He was smothering in a world of salty air. Then suddenly he was drowning.

Under his skin the fire burned on, but the rest of him was going down under an icy lake. The shock of cold water rang down his whole skeleton.

His head ached, his teeth ached, the insides of his bones vibrated with pain. A foreign force stood him up as if he weighed nothing at all. Curiously, his hands fluttered in front of him. Then the street tilted on a crazy axis, and he started to go down again, stiff and straight as a pole. Humped stones rushed up at his face. Clenching his jaw, he steeled himself for the collision, but miraculously the invisible power spun him back to his feet.

A clay pipe vibrated before his eyes. "Easy, fella. I'll untie ya'."

This time he stood there, rocking back and forth. He was taking in sips of oxygen now, but it didn't seem to help. Instead, a spasm gripped his stomach and reduced it to the size of a fist. He had knuckles in his stomach, knuckles he had to spit up. And they came, too, gristle in a burst of yellow bile. Even when there was nothing else left to cough up, the convulsions didn't abate. Instead, the seizure carried on deep within him, as if, with nothing left to disgorge, it would dredge up the organs themselves.

In the midst of the fit, he realized something. He wasn't dying. He was gagging, sucking, spitting, gasping. Wasn't that life? Confused, he wondered why he was so sick. Because of the smoke, or what he had seen, what the fire was devouring before his eyes?

Hands patted him. He floated onto a cart where he fought to sit up.

"Leave him be," the clay-pipe man advised.

A wild gong echoed down the street. Bodies flew out of the way. Iron-shod hooves rang out against the pavement. Engine Company No. 15 pounded toward the conflagration. Clinging to the shining fire patrol wagon, rubber-coated men shouted and waved their axes, driving onlookers off the street. From the opposite direction, a gleaming white-and-gold hosecar spun around the corner, a pair of dark stallions pulling the swerving wagon behind them. Which vehicle would get there first?

Somehow he climbed off his perch and wobbled back toward the warehouse. In a dream he saw the brown gash in the basement, nameless mounds curling in flame. Lost in this waking nightmare, he could not stop the two puffs of air from whispering in his ear. Le-on. He tasted clay in his mouth. He shuddered.

The firemen would have no chance. The building would be consumed down to the last brick. A wild despair seized him, his jaw went slack, and he stood like a stunned animal before the conflagration.

Yet, disconnected from his paralyzed limbs, his other mind kept observing, sifting ideas, testing theories. This thinking apparatus was part of him, yet outside his body. In its cool, impenetrable sheath, it tested its own observations and came to its own conclusions.

The firefighters didn't know it, but they had to rescue the remains.

As the men peeled off the patrol wagon, an affectionate cheer rose from the crowd.

"Got here fast, huh?"

"They got brass balls, going in there."

Coughing, doubling over, and rising again, Max wove through the eager crowd, pressing toward the front lines. Without him, how would they know where to dig, what to look for? Without him, how could they read the scraps of charred oilcloth or the story of blackened bone?

A hefty fireman pointed his halligan at the roof. Another one, looking grave, nodded in agreement. Aloof from the mob's excitement, they moved deliberately, arranging their pumper's connections and hoses, shuffling forward in their great boots for the attack.

A woman tried to drag her husband away. "C'mon, Sam, it's gonna fall on our heads."

He would point them to the trench. He'd get down on his hands and knees and dig like a dog.

Another gong rang and rang like a war cry. Vaulting the curb, Hook and Ladder No. 6 screeched to a halt. Before it rolled to a stop, men were leaping off and ripping scaling ladders from their hooks.

The steamer lofted streams of water onto the seething fire, billowing smoke blackening in response. Lit cinders rained down on the festive crowd. Flasks passed from hand to hand, and Max saw a longshoreman slip his hand up a plump woman's skirt. Leaning back against him, her eyes fixed on the smoking building, she shifted an inch or two to make herself comfortable. French sailors fresh from a grog shop staggered to the scene. A knot of American seamen elbowed each other and gave the foreigners dirty looks.

"You need a hand, fellas?" one of the Americans called out to the men in rubber coats.

"Keep outta the way there," the captain shouted. The eager mob surged forward. "Back, alla yez!"

"Max Greengrass, *Herald*," he mumbled, showing himself.

The captain tilted the shiny brim of his hat back, revealing untamed eyebrows. "Mother of God. What the hell happened to you?"

"In the basement . . . dig," he managed. "It started. . . ."

"You don't say? Mallory, keep an eye on this citizen."

A towering recruit, Mallory heaved Max over to the pumper. "Barney, cap'n says this one stays put."

Flannel sleeves rolled to his elbows, a red-faced firefighter was wrestling with a recalcitrant hose. "Damn pressure's down!"

Mallory hurled Max onto the pumper's seat.

"It's a roast," Max informed the dubious fireman. "Down in the basement."

"That so? We'll send for the marshal. Don't give the man no trouble, chief," he added, cuffing Max under the chin.

Why should he cause problems? He'd accomplished his mission. They would listen to him now.

Bearing their axes, a pair of firemen leaned ladders against the building and began to climb. In the spray they glistened like black beetles. The one on the right pried open a shutter and smashed a second-story window, revealing the roiling furnace inside. Directing his nozzle through the broken glass, he held on to his pulsing hose until the fire went from crimson to orange to sooty smoke.

"Man on the roof!" a fireman called out.

Max craned his neck. Joseph MacNamara peered down over the lip of the cornice, then backed off at the sight of the sheer, four-story drop. MacNamara. Trapped in his own fire. Had he gone back for something? Waited too long?

Max stood up and shouted at the top of his lungs. "Back stairs! Around the back!"

The throng took up his suggestion. "To the back. Back stairs!"

Max could see the bartender shake his head and lift his palms. Finally, the dark figure receded. Stepping down from the engine, Max tested his balance. The wobbles were going away. Pushing off, he let the mob sweep him around the side of the building. Beating at the crazed spectators, two cops managed to impede the charge, allowing a few firemen to haul ladders around to the rear of the building.

Engulfed in flame, the wooden staircase was disintegrating, fiery steps, fiery railings sailing down, light, half-consumed. Fully extended, the first ladder reached the third floor. Punch-drunk, Max staggered to the rear of the building just in time to see MacNamara gazing down at the burning platform below him. Strips of flame licked back at the window.

"Take a flyer!" a reeling sailor cried out.

"Shut your trap, Wheatly!" a fellow seaman shouted.

A second, taller ladder rose skyward, this one reaching to just below the cornice. Still, MacNamara would have to climb over the stonework, dangle his leg down, and find his footing. His helmet low over his face, the second fireman grappled hand over hand up his ladder. Stephenson's rag dipped a foot into the empty air, and the crowd fell quiet. His rescuer grabbed his ankle and guided it to the ladder's top rung. The two of them were safe now.

What luck: he would get to see MacNamara hang. Max had never had much taste for the carnival of public executions, but a spiky flower opened inside him now. Some jackals didn't deserve to exist. After Byrnes applied the third degree, MacNamara would cough up Weems, Mrs. Edwards, Marianne Granger, and the rest of them.

Lost in a reverie, he wondered how Hummel could hold him responsible for reporting the insurance ring's private business if Police Superintendent Byrnes made it public.

And didn't Max have some intelligence to trade with Byrnes? Couldn't he go into business for himself?

All the bartender had to do was set his weight, turn around, and lower himself down.

It was hard to understand what happened next. Max thought he saw another small burst of black smoke roll off the roof. The two dangling men grew hazy for a split second, and then the ladder rocked back from the bricks.

For a moment it hung there at an impossible, vertical angle. A pair of firemen rushed over and positioned themselves under the teetering ladder just before it began its sickening backward plunge. The barrel-chested MacNamara flew off first, the fireman a heartbeat later, a pair of dead weights dropping toward the unyielding pavement below.

Without a word to each other, two firefighters on the ground separated, spread their arms and legs wide, and fixed their eyes on the plummeting bodies.

All they had to do was cushion the hurtling men. They might end up with a few broken bones, but the nose-diving victims would likely survive. Then at the last second two sailors staggered under the plunging bodies, too, flinging their arms out and jostling one of the rescuers, knocking him off balance.

The plummeting fireman hit with a moist sound, a bag of laundry splatting on the Belgian paving stones. A single animal, the mob groaned. A black rubber hat bounced into the gutter. At the same instant, MacNamara hurtled into his savior's arms, knocking the fireman flat on his back. His crushing weight pressed the firefighter flat against the stones. The captain, blind with rage, grabbed one of the American seamen by the throat. It took a pair of his comrades to drag him off.

Joseph MacNamara stood up unsteadily and brushed himself off. With the back of his hand, he smeared soot off his jaw. Before he could wander off, a higher-up in a blue cap grabbed his elbow. "Don't go nowhere's, you! I'll split your head wide open, hear me!"

"Mary, Mother of God!"

"The hell with God! Get a doctor!"

Faces blackened by the fire, a cadre of firemen swiftly lifted their comrade's limp body and bore it to their water-streaming truck. The mob fell quiet as the rag-doll corpse flopped onto the hook and ladder. A heavy brow, a pug nose, a shock of black hair. The last mask of disbelief. The streak of dirt across cheeks and nose, such an even line, couldn't obscure the man's beardless face. An odd scuffle took place, one rescuer yanking on the victim's rubber boots, the other bulling him against the truck panel and shouting: "Conroy! Leave him be! You daft, or what?"

The team of horses, glassy with sweat, stamped impatiently. Then the mad gong started up again, the stunned crowd parted, and the horses, as if sensing the grave moment, bolted forward.

A hand shook his shoulder hard. It wasn't one of the friendly hands that had transported him from the pavement and lofted him to safety. Spinning, he came face to face with a man in a blue hat. Its shiny brim had a military caste. Under a thatch of wild eyebrows, black eyes blazed.

"You were playin' with matches in there, wasn't you?" the captain roared.

"That's the bug." MacNamara croaked. Then he doubled over, spitting blood and ash.

"What? No! Max Greengrass. *New York Herald*," he muttered ritualistically. He looked around for his savior, the clay-pipe man. Vanished. "I was tied . . ."

"Yeah, yeah. You're under arrest. Arson, first degree."

He tried his best to explain, but his tongue was thick in his mouth.

"There's a roast down there . . . remains . . . kids. . . ." He wouldn't say Leon aloud. He wouldn't pronounce the sentence himself. "You've got to dig."

"Yeah, yeah. Don't worry. We'll dig all the way to China."

"You're arresting me?"

"Nah. Mallory!"

The raw-boned recruit emerged from the crowd, his iron grasp shoving Max's arms behind his back. Pain shot through his shoulder. "Jeez, you're dislocating—" he protested.

"I'll dislocate your fucking head, mister," Mallory muttered.

Then he passed through the pain to the protected place inside his other mind. A novel idea drifted to the surface. He wanted to get arrested. "Great. Get me to Byrnes. Go ahead. He's looking for me anyway. But there's your pyro. Take him too. And for Godsakes, check out the basement."

"Shut the fuck up!" the captain growled, shaking him.

A strangled sound was pouring out of him. The back of a hand seared his face, but he was down to the knuckle and bone of himself, and he couldn't stop.

"Stick a rag down his throat, why don'tcha?" the captain said in disgust.

"It's always the shitbags who get out alive," Mallory spat.

"You wanna see Byrnes? Quit your fucking howling."

"Yeah . . . he'll vouch—" His voice shook.

"What's the game?"

The stink of charred wood swirled around them. The smoke ran up his nose, congealed in his mouth. A skin of charcoal coated his tongue. "Nothing, I'm just going to call . . ." Grit trickled down his throat. A burst of coughs came up dry. His chest ached. ". . . call my paper from Byrnes's office, and then I'm going . . . I'm going to tell him how you blind monkeys wasted your time manhandling me."

"What'd you say your name was?"

"Max Greengrass. *New York Herald*. What's yours?"

"Never mind that," the captain said warily.

"Forget it. You know who owns that building?"

"You're the prophet. You tell me."

"Holy Trinity. This one here works for them."

MacNamara managed to cough out a few words. "Damn bug's . . . lyin' to save hisself."

Max shrugged. “And they’re going to collect their insurance, too.”

“What’re you, daffy? You think a silk-hat church like that’s gonna act like a cockroach landlord?”

“It’s not that kind of insurance. Listen, give us both a ride over to Mulberry Street . . . I’ll bet Byrnes knows this joker, and if I’m wrong I’ll write my own ticket to the Tombs.”

Burning cinders drifted down. Oily smoke leaked from the smoldering warehouse. The bleeding brown trench. Nobody’s bundles, tossed into a hole. They came to him from a filmy dream. Mrs. Darling wouldn’t dare. Didn’t his sister say she was all paid up? But so what if Faye swore up and down; she probably owed plenty.

His face smeared with soot, the captain didn’t seem to notice the quarter-sized burn high on his own forehead. Max’s nose ran.

With the back of his hand, the captain rubbed his ash-grimed cheek. “You got a press card?”

Max dug in his pocket. The cloth was moist and sticky in there. Finally, he produced the tattered document.

“The marshal’s gonna wanna see this.”

“Hey, I need—” he started to remonstrate, but then he took another look at the weary captain’s seamed face. “Yeah, sure. Tell him I’ll run it all down for him.”

Before he mounted the fire wagon, he stuck his head in an overflowing bucket. Droplets of blood floated in the brown water.

“Take both of ’em like he says, Mallory.”

If he could only break Darling’s door down, hunt through her rooms. “I need to stop—”

“You’re stoppin’ nowheres,” the captain swore.

chapter thirty-nine

Down at Mulberry Street headquarters, Max cleaned up as best he could. A sympathetic sergeant scrounged up a bit of plaster for the tiny cuts under his eye. At a utility sink, he washed his face and the ring of soot that graced his neck. Wetting his fingers, he combed his hair back and fluffed up his mustache. He looked as if he'd gone a few dozen rounds with John L., but no worse.

The police superintendent didn't show up for hours. On the hard bench, Max faded in and out of existence. Finally, Byrnes rumbled past him and slammed the door. Max stared blankly at the walls. Creeping time would come to a close. In a minute or an hour or a day, he'd gain his audience.

At long last the heavy door swung open.

He had no nerves any more. In the past Byrnes had inspired fear, but now Max faced the great detective with nothing more than an inward shrug. He noticed the pallor under the police superintendent's ruddy complexion, and the brittle note in the cop's voice.

In a flat tone, Max laid out the details. In his other mind he tore through Darling's flat, his fingers closed on her throat, and he shook her until she came apart.

"You better have the show-and-tell, boyo. I can't go around spouting off against people of that standing."

"Go dig up that basement. You'll see."

"Ain't you the fair-haired boy? You look like you went through a meatgrinder."

Byrnes glared his practiced glare, but Max barely noticed. A radical resignation gripped his soul. In a queer way, fatalism felt the same as confidence.

"It's a nice trick," he explained in a voice not his own. "The mother's desperate, the kid's going to croak anyway. She takes the buyout, money in the hand, and our Mrs. Edwards says 'Don't worry. If anything happens, we'll take care of the stone.'"

Byrnes's eyes narrowed to slits. "Only she don't buy a stone, is what you're telling me?"

"They can insure the same kid five times, too, if they want to. You think one company knows what the other one's doing?"

"The agents are selling all over the tenements. Am I right?"

"And the other vultures are speculating. The odds are in their favor. If they have to, they help them along."

Byrnes's great mustache bobbed and quivered. "If we weren't so damned civilized, we could simply toss 'em in a pit with a bunch of sharpened sticks."

"Just pick up Edwards and Granger. You've already got MacNamara, right?" For the moment, he kept the Reverend Weems's name to himself. The minister's denials would put the icing on the cake. Then there was his speech. Max had a few questions about that, too.

"Don't go telling me my business," Byrnes said sharply. "We've been on the trail for months, right, boyo?"

"As far as I'm concerned, it was a brilliant piece of police work."

What amazed him was that he didn't care any more. His whole being had been poured into the newspaper business, but now he saw from this new, curious distance, that if he were pitched out onto the street tomorrow, he would still be living in the same skin. The sun would still pour down, good whiskey would still taste smooth, a lean steak would still make his mouth water, the hollows of a woman's body would still make him ache. Freedom was curled up inside despair.

Just let Leon live.

"You can say this," Byrnes quoted himself thoughtfully. "'We have been investigating these brutes for some time, and we have finally caught them red-handed. I've held my position for many years, but this is the single most heinous crime I've ever witnessed. I hope never to see its like again.' Got that?"

"Every word. I'll need interviews—"

"Not 'til after we interrogate. We'll see if you're going off half-cocked, Greengrass." A deep crease appeared between Byrnes's small black eyes.

Max noted all the mechanics of intimidation, the guttural tone, the jutting chin, the fists going white at the knuckles, but it seemed a dumb show. He could almost make out the smile flowering under the formidable mustache.

He also noticed that Byrnes knew his name.

"You'll put in the word with Abie Hummel? If he follows through," Max snapped a fingernail at his notes, "I'll be out on my ass. This story will never see the light of day."

A naked gambit, but the only one at his disposal. Then again, he was learning that the game was played mostly on the surface.

"Don't get wise. Abie's not such a bad fella. You seen his Saratoga column? He'll give you some good tips if you get on his right side."

"Just talk to him, right? Keep him off my back." He kept his voice flat, but Byrnes was his only hope. He prayed he was offering the superintendent enough in exchange.

"Sure. But Abie's his own man. You can't ram nothing down his throat."

Byrne's words didn't inspire confidence, but they were all he was going to get. Resigned, he turned his mind to more pressing matters.

Leon. A dank sweat trickled down his spine. One way or another, Belle would be home by now. A wave of fever swept through him. His elaborately constructed calm shook. Willing himself blank, he kept dread at bay.

Reeling home from Mulberry Street a few minutes past eleven, he was surprised to see a light burning in Mrs. DeVogt's parlor. Scraps of fog were blowing off the river, diffusing the lamplight. In the haze his own footsteps were muffled, his own breathing unnaturally loud. Out of sight, iron wheels rattled on stone. A foghorn blew an aching note that vibrated in his chest. At the foot of the steps he hesitated. Could he face another human being?

Capes of mist saturated his thin coat. Reflexively, he put up his collar and climbed to the front door. Belle was sitting up, reading a fat Russian novel. Startled, she placed the book face-down on the arm of the sofa. Something called *Anna Karenina*. Judging by its size, it must have been a Count Tolstoy production. How she ever waded through these tomes was a mystery to him.

"How's tricks?" The line was all wrong. So was his leaky grin.

"Your face!" Half-mooned scabs marked his cheeks and forehead. Her heart clenched. Some incompetent had applied a messy poultice under his right eye. She'd have to get her bag without waking the baby.

He patted the skin absently. His back was slick with sweat. "Occupational hazard. What're you doing up in the middle of the night?"

"I finally got Leon to sleep."

Chills ran hot and cold down his spine, and he wondered if he was getting the grippe. He had assumed, denied, pushed it out of his mind. Or into his other mind, where he swathed fear in forgetfulness. The brown gash in the ground. Oilcloth and string. "Leon? He's all right? I thought . . . I mean, I got it into my head . . . What's he doing here?"

He was in a dream world, she realized. His eyes, usually so full of light, had a dull sheen, and he seemed to be staring at some invisible place in the distance. "Faye is who-knows-where by now. Where else should I take him?"

"He's okay?" Electrified, the hair stood up on the back of his neck. Jesus Frigging Christ. The kid was in one piece. The swollen sensation in his chest surged up his throat, but he fought it back down. No reason for Belle to see him bawling.

"His fever's down."

"Mrs. Darling, she was taking care of him?"

"Oh, she wouldn't harm a hair on his head. Faye gave her a publicity picture. She signed it, too." She reached out and touched the spray of cuts on his cheek. "Does that hurt?"

"Only when I breathe. Can I see him?" All he could think about was smelling the top of the boy's head, counting his fingers and toes.

"Wait. Later. You know what's an infection? If it gets into your blood, you won't like it."

When she returned, she arrayed her astringents on the rosewood end table.

"Is this going to sting?" he asked, in mock horror.

"If it doesn't, you're dead to the world," she said, soaking a strip of linen with alcohol. With efficient strokes, she cleaned out the small wounds.

Unfortunately, she had set his whole face on fire. "Yeow," he murmured, gritting his teeth.

Her knees brushed his leg. As she worked, she stood up to her full height of five feet two inches. Leaning over, she seemed unaware that her breasts were resting on his shoulder. "Now I'm going to wrap you up."

She produced a scissors and cut long strips of clean cloth, which she proceeded to fix over the burning cuts. Pain alternated with awakening desire. In his cottony state of mind, he felt something give way inside him. He looked over her armada of antiseptics. He felt her fingers busy pressing, pasting, and winding. Raising his eyes, he saw her deep concentration and the way the tip of her tongue poked from the corner of her mouth.

"Are we friends again?"

"Stay still. Somebody said we were enemies?"

"Do you want to get married?" He wasn't sure who was asking the question or where it came from, but it seemed to make sense.

The snipping and patting ceased for a moment. "To who? John D. Rockefeller?"

"To me."

She stepped away, put her hands on his shoulders and gave him a searching look. "Did you ever hear of 'soldier's heart'?"

"No."

She placed a chaste kiss on his head. "You can ask me again sometime. When you're not in shock."

Leon was sitting up at dawn, babbling to himself in his cradle. When Max slipped into the room, the boy laughed, then ducked his head, shy and amused. All of him appeared intact. His high forehead, his purple birthmark, his big ears, his funny upper lip. Max lifted him up and turned him high above his head. Leon squealed in delight. Lowering the boy to his shoulder, Max sniffed his hair; that fresh, indefinable smell of a new human being.

"She's coming back soon, kiddo. Don't worry. How 'bout this? Do re mi fa so la ti do?"

The serious look passed from the child's features. "Do re mi. . . ."

Tangled in her sheets, Belle rolled over and groaned.

"See that? You woke her up."

"Lemme down, Unca Max."

With obvious pride, Leon toddled across the room, fast and steady. Wasn't he a squealing bundle just a second ago? You could see the kid had gumption. What about the others? A chorus of bones. But the elation he felt after finding Leon alive and well, it was only human, wasn't it?

When Belle sat up, her curly hair shooting out in all directions, her sleepy features looked blurred. His heart stopped. Without her rice powder and lipstick, she looked painfully young. Yawning, she reached out for the kid. "Give him here. We'll have to get him off the bottle soon."

"I'll fix you a tray," he said, scuttling downstairs to the kitchen.

By the time he returned, she'd conquered her hair with tortoiseshell combs.

"That's so sweet," she said, sipping her coffee and taking a bite of a fresh roll.

"What'll we do with him? We both have to go to work."

"Don't worry. Mrs. DeVogt said she'd watch him while we're gone."

"She can't do that every day," he said, suddenly filled with domestic anxiety. How long was Faye's damn tour going to last? What did she expect him to do while she lollygagged all over the East Coast?

"We'll have to wire Faye. Can you do that from your office?" she asked, her brow furrowing with light lines.

"Sure. The two of them aren't running back home anytime soon, I'll tell you that," he said.

"I know. She can send money, though. Once she gets paid."

When it came to coughing up, Faye was prone to convenient lapses of memory. Belle wasn't just helping with the Leon fiasco, she was helping him manage his sister too. She fell into the role so naturally, he didn't have to ask. What bliss. He'd never dreamed of sharing Faye's disasters with anyone else. "You think you can find somebody we can trust?"

"I know a woman on Carmine Street. If you're not worried he'll eat red sauce."

"He can kiss the Pope's ring as far as I'm concerned. As long as he's safe. This is gonna hamstring you, though. It's not your responsibility."

"Shut up. It's nothing."

"Ha! I'd like to see *something*."

chapter forty

At the rectory, the housekeeper, a tight-lipped woman with formidable hips, insisted that the Reverend Weems had left for the day.

The vestibule was a tight fit. Max shuffled his feet, searching for a polite stance. "I can wait," he said blandly.

"He might not be back 'til tomorrow," the servant insisted, inserting her bulk into the sliver of space between them.

"Ahh. Well, tell him that Max Greengrass from the *Herald* wants to give him a chance to tell his side of the story."

In the waning light, he found a stoop down the block from Weems's residence. He could make his deadline without the minister's remarks, he supposed, but he was greedy for the tortured rationalizations the clergyman was sure to offer. It was one thing to write up what he had witnessed in the cellar, but quite another for a man of the cloth to try to explain it away.

Waiting made him jumpy. He got up, sat down, stretched his legs with a short walk, then returned to his post. Sitting still was almost impossible. When he wasn't in motion, he couldn't forget; and if he remembered, he would have to feel; and if he had to feel, he feared he would drown. Or unleash his formless rage. Playing the newsman kept the storm inside his skull at bay.

Around twilight, the Reverend Weems emerged, gripping a carpetbag.

Unfolding his stiff body, Max intercepted the gangly clergyman at the corner.

"Max Greengrass from the *Herald*?"

Waving down a cab, Weems refused to acknowledge his presence. Max grabbed the minister's sleeve, but he shook the reporter off and hurled himself into the hack. Why was he running? Why wouldn't he answer a few simple questions?

Racing alongside the cab, Max fired off one question. "Your church owns a warehouse on Schermerhorn, doesn't it?"

In his self-made bubble, Weems gazed into space. Did he know what his cousin, Mrs. Edwards, had been doing all along? Wasn't flight an admission of guilt?

"I know about the insurance policies," Max shouted as the vehicle picked up speed.

Weems stared straight ahead, as if he hadn't heard a thing. On the run, Max caught a glimpse of the minister's grim face. Then a produce wagon practically knocked him down. Skidding and tilting on the uneven pavement, the cart bounced past him, a bushel of red potatoes cascading to his feet. Dodging the soft missiles, he tried to hail another cab.

The first empty one, rolling in between the far curb and a flatbed piled high with lumber, rattled by out of reach. Another driver took a look at him waving frantically from the curb and snapped his reins, his gray gelding bolting forward.

By the time Max secured another hack, Weems was bobbing along two blocks further downtown. Cutting into the streaming traffic, the cabby roused his nag with a slashing whip. Bearing down on them, the massive Sixth Avenue horsecar rumbled along its rails, but the cabby's light carriage bounced across the tracks a foot ahead of the streetcar's pounding team.

Tentatively, Max opened his eyes. A lumbering coach rocked a bare six inches away.

"Where to, mister?"

"You on hop or what?" Weaving in between a furniture truck and a brass-fitted landau, Weems's cab veered right onto Twentieth Street. "Next block, hang a right."

Twentieth became a wall of traffic. Max leaned out of his vehicle just in time to see Weems jump out. Hauling his stuffed bag, the churchman trotted toward Seventh Avenue, then disappeared around the corner. Max threw a coin at the hack and leaped out too, but by the time he reached Seventh Avenue, Weems had disappeared. A girl chalked boxes on the sidewalk. Nearby, her friends turned a rope and chanted. A raw construction site provided the main attraction, sidewalk engineers smoking and peering through the rough plank fence. Half-heartedly, Max jogged uptown toward Twenty-Third, just in case.

Twenty yards in front of him, Weems materialized, kneeling, his carpetbag split at the seams. Helter-skelter, the minister was stuffing his linens back into the satchel. Max took a few more steps before the clergyman looked up. His eyes fixed on the reporter for a heartbeat, and then he took off, socks, underwear, starched shirts, and black clerical garments spilling out behind him.

Several small boys swarmed over the bag's strewn treasures. Weems had a deceptive, loping stride, and was running at a good clip. Max was losing ground, and then he almost bowled over a portly businessman. The sidewalk was choked with window shoppers, deliverymen, salesmen, liveried toadies, beggars, coachmen, and a circus of loose children. At the end of the block, the uptown Sixth Avenue blasted its steam whistle and pulled out of the elevated station.

Max had to stop him. If Weems made that train, he could catch the Northern New York Railroad at 145th or disappear into the wilds of St. Nicholas Avenue. The engine's roar slowly faded, but in a minute, though still invisible, another locomotive came chugging in. The downtown cars. Suspended two stories above, the fanciful Gothic station looked a mile high. Max took the covered pavilion stairs two at a time. When he reached the platform, he caught sight of Weems leaping onto the first car. Then the doors slid closed, and he heard the first burst of steam. Racing toward the end carriage, he saw a pair of young men on the last car's rear platform urging him on.

His legs were knotting up with cramps.

The great iron wheels started rolling. He'd done it before, dozens of times. The gate was down. The train lumbered along the edge of the platform, slowly picking up speed. His heart in his throat, he timed his leap and vaulted aboard. Staggering, he grabbed a railing with his bandage-wrapped hand, the two sports righting him and pounding him on the back.

"Almost fatal," one young man laughed.

"You shoulda seen what Carl here did last week on the Third Avenue. Suicidal."

Max peered into the rear carriage. Packed tight as a can of tinned fish. Weems was three cars ahead. He had to make a plan. He could leap out at the next station, race forward and jam himself into the next car. The conductor might close the doors in his face, though. It made more sense to hang off his current perch and scan the emerging hordes at every station. He could always take a flyer onto the platform if he saw Weems slipping away.

The Jefferson Market Courthouse threw a shadow across the Eighth Street platform. At Amity Street a gaggle of factory girls tumbled out of the train. Weems was a head taller than the black-shawled Italian women passing by. He'd stick out like a sore thumb if he plunged off at this station. At Chambers, passengers poured out for the steamship lines and the Erie Railroad Ferry, but the minister wasn't among them. He was still aboard. Either that or he had melted away earlier. Its wheels grating, the train jerked a block east past Printing House Square, the Post Office, and City Hall. At every stop Max tensed, ready to lunge through the doors, but Weems didn't show.

St. Paul's Georgian spire sailed past as the Sixth Avenue thundered toward the tip of the island. Commercial blocks of brick and brownstone, the treetops of Battery Park all sped by two stories below. With every stop his spirits sank. Weems must have evaporated into the departing crowds, but Max had no choice. He had to hang on now until the end of the line.

South Ferry station was a madhouse, a thousand voices rising and falling like breakers on the shore. Passengers from every El converged, switching lines, heading for the Staten Island Ferry or the sidewheeler to Coney. The great terminal stank of horseshit and brine and an underlying, sickly sweet aroma. Max elbowed his way off the Sixth Avenue and threw himself into the roiling mob. Turning round and round, he couldn't see more than two feet in any direction. He jumped as high as he could, but couldn't make out the clergyman in the dark masses of passengers coiling around him. Then he saw the iron girders.

Fighting his exhaustion, he shinnied up several feet above the river of bobbing heads, derbies, homburgs, straw boaters, feathered hats, and shawls. Dark tributaries spilled out toward the Third and Ninth Avenue lines.

Far downstream, Weems's gaunt form shuffled along in the packed crowd.

Ducking his head, the minister passed under the Third Avenue sign. Against the tide of Ninth Avenue riders Max jostled his way, turning sideways, making himself small, shoving until he was swept up by the powerful counter-current of east side riders. Every few minutes trains rumbled in and out of the station.

Near the Third Avenue line's platform, the crowd thinned just enough, and he ran, weaving in and out of the slump-shouldered garment workers. Caps and shawls predominated now. The peacock feathers and birds of paradise had migrated to the west side trains. At the last moment he hurled himself into the middle carriage, forcing himself into a few square inches of space, but then the doors refused to close. A man with an inflamed face seemed to blame Max and tried to shove him back onto the platform, but the reporter put his head down, spread his legs for balance, and refused to budge. On the third attempt, the doors slid shut, and the train shuddered and jerked forward.

He didn't know where Weems was now, in the same packed car or up front behind the locomotive. At first the east side train ran on the narrow streets themselves. Water Street. Coentis Slip. Front Street and Old Slip. Irate passengers trapped in the center of the carriage called out their stops but remained ensnared in the dense core of bodies. In a jumble Max saw a sail puffed with wind, tenements, coffee and spice warehouses. Climbing a gentle grade, the steam engine dragged its human cargo to the elevated tracks. At Fulton Street, too narrow to accommodate the usual iron stanchions, engineers had built the station right into the United States Hotel.

A force boiling deep inside the carriage suddenly blew Max out onto the platform. Enraged riders already two or three stops past their destinations exploded from the car. The door to the hotel flew open. Disoriented, Max saw a brown-haired woman shaking a leather cup behind the check-in desk. A dice cup, he registered. A lobby jockey lobbed a gob of phlegm at a brass spittoon. Twenty feet down the platform the Reverend Weems, also flung out, gazed around, goggle-eyed. Quickly recovering his senses, the clergyman ducked his head and headed for the hotel.

In bad sack suits, several drummers clustered around the front desk, betting on the next roll. A murky painting of the Hudson, the river little more than a brown stain, dominated the room. A worn couch and a few chairs huddled around a colorless rug. Weems stalked toward the desk, unaware that Max was at his heels.

"Eight's the play," a slack-spined salesman called out.

"Bets, gentlemen," the brunette called out. Traces of former beauty marked her lined features. A sprinkling of cornstarch on her throat didn't quite hide a rash.

Weems forced his way between the players. "May I pay for a room?"

The bones clicked across the desk. Three and three.

Blood pounding in his temples, Max lunged and grabbed Weems's elbow. "You got a house dick, lady?"

"You registered?"

"This man's assaulting me," Weems said in an even tone, jerking his arm out of Max's grasp.

"He's behind that fire on Schermerhorn today. Call the cops, the fire department, something, come on," Max urged the brunette.

At the mention of arson, Weems's hawk-nosed face drained of color. His tic of a smile quivered, a muscle spasm in the corner of his mouth. His Adam's apple bobbed in his stringy neck. Suddenly he bounded toward the door. Max snatched at him but caught nothing but air. By the time he burst outside again, Weems was craning his neck at the end of the platform. Max threw everything into his last dash, his short, choppy strides propelling him forward.

A small shape in the distance, a Forney blasted its high-pitched whistle.

Max caught up with Weems as the train thundered toward the station. Lowering his shoulder, he knocked the minister against a girder. Whippet-thin, Weems went flying, but he caught his balance at the last moment. Dodging Max's grasp, he tried to scuttle back down the platform, but Max cut him off. If only the sonofabitch would stay still for a minute. The man was all arms and legs. Retreating, Weems escaped a second time, but his ankles seemed to tangle and all at once he was teetering on the platform's lip, an expression of horror on his bony face.

There was plenty of time. Weems's spine arched back, his head went in the other direction, his spastic arms sawing air. All Max had to do was reach out, loop his arm around the minister's waist, and reel him in to safety. Hooking one arm around a nearby girder would anchor him. . . . The split second lasted forever. Weems's face turned to fish flesh, his jaw went slack, his stringy neck stretched to the snapping point. He gave Max a beseeching look. In the compressed moment, Max gazed, mesmerized, as the clergyman's disbelief turned to white-eyed terror.

Max heard the train's roar in his ears. He tasted the dead fire's ashes on his tongue. There was a trench in a warehouse basement. . . . What about the others?

Flailing, Weems flopped backward and down to the track bed, his skull striking a rail, the sound of the blow blotted out by the approaching uproar. Now the steam engine tore through space, growing enormous, its ear-splitting whistle blowing over and over, its iron wheels locked and skidding, throwing up sparks. The screech of metal on metal became unbearable. The maroon cars blurred past, bucked, then ground to a stop.

The Forney's stack was pointing at a crazy angle. Max's stunned eye traced the outlines of the spark arrester first, moved to the tilted cab and then further down to the string of cars, bunched and thrown from the tracks. Then his gaze drifted back to the polished locomotive. Beneath its wheels a bloody clump of hair and a white, wormy substance.

He hadn't shoved the man. He'd been perfectly neutral. No one could accuse him of a thing. But he knew what he had done by doing nothing at all.

Slowly the upended cars bled their dazed passengers. A stout man in a celluloid collar emerged blinking, a faraway look in his eyes. Hand on her wide-brimmed hat, a young woman lifted herself through the door and scrambled up to the platform. A long-necked, stately broker held his arm out to a matron and led her to a service ladder. Picking his way down the line, the engineer paused and squatted, shaking his head as he examined the wreckage.

Then he came upon the crushed man, and he let out a groan. Max had to turn away.

Curses ripped the air. A flagman raced down the tracks to head off further disaster.

Murder by omission. Drifting in another world, Max wondered if there was such a thing.

The self-accusation was absurd, wasn't it? It had been an accident. Weems had fallen fleeing a simple interview. If he wasn't guilty as sin, why had he run away like a criminal? There had only been a split second to reach out. Anyway, suppose he had gotten a grip on the flailing minister? He might have been dragged down and mashed under the Forney's wheels himself. It had all happened in a blur. How could an act of self-preservation become its mirror image?

Unfortunately, his other mind saw it quite differently. Hadn't there been all the time in the world? A hundred thoughts had flashed through his brain between the premonition and Weems's dying fall. The minister was a light, gawky creature. Bracing himself on that girder, he could have righted the staggering man and kept himself perfectly safe. When he had refused to reach out, he wasn't saving himself, he was choosing to let Weems tumble to the tracks. His paralysis was really an act of revenge.

And so what? Who would know? *He* would know. He would remember. In the nightmares he knew were coming, *he* would be the one losing his balance, fluttering and plunging under the grinding wheels. Inside these dreams, he would reason with himself, he would recall that he was alive, but it would do no good. In his dream-life, logic was a paltry force.

An automaton, he groped for his pencil. His warring thoughts deadlocked, cunning took over. Who would shape what had happened? Who would create cause-and-effect where there had been none? The body on the roadbed deserved attention, but was it more than a sidebar? Had Weems tripped over his own feet? Or thrown himself in the steam engine's path in despair? Who could tell?

"A terrible accident on the El road . . . train derailed . . . a fatality." The inked keys struck paper. The platen gripped. The barrel turned. The dry description had practically composed itself.

Had he made indecision an act of retribution? He couldn't quite recall. In that endless instant, so many thoughts had flooded his mind. How could he feel such self-loathing and indifference simultaneously? Because he had killed the right man for the wrong reason? Killed? Ridiculous. An oversight, muscle failure, a miscalculation, a natural impulse to survive.

Yet he couldn't shake the sensation that he had made a decision before reason entered into it. Then it was out of his hands, wasn't it? To the outside world, the affair was cut and dried. In five grafs he'd fixed Weems's fate. You could read all about it in tomorrow's edition.

From Printing House Square he caught a cab to Mulberry Street. Across from the yellowed marble station, three reporters on a stoop suspended their card game, eyeing him as he bounded into the inner sanctum. Leaving half a dozen petitioners waiting, the secretary hustled him into the police superintendent's office. Without a word Max slid Mrs. Edwards's ledger across Byrnes's desk.

"What've we got here?" The detective riffled the pages.

"The addresses of all the church property. I marked the baby farms I found already. There have to be others. Policy numbers are in the back." All his energy was rushing back. And Leon was ensconced safely on Carmine Street, learning the pleasures of pasta. There was a still place, for once, in Max's restless mind.

Byrnes flipped through page after page, whistling under his breath. "My investigators came up with this when they searched the lady's premises, didn't they, boyo?"

"Sure. Nice job. Did you pick them up yet?"

"We nabbed the two women last night. Don't worry, they're spilling. You know the fella did the swan dive?" Byrnes asked.

"MacNamara?"

"Hudson Duster. Right in line for the crown after Dinny Watson."

"Royalty?"

"Oh, yeah. We've got him in our picture gallery." Byrnes drew a print from his drawer. The stark likeness of Stephenson's long-jawed rag. "For your picture artist." Leaning forward, intimate as a pal at a long polished bar, he gave up a choice tidbit. "The Dusters're moving into legit stuff fast."

Leaning back in his chair, Byrnes cracked his knuckles and lit his dead cigar. Who knew better than the great detective? The superintendent had invented the picture gallery, his web of informers extended from Jay Gould's banking house to Battle Alley. It was hard to fight the undertow of Byrnes's good will, but where was the Reverend Weems in this equation? Or Holy Trinity?

"Are you saying these ladies took their marching orders from MacNamara? That's a little hard to swallow."

Dark lines radiated down from the police chief's brow. His black eyes narrowed to slits, his glare striking Max with the force of a blow. More than one man had withered under this fierce expression, but Max knew all the elements of the performance. Leon was still alive. He felt an unreasonable peace.

Radiating confidence, Byrnes launched into his argument. "Why not? You think these gangs are a bunch of dumb brutes? The public has the idea they just pinch goods off the docks, but they've got curb brokers in their pockets, too. After-hours trades, penny stocks, that sort of thing," he added for good measure.

"I don't know. The Dusters and a bunch of society quiffs? They were paid off as muscle is my guess. They're not running the scam themselves."

Bristling, Byrnes lit into him. "You're lecturing me about Wall Street, boyo? If you want to know something, the Whyos have their own broker."

"Is that for attribution?"

Byrnes growled in the back of his throat. Max held his fierce gaze. Then the detective threw his head back and laughed. "You sonofabitch, Greengrass, you print that, I'll skin you alive."

"I guess that's a no-no. Well, when you chat with Mr. MacNamara, ask him if he remembers shooting an insurance agent named Martin Mourtone at Stephenson's. Jog his memory." He didn't know where his newfound calm was coming from. Maybe he didn't care what happened to him any more. Maybe he'd filled his quota of dread.

"What the hell do you know about that?"

"I saw the fella. Martin Mourtone. Insurance agent. Somebody misplaced the back of his head."

"Never heard a word about it."

"Yeah, well, the body got up and walked away. Just as a favor, put it to Abie."

"What's his reason, MacNamara?"

"Mourtone found out about the buyback routine. An African named Harry Granger set up a meeting at Stephenson's so MacNamara could do the deed. Granger's the Negro who ended up in pieces in a barrel, so I guess they didn't trust him to keep his trap shut. Remember that one?"

"That rings a bell."

"Ask him about that escapade, too. I've got another question. Do you think they were using more than one insurance company?"

"You're a little bulldog, ain't you? As a matter of fact, they squeezed 'em all every which way. As many settlements as they could get. All they need's a sawbones to pronounce. We've got his name, too. Old rummy. A Dr. Slurry. Now there's a business with a future," Byrnes added thoughtfully.

"Jesus, you think somebody else will try it?"

"Unless the companies stop issuing those policies. What're the chances of that? I made some inquiries. Since the eighties they've been raking it in. Twenty-five percent of the policies they write are on kids under ten."

"How much can they make on policies that sell for a few cents a week?"

"More than a few cents when they're issuing over a million policies. Some reformers tried to outlaw it in Massachusetts. England, too. Creates a bit of an incentive, don't it?"

"When can I get my interviews? I'll need the coroner's report, too."

"Sure, sure. As soon as we can make them available."

"By the way. Who were the policies payable to? Did you check that out?"

Byrnes's answer came a heartbeat too late. "Ah, this Edwards far as I know. She was working for her own pocket."

Keeping his own counsel, Max let this assertion pass.

chapter forty-one

As it turned out, Joseph MacNamara's jaw had broken itself in several places. Under treatment at Bellevue, he wasn't moving his mouth too freely. Mrs. Edwards had been spirited away overnight, and none of the court officers seemed to know where she had gone. Only Marianne Granger, unable to make bail, remained locked in the Tombs.

A pot-bellied guard led Max over the Bridge of Sighs and into the prison proper. Packed holding tanks lined the first corridor. A man was singing an air involving County Cork until an intimate friend began to choke him during the refrain. Another inmate bemoaned his fate. "Sonofabitch Cleveland," he reasoned. "He got it in for me."

"You putchyerself in here, birdbrain," another prisoner hooted.

Max followed the guard to a lower level. The air grew colder, and the bricks were prickled with moisture. In the muffled silence, he heard his own shuffling and sucking for breath, inmates muttering and snoring. When the turnkey reached an iron gate, he called for the next booly dog. Holding a guttering candle aloft, this putty-nosed creature drew him deeper into an airless passage.

Huddled in the corner of her cell, Marianne Granger stared back at them. Tense. Watchful. When the flickering light fell on her, she seemed to withdraw into the wall itself. He had steeled himself against his own rage—wasn't he face to face with the fiend who had tried to kill him?—but instead the sight of the frightened African filled him with pity. Who knew how many kidney punches and well-placed knuckles had been applied to her during questioning?

"Lookit that. Her own digs. This nigger, she's got the pull."

"Were you holding the other woman here?"

"That high-hat bitch? They bailed her out jack flash. All's I got for you is the nignog. Wanna go back?"

"No, no. I have candles. Just let me in."

He dropped a few coins into the turnkey's hand and swung the cell door open. Once inside, he settled himself on the plain plank bed, lit the wick on a fresh candle and opened his parcel. "Would you like something to eat? Ham? Cheese? Some fresh fruit? I've got bread and two beers, too."

"What you doin' here? I thought you was . . . Oh, Lord."

"Just doing my job. For the paper."

"I didn't hit you, mister. It were MacNamara. He the one. Not me."

"I know that," he lied, trying to soothe her. "Drink?" He groped in his pocket, produced a church key and popped a bottle.

She snatched it and took a long pull. "They gonna shoot me with the electricity? My lord, I'm thirsty." She took another swig. He passed her a hunk of bread. "Lemme see some of that ham you got. You know what they feed you?"

"I've got a good idea."

"Them little white worms in everything." She tore into his offerings, devouring the meat and cheese first.

"I can help you."

"Reporter cain't do nothin'."

"I can tell people your side."

"Black got no side. They put the whole thing on me. Harry and me, we jus' try to feed our family."

"Wasn't it MacNamara's idea?"

She let go a derisive laugh. "Joseph? Half he nose gone."

"What are you talking about?"

"He a Duster. All they cares about's snortin' up. He mind, I'll bet it got a hole in it. That what they sayin'? That Joseph the one? They try to put it on him and me? You'll put it in your paper? The way it really happen?"

"That's what I get paid for."

"I never done it my own self. They jus' uses me to dig the hole. . . . You write that. They the ones who . . . oh, Lord, they goin' tie me to that chair. They says you hair catch on fire, when you in that chair you spit out the electric." Her voice quavered, but she fought back her tears. "I'm feared, mister. What my kids gonna do, they momma die like that?"

Now her tears came sudden and unrestrained. She gripped his arm so hard he recoiled, but she wouldn't let go. He dug for his handkerchief and waited for her to stop shaking. For a long time they sat in silence.

"You think you c'n help. You ain't fibbin'?"

"I can put it in the paper so everybody knows." He waited until she blew her nose again. "So who thought up the insurance fraud?"

"They ever kills a lady with the shock?"

"If I can get your story out. . . ."

"Electric expensive. Maybe they don't wanna waste it on no black bitch." Her sly joke took him aback. He'd never realized Africans had such a bitter sense of humor. "Got that other one?"

He passed her the second beer, she took a long swallow and fell quiet. Sensing he shouldn't press too hard, Max waited. In a distant cell, a woman wailed, a high-pitched, looping cry that sounded barely human. In a ragged chorus, curses resounded through the lockup.

"It happen by accident," Marianne said finally. "Harry find a little momma at a house on Sullivan, she cain't pay the ten cent. They a lotta them, first they buy the policy, parade aroun' like they doin' the right thing," she added with scorn.

"He was selling policies in a brothel?"

"Why not? They the girl got the coin. Half of 'em droppin' baby and then they go runnin' off. Money go to French dress, the gin bottle. Then they fly the coop."

"So Harry bought the policies back?"

"Nah, he jus' tell the lady, Mrs. Edwards, about this girl Ruthie. Black girl from Camden. How she stop payin' the ten cent."

"Where did he meet Mrs. Edwards?"

"Mrs. Edwards in there collectin' the rent and preachin' to the girl. Tellin' 'em how they dirty and all."

For a moment he sat there, stunned. Weems was railing against parlor houses while the church pocketed profits from the same source. The hypocrisy was almost too raw, yet it had the ring of truth. Why did he cringe in disbelief then?

"And what did she say?"

"She know about Ruthie 'cause Ruthie stop paying the lady takin' care of her kid, too. Mrs. Edwards, she know everybody in the building. Madame. Baby lady. Ruthie got kick out, she cain't pay nobody."

"Kicked out of the brothel?"

"Yeah, so Harry start to think. He do all kind of number in his head, and he say if somebody buy back the policy from Ruthie for less, everybody be better off. Put that in the paper, mister. It were to help a poor girl."

For a humanitarian, Marianne Granger had quite a lot of blood on her hands, but he let her self-serving claim pass. Was it possible that a Negro had thought up such a perverse scheme? And if so, wasn't it proof that the black race was equal to the rest of mankind? "And Harry made some money too, didn't he?"

"Sure. He keep collectin' the premium from the lady who buy back the policy. Harry say the Jew, the white man, they make money outta paper. Why not the black man? But it were only to help," she insisted.

"So Ruthie's baby passed away and Mrs. Edwards collected, right?"

"Yeah. She buy more policy then. She after Harry to tell her about all the jazzin' momma don't pay. They happy to sell. They ain't eatin' they own self. Mrs. Edwards a religious lady, she doin' a good deed she say."

"Was Harry the only one who found . . . ah . . . clients for her?"

"Nah, once she figure it out, she ask all the baby lady, do they have any with the policy. She take 'em from Harry when he find 'em, but she go out on her own. She take rent at a lotta buildin', and the girl, they droppin' 'em every which way."

"And Harry told Martin about the buybacks?"

"Yeah. He say they should do the same thing the lady doin', but Martin, he don't want to buy 'em back. He say it look like they helpin' but maybe they hurtin'. Speculatin' like that."

"The odds were good, though, weren't they? Don't a fair number die anyway?"

"They mostly weak, they mother don't have the good milk. Harry say 'Why not pay the girl and collect our own self?' But Martin, he don't like that idea."

"Do you have any idea who might have killed your husband?"

"We was goin' good, he don't have no enemy. Everybody like Harry. But he carry aroun' too much cash after he collect. . . . Some nigger probably cut him."

He didn't have the heart to tell her that her own friends didn't want Harry talking, any more than Martin. If MacNamara himself didn't do Harry up, another Hudson Duster had.

"Mrs. Edwards said it was for charity?"

"She give it to the church, she say. Girl in her buildin' droppin' every day, and she got buildin' all over town."

"And there are baby farmers in a lot of them?"

"Little ones every which place. Gots to have the ladies take care of 'em."

"I see. Who cashed the policies? Edwards?"

"They make like the church cash 'em. Girl sign over to the church. Harry say nobody ask no question if it be the church."

"You saw the Reverend Weems come around?"

"That skinny teeth man? Yeah, he tell us how we doin' God's work 'n'all. The lady, they believes him, too. They do the business one, two, three."

"They smothered them, didn't they?"

"They the one who do it," Marianne responded. "Not me. I gots children of my own. They use the handkerchief and stuff."

"And then you took them downtown to bury in that warehouse?"

"They gots other basement, too. Other tenement."

"Can you tell me which ones?"

"There one on Desbrosses, and two on Greenwich I knows of. They got dirt basements. They fills 'em up."

He flinched at the specter of these hidden Potter's Fields, but they were a natural outgrowth of the business, weren't they? Efficient depositories that completed the transactions.

"Were they all in abandoned buildings like the one on Schermerhorn? Do you know any addresses?"

"I don't exactly know no number, but nobody live in 'em. Yeah, they abandon."

He didn't know if she would understand his next question. "Did they ever talk about science?"

"I don't know nuffin' about no science." She hesitated. "Sometime they talk about blood. . . . You know, weak blood, strong blood. Maybe they know what they talkin' about."

"Whose blood?"

"People blood. Like they makin' a mule or somethin'."

Christian purity and the Reverend Weems's modern thinking dovetailed in a way, didn't they? How convenient that progressive science and spiritual ideals came together so neatly.

"Did they talk about the Immigration Restriction League?"

"Some society they work for. They has these preachers talk at they house."

"Did the Reverend Weems give talks over there?"

"Him and his other preacher friend. They talk about it like I'm not there. Like I don' understand nothin'. I know what they sayin'. Too many mick, too many dago, too many polack, you know."

"I see. Didn't Mrs. Edwards have any qualms?"

"Any what?"

"Misgivings."

"Nah. She do it jes' like they chicken. I seen it on a farm down South."

"Did you tell the police about the League or Reverend Weems?"

"The superintendent, he come in here."

"Byrnes?"

"Yeah, but he don' listen. He say sign this paper."

"And you told him about Reverend Weems."

"So what?"

"It's personal. Oh, one more thing. Were any of the infants white?"

"White? Sure they white. They Jew, dago, mick baby. A 'course, nigger too."

"I mean white-white."

Her derisive laughter stopped his heart. "Mrs. Edwards, she don't drop nones I knows of."

After his articles on Holy Trinity's real-estate empire ran their course, Belle took him to meet some people at the Henry Street Settlement House. The gathering included Belle's mentor, Lillian Wald, the woman who had invented home nursing; Jane Farmer and Alice Montgomery, two humorless acolytes who reminded Max of nuns; an austere millionaire reformer, Mrs. Spencer-Morris; and Mr. Schiff, whose philanthropy drew on his banking fortune.

In other words, exactly the sort of assembly that made Max itch. For one thing, he sensed that his snappy yellow vest wasn't going over well in this crowd. Yet somehow, by sheer accident, he'd earned a place among them. And he knew how much Belle wanted him to cooperate with these secular reformers. At least the Henry Street Settlement went light on Christian love, so he found he could bear its atmosphere. Up to a point.

They sat in a stark room and drank tasteless tea. At the head of the table, Mr. Schiff, a martinet not so different from Colonel Fisk, made a proposal: "I've been speaking to Mr. Gilder and we're forming a committee. We'd like you to testify as to the conditions you've seen."

"Your articles were a revelation," Miss Wald put in.

"We're looking into legislation to stop this despicable insurance business," Mrs. Spencer-Morris added.

"I've seen a dozen of these hideous baby farms," Miss Wald observed. "But I had no idea how organized they were."

"That's the Reverend Parkhurst's whole point. Even the bootblack pays tribute for his miserable corner," Schiff declared.

Max blushed. If only this crowd knew how much blood had been left on the newsroom floor, how much had been misrepresented, and how much of his story he'd been forced to slash before even a semblance of the truth was allowed to take shape on the page! He had to laugh. With their implacable naïveté, Schiff, Wald, and Mrs. Spencer-Morris could never imagine his negotiations with the revered Police Superintendent Byrnes or his battles with Stan Parnell.

When he'd shoehorned Marianne Granger's accusations into his first draft, his editor had jumped all over him. "You can't build a case around one nigger lady's accusations. Byrnes says she's just trying to save her own skin and this MacNamara, he's pleading out on the arson charge."

"Did he admit to the murders?"

"What murders?"

"Mourtone and Granger."

"Do you have wax in your ears? He pled out on arson. That's it."

"In return for his testimony."

"Sure. He nailed Edwards and her friends. Byrnes tied it up with a bow."

Max had dug in his heels. "Okay, forget Mourtone. You can't cut the whole section on Weems and the immigrant angle."

"Why not? Where are your sources? You don't have a leg to stand on."

"Okay, forget the League. I can draw the dots between Weems and the racket. We can get balance, Stan. Let me quote Granger and get Fisk to deny."

"No can do. It's bad enough I've got Mutual and Prudential burning my ear off. They say you're going off half-cocked."

"I quoted Gordon Lark from Accident and Life. Didn't you see that?"

"Just forget about Weems. He's dead and buried. The ladies are coughing it up. Why go out on a limb?"

For a day after that argument, Parnell had let Max languish on the space-rater's bench without a single assignment. He'd pushed too hard. Two more days went by. Nothing. He was sure he was going to be eased out. He would have to make his case one last time.

The next morning, steeling himself for the guillotine, he had pushed open the frosted-glass doors. Copy boys were racing around like mad monkeys. Typewriters ping'ed at the end of each line. Swanson dipped his pen into an inkpot. Corelli fixed his pince-nez on his nose and held his handwritten copy at arm's length. Nick Biddle peeked over the back of a young secretary, generously pointing out her mistakes. Two phones rang. The familiar undertone of muttering, sighs, and complaints merged into a single humming noise, the hiss and rattle of the sentence mill.

Parnell had studiously ignored him.

Max had intended to assault the throne and press his case right away, but he had all the time in the world to get fired. Instead, he wandered over to his scarred desk and made a small pyramid of notebooks, ink bottles, pencils, and pens. Then he gathered his clippings from the bottom drawer. Gazing at this homely pile of possessions, he saw the finality of his predicament. Craning his neck, he stared up at the ceiling. A black, furry dust clung to the stamped tin. If he was fired now, he would never get a desk at the paper's elegant new digs on Herald Square. It would take him years to climb back to the same roost at some other paper, if one would have him at all.

He barely heard Parnell call his name, but he was fully prepared for a curt send-off.

"Go down to payroll and sign your papers, Greengrass," the editor told him. "Maybe then you'll get off my back for a while."

Minsky, the paymaster, made it official. The *Herald* had hired him as a general assignment reporter.

He felt a muted elation, but that soon faded. The grind was exactly the same. A kitchen fire and a horsecar fracas. A wolfhound who howled "On the Banks of the Wabash" to piano and strings. A suicide at the Metropolitan Hotel. A double wedding for Siamese twins. His first check seemed a bit skinny, but he took Biddle out for a cocktail anyway.

"You racked up so many sticks," Nick observed, with his unerring instincts, "they had to take you on to save money. Why do you think Harding Davis won't go on the payroll?"

"Because he piles up so many inches?"

Back at his desk Max did the calculations and found that the paper would save, on average, $3.45 a week by putting him on salary. He'd have to put the touch on Belle for that new suit.

The Henry Street Settlement House was unanimous in its praise, yet how could he explain to Mr. Schiff that Superintendent Byrnes had resisted the very investigation he was now taking credit for? Or to Miss Wald that a man could be murdered and evaporate the same day? Or that he had settled for a limping approximation of the truth? Or that the *Herald*'s headline editor might tell this version of the story:

MIDNIGHT BAND OF MERCY IN EUTHANASIA-FOR-PROFIT SCHEME

Superintendent Byrnes Cracks Ring
Mrs. Edwards and Cohorts Confess to Insurance Murders
Fiendish Negress a Partner in Crime

Then there were the crosscurrents. Even as he fought Parnell tooth and nail, he saw the wisdom of his editor's remarks. Mrs. Edwards had confessed but declined to implicate either the church or the Immigration Restriction League. MacNamara had offered up a few bare facts, along with a handful of his teeth. Though Max knew in his bones that Marianne Granger was telling the truth, his sources *were* thin. He'd had to settle for half a loaf, but look at how much of the shadow world he'd dragged into the light.

"I'd be happy to talk to the committee. Let me speak to my editors."

"You'll ask them if you can share your notes?" Schiff persisted.

"I'll raise the issue." There was no way in holy hell he'd let them see his raw scribblings. "But don't worry. I'll give you more than you can handle."

"That's marvelous, isn't it, Mr. Schiff?" Miss Wald said.

His face was burning, and he didn't dare look at Belle.

Years before, when he'd started out scrambling for squibs, he'd had no intention of illuminating anything at all. Now he was being lionized as the Second Coming of Jacob Riis. Little did his admirers know that he had a permanent case of newspaperman's disease. Yet he wondered if now he hadn't been infected with the worst impulse of all: to render justice. Belle said that to be a whole human being, you had to take a position, and he saw her point. But sides had sides, and he wasn't quite sure where to stand. He was in sympathy with her certainty, but he couldn't quite shed his undermining cynicism.

On the subject of Miss Rose, he had no ambivalence whatsoever. He loved her, and he was even willing to flirt with goo-goos—though he drew the line at temperance fanatics—to keep her close.

chapter forty-two

Loving Belle wasn't a simple thing. She was a prickly pear, an interrogator with a ferocious curiosity. Sitting with him on Mrs. DeVogt's steps, she wouldn't let the case go.

"He made a big speech, your Mr. Weems," she began.

"Yeah. So?"

"You don't know what these people believe?"

"Sure. They want to slam the door shut and keep out all that riff-raff from Europe. Lucky for us, you got in."

"And it's my ambition to be the death of them," she laughed. "You watch. Soon they'll pass laws to keep us out."

He was more interested in curling her hair around his index finger than talking politics. Anyway, he figured she was blowing things out of proportion again. "That's daffy. No one's gonna follow a line of crap like that."

"They fill a hall plenty of times."

Personally, he wasn't worried about the lunatic fringe, but he figured he'd humor her. "Yeah, that they do."

From the step above her, he leaned down and kissed the nape of her neck. He spread his legs, and she let her head fall back on his knee. In the lamplight, the street was wet and gleaming. "I like the way it looks after the rain," she replied.

A maroon phaeton rolled by, the soothing sound of its chestnut's hooves echoing down the street. Craning her neck, her back arched, she drew him down and kissed him full on the mouth. Her darting tongue explored, questioned, penetrated. Her fingers were in his hair. That night, she slipped into his bed in her sheer chemise, shook her thick black hair loose, and ran her hands under his nightshirt. Covering his mouth, she straddled him, and he almost fainted.

She brought a sheepskin with her, of course. She was a visiting nurse, and she'd seen everything. Every night she came to him now, and Mrs. DeVogt, true to her creed, never said a word.

It was a dream to make love to her, and to have an ally too. He was forgetting how it felt to be alone, to live completely inside his head with the whole world arrayed against him. If he had to show up at the Henry Street Settlement House once in a blue moon, it was a small price to pay.

When her mother fell ill again, Gretta said she didn't know how long she would be away. She looked magnificent, but more distant than ever. In fact, Max had the strongest premonition that she would live her life out alone, but perfectly content, hauling her fifty pounds of cameras around town, retreating to her cottage by the harbor, then setting out again like the tide.

On her way to Staten Island, she asked him to walk her to the train. His affair with Belle was out in the open by then. Consequently, Gretta had become a trace more formal. He responded in kind, but her throaty voice still thrilled him.

"Am I right, then, that Martin's been forgotten, that there will be no case? You're on to something new?" she asked.

"It's all played out. I'm sorry. At least *you* know what happened."

When they reached the El, she offered her gloved hand. "Yes. It was kind of you to explain it all . . . and to risk so much for me."

"Forget it. I had plenty invested myself."

"If you ever need a picture, a wedding picture, I'll be happy to be the one. As a favor."

"Ahh, that's generous. I'll mention it to Belle."

Belle's Russian eyes turned to slits when he repeated the offer. "Tell that cow to keep her camera to herself," she snapped.

When they went down to City Hall, Faye's friend, the publicity photographer Ira Gold, made two plates for them. In Max and Belle's wedding picture, taken in the municipal chapel before a few dozen Syrians, Sicilians, Bohemians, Polish Jews, and Greeks, and a smattering of Norwegians and

Swedes, the rectangular sign saying "Marriage License: $1" appears to be growing out of the groom's head.

Belle wore a fitted wide-lapeled jacket with enormous sleeves and a jaunty boater. Max appeared in a morning coat, checked bow tie, and white vest. In glistening taffeta, Faye struck a dancer's pose. She knew exactly how to trick the lens and make her double chin disappear. For Faye, the full profile amounted to professional suicide.

The ceremony seemed to lift Faye's spirits. Ever since Danny had absconded with the widow Sutherland, the New Haven heiress whose deceased husband had invented the Deliverance Coffin, she'd been deep in the dumps. As far as Max was concerned, Danny had revealed his true colors, and he'd better not show his song-plugging face again in New York if he knew what was good for him.

Faye seemed more indignant at the inventor Sutherland, whose device offered an escape mechanism for the buried-alive, than at Danny. "You know how that thing works? They put some kinda ball on the body's chest, and if the corpse wriggles or something, this thing explodes and sends up a signal. That's how she made her pile!"

"We're trying to get married, Faye," Belle pointed out.

"Keith wants me to call myself Fritzie now. Fritzie Credenza. What's wrong with Faye Greengrass?"

Belle insisted that she wouldn't mind living with Faye and Leon for a while, until his sister got back on her feet, but lately she had begun to raise questions: Had he ever noticed how money ran like water through Faye's hands? Was there an end to her blues? Didn't she know Ira Gold was using her to get business from her actress friends? Didn't she understand that her new manager, Cookie Grimes, was a reptile? When exactly did she plan to stand on her own two feet again?

Faye had to make a five o'clock curtain, so Max and Belle went over to her room off Union Square and kept an eye on Leon until the nanny showed up. They caught Faye's last turn and then they all went out to celebrate at a new lobster palace on Broadway and 41st.

"Now we've got to keep him out of the saloons," Faye declared as they clinked champagne glasses.

"Are you kidding?" Max retorted. "I've gotta keep you buzzers outta the Tombs."

When the lobster arrived, Max had to show Belle how to crack the claws. It didn't take her long to learn.

One of Nicholas Biddle's lungs filled with fluid, then the other. Max visited him in his flat, along with a string of other reporters who tried to comfort him by drinking and smoking by his side late into the night. Biddle's withered landlady supplied moist cloths for his brow and pitchers of ice water for his unquenchable thirst. Nick muttered a blue streak about a pile of black snow and asked an invisible woman named Carla to come, dear God, come to his bed, only to break into lucid moments more painful to observe than his delirium. In one of these conscious fits, he grasped Max's hand and swore he was leaving him everything.

Max looked around the flat at the faded hangings, the Japanese prints, the worn-smooth Oriental rug, the sprung divan, the storm of clothes hanging from hooks and lamps, and found the one thing he wanted, a Roman head with a shattered nose. Its hair, carved in intricate curls, was dark with grit, its eyes skinned with dust. That night he put the cast under his arm and hauled it home.

Near the corner of Thirteenth and Sixth, he sensed his face was wet. Only then did he realize he'd been crying the whole time. Shifting the broken-nosed Roman to his left arm, he groped for a handkerchief. Biddle's life frightened him; he didn't want to die alone.

In a matter of days, Nicholas Biddle faded from existence. Scattered across his desk he had left notes in his savage scrawl, a half-finished story, nubs of grease erasers, and a congealed inkpot. The sight disturbed Max as much as his friend's death rattle. An impromptu wake sprang up at Logan's and, with pickled eggs and day-old sardellen as ballast, the reporters drank round after round to the deceased. Biddle, who had spent every cent that ever passed through his hands, left behind his Oriental furnishings, his opium layout, three suits, three shirts, and two pairs of shoes.

"Don't forget the bad debts, boys," Stan Parnell added. Booze went right to the frail editor's head. Reeling, he went on, "Not to put too fine a point on it, but he did it in style . . . left less . . . than nothing. . . ."

This observation brought a cheer from the assembly, though it had a sobering effect on Max, who was scouting for an apartment. Belle had worked out the numbers. With the right deal, they could save half their paychecks. If Faye kept up her end of the bargain.

He caught Parnell just as the editor was losing his grip on the bar. His leader smiled his lipless smile. In a wet whisper, he said, "Willy's all yours now."

With thumb and forefinger, like something unclean, William H. Howe held up Max's subpoena. The weather had turned bitter in late October, so the ruddy-faced lawyer kept a healthy fire going in his office.

"Glad we could help you with this," Howe growled, dropping the summons into the fiery grate. "We're going to miss Biddle," he sighed. Lost in thought, he fingered a lapel on his bottle-green jacket.

"We had another mutual friend who passed away recently," Max replied. "Now that matters are settled . . . just out of curiosity, did the father bury an empty box?"

"We had no reason to add to the man's grief," Howe replied. "Suppose we prevailed on him not to view the remains, which is not to say there were any, we would have had the best of motives. You wouldn't torment the poor man again, would you?"

"I wouldn't think of it," the reporter agreed. Howe's gnomic pronouncement would have to do.

Intently, Max watched the summons turn to ash. He'd packed on some weight since he'd gotten married, a protective layer of flesh that comforted him in the vast lawyer's presence. "They say Nick was there before the flood."

"Ha! He probably crawled out of the Old Collect Pond. We worked together on a hundred cases if we worked on one."

Max's ears pricked up. He thought he knew what was coming, but he had to hear the words from Howe's lips. "He did a profile of you once?"

He was ready to draw Howe's portrait himself now. What about his murky London days? His years as a physician? Or was it horse doctor? The murders he'd witnessed as a boy. Or known too much about. He felt a curious sympathy for the man. Perhaps because he knew too much himself.

"A fine piece of work it was. Now what are we to do? I have the prettiest murder case. My client is absolutely upstanding. A masseur on St.

Mark's Place. The D.A. is trying to railroad him over some barber they found in pieces."

Howe rummaged around in his desk drawer and drew out a greenback. Max couldn't make out the denomination.

"Really?"

Chubby fingers pushed the bill across the polished mahogany.

"Absolutely outrageous. They don't even have the whole body. No head. All of his alleged tattoos skinned off. Then there's the barber's wife, a woman with a spotty reputation."

Now Max could see the figure. A crisp hundred. A very decent price for good publicity.

Max knew something William H. Howe did not, however. A witness from an old and insignificant divorce proceeding had developed a personal grudge against Howe and Hummel, and had passed on certain highly damaging information. In fact, based on Mr. Schiff's recommendation, the D.A. had confided in Max and was trying to recruit him to the cause.

"Once a month, say? Nick worked his way up to that, but you've got responsibilities now, don't you? And what they're asking for a decent flat these days, highway robbery!"

How did the lawyer know Belle was pregnant? Had he posted spies under Max's bed? They had already talked about moving out to Brooklyn where the rents were a bit saner, but who wanted to live in the wilds of Flatbush? One hundred a month would do very nicely. They might be able to buy into some rooms on the Upper West Side.

The beautiful bill sat there between them. Nostalgia for the old times sang to him, but the endgame was near. "Sorry, Willy. Can't do business that way any more."

"Why in the world not?" Howe asked, his voice tinged with sadness.

What could he say? That a few murders stood between them? Willy would profess ignorance, and who knew if he hadn't kept himself safely in the dark. It was an odd sensation to sit there across from Howe and know exactly how the great lawyer would fall. There would be no three-hour appeals to the jury from his knees this time. The case against the firm was clean and technical. Delay until death was his only hope.

"I don't know. But things are changing. Take the National League. They're talking about bringing in an infield fly rule. The infielder won't be allowed to drop the ball on purpose any more."

Under his hoary eyebrows, William H. Howe's eyes widened in horror. "Well, at least take a decent cigar. Fresh from New Haven. You're not some sort of Methodist now, are you?"

A barber, a cuckolded masseuse, and a decapitated torso. It did sound promising. He could cast it as William H. Howe's last ride. "Tell me about the barber, Willy," he said, reaching for the golden Connecticut leaf.

acknowledgments

I could not have written *The Midnight Band of Mercy* without the unstinting love, support—and criticism—of my wife, Rose Mackiewicz. Her wicked sense of humor sustained me through the dark days of composition.

Anna Tasha Blaine, my daughter, did much to bring this work to fruition. Her excitement for the material was contagious

My agent, Sally Wofford-Girand, provided wise counsel when it came time to cut those passages I loved only too much.

Laura Hruska, my editor at Soho Press, edited with precision, but without doing violence to language and structure.

Michael Rothfeld, a reporter's reporter, read an early draft and pronounced Max Greengrass's obsessions true to the trade. Marge and Ed Blaine weighed every word and gave invaluable advice, as always. Richard Lieberman, who hired me to teach New York City Literature some years back, encouraged me to try my hand at this material. The librarians at Hartwick College and the State University of New York at Oneonta obtained arcane materials, including microfilm of the *New York Herald*, and tracked down my most outlandish requests. Thanks to all of them.

E. H. Dunlop's entertaining book, *The Gilded City*, first introduced me to the actual Midnight Band of Mercy. Her correspondence was generous and gave me confidence that I might somehow solve the riddle of the group's strange crusade. Jared Day, author of *Urban Castles: Tenement Housing and Landlord Activism in New York City, 1890–1943*, helped guide me through the intricacies of late nineteenth-century real estate. Our conversations sparked a new turn in the novel's plot.

Other books that were essential include Luc Sante's *Low Life*, Richard Rovere's *Howe & Hummel*, Warren Sloat's *A Battle for the Soul of New York*, Robert Snyder's *The Voice of the City: Vaudeville and Popular Culture in New York*, Elaine S. Abelson's *When Ladies Go A-Thieving*, and Burrows and Wallace's *Gotham*. A source of true "research rapture," the *New York Herald*'s wry and colorful language evoked the time as much as any detailed history.